Copyright © 2016 by Matt Shaw

Matt Shaw Publications

All rights reserved. This book or any portion thereof may not be reproduced or used in any manner whatsoever without the express written permission of the publisher except for the use of brief quotations in a book review.

The characters in this book are purely fictitious.

Each story contained within is the property of the authors listed and has kindly been given for inclusion in this anthology.

Any likeness to persons living or dead is purely coincidental.

Matt Shaw Presents

EASTER EGGS
&
Bunny Boilers

A Horror Anthology

INTRODUCTION

Easter a time of rejuvenation, bunny rabbits and chocolate. Out of all the Christian religious seasons this has been the one that has always bothered me the most, which is odd as I am an atheist. In my opinion this should be the most revered of them all, hell they are celebrating the fact that their long haired hippie leader was nailed to a couple of two by fours, and left hanging around like a fat man at a salad bar until he died. It should be a somber occasion, I mean he gave his life for you, not me. I'm a Ginger; even the Son of God hates us. But instead of them being all referential and sad they celebrate it by stuffing their faces with mass produced chocolate eggs, and slaughtering millions of lambs, kind of ironic since he was the Lamb of God, thank God he wasn't referred to as the Panda of God, smothering it in vile mint sauce and force feeding themselves on the day of his resurrection.

Forgive the pun, but Christ on a bike, who bases their religion on a bloody Zombie? What's next the latter day Saint's Church of Holy Werewolves?

However the more enlightened of us know that the Catholic Church didn't like the fact that us locals were doing our own celebratory things at this time of year, and they did what they always do, take over the local custom and smack it down into the gutter, stab it in the back and claim it as their own, while they dump the poor rotting corpse into the nearest hole in the ground.

Easter is also a very poor time for us horror fans, with the exception of such things as weird Pagan cults barbequing innocent Edward Woodward impersonators or killer bunny rabbits, whether they are tiny like the Beast of Caerbannog or giant killing machines like those from *Night of the Lepus,*. A film I watched as a very young child, that to this day still has me think that all rabbits should be boiled alive, which expertly leads me to the reason why we are all here. Matt Shaw's rather spiffing new anthology *Easter Eggs and Bunny Boilers.* This was an odd request for me, initially I was thrilled to be asked, then my heart sank when I noticed that two of the authors concerned had been involved in two rather public falling outs with me. I know who would have thought that was possible, I'm the most happy cheerful Don of Horror out there. Who could ever fall out with me? Well I won't name names, but it was all their fault, I'm perfect I do nothing wrong, well nothing I will own up to in public. And that is the great things about projects like this, it forces you to look hard at yourself and realize that maybe you were an asshole as well, and makes you reach out with an olive branch to those who you have fallen out with.

I've not read any of the stories in this anthology but Matt has put together a fantastic line up of writers, hopefully by the time you have finished reading this anthology, (and yes it's an anthology, not a collection, despite what some idiots tell you) you'll have had a great time reading it. And if you did please leave a review on Amazon, and don't forget to mention just how awesome this introduction is.

Jim Mcleod

The Heart & Soul of Horror News, Reviews and Interviews

http://gingernutsofhorror.com/

A Word from Matt Shaw

Hello, children.

Thank you for purchasing this anthology. A project I decided to put together when I came to the conclusion there doesn't seem to be much room for horror around the Easter period - and given the fact Jesus Christ came back as a zombie and society turns into greedy slaves to chocolate and commercialism - I don't see why not. With that in mind, I approached a couple of author friends to bring you this here collection. And then - when they said 'yes' - it seemed to snowball, with me approaching more and more people, some of whom I haven't spoken to much before this project, and more and more of these people saying 'yes' to feature in this book.

Now, I feel it prudent to mention I do not own the rights to the stories collected here. They remain with the author so it may be that you might notice the stories repeated elsewhere *should* the authors decide to publish them anywhere else. All I asked was that it remained unpublished until this book was released and - thankfully - they all agreed. I say *all* but that's technically a lie. Two of the authors I approached turned me down. The bastards (insert a cheeky, smiley face here).

Now if you're new to the purchasing of anthologies, I think you're in for a treat. There are some great names in this collection - some of which you are most likely familiar with already. Having read the stories, I'm happy to report back - though - that they all brought their A Game to the collection and you're in for some real treats here. Treats which, you'll be pleased to hear, won't have to be added on to any calorie counter - like the bastard Easter eggs people might be buying for you. Also - another reason this book is better than an egg - it will last a lot longer as it is sitting around 100,000 words. A tome of a book.

There is no real rhyme nor reason as to how the stories appear in this collection, I'll be honest. I simply slotted them in as and when I received them. I did - however - put mine first and there *is* a reason for that…

I am known for extreme horror and whilst I do love extreme horror, I did not wish to bring it to this collection. Instead I wanted to have a bit of fun with my story, and lower you into the madness gently. It's something different from me to lull you into a false sense of security, and a million miles away from my Black Cover Books. Now, I appreciate this may disappoint some of you who read only my Black Cover titles and have come expecting that but - I just didn't think it suitable for this collection. Not when there is so much darkness on offer from the other authors and - with that in mind - there's nothing more for me to say other than to thank you for purchasing this collection and I hope you truly, truly enjoy it.

Until next time, kids.

Kind Regards,

Matt, The.

DESSERTS

Matt Shaw

Justin rolled onto his back and stared up at the bedroom ceiling. Instantly his tired eyes started making shapes from the shadows cast across the room by the light spilling in from the landing. He sighed heavily as his mother and father continued arguing downstairs; raised voices that stopped him from slipping into that wanted peaceful slumber. Something about there being no decent food in the cupboards, something about fed up being served slop and - father wanted a .... beer. Justin was ten years old and wasn't allowed to say the word that proceeded "beer" although he often wanted to - and sometimes almost did purely by accident. It was hard not to, given the amount of times he heard it in any one given day. His father's favourite word for sure.

A door slammed from somewhere downstairs, causing Justin's young heart to skip a beat. That would be his father storming into the living room, slamming the door behind him so that Justin's mother wouldn't dare follow, begging for forgiveness. Not that she tried that anymore. She knew better. She knew he wasn't so much as angry at her, just that he was stressed with work. She just happened to be in the firing line when he vented said stress.

It won't always be like this, she kept telling herself.

Justin often said the same thing in his own mind too, despite having no clue that his mother was thinking along the same lines. Still, the argument was over now. It always went quiet after a door slammed. It was like the act of slamming the door itself was a dramatic full-stop to the conversation.

Justin rolled onto his side and closed his weary eyes once more, desperate for sleep to overcome him and lead him to another day; a better day. He tried to clear his mind, to stop it continuing to replay the argument from downstairs - imagining the scenario play-out as though he had actually been down there, with them, for the whole time.

'All I want is to come home to a decent meal and yet day in, day out - I get this; frozen pies, frozen chips, frozen vegetables. You know how depressing this is? Never mind how crap it tastes.'

'I do the best I can with the money I have!'

'Oh - so what - you're saying this is my fault? Like - I don't know - I'm not fucking providing for you, or something like that?'

'That's not what I meant...'

'You know it's been a tough year. But - are the bills paid?'

'What?'

'Are the fucking bills paid? Yes they are. Do we have a fucking roof over our heads? Yes we do. Perhaps - if I'm not doing a good enough job... Perhaps you'd best go out and get a job? The boy doesn't need babysitting anymore. You can get a part-time job that coincides with his school hours...'

A moment of quiet while the husband thinks of what else to pick holes in and silence from the wife - who knows better than to try and defend herself when he is in one of these moods. All of it bouncing around Justin's head.

'Get me a fucking beer.'

That awkward pause as the wife tries to figure out how to tell her husband that he'd already drunk the last one over the lousy dinner he'd been complaining about. A dinner made worse by the fact it had to be warmed in the microwave because of the time he had got in from work and now a confession about the lack of drinks which leads to the living room door being slammed and the wife left - in the kitchen - wondering whether she should get in the car to go and fetch some more. It was late but the petrol station would have some still. They'd be overpriced, for sure, but if it would help with his mood - the extra money spent would be worthwhile.

Blank mind. Blank mind. Blank mind. It's quiet down there, no need to think about it anymore. Dad is watching television and mum is... Mum is probably in the kitchen cleaning. Everything is fine now. He has had his say and tomorrow everything will be better. Stop worrying about them. Everyone argues. It's not like they're going get divorced like Billy's mum and dad. GRRRR! Stop thinking about it! It's fine.

Justin rolled over onto his back again. Hard to drift off when your brain is working overtime stressing over this and that, wondering whether your mum and dad are going to break up and you're going to be left there trying to choose who you want to live with.

Justin almost wished he had to go to school in the morning. No school though, typically. Easter Holidays. Even if it weren't the holidays though - still the weekend. Easter Sunday tomorrow and after all that shouting about money and not being able to afford decent food, Justin couldn't help but wonder as to whether he was even going to get a chocolate egg. Not that he'd mind if he didn't. There was more to life than chocolate and if it was one less thing for his mum and dad to argue about, he'd happily sacrifice it.

A loud bang from downstairs caused Justin's heart to skip a beat and a sudden rush of adrenaline to surge through his body. A mumbled voice belonging to his mum followed by his father's clear roar, 'What the fuck do you think? I'm still hungry. I'm looking for something to eat!' Another bang which Justin knew - now - was one of the kitchen's many (empty) cupboards. A third bang. A rustle which sounded as though it belonged to a packet of crisps. Stamping feet leading down the hallway. A door slamming. Another sound Justin hadn't heard for a while but recognised immediately - weeping.

Justin sat up and looked over to the bedroom door. He wanted to get out of bed and creep down the stairs towards the kitchen. He wanted to put a comforting arm around his mum's shoulder and tell her that everything was going to be okay. He even wanted to see his dad - despite the mood he was in. He wanted to say the same thing to his dad that he'd say to his mother; a promise that everything would be fine. Work would turn around for him. Things would be easier for all of them.

Mind your own business! He could hear his father's voice now; dominant and filled with hostility as the stress continued to vent in the wrong direction.

It's okay, honey, just go to bed. I'm fine. His mother would send him away, embarrassed to be seen crying.

A decision was quickly made, it was best to stay in his bed, out of the way. He could check that his mum was okay the following day when everything would seem brighter. His dad would have had a sleep and would hopefully be in a better mood and his mum wouldn't be embarrassed at being caught with tears streaming. Okay. Tomorrow. He'd make sure she was okay in the morning before his dad got up and - when his dad did climb from his own pit - he'd try and give him the best day ever, even offering to help with any outstanding work even though his dad usually refused such an offer.

You'll only get in the way.

Tomorrow it is.

Justin rolled onto his side - his back to the door. He'd just try and ignore the crying. He was so tired that - hopefully - he himself would be sound asleep soon enough and he wouldn't have to worry about it anymore.

Please sleep. Please sl...

Justin sat up straight and stared at the bedroom door, distracted from his thoughts by a noise he didn't know; a scuffling noise from out on the landing. A noise not dissimilar to a pet cat, or small dog, scurrying on the carpet - stopping occasionally to investigate something perhaps before carrying on.

But Justin didn't have a pet. His father wouldn't allow it due to his own allergies - or at least that was the excuse he gave. Whether it was true or not, Justin would never know. But regardless...

What is that?

The noise stopped just outside the bedroom door. Justin didn't move from his bed, frozen to the spot; both worried and curious - a strange mix of emotions.

'Hello?'

The door was opened a crack - enough to let the light spill in. Whatever was making the noise, it was right out there. Right on the other side of the door.

'Hello?'

A rat. Or a mouse. It could have been either. The house backed onto fields. They'd had rats in the shed before now and they'd had a mouse in the kitchen. But then - the noise on the landing - it sounded heavier than either of those animals could manage. A big mouse? A big rat?

Slowly - carefully - Justin climbed from his bed and quietly touched his foot down upon the worn carpet. A creak from the floorboard and a shift of weight from behind the door.

'Hello?'

He knew there'd be no answer but it made him feel better; hearing the sound of his own voice. But what if there was an answer? What if something out there, on the other side of the door, did answer him? Would it get to him before his mother and father could if he screamed out in terror?

'Who's there?' he asked as he reached for a cricket bat that leaned against the bedroom wall. It wasn't supposed to be used as a weapon, he'd even been warned about such actions by his father but... What if there was an intruder out there? What if someone had broken in to abduct him? Surely then - and only then - his father would okay the use of the bat as a weapon. He asked again, 'Who's there?'

He inched closer to the door with the bat raised up as though it were used for baseball rather than the gentlemanly sport of cricket. With his right hand shaking and sweating - Justin reached for the bedroom door. Hand on handle. Creak from the other side. A moment's hesitation and - he pulled the door open, prepared to hit whatever was on the...

A rabbit?

What?

In the hallway, next to a small wicker basket, there was a small white rabbit. Black eyes, floppy ears and twitching whiskers. And the wicker basket? Inside - a chocolate egg wrapped in gold foil, a pretty bow of red silk tied around it elegantly.

'How'd you get in here?' he asked, lowering the bat.

The rabbit looked at him and tilted his head at the sound of Justin's question. With its head, he nudged the basket towards where the boy was standing. The boy didn't move. The rabbit nudged it closer still.

'For me?' Justin asked, spotting the chocolate egg.

The rabbit stood on its hind legs, whiskers twitching still, and nodded - long ears flapping up and down and swinging even when the head was still.

The Easter Rabbit?

Justin was ten years old. He knew Santa was fake; made up by parents desperate to keep their unruly children in hand. He kind of presumed the Easter Rabbit was the same.

If you're good - you get chocolate! If you're bad... He hops right on by...'

Before Justin could say anything, the rabbit turned and hopped away - down the landing and down the stairs out of sight. Justin wondered whether he'd imagined the whole thing but - when he looked back down... There was the egg, waiting for him in the basket. His egg.

Smiling, the young lad picked the basket up. Now most children would have thought about scoffing the chocolatey goodness for themselves - right there and then - but not Justin. His thoughts were far less selfish. His dad was hungry. His mum was upset. He'd share the egg with them! And with the thought in his head - there was no better time to do so than right now!

With the egg in hand - and the basket left on the floor - he ran down the stairs just in time to see the rabbit disappear out of the un-used cat-flap in the door; installed by the family who had lived in the large house many moons ago.

'What are you doing up?' his father's voice boomed. Justin jumped. His dad was standing in the doorway with an empty crisp packet in his hand and a stern look on his tired face.

'What's that you have there?' Justin's mother was standing in the kitchen doorway. Her eyes fixed upon the chocolate egg.

'The Easter Rabbit!' Justin blurted out. 'He was right here! He gave me a chocolate egg! Look! I mean - I thought he wasn't real but...'

'What?' his father interrupted him. 'The Easter Rabbit? Where?'

Justin - confused at his father's outburst - pointed towards the cat-flap that was still swinging. He explained, 'I thought we could share it. I heard you from upstairs. You're still hungry...'

The father pushed Justin out of the way and grabbed his rifle from where it rested in the hallway cabinet. And - with that - he was out of the same door the rabbit had used, out onto his farmland.

Justin - tears in his eyes - turned to his mum, 'I thought we could share the egg,' he said.

His mother smiled sympathetically, 'It was a lovely idea. Thank you.'

From outside - a rifle shot rang through the air.

'It's probably best you go to bed now,' Justin's mother advised.

Deflated, Justin turned away from his mother and walked back up the stairs towards his bedroom. His Easter egg - *his* easter egg - still in his hands.

Tomorrow will be a better day.

*

Tomorrow had come and the day had been just as any other day that had passed before it. There had been no more chocolate eggs for Justin, not that he minded, and no one mentioned what had happened the previous day. No one needed to. It was evident from the dinner plate - resting on the table before Justin - what had happened. His father - the hardworking farmer - had chased after the rabbit, he had pulled the trigger of his gun, he had fired his shot and he had killed the rabbit. One shot, one kill. And then his mother had ripped the fur from the body and gutted it before cooking it in the oven. No frozen pie for dinner this evening and no frozen pie for the following evening too given how far she'd managed to stretch the meat, and the fact Justin that- with tears in his eyes - didn't want to eat any of it.

'So - boy,' his father said with a mouthful of murdered rabbit, 'how's about some of your egg for dessert?' As he spoke, a small splattering of meat sprayed from his mouth onto Justin's hand, 'Sound good?'

Justin didn't answer. He didn't want to talk to his dad ever again although - for the sake of keeping the peace - he didn't make this obvious to his father. Had he not tried to do the right thing by sharing his egg. Had he not tried to make his mother and father happy. The poor rabbit. Not just any rabbit.

The Easter Rabbit.

The father was now looking up to the mother - a cold stare designed to get her attention.

'Get me a beer,' he ordered when she finally looked up.

THE END

Bio

MATT SHAW is the published author of over 120 stories. Although known as being one of the UK's leading extreme horror authors, he also enjoys spending time in other genres too - something he had always planned to do in order to have at least one book, in a wide collection, which would appeal to people from all walks of life. Shaw was first published in 2004 with his horror novel Happy Ever After - the first of his books to reach the number one slot on Amazon and the first of his books to use his trademark style of narrating the stories through the first person perspective. An extremely prolific writer, Matt Shaw is continually writing as well as keeping up to date with his readers via his (some might say) crazy Author Page on Facebook.

Currently he has half of his back catalogue being translated into Korean and German, has sold multiple film rights and has opened the doors to his own publishing company.

Matt Shaw is also one of the first authors to offer up personalised stories for his readers and the chance for them to appear (and die) in his many stories - something which is being offered up more and more by other authors in the community.

www.facebook.com/mattshawpublications

www.mattshawpublications.co.uk

Bastard Bunny

David Owain Hughes

Same fucking charade, every fucking year! he thought, looking up at the suit that was hanging on the wardrobe. *Well, not this fucking Easter. They can all fuck off*!

"Henry, do hurry down!" he heard Henrietta call from the dining room. "We're all dying to see you in your pretty get up."

I'm sure you are.

He could hear them chuckling at his misfortune.

"Poor Henry. The chap does it *every* year!" he overheard John Green say, followed by a horsey laugh from his wife Charlie.

"Nonsense! Henry loves it," Henrietta said, snorting a laugh.

Bastards! "I'll be down in a moment, dear!" Henry called, trying to remain calm. But it was proving difficult. All week people had asked and ribbed him about Easter.

'*Will you be dressing as Mr. Winkle Whiskers this year?*' or '*I can't wait to see your floppy ears and squishy tail, Henry!*'

"*Ugh*! It's enough to make a fucking saint swear," he uttered. A tick had developed at the side of his face on Monday, and had gradually worsened as the week wore on. *Good Friday*, he thought, continuing to look up at the outsized bunny costume his wife *made* him wear every Easter without fail.

'*The children love it, dear!*' she'd coo.

Little fucking monsters! I hope they choke on their mini eggs, or whatever it is they eat these days.

Once dressed in the atrocity, she would make him attend the annual church fete and run an Easter egg hunt for the children.

It drove him nuts.

Some of the younger children behaved, but not the older ones. They would often belittle him or throw eggs at him – the chocolate and hardboiled kind.

It was a grown man's worst nightmare.

It was a minefield of snot, taunts, goo-goo-ga-gas, chocolate bunnies and humiliation; a wet dream for a perverted, sadomasochist fuck-sack who has a tendency for young flesh.

Last year, he recalled, *some shit-head dumped a spoonful of ice cream down the trapdoor of my suit. The dollop of chocolate was wedged against my anus, before making a cold, slippery path towards my ankle. How the people laughed when they saw me shaking my leg like I was having a fucking fit. Then, as if things couldn't get worse, out pops the hard scoop of ice cream.*

'Ha-ha, old man Henry's shit himself!' some heinous twerp had bellowed.

"Even Henrietta had laughed," he muttered with clenched teeth. His jaw ached. "Well, 'Old man Henry' has a few surprises of his own, this year."

He stared into the rabbit's huge hazel eyes. "Mr. Winkle Whiskers my arse! Bastard Bunny, more like."

The bunny's head looked ridiculous – the ears were coloured pink and white, with one flopped over. The other stood stiff, like a defiant hard-on. The nose was minuscule, with huge, cartoon-like whiskers sprouting from either side. However, one set was longer than the other, due to Henry being held down one year by teenagers who had snipped them.

The thought made his blood boil.

Some of those teenagers' parents were currently sat in his dining room, awaiting a feast he was preparing.

'Oh, they're only children, Henry. Don't take it to heart,' Tim Nettles had said of the incident. '*Boys will be boys!*' Emma, his wife, had chirped.

"And nutters will be nutters!" he said, laughing. Looking over his shoulder, he saw his bolt-action shotgun lying on his bed. A box of cartridges stood by its side. The gleaming barrel and hypnotic walnut stock were inviting.

Turning back to the suit, he grinned. "This will be the best Easter ever!"

Whooping, he stood up and grabbed the costume.

"I may as well give them one last chuckle this Good Friday," he said, a laugh bursting from him.

Throwing the bunny suit onto the bed, he started to undress. He slipped out of his black shoes and trousers before removing his black tunic, clerical collar and white shirt.

Who'd be a fucking vicar anyway?! I've devoted my life to a false God and the worst piece of fiction ever written.

"Hen-*ry*!" his wife bellowed. "Hurry down, will you?"

"Coming, dear!" he said, before muttering, "Fucking whore."

Naked, he looked at his scrawny arms, legs and body. They disgusted him. Pushing the thoughts aside, he stepped into the bastard bunny costume and zipped it up. Before putting the head on, he glanced in the full-length mirror.

I look hideous. On the chest was a giant carrot being munched by a baby rabbit; a small basket of eggs stood by its side. *I wouldn't make a child dress like this, let alone a man in his early forties.*

Putting the head on, he then picked up the shotgun and shells and walked out of the bedroom door. As he crossed the hallway, he stopped at the room where his girls slept – Lucy, seven, and Tina, eight; the room also held a Moses basket for Jacob, his baby boy.

Looking in the room, he remembered how the girls had laced his costume with itching powder three Easters ago, which Henrietta had organised. The year before that, they'd put ants and bugs in bastard bunny's head, which they had orchestrated themselves.

He was seen as the village idiot, not a man of the cloth- a man who should be respected and somewhat feared.

He gripped the gun fiercely

Well, that will soon change! A crimson mist rolled over his vision. All he could hear were the screams of the dead and dying. *There's only so much pushing a man can take.*

Ripping his gaze off the Moses basket, he pocketed the shells and hid the weapon down the front of his costume. Filling his lungs, he started downstairs.

"Shh-shh!" he heard Henrietta say. A few titters were stifled. "He's coming. Christine, get the camera ready!"

Poor lambs. They have no idea, do they? Twelve hungry bellies are about to get filled with fish, roast and buckshot!

When he got to the bottom step, he took another deep breath. Just beyond the door to his left, he could hear them whisper and giggle.

Huffing, he bowed his head and shuffled through the door.

A wave of laughter crashed against him.

Beneath his face covering, Henry could feel his cheeks burn. He'd never been good around a lot of people in close quarters, especially when dressed like a fool.

I've always loathed fancy dress, which Henrietta knows. She loves pushing my buttons.

"Do the dance!" Christine encouraged him.

Looking at her, he drank her in. She was a fat, fifty-something slut who wore skirts way too short for her age, leaving her stocking tops visible for all to see.

No wonder that no good husband of yours left you! Henry thought, trying to avoid the sight of her thick thighs. *Even with a gin-soaked brain, he could see through your lies and knew you were screwing every Tom, Dick and Harry! Well, you're probably not interested in Tom or Harry.*

The camera flash partially blinded him as he hopped, bounced and danced the dance of Mr. Winkle Whiskers. Everyone whooped, cheered and laughed as he made a complete spectacle of himself.

That's right, laugh it up!

"Say it!" Catherine Goodson chimed. "I want to hear you say it, Henry!"

"Yes, please do!" her husband added.

"Are you ready, children?!" Henry said in a goofy voice, causing a hush to fall over his flock. "I can't hear you?!"

Some of his audience members screamed. *"Yes!"*

"Then here comes Mr. Winkle Whiskers with his basket of eggs!" Henry said, starting to hop around the room in a crazed fashion again. "Follow the rabbit, children! Boing, boing, boing..."

"Ha-ha, oh my!" Henrietta laughed. "Look at him, girls!"

"He's silly!" Tina said.

"What a fool," Lucy agreed.

"Mr. Winkle Whiskers has buried his eggs in his cabbage patch. Come and find them, children!" Henry screeched, which was a full-stop to his humiliation, as he bunny-bounced into the kitchen and out of view.

"Ha-ha, what a jester!" Henry heard one of his guests say.

"I know," Henrietta said. "It's nice having a man in his place."

"I need to get my Simon trained," Beth Gibson added.

"Best of luck!" he shot back.

Motherfuckers. All of them!

Taking the head of his costume off, Henry ducked his head back through the kitchen door and addressed his twelve guests. "Could you take a seat at the table, please?"

His wife perched herself at the head of the impressive dining table, whilst their daughters took up seats either side of her.

Turning his back, he opened the oven and removed the six large bass from the oven. After seasoning the fish with cyanide, salt and pepper, he whipped the large tray into the dining room and told his guests to dig in.

"The roast and vegetables will follow shortly!" he said, rushing back into the kitchen.

Whilst opening the oven he noticed the radio. "Hmm, why not!" Turning it on, the room was instantly filled with the sound of a band he didn't recognise. They were singing a song about breaking the law. "Catchy!"

Removing the roast, he put it onto a platter, covered it with a lid, and returned to the dining room. He noticed everyone had started eating the fish except his wife and daughters. A smile played across his face as he put the platter down in the centre of the table.

"Mm! Smells scrummy!" Charlie said.

"Oh, it sure does!" Henrietta agreed.

"Voila!" Henry said, whisking the lid off the roast.

"*Jesus!*" Christine said.

"Not quite!" Henry said.

"*Jacob!*" Henrietta screamed at seeing her son's tiny, smouldering body. It was charcoaled. When Henry put a butcher knife to it, chunks of flesh fell away, causing a scattering of black dust on the white table cloth.

"Hmm, I may have left it in the oven too long!" Henry said. "Sorry, folks!"

To his side, John Green fainted. His face smashed through his plate and slammed against the table. Blood dribbled out of his open mouth, along with a few broken teeth and chunks of china.

"Oh, dear!" Henry said.

"You sick bastard!" Simon said, getting up from his seat. But then he started to violently cough blood and vomit.

"Is the bass not agreeing with you, simple Simon?!"

"You...*Ugh!*" Simon collapsed to his knees, keeling over. Henry could see Simon's bowels had discharged in a hostile way – his excrement was seeping through his trousers and coating the carpet.

The others guests started screaming and crying.

"Don't go, people! What about dessert?" Henry said, removing the bolt-action from inside his costume. Slamming a cartridge in, he cocked the weapon and fired.

The round blasted into Christine's flabby gut; the wide spray of ball bearings tore through furniture, plates, and picture frames, and removed half of Beth Gibson's face.

She hit the deck with an earth-shattering scream, and she tried to hold what was left of her face together.

Blood splashed across the table and erupted up a wall.

With a fresh cartridge loaded and cocked, he blew a hole through Catherine's neck before unloading a lucky round into her husband's crotch. Mr. Goodson's pulped privates tore through his anus and smeared a nearby wall.

Unloading, Henry slammed another shell into the gun. From behind him, John was starting to come around.

"*Argh!*" he screamed, picking shards of glass from his face.

Without a moment's hesitation, Henry put the muzzle of the shotgun to the man's head and fired. It blew apart like a ripe pumpkin hitting the floor; portions of brain and skull matter pebble dashed the table, floor, wall and Henry.

When the dust finally settled, Henry made his way around the fallen bodies and clubbed the wounded to death. His kill count numbered nine.

Henrietta and the girls were missing.

Loading a fresh round into his gun, he cocked the weapon fiercely.

He knew they hadn't escaped the house, because he'd made sure every door and window had been locked and bolted.

Entering the hallway, he looked at himself in the mirror. His face and costume were plastered in blood, with chunks of brain clinging to his bald head.

Floorboards creaked above him.

"Are you ready, children?" he screamed manically. "Looks like old man Henry gets to have his own Easter hunt this year," he concluded, climbing the stairs to the second floor.

THE END

Bio

David Owain Hughes is a horror freak! He grew up on ninja, pirate and horror movies from the age of five, which helped rapidly install in him a vivid imagination. When he grows up, he wishes to be a serial killer with a part-time job in women's lingerie...He's had several short stories published in various online magazines and anthologies, along with articles, reviews and interviews. He's written for This Is Horror, Blood Magazine and Horror Geeks Magazine. He's the author of the popular novel "Walled In" (2014), along with his short story collections "White Walls and Straitjackets" (2015) and "Choice Cuts" (2015).

Links:

Facebook: www.facebook.com/DOHughesAuthor/?ref=hl

Twitter: DOHUGHES32

Website: http://dohughes1103.wix.com/horrorwriter

HE IS RISEN

Duncan Ralston

Fertile green fields rattled by the dirty window. Madison still hadn't gotten used to looking left out of the passenger side as opposed to right. Thankfully, Colin had taken to seating himself on the right-hand side of the car and learnt to drive quite quickly.

"Easy peasy lemon squeezy," he'd said, downshifting with his left hand. They'd been in the English countryside a couple of days by then, sleeping overnight at quaint B&Bs, and Colin had already believed he'd picked up the lingo. Madison was sure the locals thought he was bananas, this silver-haired Canadian asking for a "cuppa" and "biscuits," but she supposed she should at least count herself lucky he hadn't started imitating the accent—*yet*.

The weather channel had called for rain this afternoon, but the sky had been blue since they'd arrived at Heathrow on Tuesday. Odd weather for April, the weatherman had mentioned, particularly considering the great dump of rain that had hammered most of the northern hemisphere during the winter. Madison was grateful for the respite. Rain depressed her, and the snow and "greige" in Toronto still hadn't let up by the time they'd left the city. When Colin had suggested they travel up the Irish Sea coast to a fellow professor's country home near the Scottish border during break, she'd been leery, but anxious to spend some time with him off-campus. They'd only been dating since the beginning of first semester, and she thought this time together—away from the pressures of school and the prying eyes of the few students who knew of their pairing and found it questionable, Madison being Colin's T.A. (as opposed to his *T and A*, an insult she'd heard from several students)—just might push their relationship to the next level.

The weather had been a nice surprise. The sea air was crisp, but the sun felt good on her pale face. Colin was smiling at the road ahead, the small hatchback rumbling along a single lane of macadam carved out of the green as he slapped the wheel to an old Clash song on the radio.

"Hey, check it out," he said, his smile fading.

Madison followed his gaze. Among the green three—or was it *four*?—sharp gray stones jutted up from the earth like ancient claws. "Stonehenge?" she said.

Colin shook his head. "We're nowhere near there. The 'Henge is south of where we started. They've got standing stones all over the countryside out here, though. Nobody knows who left them, or why."

"*Nobody* knows?"

Colin gave her a curious look. "Well, I'm sure *somebody* knows. Spinal Tap, maybe."

He grinned at her, awaiting her reaction. Not getting the reference, Madison narrowed her eyes at him. The gap in their ages often showed itself in little things like this. She told her friends age didn't matter, and usually she tried not to let it get to her, but the more these differences piled on, the more she felt the gap grow wider, until someday it would yawn like the mouth of a canyon, and one or both of them would stumble in reeling.

"Speaking of hard things..." Madison reached over with a grin and squeezed the front of his jeans. She felt for his cock, and began to massage it to life. Colin gave her an odd look. He took her hand, squeezed her cold fingers a moment, and placed it on her lap.

"Not while I'm driving, luv," he said.

Madison looked left out the window as they passed the standing stones, sulking for several minutes, as "London Calling" gave way to "A Whiter Shade of Pale," and the gray slabs of rock disappeared in the mirror. Colin began to whistle along to the organ.

Though Madison liked many modern artists, and he enjoyed a fair bit of jazz—a genre completely lost on her—a love of classic rock was something they both shared. She turned to him and smiled, his shaggy silver hair riffling in the breeze from his window which was open a crack. A road sign caught her eye then, written in an incomprehensible jumble of black letters she supposed must be Welsh or Gaelic:

DRWS MARWOLAETH

"Is that the name of a town?"

Colin squinted at the sign as they passed. "That, or one of the Old Gods." He grinned at her, and once again, the reference flew over her head.

Moments later, the town rose out of the fields. First there was nothing but green, and then pitched rooftops with smoking chimneys became visible, and windows bright with sunlight, and proper roads zigzagging, where people strolled cheerily and cars drove slowly, all seemingly moving toward the same place, the northern—if her directions were correct—end of town.

Colin followed the flow of traffic—not that he could have done otherwise even if they hadn't already been heading in that direction. Men and women walked hand-in-hand. Children scurried ahead, dressed in their Sunday best, some holding bunches of yellow flowers. Store owners flipped signs to CLOSED in the windows of stone shops, put on their caps and joined their fellow citizens marching down the main thoroughfare.

"It's Easter," Madison realized.

"Oh, right," Colin said, peering around edgily like a man in a shark cage. "Well, I guess that tells us where they're all heading."

A little girl wearing a pink bonnet waved at Madison, who smiled and waved back. The girl blew into a homemade pinwheel, making it spin. "What a friendly little town," Madison thought aloud.

"Too friendly, if you ask me."

"Why do you always have to be so suspicious of everything?"

"Comes with the territory," he said, grinning at her, and she managed to get that one: he meant because he was a philosophy professor. "You're a Catholic girl, aren't you? When's the last time you went to mass?"

"I'm a C & E Catholic." Colin raised an eyebrow at her. She grinned, having stumped him for once. "Christmas and Easter," she explained. "I totally forgot this year. Usually I'm at home over Easter, and my parents would take us."

"Doesn't say much for your devotion to the faith."

Madison scowled at him. Colin had often teased her about her religion. She'd never been devout, and didn't mind his jabs so much in the abstract, but in the midst of so many seemingly dedicated worshippers heading joyfully toward church, it irked her, felt somehow *profane*.

"How about we have a look at how Easter is celebrated in the picturesque town of Derwiss Marwo... *whatever*?"

"You just want to go so you can poke fun."

"No," he laughed. "I'm serious. I am honestly interested, Madison." Colin bit down a wicked smile, crossing his index and middle fingers. "Scout's honor."

Madison chuckled. "Who even says that anymore?"

Smirking out the window, Colin honked the horn, startling an old woman before waving innocently at her as she scowled down at him from under her frilly purple Derby.

"*Colin*," Madison scolded, grabbing him by the shoulder and swatting his leg.

"Just trying to get the giggles out before we enter the Holy Place."

"If you laugh in that church, you won't be seeing my Holy Place the rest of the trip."

Colin laughed. "That's what I love about you. You're not afraid to blackmail me with sex."

Madison's smile never faltered, though neither of them had ever spoken of love before, and she wasn't sure she felt it herself. She took a moment to ponder it, and by the time she'd settled on a response, Colin had already shifted focus to the massive church up the hill.

Hewn out of stone, like most of the edifices in town, the Gothic church towered over all that stood beneath it, casting its long shadow down the lush green hillside. The churches they'd seen here had dust older than most surviving parishes in Toronto, where few buildings predated the mid- to late-1800s. The sense of history in a place like this, of *life*, was far richer than in much of the Commonwealth.

Families left cars parked along the long gravel drive, and in muddy tracks carved into the grass like at a rock concert, and ascended the rest of the way on foot. Colin pulled over into a tight space on the grass, muttering, "When in Rome," and the two of them climbed out together under the church's cool, dark shadow.

"Are you sure about this?"

"It's Easter," Colin said. "I'm sure God wouldn't approve of one of His children missing the day His only begotten Son rose from the dead," he added, rolling the *R* in *rose*.

"Don't start with the accents," she muttered, peering around to see if any of the townsfolk had heard him. "*Please*."

"I shall make no promises," Colin said in passible posh English.

Madison elbowed him in the ribs, and he slipped his arm around hers. As she leaned into his shoulder, they caught up with the group.

"Welcome, welcome," said a hunched elderly man with a shiny liver-spotted pate, his green jacket emblazoned with various medals.

"Did you see that?" Colin asked in hushed awe as they left him shuffling slowly behind them. "The two crossed swords. He was wearing a medal from World War I!"

"Is that weird?"

"Well, considering the last World War I veteran died in 2012 or so, I'd say it's a bit weird, innit?"

Madison removed her head from Colin's shoulder to study the faces of those around them, hoping no one had heard his Britishism. Everyone seemed focused on themselves or each other, wearing smiles as they trudged the gravel drive to church. A little boy in black short pants with a jacket and tie wound his way between moving legs, somehow managing to not get trampled as he hurried to the front of the line.

"Maybe it's his father's," Madison said, having lost the old man in the crowd.

Colin shrugged up his shoulders. "I suppose you're right."

Hard soles hoofed up the church stairs toward the arched doors which opened on a gloomy vestibule. The line seemed to take forever to progress, and as she and Colin climbed the stairs themselves, she saw the priest or pastor shaking the hands of every adult as they entered, and greeting the children warmly. A sign at the front announced it to be The Church of St. Francis.

"Not too late to change your mind," Colin offered.

"You're the one that should be worried. Just don't touch the baptismal water, you'll probably get scalded."

Colin showed his white teeth in a grin.

As the husband and wife ahead of them shook the pastor's hand, the pastor caught Madison's eye and smiled.

"Welcome, welcome," the pastor—preacher?—said with a slight Welsh lilt to his voice. Tall and broad, dressed entirely in black save for the white collar, his pale face stood out starkly from under black, slicked-back hair. He held out a long-fingered hand, and Colin took it. The man rested his other hand on Colin's shoulder, which Colin glanced at without expression. "Welcome to our little church and our little town."

"Little?" Colin remarked. "I'd hate to see the big one."

The religious man smiled patiently, then focused his attention on Madison.

"We do so enjoy visitors," he said, taking her hand, "but we'd love for you to stay a spell. Our little town has plenty to offer."

"Thank you, Reverend," Madison said as he let go of her hand.

"'Jack' is just fine," he said, and greeted the people behind them as the two of them moved ahead.

"He seems nice," Madison whispered as they entered the nave.

"*Everyone* seems nice," Colin said. "It's a little eerie."

"So cynical," she said. They sat in an empty pew near the back, Madison craning her neck to get a look at the vaulted ceiling high above, painted with scowling angels and morose saints, as more townsfolk piled in and took their seats. Finally, Reverend Jack entered and strode to the front. He took his place behind the pulpit, and the crowd quietened.

"Easter is a celebration of the Risen Christ... these days, it's difficult for some to believe in the Resurrection, and even more difficult to believe that Jesus brought a common man back from the dead, a man named Lazarus."

Murmurs rippled through the gatherers. Some shook their heads. "Of course, we here in Drws Marwolaeth know it to be true, as true as the rest of the Good Book. Jesus spent several days and nights in the earth—it's never quite clear how many days and nights He spent in His tomb, and nor does it matter. What matters is, crucifixion on Good Friday," he held out his right hand, palm up, "risen on Easter Monday," and he did the same with his left. "Jesus died to absolve us of our sins, and He rose again to prove that only He who created life has the power to *bring it back*."

His parishioners nodded. Colin turned to Madison with a quizzical frown, as if she being used to this sort of rhetoric might know where the reverend was leading.

"Man has always aspired to be like Him," Reverend Jack said. "It was our own St. Francis of Assisi who said, 'I want to know Christ—to know the power of His resurrection and participate in His sufferings, *becoming like Him in His death*,'" he emphasized, his gaze sweeping from right to left. "Of course, there will always be doubters. Thomas did not believe the other Apostles when they told him—"

Several pews closer to the front, the little girl Madison had seen in the street turned and slumped her elbows over the chair. She raised the pinwheel and blew into it, its spokes reflecting bright colors as it spun. Madison waved, but the girl's mother tugged on her daughter's sleeve, and the little girl slumped back in her seat.

"And now," the reverend went on, "I'd like to ask that you all go outside, and join me in clipping our fair church, in the hopes that the Good Lord will bestow upon our church, and our town, new life."

The parishioners rose. Colin peered skeptically around at them. "That's it?" He shrugged. "I guess that's it."

"What's clipping?" Madison wondered.

"Never heard of it. Likely just some folk tradition they trot out to creep out the heathens. And what was all that about the 'power of resurrection'?"

"Christ's resurrection is very important to the church," Madison said, the two of them remaining seated for the time being while the parishioners marched outside. "Easter's much more important than Christmas for Catholics."

"Are these people Catholics, you think?"

Madison shrugged. "If they are, it's very different from what I grew up with. No bells and smells. Not even a Eucharist."

"Ah yes, the Holy Cracker," Colin jibed, and Madison elbowed him again. "You'd better stop doing that, or it might become a fetish," he said, and kissed her neck below the ear. A chill ran up her spine and she giggled. The little girl with the pinwheel passed by then, holding her mother's hand, and the girl waved timidly as Madison wriggled out of Colin's embrace to twiddle her fingers, feeling slightly ashamed.

"We would be honored if you would join us for the clipping," Reverend Jack said as he approached their pew.

Madison and Colin rose to their feet respectfully. "We'd love to join you, Rev— Jack," Colin said. "What is clipping, exactly?"

A smile flashed across the reverend's pale face. "Come and see," he said, ushering them into the aisle with an open palm. "We won't bite, I assure you."

Madison stepped out. Colin followed behind her, and the reverend led the two of them out into the gloomy vestibule.

"We use Easter as a time to reflect on our own mortality," Reverend Jack was saying. "And also to encourage a renewal of life. You've likely noticed there are many lovely young children in Drws Marwolaeth, but our hope is always for more children, to carry on our way of life." He smiled over his shoulder as they stepped out into the sunshine. "If I may be so bold, do you plan to have children?"

Madison and Colin shared a brief look, shielding the sun from their eyes. "We haven't discussed it yet, Jack," she said.

"I see. Well, plenty of time, I suppose. Time," he said, seeming to reflect. "This is a very old town. Our traditions predate that of many communities in the North West. We're one of the only towns to continue the practice of clipping, a very old tradition— and certainly the only church to do it on Easter Monday, in honour of our namesake. Clipping derives from the Old English word *clyppan*, you see, which roughly translated means embrace, or circle."

He directed their attention to the townsfolk who had gathered outside, not in a group but in a line, each holding the hand of those on either side of them as the queue began to stretch around the church. It reminded Madison of "Ring Around the Roses," and the image troubled her somewhat as she recalled a time when she'd played the game with her friends, and when they all fell *down*, the other girls had pretended to be dead. She'd gone around shaking them, trying to wake them up, but nobody moved or spoke until Loren Ainsley broke into giggles and the rest of them rose around her in a chorus of damning laughter.

"What we do," the reverend said, "as you see now, is we all join hands and circle the church. Once we've all linked hands and the circle is unbroken, we round the church once to clockwise, and once anticlockwise. There must always be enough of us to completely encircle the church, otherwise the point is lost."

"And what *is* the point?" Colin asked.

The reverend squinted at him. "Like many rituals, its intended purpose has been lost to time. However, we like to believe it protects us, and protects our way of life. There's something to be said for a bit of mystery though, no?"

"Some might say it's the spice of life," Colin said, and slipped his arm around Madison's. A woman approached the reverend, holding out something slate gray and globular. As Jack took it, Madison saw that it was a rabbit mask, though it was a far cry from the Easter Bunny, so devoid of cutesy as to be sinister. The reverend placed the mask on his head, tugged the strap behind it, and turned to them, only his clear blue eyes and mouth visible. "For the benefit of the children," he explained, shrugging up his broad shoulders.

Reverend Jack the Bunny trotted down the stairs, chasing behind a few straggling boys and girls, who scurried to meet the end of the line. "Run!" he cried, laughing heartily. "Run, little children! We mustn't dally or the Easter Hare shan't leave his eggs!"

Colin turned to her. "Well, what do you think?"

Madison shrugged. "It's bizarre. But it's kind of sweet."

Colin embraced her and kissed her temple. She hugged him back, then started down the stairs to catch up with the others as the head of the line emerged around the other side of the church. Colin took the hand of a young dark-haired woman with high Irish cheekbones at the end of the clipping circle, and Madison took the hand left over. The old veteran took her free hand, smiling warmly at her from what had been the head of the line as they continued their stroll. Jealousy tweaked at Madison's nerves as the fair-skinned woman smiled back at Colin, but she trusted him. He could have slept with just about any woman in school, and he'd chosen her. If he'd been in the mood to sleep around, he'd have suggested it by now, and he certainly wouldn't have dragged her all the way out to the other side of the pond to do it.

She let the cheerful townsfolk merry-go-round her to the side of the church, where the crumbled, mossy gray stones of an old graveyard became visible on a green hill, the flat gray sea beyond it. Madison looked up at the steeple and bell tower, meeting the googly eyes of a gargoyle made to look like a monkey sticking out its tongue. Ahead of Colin and the dark-haired seductress, the pinwheel spun in the girl's limp pale hand as the wind took it, the girl herself hidden behind trudging legs.

Reverend Jack the Rabbit sprung from a doorway, throwing up his hands, and several people screamed, including the dark-haired woman, who smiled embarrassedly over her shoulder at Colin. They all laughed when the reverend raised the mask, and he smiled down on Madison as she passed.

"I hope we don't ruddy go 'round for very much longer," the old veteran said to Madison as they marched around the back of the church.

Madison smiled politely. She considered asking him about the medal Colin had pointed out earlier, but a woman's voice called out, "Now, round and round anticlockwise!" It took a bit of fumbling, laughter and apologies for people to get themselves turned around and traveling in the other direction. They passed the doorway where the reverend had jumped out and scared them, and for a moment, she felt Colin's hand slip from hers before snatching it again.

"Do you have the time?" the old man asked over his shoulder.

Madison twisted the hand he held to look at her watch. "It's quarter to two."

"Quarter of two, already? *Cor*, I'll need my kip in an hour!"

Madison didn't know what a "kip" was, but she smiled in sympathy. Colin's cold fingers grasped hers tighter, and she turned to smile back at him, startling when she saw that a freckled young man with thick, dark eyebrows held her hand instead of Colin. "Where's my boyfriend?" The young man scowled at her. She called out Colin's name, prying her hand loose from the young man's, who held tight. "Have you seen my... my boyfriend?"

The young man continued forward, shoving her brusquely out of the way. Men and women gawked at her, suddenly not so friendly. The fields were empty. Gray clouds scudded across the sky. "Colin!" she cried, hurrying along in the other direction, disoriented by the blur of townsfolk trudging forward. "*COLIN!*"

The little girl's pinwheel stood alone in the grass, spinning in the wind. A simian-like gargoyle stood on its perch displaying its genitals, mocking her.

Madison stopped running when she reached the doorway, a part of her already certain Colin had slipped off with the dark-haired woman into some dark corner of the church. Everyone was out here, mindlessly circling. Inside, they would have privacy. She had to get in. The queue kept moving forward, blank stares meeting her frightened eyes, no one kind enough to break the circle and let her through.

"Excuse me!" The townsfolk gave her bewildered looks. "Get out of my way!" she shouted, ducking to squeeze in under the arms of an elderly couple, pulling their hands apart and temporarily breaking the circle. She stood in the alcove where the reverend had hidden, hugging the door in bewildered terror as the glowering eyes of the crowd still circled.

Nervous about turning her back on them, Madison kept an eye on the clipping circle and tried the doors. She spilled into a small dark vestibule as they opened. She closed them behind her, cold eyes peering in at her as the doors came together.

"*Colin!*" Her own voice echoed in reply. Madison pressed her palms against her eyes, adjusting them to the darkness. The small, round chamber contained a door and a winding set of stone stairs. She tried the door, found it locked. Upstairs then, or back outside with the insane people and their poor, oblivious little children.

Madison called out his name once more on the stairs. The damp walls were cold to the touch, but the height made her nervous. She felt her way up to the top, where another door muffled voices in whatever room lay beyond. She pressed her ear against it, not ready to get caught by surprise, worried she might die if she saw Colin with another woman. Difficult to identify the sounds beyond the door: moaning or talking or some kind of rhythmic chanting.

Only one way to find out, she thought, and twisted the knob.

She saw Reverend Jack Rabbit first, standing at the far end of the bell tower, reading from a book he held out in one long-fingered hand. Candles burned and smoldered from crevasses in the walls. Below the old brass bell, Colin lay shirtless on a stone slab. The dark-haired woman lifted his head by his beautiful silver hair and before Madison could raise her voice in alarm, she dragged a curved blade across his throat.

The blood came in gouts, splashing the dark-haired woman's coat and showering Colin's chest as his tongue wriggled in strangled chokes, his warm brown eyes locked on Madison. She stumbled back, reaching out to grab hold of the arch, only vaguely aware of the steep drop behind her. Cold hands snatched her from behind and forced her roughly into the room.

The reverend pulled up his mask with a grin. "Ah... you've arrived just in time, my dear child, to bear witness to the conclusion of the ritual."

Madison struggled against the hands. "Let me go! *What the fuck is wrong with you people?*"

"Wrong?" He closed the book. "Funny you should ask. You see, this town is quite old, and so are we. Several of us are older than this church, aren't we, Carwen?"

Carwen, the dark-haired woman, winked and smiled, allowing Colin's head to strike the stone while his gurgling abruptly ceased. As the reverend crossed to Madison, Carwen unbuttoned her long red coat, revealing her pale, freckled body, small breasts with puffy, perky nipples, a triangle of dark hair in the crease below her jutting hipbones.

"What's she doing?" Madison wanted to know.

"Never mind her. Listen to me, my dear. If we're to prosper, this town needs children. You could live with us, the two of you."

Behind him, Carwen unzipped Colin's jeans and jerked them and his white briefs down to his knees. Colin's penis, slightly crooked in its thatch of salt-and-pepper pubic hair, sagged over his tightened balls while his lifeblood trickled down the slab to the cold stone floor, and his dead eyes stared vacantly at the interior of the bell above his head.

"You ki— you *killed* him..." Madison wept, as the reality of it sunk in. "*You killed my Colin!*"

"Ah yes, but the power of resurrection!" Reverend Jack said. "St. Francis was right... it is possible to know the power of resurrection! To become like Him in death. He will *rise again*, my dear. We have *all* risen again."

"This is insane!" She struggled against the cold hands, hot tears streaming down her face. "*You're insane!*"

The reverend unbuttoned and removed his collar, revealing a jagged pink scar across his throat. "Do not doubt me, Thomas," he said to her calmly. He nodded to whomever still held her tight. "Show her."

The hands let her go, and she twisted round, face to face with the young man with thick eyebrows. He pulled up his shirt, and she turned away, not wanting to see.

"Look at him, dear."

She didn't want to look, but the reverend wore the rabbit mask again, and Carwen had straddled Colin's body, crouching over his hips and thrusting herself back and forth on his limp cock, now glistening with her juices. She'd always thought she would die if she saw Colin with another woman, but here she was still alive and Colin dead. Reluctantly, Madison turned. The young man smiled at her, fingering a large open wound like a fish gill under his ribs.

"The same wound Pontius Pilate gave to Jesus," Reverend Jack said. "Do you still doubt?"

Madison shuddered. "What is this...?" she managed to groan.

"We need more children," the reverend said. "Only the dead can impregnate the dead."

"But... but he's..." She turned to her lover, tears filling her eyes, causing her vision to blur. She blinked them away, startling as Colin's prick began to stiffen, rising like a snake from the bushes. Carwen grasped it, and slipped it into her dark, wet tomb.

"He is risen," the reverend smiled, and Madison fainted dead away.

Bio

Duncan Ralston was born in Toronto, and spent his teens in a small town. As a "grown-up," Duncan lives with his girlfriend and their dog in Toronto, where he writes about the things that frighten and disturb him. In addition to twisted short stories found in *Gristle & Bone*, *The Animal*, and the charity anthology *The Black Room Manuscripts*, his debut novel *Salvage* is available now.

You can connect with him on Facebook (www.facebook.com/duncanralstonfiction) and Twitter (www.twitter.com/userbits), and at his website The Fold, www.duncanralston.com.

The Chickens and the Three Gods

By Kit Power

The four chickens our tale concerns were adopted young, within a couple of weeks of coming of age – measured by chickens, naturally enough, from the time they start laying eggs. They were taken from their siblings – two brown, two white – and placed in a small domestic garden. The home they were given was spacious, with a nesting box and feeding area. For three days they were kept in there, fussing and fidgeting and engaging in displays of dominance. Sorting out the pecking order.

In this period, they met their first God.

The first God was a Hen-Human. She brought them food, water, changed the bedding straw, took the eggs, and gave them foraging seed in the afternoon. They named her C'ra, which is chicken for 'Mother'. They loved her (as much as chickens can love, which sad to say is not a great deal) and revered her, and attempted to reward her by laying regularly.

C'ra often set them loose in the garden of an afternoon. There they ate the grass, dug for worms and grubs, and shat on the patio.

Here they met for the first time their second God.

He was a Cock-Human. He also gave them foraging seed, and sometimes he would crumb bread and throw it for them. He scraped out and cleaned their home every two weeks, removing all the accumulated shit and matted straw, and replacing it with clean. Though they saw him less frequently, his kindness meant they revered him too, and called him R'ak, which is chicken for 'Father'. In deference to him, they tried their best to shit in a particular section of the dwelling, to make his work easier (unfortunately, chickens are largely incontinent, and this effort was therefore not hugely successful).

Three weeks after their arrival, the four chickens were loose in the garden, enjoying a late summer afternoon bug hunt. C'ra and R'ak were sat in chairs, talking in the gabbling human noise, holding their strange featherless wings together, and drinking from brown bottles something that smelt to the chickens like rancid water. After an exchange, R'ak got up and walked into the Human House.

He returned with a miniature human on his wing.

The miniature human smelled like a Cock-Human to the chickens, but it was so small they couldn't be sure. It only just came up to R'ak's thigh, and was pink-fleshed save for shoes and comically large white pants. The mini-human made gurgling, oddly pitched noises that made the chickens' heads hurt, but R'ak and C'ra smiled and cooed at every sound, apparently immune to the pain.

Whilst the chickens marvelled at this, R'ak let the mini-human go, pointing in the general direction of the garden.

What followed was pandemonium.

The mini-human uttered a shriek that pierced the chicken skulls like a drill, and then charged. Its gait was lumbering and ungainly, but its purpose was unmistakable. The chickens turned as one to the source of the noise, and beheld what dwelt in its eyes.

What they saw filled them with dread. They knew one of their own.

They scattered at its approach, understanding instinctively that the herd is a bigger target. This elicited another awful shriek from the creature, and it put on an alarming burst of speed. The pink mini-human pursued one, then another, changing course seemingly at random. The chickens clucked and squawked their terror to R'ak and C'ra, but their lamentations fell on deaf ears - the two Gods simply observed, smiling.

Quickly, the chickens realised that the creature would pursue whoever it was closest to, and so began a quite horrible game of Tag, where each hunted animal would run close enough to another to draw the staggering monster's attention, until all the chickens were ragged and terrified.

Finally, one of them, more through luck than judgement, fled back into their new home. There was a moment of pure existential terror as the creature began pursuit, but C'ra suddenly intervened, plucking up the awful noise-producing thing, with a tone that implied admonishment.

The other chickens, relieved at the notion that they had sanctuary, retreated in short order to their home, and cowered until the creature was removed from the garden.

They had met their third God. They named it B'rok, which is chicken for 'Chaos'.

B'rok became a constant source of terror over the following weeks. It would kick the side of their home, and bang on the wire roof of their run. It would sometimes feed them bread, but it would break it too big, causing the chickens to fight, and often it would only wave the bread at them before simply consuming it, producing its hateful sound the whole time.

The afternoon garden forages became fraught also – the chickens simply could not relax, always on edge, awaiting the arrival of the pink bundle of miniature malevolence, and the inevitable chase that would ensue. The chickens grew increasingly agitated, and despite their continued and sustained prayers, their Gods offered neither relief nor succour.

The final straw came during one such chase session. B'rok had become more and more agile, faster and harder to avoid. A couple of times it had managed to grab at the tails of the slower brown hens, and the shrieks from B'rok that followed such moments were excruciating.

On this occasion, B'rok had managed to corner one of the white hens – the head hen, as it happened. R'ak and C'ra were indifferent, sitting and making noises. The head hen was frozen in panic. B'rok laid both hands on her wings and squeezed, gurgling its demonic noise directly into the hen's face, vibrating her thin skull and utterly enraging her tiny chicken brain.

She was the head hen, and she'd got there the way head hens always do. The paralysis broke, all at once, and she did what came naturally.

She pecked.

Her beak pierced the fleshy lump in the centre of B'rok's face. She tasted hot flesh and blood. B'rok jumped back, stumbled and fell, then threw it's head back and bellowed.

The head hen thought the sound was wonderful. Like music.

So fascinated was she by the beautiful noise (and also by the feel of fresh blood and meat in her belly), she was scarcely aware of the two other Gods running over to investigate.

C'ra swept the suddenly-musical thing up into her arms, breaking the head hen's spell, and, too late, she became aware of R'ak, swinging his foot towards her.

The blow lifted her off her feet. She collided with the wooden fence and landed badly, winded. Even in her shock she saw R'ak closing in again, making a noise she'd never heard before, deep and loud. She understood he had turned Predator, and meant to kill her. Instinct took over. She fled into her home.

She remained in there for several minutes, until the fear faded. She ventured out of the hutch and into the enclosed run, but all the Gods had gone, and the other chickens were back inside with her.

The chickens went about their business, and then the Gods returned. C'ra was cradling B'rok, who was still making that sweet sound. The injury to his face was covered, but the head hen could still smell the blood.

R'ak opened the cage, and the chickens shrank back, fearing another attack.

Instead, he grabbed their water and removed it from the cage. He pointed at B'rok, making that same low, loud noise, then at the head hen, then at their water. Then, with slow deliberation, he poured it all out over the grass, before throwing the empty container back in the hutch. He then went to the Food Place, removed The Lid, and took out a cup of foraging seed – their afternoon food. He pointed again at B'rok, at the injury, then the head hen, then he scattered the seeds on the ground outside the cage.

The cup and lid were replaced, and the Gods left.

The chickens were distraught – it was warm, they had been chased, they were thirsty – but the Gods were indifferent to their lamentations. They became hungry too, and could see the seeds on the ground, but their beaks were not long enough to reach them. Instead, they had to watch as local birds, drawn by the commotion, feasted on their seeds before flying off, unafraid. Their territory had been violated.

The chickens became angry.

That night, after a full afternoon and evening of no food and no water, they held conference in the sleeping area. Chickens have no words, of course, but through clucks, movement and scratching, they manage rudimentary communication. They expressed dismay, despair, hunger, fear, anger. Their Gods had forsaken them. They had given the chickens over to B'rok, and punished them when their leader stood up to it.

B'rok had turned the other Gods against them.

The head hen waited for a moment, then scratched once with her left foot, decisively. The others fell silent at once.

Our Gods have forsaken us. B'rok is to blame. B'rok rules them.

B'rok is our enemy. B'rok makes the Bad Noise that pains us so. B'rok chases, hurts. B'rok grows bigger, stronger, faster.

The head hen let this sink in, feeling the fear and rage rising in her sisters. Letting it build. Then:

B'rok tastes of prey.

The others burst into excited song, happy, anxious.

Hungry.

B'rok tastes of prey, the head hen repeated. B'rok is our Predator, but B'rok tastes like prey.

B'rok is dangerous. B'rok is *small*.

Sisters. Let us use our Magic.

Sisters, let us cast the ritual.

*

For the next week, things went on as before. C'ra and R'ak returned to their roles, providing food and water. And of an afternoon, B'rok terrorized the chickens and chased them around their former garden paradise. They knew better than to fight back, and instead fled to their home, only emerging again when C'ra or R'ak took B'rok away.

Over the week, each laid one egg in the Perch rather than the Nest. These eggs were hidden in a small pile of straw. The Gods did not disturb the Perch apart from the Cleans, and this was not due to happen for several days yet. The chickens were restless during this period, uneasy. They possessed only limited awareness, but some part of their animal brains understood that what they were about to do was dangerous.

Forbidden.

Still, on the night of the perfect half moon, under the light of judgement, the chickens placed their eggs on the floor of the Perch. They stood, beaks facing in, and waited for the ritual to take them.

They all moved as one, jabbing forwards and opening the eggs. The yellow and clear fluids poured together in a sticky mass, mingling with the shit and straw and creating a paste.

Again as one, each pecked, piercing the yolks, freeing the yellow fluid to mix and swirl. The head hen moved into the centre and the others formed a triangle, with her as the eye. She scratched and scratched, her feet smearing the fluid, drawing crude shapes and sigils in the paste with her claws. The others just stared, unmoving.

Several minutes passed before the symbols were complete, then the head hen raised her beak. She clucked once. Immediately, the other hens jabbed, opening three wounds in her wings. She flapped, small droplets of blood splashing the walls, until eventually a few drops fell from her wing feathers into the circle she had drawn.

As this happened, she began her song. The other chickens joined in, their voices mixing in disharmony. The sound was chickens, yet unlike any sound a chicken has been heard to make. It was eerie and discordant. It rose in the air, aided by the moon-rays, and wafted in through the brick wall of the house, into the sleeping ears of the Gods.

*

Time inside the ritual had no meaning. The chickens could feel their power rising, feel it mingling, becoming greater than the sum of its parts. They felt the Magic rise from them. Felt it touch the mind of a sleeper, then wrap around it like a snake. Felt the slumbering rise.

The head hen gave her orders, careful not to break the chant. To hold two thoughts in her mind at once was an act of almost impossible difficulty, but hatred was ever a strong motivator. And she did hate, so very much.

Eventually, they heard the door to the Human House open, and they stopped their song. The Magic had taken root. The ritual had served its purpose.

They left the Roost in a flurry of feathers and a scrabble of claws, tumbling down the run in their haste. There, they saw R'ak. His head was glowing faintly with the residue from the Magic. His face was relaxed, eyes open but unseeing. He closed the thick glassed door behind him, gently.

In his arms, he held the sleeping B'rok.

The night air was cold, and it began to stir as R'ak walked over to the door of the hutch. As he reached to open up, the arm supporting B'rok's head fell away, and it awoke with a start. Immediately, it began to make that sweet noise again, the musical sound that had so pleased the head hen. As the bolt on the hutch was drawn, and the door swung open, she understood in a flash of recognition why the sound was so pleasing to her senses.

It was the sound of cornered prey.

R'ak placed B'rok down indifferently on the floor of the run, plucking one of those small featherless wings off his own as it tried to grasp him. R'ak locked the door and stepped back. The moon lit his face. He was smiling.

B'rok made the sweet noise louder than ever, and began trying to stand. The ground was slippery with shit and spilled water, and B'rok was still groggy from sleep. The chickens' minds responded to the imperative in the sound, and swiftly surrounded B'rok before it could rise.

They pecked. It howled. They pecked some more. It howled again and flailed about, but it was too uncoordinated. Too disoriented.

Too weak.

Their attacks became more insistent, more confident, as each got the taste. The blood and flesh and the sweet, sweet song filled them up and drove them on. Blood mingled with the shit and straw and water. It looked black in the moonlight. R'ak looked without seeing, and smiled on.

Eventually, long after they'd feasted on those delicious, delicate eyes, long after the thrashing had become feeble and ceased altogether, the wonderful noise ceased. But by then the blood frenzy was upon them, and they pecked and pecked and pecked and pecked and pecked.

Bio

Kit Power lives and writes in Milton Keynes, and insists he's fine with that. His short fiction has appeared in a number of venues, including, Kzine, Splatterpunk Zine, the Widowmakers anthology, The Black Room Manuscripts, At Hells Gate Vol II, and others. His debut novel

GodBomb! was published last year by The Sinister Horror Company. Kit also blogs and occasionally reviews for The Gingernuts of Horror website, where his monthly column 'My Life In Horror' occasionally goes viral, to his utter mystification.

He used to own chickens. He doesn't any more. His daughter is just fine, thanks for asking.

Places to find Kit and his books online:

Amazon Author Page: http://www.amazon.co.uk/Kit-Power/e/B00K6J438K/
Facebook: https://www.facebook.com/Kitpowerwriter/
Twitter: @KitGonzo
email: kitpowerwriter@gmail.com
My Life In Horror: http://www.gingernutsofhorror.com/my-life-in-horror.html

Wicker Baskets

By Kindra Sowder

Little Jesse's favorite holiday, well one of them, was Easter followed very closely by Halloween. Why? Candy. And because he was an only child he got only the best candy that his parent's money could buy. He had only expected there to be candy, and maybe a bunny like he had asked for, but he knew more than likely he wouldn't be getting that this year. He decided that he would settle for a large, hollow milk chocolate bunny. He always ate the ears off first. He wasn't sure why, but it just seemed right.

He lay in his bed, waiting for his mother to come and tuck him in like she always did. He knew that his parents were in the living room putting together his Easter basket, but she would stop long enough to kiss him on the forehead and attempt to coax him to slumber. Every year they used a clean, white wicker basket and filled the bottom with iridescent Easter grass that you could purchase from Wal-Mart or even the drug store weeks before Easter actually arrived. Jesse's door creaked open and his mother poked her head inside, a broad smile on her face. Most likely because of the festivities they had planned for tomorrow.

"How's my little man doing?" she asked as she walked into the room and towards his bed with bare feet. She couldn't stand to wear socks or shoes in the house. "Are you excited to see what the Easter Bunny brings you tomorrow?"

"Mom, I'm seven, not stupid. There's no such thing as the Easter Bunny," Jesse whined at his mother.

Her smile never wavered and she responded, "Now, who told you that?" She sat on the bed and began to tuck the blue comforter in around Jesse's tiny body, her dark hair falling down around her shoulders as her dark brown eyes met Jesse's.

"Brandon told me. He said that your mom and dad put all the stuff in the basket at night and you get it when you wake up," he explained.

His mother cleared her throat. "Well, Brandon was just being mean. There is definitely an Easter Bunny."

"Can I see him?"

"No," she shook her head, still smiling, "you have to be asleep when the Easter Bunny comes. Kind of like Santa."

"You mean exactly like Santa?" Jesse asked, skeptical despite his mother's insistence.

"Exactly." She leaned down and kissed him on the forehead, tousling his hair playfully. "Now it's time for you to go to sleep. So the Easter Bunny can come. Maybe you'll get a bunny this year."

"You think so?"

"Maybe," she said with a shrug. She stood up and began to walk to the door, turning halfway between the door and the bed. "Sleep tight, sweetie. I love you."

"I love you too, Mom."

With that Jesse's mom walked out of the room and turned off the light, leaving the door open only a crack so the light from the hallway filtered in. Jesse was afraid of the dark, but refused the night lights his parents bought him so they opted to keep the door cracked open with the light on until he fell asleep. They were always awake later than him so they didn't mind doing this for their son. Not too long after Jesse's mother left the room, his eyes closed and he fell asleep, not even aware of what was about to transpire.

*

"Is he asleep?" Jesse's father asked in a whisper, standing in the hallway with his arms crossed over his chest and leaning against the wall.

Jesse's mother couldn't help but think that those blue eyes of his were still just as penetrating as the day they had met. She walked towards him and snaked her arms around his waist, his hands travelling to her lower back to embrace her.

"He wasn't, but he will be soon. Some kid at school told him there was no Easter Bunny," she sighed in irritation.

"You know kids. They can be mean. What did you tell him?"

"I told him he's real and he has to go to sleep or he won't come, just like Santa. It was all I knew to say."

"You did the right thing," he said as his nuzzled his nose into her hair. She always smelled like fresh granny smith apples and he loved it. "We just have to make sure the Easter Bunny comes so he doesn't think we lied to him."

She pulled away from him and looked into his eyes, a renewed grin spreading across his lips as she looked up at him. She loved her son so much that she would do anything for him, even make certain that he believed in fairy tales. She pulled away from him and began to walk towards the extremely large master bathroom that you could possibly even fit one of those micro houses inside of it. The floors were a dark ceramic tile and the walls were painted a light mossy green that complimented the floors well, looking sort of like a forest had made its way into the house.

"How is she doing?" she asked as she walked through the threshold and towards the side of the massive garden tub where a large cage was set up for Jesse's Easter gift.

"She's doing great, just like I told you she would be," he said. He followed her into the room and she knelt down in front of the cage, the smile not once leaving her face as she stared down at the adorable animal in front of her.

They had bought Jesse a large, white rabbit with black floppy ears and black circles around bright red eyes. It was the most beautiful rabbit she had ever seen as well as one of the biggest. She had long, white whiskers and her nose never stopped twitching as she sat down in front of the cage and reached out to open the door to let it out to jump around for a little while before sticking her back inside until the morning.

"I kind of want to keep her for myself," she said as she took the latch in her hand and pulled it up just enough to open the door and let it fall, clanking against the metal.

"And what about the kitten you want? I could always give that to Jesse instead, I guess." He stood behind her and watched as she reached in and pulled the bunny out of the cage, cradling it against her chest and nuzzling her cheek against the top of its soft head. Her free hand ran over its back, caressing the indulgent, clean fur.

"No, he wants the rabbit. We could always share her." Jesse's mother turned to look at her husband. The bunny squirmed in her arms a little bit so she adjusted her and it calmed instantly. "Plus, this is the best gift we have ever gotten him and possibly will ever get him until he gets old enough to hate us and then we're forced to buy him an overpriced sports car."

Jesse's father laughed and nodded in response. "You're probably right."

"So," she said as she lifted the rabbit into the air and looked directly into her eyes, "Jesse gets the bunny until that time comes. Until then we get to enjoy his excitement. Later he can tell us all about how he hates us even though we got him this bunny when he was seven because he wanted it so badly." She cuddled it to her chest again and kissed the top of its head, petting it as she sat there on floor.

"Sound like a plan," her husband said as he kneeled down beside her, taking his turn to pet the rabbit before his wife placed it lovingly on the floor so it could hop around for a couple hours before having to place her back in the cage for the night.

They would then take her out again and let her hop her way around the house until Jesse found her and cried with excitement. What was it about a rabbit that caused children to squeal in such a way that scared the Hell out of adults because they thought they got hurt? She would never know. She just wanted her son to be happy. They normally stuck with the hollow milk chocolate rabbit that he would eat, starting at the ears, but they wanted to do more for him this year and he wanted a rabbit so bad he had practically begged. They just couldn't say no again.

At exactly the same moment the rabbit sniffed her hand, its nose twitching in that adorable way, there was a knock on their front door that could be heard throughout the house.

"I guess I'll go get that." Jesse's father walked out of the room and continued, "Who the Hell would be here this late, anyways?"

He walked through the living room to the front door, taking the silver knob in his hand without looking through the peep hole, just wanting to get this over with. It must be important for them to come this late. It may have only been nearly ten at night, but once Jesse was down they considered it late because of the risk of waking him up and him being up all night because of it. With the other hand he unlocked the deadbolt, opening the door as soon as he heard the click of the mechanism inside the door. The door swung open to welcome the visitor on the other side.

*

Something had woken Jesse up, but he wasn't sure what that something was. When he opened his eyes it was still dark outside and the light was still on in the hallway and whispers could be heard out in the living room. His parents must have still been awake, making sure everything was perfect for tomorrow since family was coming over to take part in the Easter festivities and his grandparents always brought him something special every Easter. Plus, all of his cousins came over and they got to play. He got out of bed and walked towards his bedroom door, peeking through the crack into the hallway. Maybe he could see something and get a sneak peek of what his parents were giving him for Easter.

"Mom? Dad?" he ventured, opening the door and taking one tentative step out into the hallway just in case he'd get in trouble for being up.

That was when he saw it. A white bunny with black ears and black circles around its eyes was hopping down the hallway in his direction and he knew it had to have been for him. He gasped and ran towards the rabbit, kneeling down just enough to pick up the massive creature and hug it against his chest. It was what he had wanted. Last year they had said that there was no way he could have one because he wasn't old enough to take care of it, but this year was different. He was a big boy now and could take care of it all by himself. He walked as quickly as he could towards the living room, ready to thank his parents for the gift that they had gotten him and to tell them that he loved it.

"Mommy! Daddy! Thank you for the…"

He stopped in his tracks and froze in place when he took in the sight in the living room. His parents were sitting on the dining room chairs that had been moved to the center of the living room. They were covered in blood and their intestines had spilled out of their bellies, unfolding onto the floor around them like raw sausage links. In front of them was the Easter Bunny, sleek white fur covering its body with a pink patch over its belly and ears that stuck straight up in the air, one of them folding over. The Easter Bunny's hands were covered in blood and, sitting on the floor by his knees, was a white wicker basket filled to the brim with beautifully dyed Easter eggs. The Bunny had been stuffing Jesse's mother's belly with them, her empty eyes mirroring those of the Bunny before him. Jesse couldn't speak. He couldn't scream.

All he could do was watch as the Bunny turned towards him, raising a finger to signal that he should be silent, placing it over its open and smiling mouth with an egg still in its other hand.

"Ssshhhhh..."

THE END

Bio

Kindra Sowder was born and raised in Rancho Palos Verdes, CA until the age of 12, when her family moved to Spartanburg, SC. She graduated from high school in 2006 with full honors and as a member of her high school Literary Club and the Spanish Honor Society. In January 2014, she graduated with her second degree in Psychology, earning her an AA and BA in the field. She began to write long before this though, forming the basis for the Executioner Trilogy at the age of 15. She got married to her husband Edd Sowder in May 2014 and still lives in Spartanburg, SC where she is basing Burning Willow Press. "Follow the Ashes" has earned her nominations in the following categories: Best YA Author, Best Cover Art (cover art by Lisa Vasquez), and Best Female Indie Author in the IAFC Awards! Her work "Hello, My Name is...: A Miss Hyde Novella Volume 1" was nominated for Book of the Day's 2015 Summer Book Awards Best in Horror Award.

www.ksowderauthor.com

www.facebook.com/kmkinnaman

www.twitter.com/KindraKinnaman

My Last Easter

By Jack Rollins

The first Faberge eggs were produced by Peter Carl Faberge and his company between 1885 and 1917. The most famous of these were made as exquisite gifts for the wives and mothers of Tsars Alexander III and Nicholas II. Each ornately designed piece contained finely-crafted jewels and trinkets and they were produced every year except in 1904 and 1905 during the Russo-Japanese war. Two additional eggs were believed planned for Easter 1918, but never delivered due to the Russian Revolution.

A legend persists that Peter Carl Faberge lost a beloved nephew in the revolution and, sick with grief, created another egg in secret, one not intended for any Tsar, but imbued with mysterious properties that he believed could bring about an end to all conflict. Forever.

Tommy Pritchard stifled the disappointment well. No chocolate egg from Grandma Somerville this year. His heart had dipped inside his chest when she'd told them. His sister Charlotte, older than him by two years, ever the ten-year-old suck-up, climbed onto Grandma's bed and gave her a big hug.

Tommy kept his distance. *She's too sick to go to the shops to buy Easter eggs? Then she's too sick to cuddle me.* He hated the idea of climbing up there with her. He felt like there was this film over everything in Grandma's house and it seemed to stick to him every time he visited. Largely, this feeling came from the smell. The warm, welcoming smell of chocolate cake baking in the oven had long ago been replaced by a more clinical, plastic smell and sometimes a strong smell he recognised as being *pee*.

As his mum and grandma chatted, with Charlotte pretending she was an adult between them, Tommy gazed at a black and white photograph in a little brown wooden frame, propped on the dressing table. The man in the picture, Grandma had told him, was her Daddy—his *great* grandfather Katovich. Never having met the man, in Tommy's mind's eye, his great grandfather had taken on some sort of legendary, mythical quality —*great* meaning he was a great size, a great warrior, a *great* man. He certainly looked impressive in the picture, in his thick coat with buttons that fastened right over on one side of his chest, instead of down the middle, and a flat cap, that Tommy knew was an army hat. A thick moustache curled up at the corners of the man's mouth. He looked important. Grandma said he went to a *bolshy party*, whatever that was, and Tommy remembered her saying the man called Lenin, was a friend of his. Tommy imagined that the old band his dad liked, *The Beatles*, must have played at that party.

"Give your Grandma a hug, Tommy," his mum urged, breaking his daydream.

"Don't want to."

"Tomm-*eeeee*."

He knew that tone, and he didn't have to look at his mum's face to know exactly how it looked. She could make a dog shit itself with that scowl. Shoulders slumped, bottom lip stuck out and his eyebrows knitted into a frown that matched his mum's, Tommy trudged over the mint green carpet and leaned over to give his grandma a fleeting hug. He retreated to the chair in the corner once more, immediately, as though afraid he'd catch leprosy from her.

"Tommy, sometimes you are such a rude little boy," his mum huffed.

"Yeah," Charlotte chimed, "you are such a rude little boy!"

"That will do, madam," Mrs Pritchard warned, raising a straight finger to her pursed lips.

"Yeah, leave me alone."

"All of you leave him alone," Grandma Somerville commanded. "He's a little boy, he doesn't want to go around cuddling old women like me."

"No, he wants to cuddle Freya at school!"

"Do not!"

"That will do, you two!"

"Yes you do, *Thomas*!"

"Well, you want to cuddle Jeremy at school."

"You two! I have had enough of your bickering. Go downstairs and amuse yourselves, so your Grandma and I can have some peace!"

Charlotte barged Tommy into the wall right before the top of the staircase.

"Watch it, you nearly pushed me down the stairs!" Tommy yelped.

"Watch it yourself," Charlotte said, stomping off ahead. "I can't help it if you're blind!"

Tommy knew better than to keep it up. Either Charlotte would turn around and smack him, or their mum would come down the stairs like a tank, and give them both something to cry about.

Charlotte snatched up the TV remote and plonked herself down in Grandma Somerville's favourite seat. Tommy knew this was his sister claiming superiority in the room. "I wish Grandma had Sky," she muttered jabbing the *channel up* button, flicking from boring show about cooking, to boring show about houses, to boring show about antiques. "There's never anything on *normal* telly."

Tommy ignored her and peered out of the window, watching raindrops chase each other down the glass. *No eggs 'til we get home, and that'll be ages now that Mum and Grandma are gossiping*, he thought – his inner voice as gloomy as the weather. He glanced over his shoulder to see that his sister had settled on *CBBC* and that programme about the kids in the care home. He *hated* that show.

As he turned his attention back to the window, the china cabinet caught his eye. Long had he yearned to slide aside the glass panel and inspect the treasures within, but

Grandma never let him even stand close to the cabinet for fear he would trip and smash everything and hurt himself (Tommy often wondered what her order of priority was on that particular matter).

Tommy pressed his thumb into the gold-painted plastic ring nested in the glass and applied pressure to the right, hoping the glass plate wouldn't stick in the runner and make a noise to get him caught.

"What are you up to?"

Tommy's cheeks flushed and he snapped his hands back by his side. "Nothing."

"You were going to steal from the china cabinet, weren't you?"

"Was not."

"Were so and I'm telling Mum!" Charlotte crossed her arms over her chest and scowled at her little brother.

"Do what you want. I can't get told off for looking." Tommy turned his attention back to the cabinet. He saw crystal animals that looked dark without sunlight, or the cabinet's built-in lamp shooting rainbows through them. Ballerinas stood on pointed tiptoes, lifeless and dull. These things held no interest for Tommy, however. There was a specific piece that had captured his imagination ever since he had first clapped eyes on it.

A tripod of gold fixed a golden belt in place, within which sat an egg about as tall as his *Batman* action figure and at its fattest section, about as wide as the span of his thumb to the tip of his forefinger. He reckoned he could fit about four *Cadbury Crème Eggs* in it at a push, or maybe only three and he could eat one. Staring at the ornamental egg caused him to lick his lips even though he knew the piece was anything but edible.

The exterior of the egg was painted, but the decoration was elaborate and included a finely painted scene of the grown-up-baby-Jesus with his beard and the little towel around his rude bits, and he was hanging on a cross. Tommy rubbed the palms of his hands, when he remembered the gross story about the nails going through the middle of his hands, and through his feet. The story reminded him of that bit in *Home Alone* when the robber stands on the nail and you see it go right into the middle of the soft bit of his foot. He could never watch that and hid his eyes from the screen every time it came on.

At the foot of the cross, bright orange flames lapped at the wood and shadowy, horned figures seemed to prance and dance around, long tongues poking out between their sharp teeth.

They looked like bad-guys. They looked like *Green Goblin*, but shadows. And it looked like they were happy that the grown-up-baby-Jesus was in pain up on the cross. The picture looked like the baddies had won, and it made him feel very strange, because the bad guys were always supposed to lose.

"You like the egg, don't you?" Charlotte asked.

Tommy nodded, never taking his eyes off the piece.

"I touched it once. I held it."

"No, you didn't."

"I did. I got it out and touched it, then put it back before anyone could see."

"Liar."

"Want to see me do it again?" Charlotte asked.

"No," Tommy murmured. "I'm going to do it."

Right then the floorboards creaked as their mum moved around in Grandma's room. Charlotte's eyes turned skyward, but no more sounds came. When she levelled her gaze at her brother, her jaw fell open.

Tommy had slipped his thumb into the plastic hoop once more and pressed his free hand against the glass, sliding the pane aside. He had reached up and snatched the egg, whipping it free of the golden stand, which toppled as he had not the height to lift the egg free in a direct upwards movement, it was more of a drag. The stand collided with a crystal squirrel, which fell from the open front of the cabinet, to land on the thick burgundy carpet with a soft *thud*.

"*Look* what you did!" Charlotte gasped, pointing at the angular little squirrel.

"Look what I *did*!" Tommy exclaimed, holding the egg inches in front of his nose like *Indiana Jones* with a hard-won treasure. Turning the egg, he saw that the scene was repeated front and back, but now, able to see the piece from all angles, he noticed a hinge embedded in the back. "It opens, *look*." Tommy showed his sister the discovery.

Charlotte pounced, snatching the egg away from her brother. "I want to open it!"

"Give it here!" Tommy yelled.

Charlotte stopped in her tracks, holding the egg high above her head, where her little brother couldn't reach it. "*Shhhh!*" she hissed. "If you bring Mum down here, neither of us will see what's inside."

Tommy seethed, knowing his sister was right. He nodded his acceptance of the situation; his need to see the surprise inside this expensive-looking *Kinder Egg* outweighed his need to be the one to actually open it.

"Who is *queeeeeeen*?" Charlotte crowed.

Tommy rolled his eyes up.

"Who is *queeeeeeen*?"

"You're the *fupping* queen, okay?"

"Oooh, swearwords. Maybe I should just put this egg back in the cabinet and tell Mum about your foul mouth."

"Then you don't get to see what's in there, either," Tommy said, his wide eyes seeming to glow with this little victory.

Charlotte grasped the top and bottom of the egg and applied gentle pressure. The top portion tilted on the hinge and a blue glow was cast across Charlotte's face, turning the whites of her eyes into pools of sapphire light.

"Wow!" Charlotte gasped.

"Let me see it!" Tommy cried.

Charlotte lowered the egg so that he could share the view. Within the outer, painted egg, was a glass egg which housed some sort of swirling blue mist, crackling with contained lightning, like a tiny storm trapped in glass.

"Maybe it's like a snow globe," Charlotte suggested, shaking the piece with such violence that the inner egg dislodged and fell from the outer shell. She gasped, waiting for the crash.

Tommy pounced and caught the orb in his right hand. Both he and his sister breathed a sigh of relief. He perched the orb on his fingertips and stared into the glass in awe.

"Look at this," Charlotte cried, holding up the painted outer shell, revealing that the colours had bled away, blurring like a watercolour in the rain, revealing a skin of black porcelain beneath.

"Mum is going to kill us!"

"It's *your* fault, Tommy!" Charlotte yelled, dropping the outer shell to the carpet. She lunged at her little brother, but Tommy tucked the egg close to his chest and barrelled into her, shoulder first. Charlotte crashed to the floor, winded.

Tommy glanced back at her, stopping in the corner to inspect the orb. The swirling clouds contained within had a mesmerising effect, he found it incredibly difficult to focus on anything else. He could hear his mum's footfalls on the stairs. He knew that trouble was on the way, but he could not move. The orb seemed to thrum with a tightly contained power—he could feel it, it was like the feeling he got on his tongue when he licked the top of one of those square batteries, but in his fingertips.

"Give that here!" Charlotte snatched at the orb, knocking it from Tommy's fingers, but her own grasp failed her. The orb shattered against the wall with an ear-splitting crash.

"Look what you did!" Tommy screamed, his face turning red, cheeks burning with rage. His fists squeezed into tight balls and he turned, ready to pound his sister's face.

"What the hell is going on in there?" their mum cried from the stairs.

Charlotte stared over Tommy's shoulder. "Look!"

Tommy turned to see that the storm from the orb was no longer contained. Blue lightning flickered outward, like impossibly fast tentacles, snatching at the curtains, the carpet, the door handle. The clouds swirled and stretched – a vortex of impenetrable darkness forming in the heart of the miniature storm.

"*Fupping* hell!" Tommy squealed.

"Telling on you."

The skirting board's white paint lifted and splinters of bare wood gravitated to the growing clouds. The corner of the carpet tore free of the staples that pinned it down, its threads unravelling, sucked into the vortex like dark red spaghetti.

Tommy backed away as his mum entered the room. "Right, you two! We're going! WHAT THE HELL HAVE YOU DONE?"

"Charlotte did it!"

"Tommy did it!"

The lightning forks snapped at the doorframe and wallpaper peeled away from plaster and splinters of wood darted through the air into the nothingness.

"Out! Get out!" Mum cried.

Tommy stood mesmerised as Charlotte ran to her mother's side, hugging tightly to her hip.

The curtain tore free, snapping the curtain pole as this new gravitational force refused to let go. The windowsill split and disintegrated into the darkness.

Tommy's mum grabbed his wrist and yanked him out of the lounge as a low rumbling sound filled the air. Lightning arcs flashed, blinding and ferocious in their wake, the force of their discharge thudding into the walls and furniture. Tommy could smell a metallic, burning tang in the air.

The three of them burst through the front door, into the chilly rain, in time to see the storm eating through the brickwork of the house—only a couple of bricks at first, but blades of grass rippled, standing on end, pointing at the threat. A dozen bricks collapsed inward, with more peeling away every second. The vortex seemed to gather strength with every passing moment and the lightning flashes in the lounge created a strobe effect so intense that it could even be discerned outside in the daylight.

"Keep going!" Mum ordered.

"What about Grandma?" Charlotte cried.

"I'll get her, just keep away from that... *thing*!"

"Don't do it, Mum," Tommy warned. "Don't go back in there!"

"I have to, Tommy. Grandma needs help to get out of there."

"You won't make it. Neither of you will make it."

Tommy's mum ruffled his hair and cast him a sympathetic look. "She needs me."

"We need you too," came Tommy's response, a lump rising into his throat.

Tommy watched his mum race to the front door as the storm sucked away bricks only a few feet away from her. Daffodils and gravel whipped up from around the lawn, and a lightning flash chopped a chunk out of the turf, leaving a smoking, steaming hole in the grass.

Charlotte screamed as she saw their mum stride through the front door and stop in her tracks.

"MUM!" they both cried in unison.

A bolt of lightning shot through their mother's forehead, neatly punching a tunnel right through her skull. She fell to her knees, steam rising from her white-hot wounds. She toppled forward and, unseen by the two children, another part of the storm must have crept closer to her, as her hair rose on end, tearing free from her scalp, pulling chunks of flesh away. Skin peeled off in layers, down to fat, the muscle, then bone as gradually, another fringe of the storm drifted into view, consuming her body.

Tommy sat on the pavement, hands over his eyes, rocking back and forth. Charlotte raced to the doorway, seemingly oblivious of the fact that what had happened to her mum was bound to happen to her.

Amid the blue glow in the lounge, flickers of orange appeared as textiles, paper and wood caught fire at the force of the lightning strikes. The window frame buckled inward, pausing as the fixing bolts held fast.

Tommy found that he wasn't alone on the street. His grandma's neighbours had come out to see what the fuss was about. "What the hell is that thing? Some sort of gas cloud?" one of them cried.

"Is Hanna still in there?"

"Tommy, where's your mum, son? Can anyone see Justine?"

"Quick, fetch your Dad! I think it's a fire. I think old Hanna's trapped."

Jonathan, who lived right next door to Tommy's Grandma, grabbed Charlotte and dragged her away from the doorway. "Come on, sweetheart. You need to get away from there! It's too dangerous, my petal." The old man wrapped an arm around Tommy, pressing the siblings close together. He turned to the others gathered around. "I saw Justine, I think. It's hard to tell... she's gone."

Charlotte seemed to crumble, squeezing into Tommy's huddled form, knowing Jonathan's meaning – knowing this meant she wasn't dreaming - other people were seeing this, too. It meant that *she* had killed her mother. It meant that *she* had brought about this destruction. It meant that no matter what happened next, it was all, every bit of it, *her* fault. The crushing weight of this truth rendered her dumb. She didn't want to see any more. She didn't want to hear any more. She didn't want to know or accept any more, but the truth rushed in around her from every direction at once, like that *toonami* that hit Japan, guilt lifting her off her feet and dragging her along with its current, *drowning* her.

The window frame finally collapsed, dragging with it the lintel, bricks aligned with the first floor timber and a huge portion of the lounge ceiling. The front door vanished as the vortex expanded to fill the doorframe. More brickwork collapsed inward, the whole front of the ground floor almost exposed. Three more lightning flashes drove the crowd of onlookers back across the road.

"I've called the fire brigade!"

Jonathan turned Charlotte's head away from the scene and wrapped his arms and the thick woolly jumper sleeves thereupon, around the children's heads, trying to cover all four little ears at once. He hoped to muffle the shiver-inducing screams of their terrified grandma, as the unyielding cloud ate through the lounge ceiling and in turn, the bedroom floor around her.

As the vortex expanded upward and outward, so too did it grow downwards, swallowing the ground, tearing at the foundations of the building, feasting on the water pipes, the electrical cables, the gas pipes, which snapped and hissed and rumbled beneath the ground, as they, much like the threads of the carpet had, slid like spaghetti into a hungry mouth.

The fire engine sirens came, distant, but growing and Tommy knew that it was pointless. He had seen into the eyes of this beast. This was something *great* in every sense of the word. Something huge. Something powerful. Something unstoppable. He knew that this nothingness, this storm, would eat and eat, forever, until there was nothing left.

This is the end. This is how it ends. This is how *everything* ends.

I've had my last hug from mum.

The lightning bolts smashed through the roof tiles, sending sharp, grey shrapnel raining down onto the street. The crowd broke for cover. Jonathan leaned over the two children, shielding them with his old, bent back.

I've already had my last kick of a football with Dad.

Lightning thudded beneath the ground.

I've had my last chocolate egg ever. My last Christmas, my last birthday, my last Easter.

Grandma's roof collapsed.

I won't see Batman fighting with Superman, or Iron Man fighting with Captain America at the cinema.

The front of Jonathan's house began to crumble.

I should have given Grandma a better hug.

The lawn was half-eaten and Jonathan pushed the children back, further down the street.

I never told Freya the Valentine's card was from me.

Toby, Jonathan's black Labrador raced around the house from the back garden, streaking towards his master. Tommy reached out and stroked the animal who whimpered and nuzzled into Jonathan.

Tommy turned to face his sister. "Charlotte?"

Lightning thudded underground, sending shockwaves through the pavement. It felt as though the ground would cave in at any moment, a notion amplified by the cracks tearing through the tarmac and paving slabs.

"Charlotte, I love you."

Gas hissed through growing cracks in the tarmac. The neighbours in the crowd babbled louder in a jumble of concerned remarks and warnings.

"What?"

"I said I love you!"

The sickly sweet smell of gas everywhere. Lightning thudding beneath their feet. Panicked cries. *Screams*.

"What?"

"I said I-"

End.

Bio

Jack Rollins was born and raised among the twisting cobbled streets and lanes, ruined forts and rolling moors of a medieval market town in Northumberland, England. He claims to have been adopted by Leeds in West Yorkshire, and he spends as much time as possible immersed in the shadowy heart of that city.

Writing has always been Jack's addiction, whether warping the briefing for his English class homework, or making his own comic books as a child, he always had some dark tale to tell.

Fascinated by all things Victorian, Jack often writes within that era, but also creates contemporary nightmarish visions in horror and dark urban fantasy.

He currently lives in Northumberland, with his partner, two sons, and his daughter living a walking distance from his home, which is slowly but surely being overtaken by books...

Jack's published works are as follows:

The Séance: A Gothic Tale of Horror and Misfortune

The Cabinet of Dr Blessing

Dead Shore, in *Undead Legacy*

Anti-Terror, in *Carnage: Extreme Horror*

Home, Sweet Home in *Kill For A Copy*

Ghosts of Christmas Past in *The Dichotomy of Christmas*

Jack can be found online at:

Twitter: @jackrollins9280

Facebook: www.facebook.com/doctorblessing

Website: jackrollinshorror.wordpress.com

Lepus

By

Stuart Keane

It all comes back to that fateful day.

That's when it all began.

The feelings, the heartbreak. The overwhelming emotion.

When I realised I'd lost her.

My one true love.

I don't remember anything beyond the final conflict, that particularly fond memory bank in my brain has since bankrupted. Gone. Shut itself down. I think it must be something to do with the agony, the residual pain. I once read that crippling emotional defilement can change a person completely, make them think differently, like rerouting a railway track or resetting a server. The destination is forever changed.

It all comes back to that fateful day.

'I want you to leave,' she said. Calm, but forceful. A request, not a demand. Yet.

She stood in the corner of our kitchen, her back to our American fridge freezer. Her yellow vest and cream yoga shorts were drenched with expensive red wine, a result of a mass spillage caused by shock and tremendous horror. I could see the crimson beverage trickling down her wonderful thighs. Her attractive olive skin was glowing a lowly pink beneath the glaring lights. Her aggravated poise screamed defiance. She was in the right, and I was in the wrong.

My 'confession' was for naught.

In her eyes, anyway.

But I refused to leave. After all, it was our house; both our names were on the deed and we both had a right to it. And I wasn't finished with this discussion, not by a long shot. I loved that woman. My response was simple. 'What about Shaun? I won't leave him.'

'He's no longer your responsibility.'

But he was. And I let her know it. 'You can't raise him alone.'

She sneered in my direction. 'Watch me.'

Defiance. I had no answer to that. Which would be my final downfall.

'I want you to leave,' she repeated. This time, there was a hint of vehemence. An inflection in her tone. It made me shudder, surprised me; I'd never heard Kay raise her voice before; we were pretty happy together. Then came the crucial words.

'I won't say it again.'

BAM.

There it was.

There's something definite about that type of sentence, from a relationship standpoint. For some reason, I knew we were over then, and that there was no going back. I'd effectively destroyed our relationship. It was dead and buried.

One action and it was all over.

It all comes back to that fateful day.

Push the server button, and flick the railway switch.

That's when my life changed forever.

I want Kay back.

I was determined to make it happen.

I just hope she hasn't moved on, it's been a few months since we last spoke. Seven to be exact.

Kay's an attractive woman. Just over five feet, slim, toned, long brown hair, with the amazing olive skin that enhanced her fabulous smile and those stunning brown eyes. Her laugh always made me smile, an automatic reaction, one that happens when you're happy with the one you love. I remember the special moments we shared, the moments no one would ever take away from me.

Yes, she was probably seeing someone else now, probably grooming him into a potential father figure for Shaun. Maybe she was holding off, ensuring the boy was settling in with the drastic change, a huge adjustment that can easily destroy a childhood. Maybe she was holding off because she still loved me. Maybe she wasn't seeing anyone.

A man can hope. I can hope.

Dreams come true, don't they?

I push the optimistic thought from my mind. For now.

One step at a time, I think. Reuniting with Kay was part two.

Part one sat before me, and you don't want to *mess* this up. Otherwise, it will all be for nothing and Kay will be lost forever. I feel a smile creep over my face.

It's beautiful.

I check the suit and slowly run my appraising eyes over it. I reach out and reluctantly touch it, stroking it gently, feeling the downy fur tickle my warm palm. I feel stiff gooseflesh prickle on my forearm. The reaction I was hoping for. I know it's a job well done; it's a magnificent work of fashionable art.

It's finally ready, complete.

I check the thick black stitching; ensure the loops are pulled taut, that no small hole or crevice remains. I tug on them gently, not too hard; I don't want to rupture the seams. I check the sleeves, and the legs. I turn it over, check once more. Lift it by the shoulders, and at that point I almost drop it. The fur is still a little slick in places. I must remember that.

Overall, I'm happy.

I gaze over my shoulder and stare behind me, beyond the bedroom door – or archway, the cunt of a landlord never allotted me a door – and into the miserable kitchen. I hate this apartment, this fucking two-room living space with its yellowed white cooker, crispy cigarette burns in the wallpaper, and a beaten sofa with obvious semen stains on it. A living room/kitchen combination and a bedroom. The bathroom is just off the kitchen through a wooden sliding door, the tub and toilet both snot green. I can't get the brown stains out of either. The room doesn't even have a sink.

I hear the landlord berating me in my mind's eye, a man down on his luck, with no money and no prospects. Taking advantage of my fragile situation. *'Whadda ya need two sinks for?'*

So I can fucking drown you in one, you cunt.

I close my eyes. I can hear my teeth creaking as I subside my anger, my fingernails digging into my palms. I feel the skin break, which is becoming a common occurrence. His voice comes squeaking back to me and I groan, loudly.

'What more does a man need?'

I need a flat. I need working amenities, and I definitely need a fucking door on my fucking bedroom...I look at the suit and feel my anger washing away. I hadn't said those words, didn't dare. I needed a place to stay, somewhere to live, a quiet abode to plan.

'You take, yes?'

Let's just say part three of this plan involves gutting the money-grabbing bastard.

Priorities. Get Kay back, return home, and be happy. Kill my fucking landlord too.

Easy enough.

I need to get him out of the picture before he reports me. I haven't paid any rent in two months, and those bastards don't let it lie. I'm also ignoring all calls and any knocks on the door. My plan is so close to completion, it would be an absolute disaster if it failed now.

I think he might also have something to say about the sixty-three skinned rabbit corpses on the living carpet too. The stench is something else entirely, the kind that gets right up your nose and lingers for days, deep in your throat, so deep you can taste it. A putrid odour that makes you choke and cough.

I began making the body suit from their stripped fur about two weeks ago. An entire suit patched together from the fur of the dead rabbits, with a rough hole in the face so I can breathe and, well, see where I'm going. I also have armholes so I can use my hands. There's no point crippling myself out of the box.

The body is stitched together perfectly, the result of long hours and dedication. My fingers are still stinging red and blistered from all the sewing. The ears on the suit, a bunny's prominent feature, are comprised of seventy-one torn ears in total, all twisted and bunched and tacked together into a rough shape, like a slim oval for each ear. Despite cleaning them, some remain spotted with blood. I hold it up in front of me, for one last look, and smile.

Beautiful.

Terrifying but beautiful. A true work of art.

The rabbits went to a good cause. I glance down at their strewn carcasses. Some of the meat is green and slimy; the rasping of buzzing flies is familiar to me now. Even the writhing maggots no longer gross me out; especially when I hear several of them thudding on the carpet.

Nothing bothers me anymore.

After all, it's a time for celebration. I'm getting my Kay back.

And where better to hit her in the emotional weak spot than with the kid.

Shaun. The boy. Sprogus Maximus as we used to call him.

It's Easter, and he's getting a visit from the Easter Bunny.

I can't do this in public; it's too obvious and too weird. I know people dress up as the Easter Bunny all the time, it's somewhat a tradition, but I put a particularly special spin on it. A lot of personal effort, I hope Shaun appreciates it.

And Kay, but mainly Shaun.

The suit is void of blood and sinewy gristle, but I didn't clean it properly, not like those fur companies, I can't afford chemicals and such. Can you even wear rabbit? Anyway, there's a chance it smells a little now, I wouldn't know since the stack of bodies in my living room has completely obliterated my sense of smell. Everything reeks like dead rabbit to me, so if I stink right now, prancing through the woods in a man-made bunny suit stitched together from dead carcasses, I wouldn't know. That stench is unreal, and my eyes are watering. Hell, if I focus enough, I can still hear the heavy maggots thudding against my threadbare carpet.

Anyway, the woods.

Shaun is on an Easter egg treasure hunt today, the same as the past three years. Kay loves bringing him here, and I don't blame her. The woods are stunning and beautiful. All tall, arching oaks and dipping, winding ravines of dirt and grass decorated with a rainbow plethora of fallen leaves. The maze-like trails provide a natural home to deer and badgers, squirrels and hedgehogs, all harmless if left alone. A large lake runs through the centre of the woodland, with a sturdy timber footbridge across it, providing one of the most picturesque views in the country.

But I'm not here for the view.

I'm here for my family.

It's not long before I spot them through the trees, Shaun skipping alongside his mother, keeping pace with her, her long, muscular legs walking with elegance and poise.

She holds his hand, keeping him close. He has a huge, gratified smile on his face. Kay is carrying a pink bag that bulges and rustles with chocolate treats. I imagine eggs and bars and all sorts of confectionary goodness that does a child no good at the tender age of four.

My plan is working thus far. They're heading to the car casually, the Easter fun finished for another year. I track them through the woods, taking the odd step as they gradually close on my position, and I sidestep, inches from Kay's blue Audi. I glance down and notice a grey rabbit staring up at me, confusion in its beady eyes. It cocks its head sideways. I hold my hands up, growl gently and watch it scarper, scampering off into the brush.

I chuckle, but now is not the time for hilarity.

I relocate Kay and Shaun. I need to time it right.

Kay turns the narrow bend, out of the woods. I hear footsteps on gravel now, crunching and scuffing. I hear a stone clink off the bumper of a vehicle. Distant murmurs from a crowd of people chatter across the woodland silence, but none are nearby. I don't see any other movement through the trees.

Kay releases Shaun, motioning for him to stay still. Hushed whispers. She pulls the car keys from her pocket. Using her thumb, she pushes a fob and unlocks the car. Its lights flash twice. Kay opens the passenger seat and ushers Shaun into the car, smiling, being the doting mother. The door thunks shut and she walks around to the driver's side, opens the door, and climbs in.

Which is when I make my move.

I open the rear door closest to me, slide into the car, and shut it behind me.

'Hello, Kay.'

She gasps in surprise and turns around, shocked.

I smile. 'Hi, darling.'

Kay smiles nervously, I assume for the kid. 'What do you want?'

I narrow my eyes, momentarily confused. 'Excuse me?'

'Take my purse and the car. Please. But don't hurt my little boy.' She tosses her purse at me. It smacks me in the chest and I feel a sudden blip of remorse, guilt. She leans over to Shaun in the passenger seat, covering him from potential harm.

'Kay, it's me.'

She reluctantly looks at me, recognition dawning in her soggy eyes.

'It's me. Lee,' I say, lowering my voice, trying to sound harmless.

'Lee?'

I nod. Say nothing.

Her eyes widen as she sees my face, hidden below streaks of dirt. She quickly wipes her eyes, her jaw knotting in a flash of anger. She strokes Shaun's hair and smiles at him, easing his innocent worry. Turning to me, she says, 'Lee, what are you *doing* here?'

'I came to celebrate Easter with Shaun.' I turn to face the kid. He's looking at me dumbfounded, eyes wide, a melting Curly Wurly halfway into his mouth. I wave. 'Hi, Shaun.'

He glances to his mother. 'Mummy?'

I watch Kay, see her make a calculated decision, the instinct of a mother protecting her young from a possible threat. I can see it in her eyes, those gorgeous brown orbs that mesmerise me so much. It takes her two seconds to latch on.

'This...this is the Easter Bunny, sweetie. He came to say hello. He's just a bit tired from hiding all the eggs.' Shaun slowly turns his head to me, youthful wonderment on his face, which is when Kay shoots me a glare. She's keeping up the pretence for the kid, smiling in his eye line.

Good. Makes things easier.

'Hi, Shaun,' I say, acting the part. 'What did you find in the Easter egg hunt today?'

Shaun looks from me to his mother. She nods. 'You can tell him, sweetie.'

He looks back at me, a smile threatening to burst onto his adorable face. I can't tell if he's amused or terrified. I catch a glimpse of myself in the rearview mirror, partially hidden in the shadows of the back seat, and decide it's a bit of both. He swallows. 'I got lots of chocolate.'

I put on a high-pitched voice, the kind pet lovers use on their suffering dogs. 'You did? Like what?'

He swallows again. 'Curly Wurlys, Mars bars, Snickers, Rolos.' He sticks his tongue out, thinking, and then looks in his bag, checking his haul. 'I also got Toffee Crisps and Tob...tob...tol...'

'Toblerones?'

'Yeah, the ones like a pyramid.'

I can't help but smile. I clap slowly, and flick my gaze to Kay, the smile disappearing from my face. She's watching me with nervous anticipation, breathing steadily, her eyes burning a hole through me.

I wipe the sweat from my face. 'I bet your mummy is very proud of you.'

'I am,' she says, all too quickly. Not taking her eyes off me, she tenses in her seat. 'Shaun, honey, I need you to stay here, okay? Put your seatbelt on.'

Shaun did as he was told. I nod. Excellent parenting.

Kay nods too, smiling. 'Good boy. Now, I need to get out of the car, okay? Mummy needs to talk to the Easter Bunny.'

'Okay, mummy.'

Kay unlatches the door and backs out of the car. I feel the cool air washing into the vehicle. It's bloody hot with this suit on. I slide across the rear seat, the leather swishing against my makeshift rump and tail, and exit on the same side. I turn and wave to Shaun, who ignores me. As soon as I stand up and close the door, Kay hits the fob and relocks it, shutting Shaun away safely. For now. She quickly pockets the keys.

'What do you want, Lee?'

I reach up and lift the rabbit head off, placing it on the ground beside me. The cool air is a relief to my dripping face. I knew I should have shaved this morning. I begin to scratch my chin feverishly. 'I want to give us another shot.'

Kay laughs. 'Another shot? No way. You blew it.'

I shake my head, disbelieving her initial stance. 'I want us to be normal again. These past months have been terrible. I can't live without you, Kay.'

'We were never normal to begin with. Not...not after what you told me. Our whole relationship was a lie.' She said it with certainty, absolute clarity.

'It wasn't. What we had was great.'

'We had nothing. I dread to think what was going on in your sick mind the entire time. I never knew what you were thinking, not once. In hindsight anyway.' She looks me up and down, studying the suit, which is now dirty and soaked with sweat. Her eyes narrow. 'I still don't.'

'Don't you get it? This is the solution to all our problems.'

Kay takes a step backwards, which disappoints me a little. Doesn't she get that I'm trying here? I close the gap again, and she backs off once more. She's now level with the bonnet of the car. Her eyes wearily watch Shaun. 'Don't come any closer, okay?'

I feel my stomach drop an inch, which makes me stagger. "Why?'

'Lee, you're not well, you haven't been for some time. You need help.'

'I don't need help, I'm perfectly normal. We can be a family again.'

Kay shakes her head. 'We were never a family, let's get that straight. I can't believe you. I can never trust you again. The deceit, the...the...it's disgusting.'

'Like I said, this suit solves our problems.'

'Fuck the suit, okay? What the *fuck* is wrong with you?'

'Kay? Don't swear, okay? I'm only trying to help. This solves our problems, why won't you listen to me?'

Kay held a hand to her mouth. 'You deceived me for so long, with those horrible thoughts in your head. To think you...for so long you...you were thinking of that...urgh.'

'Thinking of what? How much I loved you? How watching you made me happy, gave me butterflies? How I admired you? Got hard just watching you, thinking of us in that way?'

'Stop it!'

'What?'

'Stop saying those things, it's not right.'

'Why not? We had something special. Don't you realise I love you?'

'And I love...loved you too. But not anymore, too much has changed. I can't be around you, it's not fair on me and it's definitely not fair on Shaun. He shouldn't be exposed to that...to you.'

'Kay please? Give us a chance. I've worked for this, put a lot of effort into it.'

'What, a rabbit suit?'

'It solves our problems...'

'Why do you keep *saying* that?'

'Because it means we can *fuck!* Okay? We can finally have a normal relationship, be together in that way. It's normal now. It always will be...' I find my sentence trailing off.

Kay said nothing. A tear rolled down her face. Then, she gagged and vomited, bright yellow bile spattered the gravel. Right at my feet. I stepped back a little. She backed away, a hand out to keep me from her. 'I want you to leave.'

And there it was, the same five words that started it all before. The sentence that ended it between us. It was starting all over again.

I'll be honest – I was a little pissed.

Ungrateful bitch.

'I'm not leaving, not this time,' I muttered.

Kay coughed. 'You need to leave. Now.'

'Fuck you, Kay. Not this time. This is our second chance, so we do things on my terms. We're destined to be together, okay? And I'm not losing you again.'

Kay cried. It took me a little by surprise. The tears trickled down her face. I saw her face sag a little, as if a great worry was lifting from her shoulders. I took it as a good sign. I'd worn her down, convinced her. The suit worked!

Now, I needed to tell her why it was so important.

But I didn't get a chance.

Kay stepped forward. 'What would Mum and Dad say?'

That stumped me. 'Huh?'

She grimaced. 'If they were alive, if they hadn't left the house to us in the will, in both our names, what would they say?'

'They'd be happy; parents should want their children to be happy.'

'They'd be happy that their son was an incestuous little bastard who fantasized about his little sister. Happy that for three years, three horrible perverted years, you eyed me up and imagined me naked, and imagined being inside me, and imagined... fucking me. I dread to think what you did on your own, in our house. You're a sick bastard, Lee, and it needs to be sorted. You need help.'

I smile, which must have shocked her. 'That's why the suit can help. Rabbits fuck their own siblings; they can have sex with their own, mate and be happy together with their own. Don't you get it? This suit solves our problems.'

Kay said nothing. She closed her eyes and shook her head. It made me a little sad.

'Come on, Kay, I'd make you so happy. Why not give us a chance? I'd be the perfect father for Shaun, the perfect lover for you. We know each other so well. I can make you so happy.'

Kay opened her eyes, those wonderful brown eyes. Her face looked like it had aged thirty years in a heartbeat, the wrinkles amplified by her tears, her cheeks a sore, puffy red. She swallowed, looked to the sky, and then looked at me.

'It's over, Lee. Over.'

I shake my head. 'No. It can't be. I worked so hard. Give it a chance.'

Kay steps towards me. 'It won't work. When you tried to kiss me? On that night? That ended us. You're no longer my brother. A brother doesn't think of his sister naked, a brother doesn't hit on his own flesh and blood. A brother doesn't rely on his wealthy sister to get by, and then try to take advantage of something that seems like one thing, but it quite another. I loved you as a sibling, nothing more. You can't think it was anything else, it will *never* be anything else.'

I stand there, shocked and gutted. The bottom fell out of my world right there, on the gravel, with a four-year-old boy in the car beside me, and the love of my life inches from me. My head spun, my life collapsed. Tears formed behind my eyes for the first time in six months.

Everyone I wanted in my life was right there, close enough to touch and cuddle and savour.

And I couldn't have any of it.

'I want you to leave,' she said again.

I lunge for her, my inhibitions shattered, my common sense no longer controlling me. Kay isn't the love of my life; she just made that perfectly clear. She abhors me, despises me.

Which means she's just like the others; a victim.

But before I know it, I'm pinned to the ground, gravel scattering round me and digging into my knees, bouncing up and hitting me in the face. I have the weight of two men on my back, pinning me down, restraining me. I look up.

Security. They must have been curious about the suit. I curse myself for the obvious flaw in a plan obscured by emotion and feelings, by the urge to reclaim my one true love. I see Kay step back, behind the two men dressed all in black.

I realise I may never see her again.

*

I don't know when I blacked out. It must have been a combination of the heat, the anger, the utter shock of Kay cutting me off. I will win her back one day. There are other methods. I'm beginning to think the bunny suit wasn't the best way.

The bunny suit.

I kick the head at my feet, hands restrained in cuffs. It clatters against the bench beneath me. I look out into the police station, which is empty and dark for the night. Everyone has gone home. I see shadows of empty desks and idle monitors. A clock ticks patiently across the room. No one is here, just me and my cellmate and the silent darkness.

That's the problem with a small police force, no night workers. In this neck of the woods, they are on call from home. Which means we're alone for the night. I'll be here for twenty-four hours, maybe more.

The cell is empty bar one other person. A giant of a man, a walking redwood in clothes. He's looking at me suspiciously, a leer on his pockmarked face. He's rocking a giant black beard, which covers most of his barreled chest. He's wearing some kind of band t-shirt, the name covered by the beard, but I recognise the design, the fit, faded black cloth taut over a bulging beer belly. He taps his green wellington boots on the concrete, the rubber squeaking, his jeans rustling on the wooden bench beneath him. I notice the wellington boots have white smears down them.

I look up. Say nothing.

He leans forward. 'What you in for?' A gravelly voice, as if he recently gargled with barbed wire and acid. I see his stoic eyes are bloodshot, and there are flecks of dried blood on his shoulders. A strange fellow all in.

I consider an answer. No longer give a shit. 'I tried to kidnap my...sister.'

'Why?'

'I love her,' I said, truthfully.

'That's sweet, but stupid. Ain't no one gotta kidnap a sister to declare that. Send her a card or flowers.' He scratched his knee and flicked something invisible from it. 'Me, I don't like me no woman. Too many hassles and politics. I prefer someone who can't talk back. Give me a bit of butch cattle ass any day.'

I look up. See the menace in his eyes, the animalistic rage there, one unbound by society's rules. It comes to me in a rush, one that makes me flinch. I feel my stomach tightening.

Realise the bars are going to be a hindrance. There's no escape.

Then it clicked. I now know why Kay was so distraught. How she had felt when I confessed. The taboo of the situation, the shock, the imminent fear, the awkward uneasiness. I feel my eyes roaming to my cellmate.

He grins. 'And I never fucked me a giant rabbit before.'

THE END

Bio

Stuart Keane is a horror/suspense author from the United Kingdom. Currently in his second year of writing, Stuart has started to earn a reputation for writing realistic, contemporary horror. With comparisons to Richard Laymon and Shaun Hutson amongst his critical acclaim – he cites both authors as his major inspiration in the genre – Stuart is dedicated to writing terrifying, thrilling stories for real horror fans.

Stuart currently has several works on Amazon – The Customer Is Always..., Charlotte, All or Nothing, Whispers – Volume 1: A Collection, Whispers – Volume 2: A Second Collection, Cine and Grin. He also featured in the #1 best-selling Behind Closed Doors anthology with several other authors, including Matt Shaw and Michael Bray. He recently signed a publishing contract with Matt Shaw Publications to bring his work to the masses.

He is currently a member of the Horror Writers Association (HWA) and an editor for emerging UK publisher, Dark Chapter Press.

Stuart was born in Kent, and lived there for three decades. A major inspiration for his work, his home county has helped him produce numerous novels and short stories. He currently resides in Essex, is happily married, and is totally addicted to caffeine.

Feel free to get in touch at www.stuartkeane.com or www.facebook.com/stuart.keane.92

He can also be found on Twitter at @SKeane_Author.

"Little Bunny"

Glenn Rolfe

"Little bunny," Marlow Shuman whispered. "Where the hell are you taking me?"

A fluffy brown hare the size of a cat zigzagged across the path before Brenner's Woods. These woods had been off limits as far back as she could remember. The haunted place was full of snakes and spiders and ghosts. When they were little, one kid from her neighborhood, Tommy Schafer, ignored these warnings by invading the grounds daily. While he came back each and every time, poor Tommy never came out quite the same. He was arrested years later and found guilty for the abduction and murders of nine children.

And yet, knowing what she did, that this was a place of pain and scars, a patch of this spoiled earth to be avoided, here she stood at the precipice of its promised darkness. And why? Because of this snuggly little rabbit?

Alice chasing down a fantasy.

I'm asleep. That's it. I would never....

"But you already have," said a voice smooth as silk and slippery as a dream.

"Hello," she said.

The little bunny was gone.

Marlow no longer stood on the roadside gazing at the entrance to Brenner's Woods--she stood in the thick of it. Her heart raced. Dead trees reached for the moonlit sky above. The moist soil beneath her sneakered feet reeked of rotten eggs.

"Are you there?" she said.

A shadow shaped like a man moved into view. When he stepped forth, his wrongful grin on full display, she ran.

Skeletal branches raked her arms and face. She could hear him panting, feel his warm breath on the back of her neck, hear him in her mind whispering of the awful things he'd done. As impossible as it was, Tommy Schafer's fingertips caressed her throat.

"Marlow, what are you doing?"

Marlow stood at the path's entrance. The blinding daylight shocked her.

"Come on, are we going in or not?" Jenna said.

Marlow brought her hand to her brow, shielding her eyes from the sun. Her fifteen-year-old sister, Jenna, dressed in cut-off jean shorts and a Ziggy Stardust t-shirt, her long brown hair pulled in a tight ponytail, stood in front of her with her hands on her hips.

"I...," Marlow tried.

"Are you all right? You look sorta pale."

"I'm...I'm fine. It's just that... you can't be here."

"Don't be silly. You wanted to come."

"I just stepped out for some fresh air..."

Marlow craned her head. Their house was nowhere in sight.

"What the--"

When she turned around, her sister was gone. The little bunny hopped toward her, gazed with its queer, dead eyes, and hopped back onto the path.

Why had she thought her sister was here? Jenna had taken her life this past Easter.

"She's with us. Come see," the voice said.

Marlow scanned the trees. They were in full bloom, no longer the horrifying dead things she'd seen before. Beams of golden sunlight shone through the given spaces between perfect green leaves and fell across Jenna's blue eyes.

Marlow stepped forward.

"Jenna?"

Feet shuffled and then padded down the path.

The little bunny bolted out of sight.

"Wait!" She felt stupid calling out to her dead sister.

"Maaaarrrloooow…"

"Jenna."

For the second time in her life, Marlow entered Brenner's Woods.

Life's colors withered. The trees and path were drenched in blue shadows.

Impossible.

"Maaaaarrrloooow…"

She followed her sister down the trail.

She'd chased Jenna down this path this past winter, a few months before her sister's suicide. Jenna had confided two things to her that night: that she was a lesbian and that she'd been raped. Marlow's world tipped off its axis. Her little sister's revelations were a sledgehammer of truth straight to Marlow's guts. A whirlwind of questions dismantled her worldview. Marlow had reached out to hold her baby sister, but Jenna had shrugged her off and lit a cigarette. There were no tears, no fallout. Just Jenna by the open window, gazing out at the forest, *this* forest, her sister's favorite singer crooning about the spiders from Mars, and smoke drifting out into the cold afternoon toward the setting sun.

"I've been there," she said.

"Where?"

"The woods."

"When?"

"Last summer. I heard…a voice."

"In there? Are you mad? You shouldn't have."

"I have to go back."

"What?"

"There's something I need to see. I need to know for sure...that I'm not going crazy."

Jenna turned to her.

"Will you come with me?"

"Into the woods?"

Jenna walked over to the record player by her bed, lifted the needle from the black circle, silencing David Bowie, and grabbed her jacket.

"You don't have to understand, in fact, it might be better that you don't, but I can't go back alone. Please, come with me."

By the time they had got to the path, the sun had set and the temperature dipped below freezing. Jenna had produced a flashlight and shined the light into the dark. Tiny animal footprints--rabbit footprints--led the way.

Marlow recalled the sour smell in the air, even on that frigid afternoon. The turning in her stomach brought visions of maggots eating their way out of a fresh carcass. She wanted to stop and found herself trailing behind as Jenna rounded a corner and vanished. As the clearing came into sight, Jenna ran into her and began shoving her back the way they had come.

"Go," Jenna said. "Run."

Marlow shook the reverie from her head.

What am I doing?

The trees around her were charred. The earth squished beneath her feet. The stench of rotten eggs returned.

The blue shadows swirled and took form.

Tommy.

The fingers of his left hand were tangled in a head of dark hair.

"No...," Marlow stumbled backwards.

"You finally came," he said. He twirled his wrist. Jenna's blue eyes spun into view.

"We've been expecting you."

"This isn't real. I'm dreaming. This isn't happening."

Tommy stepped forward.

She lost her footing. Her rump plopped into the mushy soil.

"These were my secrets," Tommy said continuing his approach.

Marlow placed her hand down trying to scramble away from him. Something sharp spilt the flesh of her palm.

"Each one precious..." Anger slithered into his voice, his brown eyes morphed into pure onyx orbs. Hatred radiated from him, a tangible ghost reaching out.

She raised her arm. Dark fluid dripped from her pale hand.

Her gaze landed on the bone fragment poking from the ruined earth.

Oh my God.

All around her, skeletal remains began to rise.

His secrets.

Jenna's head landed beside her with a soft thud. The blue eyes she'd known all her life turned black and drooled from the skull.

Marlow screamed, scrambled backwards, and stood.

Tommy struck his best Jesus Christ pose, arms outstretched, chin tilted to the sky.

"This place welcomed me with open arms. It calls out to those who will listen."

Taking two more steps forward he backed her into a tree.

"Jenna...said something about a voice..."

He grinned.

"What did you do?"

"She didn't even scream. She just laid there and cried."

"And what you did to those children? You're a monster."

He grabbed Marlow by the jaw. "Now you're starting to get it."

She wanted to spit in his eyes. She wanted to lash out. He leaned in close and brought his tongue from her chin over her lips, flinging it off the tip of her nose.

She trembled.

He let go and backed away.

The skeletal wasteland vanished. The blue world returned to normal. Sunlight rained through the trees.

"Where are you going?" she said.

He walked on.

"What the hell is going on here?"

"We'll be waiting," he said.

Then, he disappeared.

Marlow watched as the little bunny came hopping along.

Sliding down the tree, she sat on the ground, and placed her face in her hands.

I can't tell what's real anymore.

She felt something small and cold on her exposed ankle.

The little bunny rubbed its wet nose against her and bit her.

"Ah!"

The rabbit hurried off toward the path.

Marlow looked at the blood running from her ankle to the ground.

Dream or otherwise, she was through here. She was finished with that damn rabbit and these ghosts, and this damn fucked up fairytale…or nightmare..

She climbed to her feet and ran.

Ghost children lined either side of the path, Marlow felt like one of them, drifting through this horrible dream.

She passed Missy Hewitt and her stuffed Rudolph the Red Nosed Reindeer, she passed Bobby McGillicuddy and his best friend Nathaniel York, and Maggie Joyce, and the Shaw twins, Kylie and Kelsey, and three children she didn't recognize. Tommy stood grinning against a Maple tree. He gave her a weak wave as she rushed by.

Jenna waited at the exit, wearing the white dress with the lace-like, full-length sleeves they'd found her in that Easter morning. The blood stains still present from the cuffs to her elbows and in splotches from waist to hem. Her blue eyes intact.

Marlow stopped and tried to catch her breath.

Marlow raised her chin. "What is all of this?"

"Do you remember that day we came out here?"

"So what? What's that to do with any of this?"

"It wasn't my first time in this place."

"I saw her body. Missy Hewitt's."

"It wasn't your fault."

"I should have said something sooner." Jenna dropped her gaze. "I never stopped seeing her. Or him."

"That day I brought you with me...I was trying to be brave. He had hanged himself the night before in his cell, remember? It was all over the news."

Marlow did.

"I knew, somehow, I knew...he'd be here," Jenna continued.

Marlow wanted to hold her.

"I needed you, your strength, to face him, but when I got to the clearing it wasn't him..." Jenna brought her black gaze up to meet Marlow's. "It was *all* of them."

Marlow's blood froze in her veins.

The little bunny bounced its way to Jenna's side.

"I didn't say anything. They told me not to."

"Who?" Marlow said.

Jenna bent and picked up the bunny. Marlow wanted to warn her, but the rabbit nuzzled to Jenna's bosom.

"I tried to protect you, I really did, but here you are."

"Jenna, I still don't understand…"

Jenna, with the bunny cradled like a baby, stepped aside.

"Will I see you again?" Marlow said.

"Sooner than you think."

Jenna faded back into the trees until she was gone.

*

Marlow opened her eyes. She lay on the ground by the road. Glancing to her right, she saw Brenner's Woods. She tried to gaze through the trees for any signs of them. The children, Tommy, Jenna, the bunny.

She was alone.

And it was that hollow feeling that followed her home.

She was numb. She knew she should feel something, but she didn't. She walked into her house. Her mother worked late and wouldn't be home until midnight. She went into her room, walked to her dresser, and picked up the photo of her and Jenna.

Jenna's crystal blue eyes were pure black.

Marlow dropped the portrait. The frame hit the floor and shattered.

The voice slithered through her mind.

We need you, Marlow...we're so lonely... it can be our secret....

"No, leave me alone."

She knelt down, picked up the photograph, shaking it free of the shattered glass, and gasped.

Her eyes now matched the pitch black of Jenna's.

The pattering of feet drew her attention to the door.

The little bunny waited.

THE END

Bio

Glenn Rolfe is an author, singer, songwriter and all around fun loving guy from the haunted woods of New England. He has studied Creative Writing at Southern New Hampshire University, and continues his education in the world of horror by devouring the novels of Stephen King and Richard Laymon. He and his wife, Meghan, have three children, Ruby, Ramona, and Axl. He is grateful to be loved despite his weirdness.

He is the author the novellas, *Abram's Bridge*, *Boom Town*, and *Things We Fear*, the short fiction collection, *Slush*, and the novels, *The Haunted Halls* and *Blood and Rain*.

His first novella collection, *Where Nightmares Begin*, will be released in March, 2016.

He is hard at work on many more. Stay tuned!

Twitter: @Grolfehorror

Website: https://www.glennrolfe.com

Run Rabbit, Run

By

Michael Bray

Anyone who loves their life will lose it, while anyone who hates their life in this world will keep it for eternal life.

-John 12-23-25

He looked at himself in the mirror and pulled at the neck of the rabbit suit. It was tight and hugged the crest of his gut like a second skin. His face peered out of the circular opening in the outfit, huge ears dangling down at either side of his head. His eyes, cold and dark, glared at himself. He pushed his teeth forward from his lips and gnawed on imaginary carrots, twitching his nose.

Yes.

The suit was hot and itchy, but the children would love it. Just as he loved them.

Suddenly, the crotch of the suit was even tighter. In the reflection on the mirror, he could see the desk and his clergy clothes draped over the chair, his old well-thumbed bible behind it. He had long ago stopped believing in the words it contained or the message it tried to convey. He had seen the truth of the world and it was a bitter, horrible place. Also, on the table were the dozen Easter eggs, all in their respective packages advertising the companies who turned over millions every year. Huge machines which churned out products for the greedy populace to consume. He grimaced and realised just how empty he was. How tired and jaded with the world he had become. There was no hope for redemption, no cure for the greed and selfishness which had corrupted every generation. He was almost fifty and had seen more depressing events and listened to more depraved confessions than any man should ever have to endure. People, he realised were the problem with the world, and no amount of guidance would ever change things. People never listened to the clergy. They see them as kind, polite people who don't know anything of the darker side of human nature.

He glared at the robes draped over the chair and realised how much of a sham he felt wearing them. A fraud, an anonymous face in a world built on hatred.

No more.

He would make a statement. He would show the world the error of their ways, he would show them that Easter wasn't just about gluttonising on processed chocolate and filling the pockets of the industries that supplied them. He would show the true meaning of Easter. For once, he was sure people would listen.

TWO DAYS EARLIER

"You really don't have to do that, Mr Rose."

Gerald hadn't been listening. He smiled at the woman and tried to find the thread of the conversation. "I really would like to. The church is more than happy to help the children at this time of year."

The short podgy woman going by the name of Glenda formed a smile on her tiny featured face and wrung her hands. "It's kind of you, of course, Mr Rose, but we couldn't possibly afford-"

"Nonsense," Rose said, smiling and holding up a bony hand, the blue ghosts of veins visible under the skin. "I want to do this. This community has welcomed me since I joined it last year. This will be my pleasure."

Glenda smiled. "It's so nice to have such a caring, thoughtful individual join our community, especially where the children are concerned. More tea?"

She gestured to the teapot, but Rose shook his head. "Not for me, thank you."

Glenda nodded and poured herself a fresh cup.

"If you don't mind," Rose said, smiling at Glenda as she put spoon after spoonful of sugar in her cup, "I'd like to deliver them personally."

"That's most kind, reverend Rose, but I'm sure one of the boys can take them."

"I insist. It's a good way to teach the next generation the values of the church and the true meaning of Easter."

"I understand, Reverend, although, I have to admit, I'm partial to the occasional piece of chocolate egg."

More than a piece, you big fat cunt.

The words almost spilled from his mouth, but he stopped them at the throat. Instead, he gave her a thin smile and tried to douse the flames of rage inside him. "As I said, Glenda, I would be more than happy to take them."

"Thank you reverend, thank you so much. I'm sure the children will be most thrilled with the gesture."

"How many are on the ward at present?"

"Twelve," Glenda said as she slurped her tea.

"Twelve," Rose repeated. He flicked his tongue against the back of his teeth then gave her his full attention. "Very good. Twelve it is. On Sunday, I shall deliver the twelve eggs to the hospital."

"Excellent, you are so kind."

Rose smiled, looking at the flabby excuse for a human and wondering how she was still alive. He imagined her arteries filled with grease, clogged up and trying to push blood around her obese frame. He realised just what a waste of flesh she was. The very picture of greed and gluttony.

"Reverend?"

He blinked and focused on her, letting the thoughts drift away into the back of his mind. "Sorry, I was somewhere else then."

"I was asking what time would you be attending the hospital on Sunday? So I can inform them."

"After morning service. Around lunchtime."

"Very good, I'll let them know."

Rose stood up, his sore knees groaning under protest. Age was catching up to him, there was no denying it.

"Slice of cake before you go?" Glenda asked, motioning to the silver tray.

"No thank you. Not for me." Rose said, sure it wouldn't go to waste. He didn't think his seat would be cold before Glenda was shovelling it down her gullet.

"Well, if you're sure." She said, her mouth puckering into what he supposed was a pout.

"I am. I really must be going. Thank you, Glenda. I'm sure this will be a gesture the children will never forget."

*

The shopping centre was busy. It was the school holidays, and as a result, children were being dragged around the shops by short tempered mothers who longed for them to return to their classrooms. Rose didn't like crowds. He hated having to be so close to people, to disease and illness, to people who might cough or breathe on him. He was wearing his normal clothes, not wanting to be stopped by strangers or be on the receiving end of strange looks from people surprised to see a reverend outside the confines of his church. The trousers he was wearing were rubbing his inner thighs, and combined with the sweat was making walking uncomfortable. He had also been having trouble with his bowels of late. Sometimes he would break wind and defecate at the same time without any pre-warning. His stomach growled and churned as he walked the chocolate aisle, placing mass-manufactured chocolate eggs into his basket at random, making a mental tally of numbers. Towards the end of the aisle was a small boy. Rose looked at him as he browsed the collection of chocolate delights. Rose moved closer, one wheel of his shopping trolley squeaking. He couldn't take his eyes off the boy and was delighted to see there was no sign of any adult supervision. He brought his squeaky trolley to a halt in front of the oblivious child.

"Lots of choice, isn't there?" Rose said, unable to take his eyes off the child's delicate features.

The child blinked and turned to face him, hair soft and blonde, eyes blue. "I thought the Easter bunny brought them," he said.

Rose smiled. "How old are you?"

"Seven."

"Seven," Rose repeated.

He followed the child's gaze to the array of eggs as his stomach churned and the front of his trousers grew tight. "Where is your mother or father?"

"Buying stuff. They said I could come and look at the eggs."

"What's your name?"

"Ben."

"Do you know the real meaning of Easter, Ben?" do you know it's about more than chocolate eggs and gluttony?"

Ben glanced at Rose then backed away, sensing all was not right.

"Do you know that the real meaning of Easter is to celebrate the resurrection of Jesus Christ and that the idea of giving eggs wasn't always about chocolate. No, the first Easter eggs were decorated chicken eggs. The idea was that the shell represented the tomb, the embryo inside the life that would be born and break out and live again."

There was more he wanted to say to the boy, but his stomach was cramping and gurgling. It let go, and he broke wind with a sharp snap. He grunted and his eyes rolled back. He could feel the warmth down there and knew it had happened again. He couldn't smell it yet, but knew it was only a matter of time. He sighed, then pushed his trolley on, wet cheeks sliding together as he went to pay for his goods.

*

He looked at himself in the mirror and pulled at the neck of the rabbit suit. It was tight and hugged the crest of his gut like a second skin. His face peered out of the circular opening in the outfit, huge ears dangling down at either side of his head. His eyes, cold and dark, glared at himself. He pushed his teeth forward from his lips and gnawed on imaginary carrots, twitching his nose.

Yes.

The suit was hot and itchy, but the children would love it. Just as he loved them.

Suddenly, the crotch of the suit was even tighter. In the reflection on the mirror, he could see the desk and his clergy clothes draped over the chair, his old well-thumbed bible behind it. He had long ago stopped believing in the words it contained or the message it tried to convey. He had seen the truth of the world and it was a bitter, horrible place. Also, on the table were the dozen Easter eggs, all in their respective packages of the companies who turned over millions every year. Huge machines which churned out products for the greedy populace to consume. He grimaced and realised just how empty he was. How tired and jaded with the world he had become. There was no hope for redemption, no cure for the greed and selfishness which had corrupted every generation. He was almost fifty and had seen more depressing events and listened to more depraved confessions that any man should ever have to endure. People, he realised were the problem with the world, and no amount of guidance would ever change things. People never listened to the clergy. They see them as kind, polite people who don't know anything of the darker side of human nature.

He glared at the robes draped over the chair and realised how much of a sham he felt wearing them. A fraud, an anonymous face in a world built on hatred.

No more.

He would make a statement. He would show the world the error of their ways, he would show them that Easter wasn't just about gluttonising on processed chocolate and filling the pockets of the industries that surprised them. He would show the true meaning of Easter. For once, he was sure people would listen. ALL REPEATED FROM EARLIER?

There was a knock at the door, and he broke his gaze to answer.

The whore looked young, just as he had specified. She wasn't truly the age he desired, of course, too many nights walking the streets told the truth behind the lie she was trying to perpetrate. The dark rims under the eyes, cherry painted lips scabbed and cracked, but she was playing the part nonetheless. School uniform, white shirt open to reveal a black bra which she barely filled, nondescript tie pulled loosely around her neck. Her hair was bleached blonde and in pigtails.

He recognised the look when she saw him, the one it always was. Revulsion, disgust, fear. Another crack in her character. He knew well enough that girls actually of the age he desired were much easier to fool than the tramp standing on his doorstep. He supposed it could be that she was wary of the rabbit suit.

"Come in," he said, motioning to the shadow filled room at his back.

The whore complied, knowing that fear wasn't going to pay her rent or feed her habit. Rose closed the door behind her.

The whore looked around the room, then set her eyes on him. She was trying to hide it, but he could still see the fear that burned in them. "What's with the outfit?" she said, black stumps of teeth behind her lips the consequence of crack addiction.

"How old are you?" Rose asked.

"Seventeen."

"No. play the character. How old are you?"

The whore stood, and itched at the scabs on her arms, unsure what was happening. "How old do you want me to be?"

"Young," Rose said. He could feel himself stiffening against the costume again.

"Alright, I'm fifteen."

"Younger."

"Twelve."

Rose shook his head. The whore grimaced and lowered her eyes. "Nine. I'm nine."

"Good. Very good. Get on the bed."

Another moment of hesitation was followed by the realisation that it was too late to back out now. She was no stranger to weird stuff, but even so, she wanted out as quickly as she could.

"What's your name?" Rose said in a near whisper as he walked to towards her. She was kneeling on the bed, not realising that the fear she was struggling to hide was making the experience infinitely pleasurable for him.

"Amy."

"Not tonight. Tonight, I want you to answer to the name of Ben."

"Ben?" She repeated this time, the fear wasn't something she could disguise or hide.

"Ben," Rose repeated as he started to touch himself. "Have you been a good boy ben?"

She nodded, glancing past Rose to the door.

"Remember the story I was telling you yesterday about Easter?" Rose went on as he pulled down the zip at the front of the costume.

She nodded, hoping that if she just went along with it, everything would be alright and she could leave.

"Remember how I told you Easter wasn't about just chocolate? How you thought the Easter bunny brought them?"

The girl nodded again, involuntarily shuffling further back on the bed as he approached, his knees bumping into the bottom edge of the mattress.

"Well, I'm the Easter bunny, and I've brought you something much more delicious to chew on."

He took it out, showing it to her. "I want you to put this carrot in your mouth. Don't tell mummy, though, it can be our little secret."

He clambered onto the bed and pulled her towards him. She started to squirm, but it seemed he enjoyed that more. Eventually, she let him do what he wanted to do, endured the awful, twisted things he said. When it was finished, she left, eyes streaked with makeup, taste of his seed in her throat. As she stumbled away from the house, she started to cry.

SUNDAY

Rose walked own the wide, white hospital corridor, whistling to himself. He had decided against the rabbit costume. There were too many stains on it after his time spent with the whore. Instead, he was pristinely dressed in his reverends attire. Perfectly pressed black clothing, white collar around his neck. He had washed and changed and was carrying his bounty of gifts in several plastic bags which rustled at his sides. It was a glorious day, and golden grids of sunlight came through the windows and left dazzling patterns on the floor and walls. The warmth on his cheeks felt good. He arrived at the nurse's station and smiled at the pretty brunette behind the desk.

"Reverend Rose, I'm here to see the children."

The nurse smiled in recognition. "Of course, Glenda said you would be dropping by."

"Thank you."

"You know, it's so kind of you. To bring gifts for the children is really thoughtful."

He looked at her and smiled. "I like to do my part. I love children, and would like to help them if I can."

"The children here are vulnerable, many of them in need of someone they can trust." The nurse said.

Rose looked towards the ward doors. He could hear them chatting and laughing, then felt a rousing in his trousers. "I think I'd like to make this a regular thing. Really spend time with the children, building a trust, building a special bond. Tell me, how old are the children on this ward?"

The nurse shrugged. "It varies, most of the children are aged between six and twelve."

"Six and twelve," Rose repeated, stifling a little smile. "Good ages. Minds still young enough to mould."

Bodies still fresh and tight he almost added, but only cleared his throat instead.

The nurse's smile faltered, and Rose thought that she might, for a second, have seen his true intentions.

"Anyway," he said, standing straight. "I better go in. Thank you for your help, nurse." He walked towards the ward and turned the corner out of sight.

*

He stayed for an hour, getting to know the children, ensuring each of them got an egg. When he could he talked to them about the true message of Easter. For the most part, he just looked at them and played increasingly depraved scenarios in his head. He checked his watch, then stood, knees grumbling. He didn't speak to any of the children as he made his exit. They had lost interest in him and were chattering as they tucked into their chocolate gifts, chewing noisily. Another check of his watch told him it would be soon. He walked back the way he had come, stopping again at the nurse's station.

"The children like their gifts," Rose said, glancing back over his shoulder.

"I'm glad, I'm sure they will never forget this."

"No, I do believe you are right. Goodbye, Nurse." Rose walked away, enjoying the sun on his face.

The rat poison he had laced the eggs with wasn't guaranteed to work. He had read about it on the internet. It could cause blindness, or even catastrophic organ failure at best if ingested, coma or death at worst. He was hoping for coma for the most part. That, after all, would be the best way to convey his message, although their fate was now in the hands of the almighty. He liked that. Administering the poison had been tricky, and in the end, he had needed a syringe to inject the plastic covering on the front of each egg, each time using a differing and random amount of the poison, which he had diluted with a strong bleach. He supposed it was a lottery as to who got which and what happened to them. There was some doubt whether the children would notice something wrong, a smell, a residue, but he had watched them eat the eggs without question, stuffing their greedy little faces.

"The children are the light of life, and their bodies shall be the shell of their tomb," He muttered to himself as he made his way towards the exit. He would go home and watch the news and wait for the police to arrive. He would even wear the rabbit costume whilst he waited. It seemed appropriate.

THE END

Bio

Michael Bray is a horror / thriller author of more than ten novels. Influenced from an early age by the suspense horror of authors such as Stephen King, Richard Laymon & Brian Lumley, along with TV shows like Tales From The Crypt & The Twilight Zone, he started to work on his own fiction, and spent many years developing his style.

With books sold in over forty countries and rights optioned for movie and television adaptations of his work, he recently signed with Media Bitch literary agency where he intends to take the next step in his writing career. He currently resides in Leeds, England, with his wife Vikki and daughter Abi.

Where to find Michael Bray online

Official website: www.michaelbrayauthor.com
Facebook: www.facebook.com/michaelbrayauthor
Twitter: www.twitter.com/michaelbrayauth
Instagram: www.instagram.com/michaelbrayauthor
Google +: www.plus.goggle.com/michaelbrayauthor

WHEN A BUNNY SNAPS

Jim Goforth

It wasn't the requirement to be cavorting around in the miniscule costume that made her look like Easter Slutty, or some reject from the Playboy Mansion, nor the long hours spent teetering on ridiculously high heels doing a balancing act with drinks trays and the like, that shredded Bunny's nerves.

No, on a night like tonight where an establishment such as Fantasy Dress did some of its best business, that tiny, barely there namesake outfit, complete with rabbit ears and a cute little fluffy tail perched above a thong and her tight buttocks and those stiletto heels were what pulled in the big tips, so she took all that in her stride. She knew how to work it, she acknowledged what the punters came there for and she knew at the end of a gruelling shift, she'd be sitting pretty.

What really got under her skin was the utter sleazeball motherfuckers that seemed to pick nights like tonight to come crawling out of the woodwork in droves, migrating towards Fantasy Dress like a plague of lecherous locusts. Which was ironic, given her tiny, revealing attire, high heels and whatnot, and her acceptance of the fact that males mostly came along to ogle, drool and fantasise, but all the same the behaviour of these pricks ground her gears. Dredged up old bad memories. Recollections she'd tried to inter some time ago.

It wasn't all nights they were like that either. For the most part, they understood their place, they played by the rules, they respected the no touching the waitresses policies and all of that shit. Of course there was always as least one knucklehead either getting himself overly liquored up or too turned on just by being in the proximity of nubile, nearly nude waitresses, but security were usually on the spot pretty stringently.

But the big nights, the special events, the holidays...

That was when the freaks came out.

Fantasy Dress itself was nothing grander than a bar/restaurant with a flair for theme specific costumed staff. With a twenty four hour operating license, its main selling point wasn't the food it dished up, the ambience or in fact, that twenty four hour operating license. It was the costumed staff. All nubile, buxom young women dressed in risqué, skimpy attire revolving around certain themes, depending on the day or time of year. These women were in costume all year round, with management paying close attention to the calendar, current trends and all kinds of criteria to keep the interest in what the girls were wearing maximised, but while the patronage of the place was always pretty high, it was holidays and special annual events when business was booming and finding space in the joint was a hell of a mission. On days like Christmas, Easter, New Year's Day and the like where there was precious little else open, let alone for twenty four hours, Fantasy Dress was killing it. Hence the big tips for those like Bunny, tasked to deliver food and drinks in minimal clothing, to exuberant customers who nine times out of ten couldn't care less what they were eating. It was all about having those attractive females with barely restrained breasts and exposed asses, long legs and intoxicating perfumes swanning all around them, being able to ogle the abundant flesh and knock back a few cold ones in comfort.

It wasn't a new concept, not a novel idea, certainly nothing which hadn't been done before countless times, just a standard run of the mill licensed establishment acting as a gimmick outlet for folks to accumulate and spend dollars, but Fantasy Dress shrewdly zeroed in on base human desires and predictably it paid off.

Tonight was Easter. The biggest calendar night of the year for Bunny when it came to getting into costume. Her boss and fellow staff played up the fact that her name genuinely was Bunny, often encouraging her to show punters her driver's license and have her dress as the sluttiest bunny on the block. It meant big bucks for her, but it also meant a fuckload of sleazy attention. Even donning a sexy Santa outfit or enticing elf at Christmas or any number of revealing twists on supernatural beings around Halloween, didn't generate quite as much fixation and attention for Bunny as that event in March or April did when it rolled around every year.

She didn't even need to go to any elaborate lengths with the costume either, like some of the girls did. A stupid pair of rabbit ears on her head, draw some cute little whiskers on her cheeks with eyeliner and a fluffy tail attached to her thong or whatever minuscule type of underwear was going to be likely to attract the most attention and she'd have the patrons showering her in cash. And unfortunately, unbridled lascivious attention of the worst kind.

*

"I'm taking a break now!" Bunny called, trying to make herself heard over the medley of sound comprised of raucous drunks, tittering idiot girls, music and general crowd noise.

The intended recipient of her statement, her boss, didn't appear to have caught it, but a fellow staffer closer to her did. Mara, pushing forty, but still looking stunning and able to keep the men's eyes on stalks was a Fantasy Dress veteran and essentially the one all the other girls took their cues from when first starting up. She was a fixture in the place, part of the furniture. While multitudes of younger women came and went through the place in a staff turnover that resembled a revolving door, Mara held her position with an admirable tenacity.

She nodded to Bunny and started to wave her off on her break, then looked as though she'd changed her mind.

"Sure hun, go on and take a load off, but first can you shoot this lot of drinks over to table twelve?"

"Table twelve? Oh hell no, those guys are a pack of obnoxious, degenerate assholes. That dick with the buzzcut and pink shirt told me he'd 'love to smash in my back door and use my perky little cottontail as a jizzrag'. Amongst other pleasantries."

"Charming." Mara pursed her lips in disapproval, though whether that was in response to what the vulgar jackass had to say or Bunny's refusal to carry out the request, wasn't clear. She wasn't Bunny's boss by any stretch of the imagination, but she had seniority, influence and an apparent untouchable status when it came to getting her way and holding onto her position. Still, she didn't draw the attention that Bunny did…

"Not the word that immediately came to my mind."

"I suppose not."

"I'm sure Kathy will do it. She thrives on what some of these idiots say. She encourages them." Bunny suggested hopefully. "I don't know what it is about Easter… every year it's the same thing for me. I'm a freak magnet."

"Of course you know what it is hun. It's your cute little cottontail. Anyway, go on, run along and take your break. But no tarrying; you know we're short on numbers tonight and we need every hand on deck."

"No worries," Bunny hastened past to grab her jacket. It wasn't a particularly cold night and she wasn't planning to walk out on the main street wearing less than underwear like she was off to attend some Hooker Halloween party, but nor did she fancy standing around out in the back alley having her smoke break in minimal attire. Some of the girls didn't give a rats about standing around in their skimpy costumes either in the back alley or those bordering the building, hell some of them even wandered right out the front and mingled with the passing foot traffic and folks on congested sidewalks on a busy night, trying to coerce and persuade more punters to come and join the party, but that wasn't Bunny's game. When she went for a break, she wanted it to be a fucking break away from the madness and crowded mayhem inside, not a parade right into another circus out on the city streets.

The jacket was long enough so the hem of it would mostly come down past her ass, so unless she bent over to touch her toes or some such shit, she wouldn't be flashing her bare buttocks and cute little cottontail for whatever breed of miscreant might also be frequenting the alleys. Bunny had no plans on doing that. What she wanted to do was take her infernal six inch stilettos off and rest her aching feet, indulge in a cigarette to calm herself and regain some composure and then steel herself for the final leg of the night. What she really wanted to do was knock back a couple of shots of top shelf vodka, but that was a strict no-no. Fantasy Dress head honcho Pasch was reasonably lenient in regards to some aspects of what the girls could get away with, but drinking on the job or with the patrons, accepting drinks from them, being under the influence of any substance was grounds for immediate dismissal. He wasn't even keen on them smoking, but that was one concession he granted, albeit grudgingly.

Bunny deliberately aimed for the facilities, then abruptly veered towards the staff exit door. She surveyed the busy interior of the place, ensuring no eyes were on her or watching her depart, then surreptitiously ducked out. Mara knew where she'd be headed of course, but it was a fair bet Mara had no plans on taking a break herself at the moment. Bunny's reason for not wanting anybody to see her exit was simple. Her break was her time to herself; that was it. She didn't want to engage in small talk with anybody, didn't want to be drawn into any conversation, she didn't want company at all.

She supposed there was minimal likelihood of any of her co-workers deciding to join her, since as Mara had pointed out, they were short-staffed. Bunny hadn't needed any reminding of that. She was only too painfully aware of it. Jessica had called in sick, Esther was a complete no-show and Karen pulled a half shift, ducking out early with some other pressing concern. Which all made it a hectic hell for those left to contend with the late night Easter crowds, despite there being a relatively large number of girls rostered on.

On any ordinary night when Fantasy Dress was down on numbers it was something bordering on a nightmare; on a short-staffed Easter night, it was astronomically catastrophic. If it weren't for the fact that she was legitimately owed breaks, she'd have been surprised if Mara would have granted her the opportunity to take one.

There were a handful of milk crates and other assorted things various members of staff, and even patrons who wandered into the alley for a smoke or other activities, had assembled to sit on and Bunny gratefully made her way to a crate now, keen to get off her feet and out of the heels. She hadn't given it too much thought about being barefoot out here, but now she did. Though it was kept as clean as a city alley outside a popular alcohol serving establishment could be, there was still an accumulation of all kind of perilous shit out here. Potentially discarded needles, empty beer bottles, cigarette butts, condoms and a vast assortment of things Bunny didn't really want to entertain thoughts about or to put her feet down on.

As luck would have it, there was a whole newspaper, sitting folded atop a dumpster as if somebody had stepped out to have a cigarette and peruse the sports section or the funny papers, and then just left the item behind. Bunny didn't waste time grabbing that and spreading it open in front of the crate, before kicking off her shoes, digging her smokes out of a jacket pocket and sitting back to relax. Or at least as much as this tiny window of opportunity for some semblance of relaxation offered.

It didn't last long.

"So, that's where you got to." A new voice intruded on her thoughts, cutting brusquely through them with a low-pitched, unwelcome timbre. "Was wondering where my favourite Fantasy bunny had taken her fine ass off to."

Bunny must have been in some kind of reverie, or hardly paying attention at all, for she hadn't seen the newcomer exit Fantasy Dress, though quite obviously, that's precisely where he'd been.

Standing a few feet away from here, dressed as usual as though he'd just come from a business meeting was Josiah Christian, wealthy married businessman, habitual barfly and frequent Fantasy Dress patron. Especially on special events and holidays.

"Hey Josiah," she answered shortly, eyeing him warily as he fumbled around to obtain himself a cigarette. He was weaving a fraction unsteadily in his wingtips and she could tell he'd already had plenty to drink. Funnily enough she hadn't yet encountered him inside tonight.

Maybe she'd been too preoccupied by all the other sleazy, degenerate fuckwits to notice the regular customer sleazy, degenerate fuckwit. Didn't seem likely though. If he'd been around, he'd have been all over her like a rash, as usual.

"You know Bunny, I've been thinking. Been giving it some serious thought. I've slid a whole pile of money your way haven't I? A right fuckload in fact. Daresay enough to put your baby bunnies through college if you ever decide to pop some out. That'd be a shame though, subjecting that tight, hot body to the ravages of pregnancy, but I digress. As I was saying, I'm pretty generous with my tips aren't I? Pretty free and forthcoming, right?"

"Yes, you are," she answered cautiously. "That's your prerogative. I don't ask for it. I'm just doing my job. And I guess I must be doing it well if you feel so inclined to give me handsome tips."

"Oh come now Bunny." Christian laughed and it was an ugly sound, free of mirth and loaded with something far more unpleasant. "You and I both know, it isn't because your abilities to dispense drinks and plates of food, and peel off brainless banter to packs of equally brainless gawkers, is superior to any of the other pieces of costumed trim shaking their asses to and fro in there."

"Nice talking to you Josiah," Bunny said, quickly extinguishing her half-finished cigarette. "Break time is over. I've got to get back to it."

"Hold on a second. Wasn't done talking to you, was I?" He was right in front of her before she'd acknowledged he'd moved, temporarily glancing away from him towards her heels.

In the grand scheme of things, he wasn't a big man; certainly not a seven foot behemoth or anything of that nature, but when he was abruptly that close to her, his bulk seemed far greater than hers. She could barely see anything beyond it; his frame blotted out most of the light filtering in from the alleys on each side of the establishment and the so-called security lights out here were acting up once again.

"Yeah. Not done saying my piece, am I? Like I said, I've shelled out something of a small fortune to you and it's sure as hell not because you can carry out menial tasks any better than any other undressed waitress wench. So, with that said, how about a little appreciation, you feel me?"

"I appreciate what you do. I appreciate all my customers. Especially the regulars," Bunny kept her eyes on him now, feeling around with her toes for her shoes. Even though his form blocked out much of the light, making him mostly a silhouette, enough of it spilled over his shoulders to display his face. That visage was flushed, both with the effects of the apparently large quantity of alcohol he'd consumed and something else. Something ugly. Something foreboding. Something she'd seen many times before. Right before things went to hell in a hand-basket for her.

"See, I don't really think you do. A vapid smile, an autopilot response and a tuck the cash away without a second thought for where it came from doesn't exactly scream appreciation to me," Christian said. He was smiling now, but there was nothing affable in that expression. Beads of perspiration formed on the glistening pane of his forehead, rolling in lazy trickles along the curves of his eyebrows. A sweat moustache adorned his upper lip and as he leaned in closer to Bunny, he poked out his tongue which crawled like a fat pink slug from one corner of his mouth to the other. "You pop on your cute little rabbit ears, slap a fluffy little tail on your ass and gallivant around playing the bunny. Fancy that. Bunny playing a bunny. And that's your shtick, and it works for you. Shit, you don't even need to go to any real trouble with your costume, do you? I mean some of those bitches in there must spend hours getting their ensemble together, but you...well, it's all too easy for you. You know this Easter gig is your gig, it's going to pay off no matter what little effort you put into it. But here's the thing I really want to know. Do you fuck like a bunny? Because that would be something else."

"I need to get back inside..."

"Correction," Christian loomed over her, an ugly chuckle bubbling out of him. *"I'm* the one needing to get inside. Inside you. Come on, it's Easter, Bunny. And you know what I want for Easter, Bunny? I've got some real swollen cream eggs, if you catch my drift. And what I want is to unload some of that cream in a sexy Fantasy Dress Easter Bunny. Paint her eggs white. Fill her basket. Easter bonnet facial."

"Go home Josiah. Go home to your wife. Unload your cream eggs with her. I'm sure that would make her Easter."

"You kidding? If I want to fuck a cold fish, I'll...well, fuck a cold fish! Not happening Bunny. I'm after a hot piece of tail and yours is it!"

She'd already known how this was going to play out, so why she'd let him manage to spew out as much as he had already, she'd no idea, but now she made her move to run. She only had one shoe on, but fuck it, she could come back for the other or finish the shift in bare feet, or fuck knows...

Right now, escaping this situation was imperative.

She lunged to the right, trying to hook her toes in that errant shoe as she did. He socked her right in the midriff with a short, sharp punch from the hip and the impact was immediately devastating. She crumpled, the breath and the desire to scream-along with the ability to do so-smacked out of her in a shocking, brutal blow. Spreading the newspaper out in a bid to keep her feet from coming into contact with whatever unsightly substances stained the alley was all to no avail, since she landed on her rump on the solid questionable surface anyway.

Christian didn't let her slump all the way down though. Painfully winded, shocked and attempting without a great measure of success to suck air back into her lungs, Bunny probably would have collapsed if he hadn't hooked his arms under hers and hauled her upright. For a guy who'd seemed pissed out of his gourd, he was remarkably quick, adept and light on his feet. Maybe that was all a charade, to suck her into thinking he was a little more harmless than he was. It didn't matter; she could barely breathe, she was hanging limp in a powerful grip and a melange of heady cologne, rum, tobacco smoke and sweat was infiltrating her nostrils. The swirl of odours was a nausea-inducing one, making it just as hard to breathe as the solar plexus punch had.

"Come on Bunny, see what you made me do?" Christian grunted in her ear as he hefted her clear of the milk crates and beyond. "I didn't want to do that, no, but you made me, didn't you? That one's on you. Here I am talking about appreciation and you doing something like that just shows me you don't appreciate one goddamned thing I do for you."

Gasping and choking on what felt like great clouds of that hideous marriage of smells emanating from Christian, Bunny's thoughts were swimming in an illogical mire. She should have been a jumble of panic and desperation; instead she was mulling over the stupid vain effort to get her feet back in her high heels. *How the fuck was she going to run in high heels anyway?*

Not that the couple of seconds expended on trying to get her foot inside the shoe would have amounted to jack shit, had she tried the bolt earlier.

Now she was being hauled bodily away from the brighter area of the alley, back into darkness beyond the erratic spread of dumpsters, her feet dragging along the rough terrain. Vaguely, she felt pinpricks of what could have been busted shards of glass or jagged pebbles scraping at her unclad foot, and the notion that a discarded needle might be down there somewhere just waiting to spike into the bare skin fought with the other ridiculous notions clamouring in her head.

"This didn't have to be hard Bunny," Christian said, his voice grating in her ear, little more than a hoarse whisper. The cloying sweet scent of his cologne, swimming amidst that waft of alcohol and smoke was overpowering. It was nullifying her ability to get her breath back at all. He must have bathed in the stuff, on all counts.

As she realised she was so far back beyond the scatter of bulky dumpsters that she could no longer see the door back in to Fantasy Dream, or any other avenue of escape, Bunny's random procession of irrational cogitations and vagaries fled. Cold, hard terror rushed in. True fear. The acknowledgement of what was about to happen to her. The same as it had before on so many more occasions than she cared to count.

Now she started kicking and struggling, flailing like a wild animal. Legs flew out in desperate bids to strike anything, as did hands. Christian might have been with it enough to move fast, punch the wind out of her and ensnare her, but his relocating of her further in the shadowy climes of the alley wasn't without its flaws. Hooking his hands under her armpits left her hands free and she struck with them now, clawing with her ruby red nails, trying to scratch and gouge at any flesh she could find. She was aiming for eyes, but for the most part was getting tangled in the slicked down, product-laden mess that was his hair.

Christian slapped her. For some reason it was more of a shocking blow than the brutal midriff punch. He slipped his right hand out from under her arm and slugged her square across the face with an open palm that didn't skimp any on the force. It knocked her head sideways, rattled her brains and blasted a savage sting throughout her whole cranium. Teeth cracked together, biting the inside of her cheek with a ferocity that must have ripped skin away. She felt the coppery taste of blood immediately fill her mouth.

"You don't touch the hair! You *never* touch the fucking hair! You can't afford this damn hair, not even with the amount of dollars I habitually stuff into your tiny little G-string," Christian growled. "And let me tell you Miss Flopsy Mopsy Fucking Cottontail, you might think you're a cut above other whores shaking their ass in less savoury establishments here because it's some kind of costumed eatery or what-have-you, but I can assure you, you're no better than any common stripper. You're *not*. I tried to be nice about this Bunny, but you were having none of that, so now it's got to be the hard way."

He delivered another slap, this time with the other hand. Doing so meant she was completely freed from his grip, but forced back against the wall of the alley as she was, she was in no real position to be doing much about that. Even less so when the second slap connected and left a stinging imprint on her left cheek, twin to the one on her right.

Before she could collect any thoughts-most of which were now piecemeal snatches of fear and helplessness anyway-Christian had her in his hands again, spinning her around, yanking both arms back behind her. Her face ended up jammed against the hard, unrelenting rough texture of the wall, as Christian ripped her jacket from her and hurled it away behind him.

"Come on Bunny, it's not even cold. Why are you hiding all the good stuff under this? Shit, nobody's out here to see you. Nobody's going to come out and see you either. I mean you've still got those bunny ears on, your fluffy little tail sitting on this perky Bunny ass..."

Now the slap he gave her bounced right across her exposed ass, from one buttock to the other and the force he delivered it with, combined with the unexpected shock of it happening, jarred her face hard against the wall again.

"I was thinking I'd love to just leave that tail on there while I fill your basket, but I've a better idea. Bite down on it. A little deterrent from opening your trap."

Bunny felt his hand at the small of her back and then slide down to rest where the prop rabbit tail was affixed to her thong. A split second later, it was gone, yanked away, and the waistband of her thong was snapping against her skin with another unwelcome sting. Then Christian was forcing the fluffy item against her lips, fingers probing to prise her mouth open. While below, the fingers on his other hand started to probe, fondle and grope elsewhere.

The brutal invasions threw her right back into the deepest, darkest corners of her mind. The ugly, fearful shadow realms where she tried to kept horrible past events buried and locked away. Now they came free, digging their way up out of their mental imprisonments, clawing, revealing hideous faces and hideous truths. So many prior assaults of this nature. So many others who'd taken what they wanted with impunity and callous force.

Bunny snapped.

As Christian's face loomed in close to hers to whisper some further demeaning remark or crude riposte, she twisted her head to face him and promptly kissed him. It was enough to stupefy him and he temporarily ceased his ministrations, taken off guard. She launched with her mouth again, but this time was no kiss. Her teeth, already awash with her own blood, clenched onto his cheek and sheared into the flesh. Tasting a great mouthful of that less than fragrant odour brew he exuded almost quelled her fervour for the attack, or would have done on any other occasion. Not this time. Bunny had lost it. There was no stopping her now.

At the same time, she bent her leg, the one with a foot successfully encased in a six inch stiletto and then thrust it back down with a stabbing momentum. The heel punched into Christian's foot, the downward impetus driving the stiletto point in to his wingtips. Those fancy intricate detailed markings on the toe cap might have been nice to look at, but they weren't much defence against the furious attack.

Christian reeled away with a series of agonised sounds that bred shocked curses with hoarse screams, and only then, when he'd released her, did she unclamp her teeth from his ruined cheek. He clapped a hand up against the rend in his face and blood spilled from between his fingers. His eyes were wide and stupefied, the former glaze of lust and inebriation abdicating to pain and utter shock.

It wasn't enough to keep him from charging back towards her, but she wasn't blithely sitting by waiting for him. She'd bent her leg up again and this time the high heeled shoe was clasped in her hand. As he came into her orbit, she swung it and popped him right in the corner of the eye with the wicked heel point. It punched in under the eyelid and the intrusion of the foreign object in the eye socket was enough to dislodge the eyeball, pushing it out in a grotesque protrusion. As blood welled out in tandem with this aberrant sight, Christian released a thin ululation of noise that was anything but manly. On any other occasion, the mere vision would have been enough to bend Bunny double and have her retching and hurling up her guts, but now she just viewed it with a cold, detached satisfaction, inwardly thinking she should probably do something more to shut up that ridiculous noise he was making.

So with that in mind, she took another swing with the stiletto. This blow was less of a direct hit and far less satisfying than the first lucky strike. It glanced off his nose and raked a thin red line along it. Hardly the impactful violence she'd been hoping for. She fared better with the next one. Christian's gaping mouth, issuing that air raid siren of astonished agony was a prime location to park her stiletto, so she did just that, thrusting the heel over the flapping meat of his tongue and into his throat. She tried to stuff the rest of the shoe right into his mouth, albeit with little measure of success. Clawing hands were abandoning the flap of bloody skin hanging off his cheek and the freaky protuberance that was his eye and grabbing at the shoe instead.

Bunny wasn't done. Bunny wasn't anywhere near done. This alley, which up until very recently had been a source of sanctuary and solitude for the most part, and then turned brutal traitor to play host to a forceful violation, now became her friend again.

Those errant beer bottles, even the milk crates, those cast off hypodermic needles...

They weren't items of refuse to avoid with extreme prejudice anymore. They were handy pieces of weaponry, implements to add suffering, agents of vengeance. And that wasn't all.

She didn't just carry her cigarettes, essential items of make-up and other paraphernalia in the pockets of that jacket when she ducked out for a break.

The scum of the earth, the sleazes, the degenerates, the Josiah Christians of this world had taught her plenty of harsh, degrading life lessons. She toted a knife inside that jacket. Not just any simple knife, but one procured from an unsavoury face from her past. An SOG Flash II folding knife.

After she clubbed Josiah Christian in the back of the head with a section of broken brick and dropped him in a sprawl on the alley floor, she took her time regaining her jacket and fishing that knife out of the pocket.

*

In a drunken wave of humanity, Julian Maundy and his equally inebriated pack of friends finally vacated Fantasy Dress. A couple of them were completely pissed, falling down drunk, but most of them were still holding it together despite having consumed enough alcohol between them to put a small liquor store out of business.

They hadn't left the premises entirely willingly, knowing full well there was precious fuck all else they could do once they departed Fantasy Dress, but when it reached the point when even the sluttiest waitress, Kathy, was complaining about their raucous, crude antics, it was time for security to move in and move them on.

Left with little other option in the small hours of the morning, they splintered into smaller knots of twos and threes. Some wandered off with ambitions of perhaps hailing a cab home, others departed in erratic, wavering lines with no idea where they were going.

Julian and a few others hung around the general vicinity, loitering, under the belief that some of the lingerie girls would be clocking off soon enough. With plans to accost any that did happen to do so, the bunch smoked and stalked around the nearby streets, keeping eyes out for any women at all drifting into their orbit. There must have still been a couple of twenty four hour places open, because there was a reasonable number of pedestrians and traffic around, even at this late hour, but with their single-minded mission keeping them from thinking outside the box, the crew of liquored up men didn't contemplate travelling too far afield from their chosen hunting ground.

At some stage during their predatory prowling, constant trading of vulgarities and demeaning ripostes about the girlfriends that several of them already had, but didn't have any intention of going home to, Julian felt eyes on him. Even in his state of intoxication, he felt as though somebody was watching him, eyes boring into him like lasers and he drifted away from the others, curious. He wouldn't have believed it if somebody made mention of knowing when you're being watched while he was sober, but for some reason, whilst pissed as a newt, he could well and truly appreciate it. Then he saw her.

He couldn't believe it. Whatever god looked out for maggoted fuckheads was smiling down on Julian Maundy right now.

A few businesses up from Fantasy Dress, peering out from between two of them was the very waitress he'd had the biggest hard-on for whilst in the joint. She was staring straight at him, something of an alluring smile plastered on her sexy face. The hot, albeit aloof, blonde. Nah, more like fucking frigid blonde who'd had no sense of humour or interest in him and his friend's endless procession of sexual come-ons. Shit, a gal working in a joint like that, dressed in less material than he'd need to lace his shoes and she wasn't down to hear some horny remarks directed her way?

Looked quite remarkably as though she'd changed her tune somewhat.

She even still had those bunny ears she'd been wearing inside, atop her head. No disgusted looks on her face this time, no, she was all smiles. Dare Julian think it, slutty smiles? Come-on smiles? She was still in that tiny outfit she'd been wearing in Fantasy Dress and nothing more. He bet if she were to turn around she'd still have that fluffy little cottontail adorning her ass.

Goddamn, Julian loved Easter. Not for any of the religious horseshit, nor the candy or what-have-you; shit he didn't even like chocolate. What he loved it for was the fact that it seemed every single year, without fail, he had an uncanny knack of picking up and getting laid. In almost any kind of situation something would happen, resulting in him getting his end wet. Most times he actively pursued that goal, but others he didn't and things just fell into place, leaving him riding triumphant while his stupid girlfriend was none the wiser. Just like now.

And this blonde stunner wasn't just some lingerie waitress bitch dressed up as a slutty bunny, she was a bona fide Bunny. Her name was Bunny, for fucks sake. This was fate, had to be. She was the Easter Bunny. At least as close to any kind of Easter Bunny as Julian Maundy was ever likely to believe in.

Happy Easter, Julian.

The blonde with the bunny ears and the name Bunny on her driver's licence, took one step out from where she'd been hiding-or waiting, Julian wasn't sure which-between establishments. She surfaced from the dark shadows that stretched back between those buildings just enough to ensure he saw her properly, then she beckoned with a come hither finger that was a pretty clear indication of her intentions to Maundy.

He couldn't be one hundred per cent sure he saw everything after that quite as plainly or whether his brain was clouded enough by alcohol for his eyes to play some tricks on him, but she turned around and thrust her ass out, popping those bare buttocks out in a motion that wasn't difficult to mistake. It was her fluffy little costume cottontail that was making him think his eyes were deceiving him. While she had her butt sticking out, wiggling it tantalisingly, that tail he'd been making lewd comments about all evening didn't seem to even be there. Yet when she slapped her ass with one hand, the tail reappeared.

Did she have it in her hand or what? Julian's booze-soaked brain found that small, trivial detail perplexing, but the brain he relied on more heavily than the one in his cranium spoke to him from below his waist and he didn't need any more bidding than Bunny's come-hither finger and her gyrating backside to answer that call.

Then she was gone, vanishing back into the dark between buildings.

Julian glanced back at his companions. Ensconced in a loud drunken debate, they hadn't even noticed him take leave of their presence. Even better, they hadn't noticed the woman pop out onto the sidewalk and then disappear again. Which suited the hell out of him. He wasn't sharing with them. Hadn't ever had any plans to.

He wasted no time hastening up the sidewalk, departing the immediate vicinity of Fantasy Dress and its surrounds, aiming for that dark mouth of a passageway she'd disappeared into.

Even in a sober state of mind, Julian had no qualms about entering a dark domain when sex was on the agenda. Being inebriated and fired up by the amount of bared flesh on display in Fantasy Dress only heightened his desire to rush after the sexy Easter Bunny.

It was lighter than he'd expected in there, but still dark enough that his pink shirt looked like it was a glow in the dark job. He could see vague shapes and a spill of light from the open mouth that was the other end of the passage, though he couldn't immediately see the girl. He was already fumbling with his zipper, trying to free his stiffening dick. Being pissed right now wasn't giving him a case of the flops at all, not when he knew what was waiting in the shadows for him.

"Bunny? Oh Bunny, don't run like a rabbit now."

"I'm not running. I'm right here. Waiting."

One of those nebulous forms sashayed from the clustered shadows cast by the neighbouring buildings, taking shape as Bunny herself and Julian completed the job of getting his erection out, inwardly marking up another notch for a successful Easter egg hunt. Every year without fail, he was the champion, scoring the prize egg each time while his drunken mates ended up falling over one another, talking utter shit and hamstringing their own efforts to pick up a fine piece of Easter tail.

"I overheard you before," Bunny said. "You have a girlfriend. Is that true?"

"Ah not really. I mean, she's..."

"No need to lie. I kinda have a fetish for attached guys, you know. It's a big thrill to me."

"Yeah," Julian laughed, bolstered by that knowledge. "Yeah I got a girlfriend. Stupid bitch is sitting at home, clueless."

"She lives with you, does she?"

"Sure does. Though I guess 'live' is a bit of a stretch. Bitch never wants to do shit. So, fuck her."

"No. Fuck you."

Bunny stepped right up close to him and it wasn't a fluffy bunny tail she was holding in her hand now. It was a bloodied folding knife, serrated blade extended. She punched it into the side of his neck.

As she pulled the blade back out, blood squirted in a gory spray over the bright pink of his shirt and he staggered a couple of steps backwards, eyes bulging and useless hands clapping at the stab wound. His legs went spastic and rubbery under him, and he dropped on his knees with a jarring thump that knocked his palm away from the spouting neck and sent more claret in crimson rivulets down onto the garish outfit which was fast becoming stained with a darker hue than he'd started the evening with.

"Look, you're getting blood everywhere," Bunny said and tossed something towards him. "You're so full of alcohol, that blood is going to be as thin as water and you're just going to bleed out. I doubt your jizzrag is going to help with that much, but here you go."

The fluffy bunny tail of her costume bounced off his chest, where an escalating spread of blood was soaking into his shirt, and fell onto the ground before him. For such an innocuous little white ball, it appeared to be mocking him and in his stupor of pain, he couldn't tear his eyes off it. He fixated on it, tried desperately to focus on it as though it were some inane beacon to keep his tenuous grip on life intact.

Then Bunny moved in closer, still wielding her gore dripping knife. She wasn't done with it yet.

*

At first she thought the loud hammering was issuing from inside her skull, but as she came fully awake and shook off her disorientation, Magdalena Christian realised the infernal banging wasn't a result of the hellacious hangover she was sporting. It didn't help it any, but the two were independent of one another.

The reason for that obnoxious noise being so loud was because it was the front door, the thumping reverberating around her cranium like it was being subjected to a sadistic army of tap-dancing fucktards. And instead of being ensconced in her bedroom, where the sound would be muffled and faint at best, she hadn't quite made it that far. Another night spent passed out in the lounge, mere metres from the front door.

By the time she'd righted herself on the sofa, swinging her legs over the side with an accidental motion that was far too exuberant for her head to take without kicking renewed bursts of dull, throbbing pain through it, the banging had ceased. She sat there for a second expecting it to resume, but all was quiet now.

If it was Josiah, and there was every chance the imbecile had lost his keys out on another booze-soaked, skirt-chasing, slut-ogling expedition, he wouldn't relent on the banging, he'd just keep at it with his usual idiotic obstinacy, probably punctuating it with curses and shouts. Clearly he hadn't made it home once again, but she hadn't really expected anything more.

Getting up was an effort. Her mouth was Sahara desert dry and the taste in there was feral, something she knew she could attribute to the few glasses-come on, now, the few *bottles*-of red she'd knocked back over the course of the evening.

Fucking Easter. She was no believer in anything affiliated with the holiday at all; it was either an ultra-commercial money suck, a blatant excuse to stuff faces with chocolate or a reason for the fervently religious to assemble and worship, but she did subscribe to the notion that one shouldn't be spending it alone. Yet, that was exactly how she spent each Easter, Christmas, everything. Getting acquainted with a bottle of wine, then chasing it with another and for good measure, maybe one or two more after that.

There was nobody outside. Nobody standing there impatiently with fist raised ready to start up the banging ensemble again. No inebriated Josiah hanging onto the railing or sprawled in the garden bed. Nobody departing the scene, discouraged with the lack of answer. But there was a brightly coloured, garish, cellophane covered Easter basket sitting on the welcome mat just outside the door.

"What the...?"

Stooping, she picked it up and backed inside, peering with a mixture of curiosity and suspicion at the strange item. Who the hell would bother dropping off an Easter basket to her? She hadn't received one since she was a child and all of her friends knew she wouldn't be interested in receiving one now. Not unless it was full of bottles of wine...

It wouldn't be from Josiah. That wasn't his style at all. She couldn't remember the last time he'd given her anything, aside from headaches, grief and indigestion. The days of him even being able to give her any semblance of an orgasm were long gone, buried by time and dust. She wasn't sure if he even knew what an Easter basket was, let alone any of the alleged 'true' senses of the holiday itself.

Could it be from some prospective admirer? She wasn't lacking for suitors; there were a couple of strapping young lads at the gym who always eyed her with appreciation and engaged her in flirty conversation at any available opportunity and there were others elsewhere who'd indicated they'd have no problem pursuing her if she suddenly presented herself as available. She didn't think it was any of their styles either though. No, this just seemed bizarre.

Maybe it was a complimentary gift from one of the various liquor stores that saw frequent activity from the Christian credit cards. That was perfectly feasible. Between Josiah and herself they must have been keeping these establishments in business.

She took another cursory look around outside, just on the off chance she'd catch a glimpse of somebody departing or loitering around the area waiting to see her reaction, maybe a delivery van, anything to present a clue, but there was nothing. Pulling the door shut behind her, she went back inside.

Normally she'd be brewing up a nice hot pot of coffee, but at the moment she felt as though she couldn't even stomach that. She knew anything that hit the pit of her stomach would be exiting twice as fast. Instead, she returned to the place she'd woken up, perching her rump on the edge of it while she placed the curious, gaudy item on the coffee table.

"It's too early in the morning for this nonsense," she commented to nobody in particular, though truth be told she hadn't a clue what time it was. It could have been after midday for all she knew, and since her solo drinking binges usually carried on well into the small hours of the morning before she inevitably passed out, it was a fair bet that it wasn't that early at all. In any case, early or otherwise, no time was good for looking at the utter brightness of the outlandish cellophane encasing the basket. It wasn't doing her head any favours at all, so she tore it open, ripping it away from the basket to see what it contained.

Peering at it, Magdalena saw the inside of the basket was mostly comprised of bright shreds of paper, like confetti or the streamers from those absurd little Christmas crackers, all bunched around to constitute a variegated nest. In that nest were two foil wrapped eggs, their coverings as garishly bright as the cellophane and the paper streamers. There was so much colour there it made Magdalena want to throw up and that would have been the case whether she was hungover or not.

She didn't see a note or a card or anything to indicate who was responsible for this aberration that looked like it had been pissed out by a rainbow. Maybe it was somebody messing with her. Somebody from her past when she'd been a pill popper, a raver who downed ecstasy pills like lollies. Maybe there were pills inside the eggs or something. Shit, at this rate she'd almost welcome that. She would have welcomed it *last* night. A fleeting semblance of happiness to curb the stupid notion of spending Easter alone, albeit a synthetic one.

Plucking an egg out, she held it in her hand and gazed at it. It was pliable; not at all what she'd expected. It wasn't the firm feel she'd been anticipating, had it been chocolate or plastic encasing something else, or if it was chocolate, then it was starting to melt and soften. That prospect almost made her gorge rise and bring that nausea swelling back up in her. Nonetheless, she peeled it anyway. And then she did throw up.

Even without having ever seen one in this state before, Magdalena didn't need to have done so, to know what she was holding in her hand was a bloodied human testicle. A gory shrivelled walnut of a thing in its bed of bright Easter foil, that inner layer still flecked with red spots.

Magdalena dropped it with a horrified shriek and projectile vomited an acidic stream of bile, scampering away from the offending article in a clumsy motion that bumped her into the coffee table and upended the lurid basket on the floor. The other foil-wrapped egg, which she didn't need to unwrap to know she had the grisly former nutsack resident's twin accounted for, fell out among the tangle of multi-coloured paper streamers. Falling atop this mess, apparently formerly buried under the nest was a card, bright pink in colour and speckled with blood.

The last thing Magdalena wanted to do was touch that, but morbid curiosity defeated all other cogitations. Hunched on the floor on hands and knees, still trailing tendrils of bile from the corners of her mouth, she reached out a trembling hand towards that card, snatching it between fingers that really wanted to be anywhere but there.

Happy (belated) Easter, Mrs Christian

It took quite some convincing to make your husband see that he really should be giving his cream eggs to you for Easter, but he came around eventually. I know they're a little late, but I have been a very busy BUNNY.

Yours truly, the new Easter BUNNY.

*

Magdalena Christian wasn't the only one to receive an unexpected Basket on Easter Monday.

Over on the other side of town, Jessica Abbott likewise answered a knock on the door of the apartment she shared with boyfriend Julian Maundy to find a garish abomination of a basket sitting innocuously on the floor outside.

So too did others. Quite a few others.

After all, Easter Sunday was one of those nights of the year that seemed to bring all the freaks out of the woodwork. Many of whom happened to cross the path of the self-proclaimed new Easter Bunny.

THE END

Bio

Jim Goforth is a horror author currently based in Holbrook, Australia. Happily married with two kids and a cat, he has been writing tales of horror since the early nineties.

After years of detouring into working with the worldwide extreme metal community and writing reviews for hundreds of bands across the globe with Black Belle Music he returned to his biggest writing love with first book Plebs published by J. Ellington Ashton Press. Along with Plebs, he is the author of a collection of short stories/novellas With Tooth and Claw, extreme metal undead opus Undead Fleshcrave: The Zombie Trigger, co-author of collaborative novel Feral Hearts and editor for the Rejected For Content anthology series (taking over the reins after volume one Splattergore. He also has stories in both Splattergore and Volume 2: Aberrant Menagerie).

He has also appeared in Axes of Evil, Terror Train, Autumn Burning: Dreadtime Stories For the Wicked Soul, Floppy Shoes Apocalypse, Teeming Terrors, Ghosts: An Anthology of Horror From the Beyond, Suburban Secrets: A Neighborhood of Nightmares, Doorway To Death: An Anthology From the Other Side and edited volumes 2 and 3 of RFC (Aberrant Menagerie and Vicious Vengeance). Coming next from Jim will be appearances in Tales From the Lake Volume 2, Drowning in Gore, Full Moon Slaughter, MvF, Trashed, another collab novel Lycanthroship as well as follow-up books to Plebs and Rejected For Content 4: Highway To Hell (editor).

He is currently working on two new novels with plans to wrap them up before beginning further instalments of both the Plebs saga and The Zombie Trigger.

http://www.amazon.com/Jim-Goforth/e/B00HXO3FRG/

ref=dp_byline_cont_ebooks_1

https://www.facebook.com/JimGoforthHorror

https://twitter.com/jim_goforth

https://www.goodreads.com/author/show/7777382.Jim_Goforth

https://jimgoforthhorrorauthor.wordpress.com/

https://plus.google.com/+JimGoforth/

https://www.facebook.com/PlebsHorror

https://www.facebook.com/pages/Rejected-For-Content/1601557196779520

https://www.facebook.com/WetWorksJEA

http://www.jellingtonashton.com/jim-goforth.html

http://www.crystallakepub.com/jim-goforth.php

HELP ME

Neil Buchanan

Help me.

Jo raised one eyelid. "Whu...there?"

From a million miles away, sirens wailed.

Help me.

He tried to focus and forced both eyes open. It hurt. *He hurt.* Oval-shaped walls stretched towards a warped door upright upon one hinge and his rucksack which lay discarded upon the wooden floor. His bedroom remained exactly as he'd left it the night before, empty.

From beyond the mould-encrusted window, shrouded with thick pleat curtains, pencil-thin beams of daylight poked into the room. A sudden flash of amber lights danced across the ceiling and outside an emergency vehicle raced down Rudiment Hill. The flat trembled.

A fire engine retreated into the distance, fast becoming somebody else's problem.

Groaning, Jo rummaged for his packet of Golden Virginia. He'd been dreaming. But the voice had been so loud, shouting in his ear. A woman's voice, full of urgency, desperation—

Vague and insubstantial, a memory swam before his mind's eye. From the vastness of space, a giant had peered at the world, head ablaze with fire, bigger than the fucking planet, like something out of an Olympian nightmare. An egg, dark and mottled, formed within his continent-sized hands. Eyes full of stars, glowing with the fundamental building blocks of life, had stared at him. Through him. And then...then...

He couldn't remember, something about the end of the world, but that's how it went with dreams, even drug-induced dreams. Someone, somewhere, had rules and they weren't supposed to be broken. He shook his head. A dream, that's all, a *fucking* dream. To be expected after the coke, alcohol and ecstasy binge from Friday night. Today would be . . . Sunday, maybe Monday. Stayed out for nearly the entire weekend, partying... where...oh, yeah, the squat, until he'd been sick. Actually, the money had run out and drugs stopped being magic after a while. Home then, in the loosest terms: bedroom slash lounge, kitchen, bog and door. Not even a shower or bath. All his washing took place in the sink, but that was okay, better than living on the streets.

Jo had roughed it for five years in Manchester before finding the flat and a landlord prepared to wait for his rent, such as it was, and he wasn't going back for love nor money. He rubbed his arms; his stomach felt like lead. Nausea and bile battled in the back of his throat. Yeah, he wasn't going anywhere or doing anything until he felt a shit-tonne better.

He rolled a fag, fingers barely working through the process, lit it and collapsed in his bed, which consisted of a mattress, sleeping bag and coverless pillow. Smoke trailing from his mouth, he closed his eyes and allowed the events of the party to wash over him. Had he had sex with Lucy in the bog? Yeah, he thought so. He scratched at the scars on his arms, tiny white worms, reminders that on his bad days he was still capable of feeling, even if it was pain. Lucy was a fuckin' skank. God, what had he been thinking? He'd have to avoid her for a few weeks. She'd only be round trying to snag his dole and scabbing fags and....

Jo's eyes snapped open. "Fuck."

Money. He had no money. The bastards had cancelled his dole. He was going through the process. No money to eat, let alone drugs. Which meant...which meant he'd got it on tick. And the only bloke who'd have given him that amount was Len McDurmon.

More sirens outside, the rumble of heavy vehicles as they raced past.

What had he said? What deal? An image of Len reared like a snake: tattoos, muscles and a face even his mother would disown, staring at him over a joint as if he were a piece of meat on a rack. A room full of weed, the smell pungent and offensive, crammed with Len's cronies laughing, laughing... Christ, what had been so funny? He had until Monday. That was it. Pay it back on Monday. Because he'd have his interim by then. He'd give all the cash to Len and live off bollock all for a week.

Jesus, what a wanker. But what choice was there? Len was a full-on hard bastard; the stories surrounding the man didn't need to be embellished because he was the real deal. A hard-as-you-like drug dealer with a fondness for young men. They had to be thin and small, almost girlish, like Jo. And hadn't Len spent the time staring at his arse and cock. Fuck, yes, he had. A cunt of the highest order.

Jo rubbed his scars, fingernails digging into the hardened tissue. When he felt bad, when the day was too much, when moving took a herculean effort, he considered bowing out. It was the hardest option. Maybe not so bad if you believed in an afterlife, heaven or hell, but Jo was a dyed-in-the-wool atheist, death meant nothing, an absence of anything, the utter destruction of all that he had once been. Not that he'd ever amounted to much. Jo forced his fingernail into the scar tissue until he bled. But that wasn't going to happen today, at least. And if he ever did, he wouldn't make a song and dance about it. If the world ever got too much, he'd know what to do, take a tumble from a tall building, one last trip then goodnight Vienna.

Get a grip. Jo put his hand to his heart. This wasn't going to help anyone. It was Sunday. Still a day to get it sorted. He wasn't going to be anyone's bit--

Help me.

The suddenness of the voice made him jump; he twisted about in his sleeping bag, legs tangling and fell off the mattress onto the floor.

But the sound had been so close? The room, *the flat*, was empty, unless there was someone in the kitchen or the toilet? There was no way he'd have somebody back. Not that he didn't mind socialising, but to see the contempt in their eyes... Nah, he hadn't invited anyone from the squat, which meant an intruder.

Jo scrambled, not unlike a crab to his rucksack where he kept his claw hammer – he wasn't completely stupid. Grasping the handle, back to the wall, he slowly stood up. The room swayed; he lurched forward a step. A cold sweat broke upon his brow and he licked at his dry lips. *Let it pass. Let it wash over you.*

It did. The room straightened and he set off at an uneven pace towards the door. If there was someone from the squat, he'd ask them to go. Insist upon it if he had to. He *never* invited people back, even for a shag. The flat was too much of a shit-hole to entertain guests. And he didn't want them to see how crappy his life had become. How fuckin' desperate he was.

The toilet, which stank, and hadn't in the six months he'd lived in the flat ever been cleaned, was little more than a cubicle. Empty save a lone turd floating serenely in the pan. Which left the kitchen. As he shifted about, he glimpsed himself in the mirror and stopped, mouth falling open in a silent 'o' of surprise.

A woman stared through the glass. Pale like milk, eyes wide and full of smouldering emotion, hair not just red but crimson. Energy, power, all resided within her, barely held in check beneath the skin—he blinked – and caught the suggestion of wings and tail, he blinked again and she was gone. Just him, just Jo: a scrawny, near-death drug addict with scars on his arms and shit tattoos.

No one. He laughed nervously, but the sound was flat and lacking any humour. *The drugs playing with my mind, that's all.*

The door to the kitchen was closed so he stood listening, waiting for the slightest noise. Faintly, outside, someone ran past the window.

"I know you're in there," he said, unable to bear the silence a second longer. "Get your arse out or I'm coming in. I've got a...a fuckin' hammer."

He regretted speaking. Now they knew where he was. And they were in the kitchen with all manner of weapons.

Like what? He went through a mental tick list: saucepan, butter knife, fork, spoon, there was a carving knife, but it was blunt, could barely pierce the top of a plastic sheet, let alone stab anyone. But that'd be the weapon of choice. Fuck it, he had to be fast.

Jo thrust open the door and leapt inside, eyes closed, brandishing the hammer and swinging it wildly from side to side.

The kitchen was empty. The sink full of washing up, the floor dirty and stained. Thin daylight seeped in through cracked windows. But that was all. That was it.

Outside, someone was crying, the sound strangely disjointed. It faded almost as soon as it began.

He was alone. There was no one in his flat. How could there be?

In his head then? A kind of auditory hallucination. He'd heard of those, drug-addled brain making up all kinds of weird shit as it tried to make sense of the chemical soup frying his insides.

He realised he'd been holding his breath and let it out. Just his head fucking with him. Nothing more. He almost laughed.

Help me.

Jo twisted about, jarring his arm against the wall. He dropped the hammer which in turn landed on his foot. Shrieking, he fell over.

"I can't go crazy," he whispered. "I haven't got my shit together yet."

Please.

He puked, although nothing came out other than sticky strands of bile. Again. By his ear. No, closer, as if...as if it were in his head.

Jesus, he didn't feel well. He wasn't sure how long he sat that way. A good hour, maybe more, waiting for the voice to return. Fear kept him still, rooted him to the floor as if he were an abnormal growth. When, finally, his bladder had had enough and the urge to piss became intolerable he staggered up and relieved himself in the cubicle. The urine was dark and stank of sperm and who knew what chemicals his body extruded.

Through the small window, a group of children raced past, casting fearful glances over their shoulders as if playing a deadly game of catch, red school uniforms flashing between the railings. Over the rooftops, a helicopter appeared, the machine gun fire of its rotor blades made the glass tremble. He watched for a while, before shaking his cock and shoving it back into his pants. It took a while for his brain to catch up. School kids? Which meant Monday. Not Sunday.

"Fuck," he said again, then glimpsed the woman from the corner of his eye, peering at him through the glass.

"Go away," he said. "You're in my head."

A sudden bout of cramps and he doubled over, clutching his stomach. Sweat dripped from his face and his body rushed hot then cold, enough to plant him on his arse.

The woman, *God, she was beautiful*, stared at him the entire time. She couldn't be real. None of this was real. What the hell had been in the coke he had taken? Had Len sold him something else by mistake, or perhaps on purpose -- the bastard. *If I'm going to die, then perhaps it's for the best.* He closed his eyes and tapped the back of his head against the wall. *Once, twice,* when he opened his eyes she'd be gone, *three, four,* because she wasn't real, *five, six,* never had been.

He opened his eyes. The mirror was blank. Jo hauled himself to his feet. "Mind over matter," he said to his pale reflection. "If you don't mind then it don't matter."

Jo no longer had a phone, having pawned the last model months ago, but he did possess a small television, recovered from the tip last year. He switched it on, then using the remote checked the time and date.

3:25. MARCH 27th.

He'd slept through Sunday and most of Monday. Why? That'd never happened before. Because, said a small voice in the back of his mind, you didn't stop until Sunday morning. A proper two-day bender.

He was as good as dead. Len would already be cruising the streets, searching for him. He didn't know where he lived, so there was that, but plenty of people did. He had no friends. And Len could be real persuasive when he wanted to be. He was out of time and shit out of luck. Jo pressed the palms of his hands to his eyes. He couldn't stay here a second longer and he had nowhere else to go. It was back on the street or an anal beating from Len and his mates.

No choice. None. None at all. He'd lay low for a while, that's what he'd do. Wait for his money, send it to Len, courier if he had to, maybe a bit more. Just had to avoid the mad fucker for a while.

Which meant leaving for a week or two.

An image had slowly sprung into life upon the set. A newsreader looked harried at the camera whilst behind her, a helicopter broadcast images of...was that the construction site at the bottom of the hill? Emergency vehicles, police, ambulances, fire trucks scattered like toys before it, people running in all directions. The camera zoomed to something red and meaty lying on the ground, like a vat of raw minced meat had been upended into the dirt, shreds of cloth that might have once been clothes had somehow become tangled in the mess. Underneath, scrolled the words: Thirteen dead in explosion in Manchester. Unknown cause.

His hand strayed to the volume control before he remembered himself. No time.

And not his problem.

He yanked the plug from the wall, surprised when it took the plaster with it, and shoved the set into his rucksack. Cash Generator would give him at least twenty. Enough for a train or bus to ... where... where would be far enough away from Len? Jo had no family. Mum was dead and Dad had kicked him out six years ago. The insufferable prick. Down south, Cornwall way, there was fuck all there anyway. He'd lose himself in the seaside towns. He might even find work. Easter, wasn't it? He'd find work. He was sure. And not to worry about the drugs. Those places had their own versions of Len. They'd be drugs aplenty if you knew where to look. Do that for a couple of weeks, then come on back. By then Len would have his sights on another poor unfortunate.

Help me.

Jo didn't jump as such. He half-expected the voice.

"Why?" he blurted to the empty room.

Help.

"Fuck that." Jo heaved the bag onto his shoulder and after a moment's hesitation, scurried through the flat to the back door, kicked an overflowing rubbish bag out of the way, fumbled with the key, before forcing it open.

The back garden, loosely defined, was a slab of stone surrounded by four-foot red brick walls, one of which had collapsed. The air was crisp. A few defiant daffodils poked from the neighbour's derelict garden amidst an old bathtub and broken rabbit hutch. Sirens continued to blare, muted but close by and the street, even a back street, was curiously empty considering the time of day.

Help.

"Don't start."

He set off over the broken path, but before he had reached for the gate, a black BMW pulled around the corner, slowly, deliberately, like a shark sensing blood in the water. Music thumped from inside. The fact it was Len's car was assimilated in an instant as was the reason he'd come to this end of town. On instinct rather than any rational thought, Jo threw himself over his neighbour's wall, landing on the other side and jarring his arm further. The soft crack of glass revealed he'd shattered the television set and he forced himself not to scream. Instead, he slipped free of the rucksack and rolled against the wall, face pressed into the brick, heart slamming in his chest, desperately trying to control his breathing. Surely, they'd see him. Or worse, they'd already noticed him diving across the garden and were too busy laughing about it.

Tyres crunched gravel. The rumble of the engine cut to silence. The beat of music stopped as if the musicians had abruptly died.

Help me.

No time. Go away.

The click of car doors, boots scrapping on stone, then Len's voice, deep and resonant. "George stand by the door, whilst me and Danny go in through the front."

"But Len, what with all the trouble shouldn't we just, I dunno, fuck off?"

"Screw the terrorist wankers. They're not concerned with the likes of us."

"Is that what you think it is then?"

"What else could it be?"

"Dunno, the telly said something about a giant egg."

"George, try to think once in your life. Christ, a giant egg? Fuck, man, really?"

"Yeah...I suppose it sounds a little weird."

The gate opened. Boots upon the path. He could hear their breathing, the creak of leather jackets, even smell the cheap aftershave Len liked to use. If he glanced up he'd see them striding past, all they had to do was look down and they'd notice him too, curled into a ball amongst the rest of the dirt and rubbish of his neighbour's garden.

But they didn't.

"Doors unlocked," Len said, his tone smug and contemptuous. "In we go. Remember, me first, then you all get a go."

"Uh, I don't really want to, Len. It's not my thing." That was Dave speaking, the tallest and widest of the group, voice like the dull rumble of thunder.

"Look, Dave, we discussed this," Len said calmly. "It's not about sex, is it? It's about teaching the kid a lesson so he'll tell everyone else not to fuck with us. Remember that, or we'll have every twat fancy his chances."

"But, still, it's a bit--"

"Stop being such a pussy. It's not like you haven't done this before."

"But that was with a woman."

"Same difference. Now get yourself nice and hard and join in the party, or do we have to talk about it further when we get to mine?"

"No, Len, you're right. I'll join in."

HELP ME!

The voice was so loud that Jo jumped, grunting as he did so. The strange silence that followed told him all he needed to know. He opened one eye and peered up.

They were all there, standing in his door, staring at him. Len a foot shorter than the others and not one of them could be considered small. A look of incredulity set upon their faces. Len's lips twisted into a sneer.

"'Ello. Jo, we've been looking for you."

Jo sprang to his feet, leapt across the garden, launched over the wall and into the street in an instant, certainly before anyone had chance to react. Near superhuman in its execution, at any other time he'd surely have won an award, even a television appearance.

But go where, he'd never outrun them, they were too big, too strong.

Len's car loomed large and he sprawled against the bonnet. Len hadn't locked it.

He'd have heard. The car was open. Sensing rather than seeing movement behind him, Jo threw open the door, dived inside and slammed it shut, just as Len smashed against it.

"Get out of my car," Len said between clenched teeth. Then in a sugary tone. "You've still got chance to pay the money back, princess."

Part of him wanted to, just accept what was coming, let it happen and they'd walk away. Sure, he'd bleed for a while. It'd hurt when he took a shit, but that'd be all.

No, he'd rather die. Jo stared at the dashboard, searching for the master control for the locks. He pressed the button and kept his finger on it. All four doors locked as Len thought to try the handle. Len fumbled in his pocket for the remote. The lock shifted beneath Jo's finger, but he didn't budge and the car remained secured.

"Get your ass out of my car." Len lowered his head against the glass, unbuttoned his jacket and slid it to one side. A gun sat holstered at his hip. "Don't make me use this."

"Fuck off, it's fake."

"Wanker." Len hurried around to the boot of the car. Jo craned his head around, but he already knew what Len was up to, moments later the boot was sprung and Len's grinning face appeared as he started to clamber through.

The other men gathered around and he felt like crying, not that it would do any good. Nothing was going to help anymore. His ass had a date with three large cocks and there wasn't a thing that--

Help me.

Ahead of him, Rudiment Hill dipped through an alleyway towards the crossroads and construction site. He spied the edge of a fire truck and an ambulance in the distance. A police car had parked in front of the wooden barriers, lights flashing, doors open. No time for that. Council's problem, not his.

Len was in the boot, twisting through the small space towards him, grumbling obscenities.

Rudiment hill....

Jo slid into the driver's seat and released the handbrake. A moment of nothing, then the car began to roll. Slowly at first before gathering speed. George and Dave were at the back of the car, they slapped their hands against the metal, dragging it to a stop. Dave ran around the front and placed his considerable bulk against it.

"Sorry, Jo, I really am," Dave said, "but we can't let you piss off with our boss's car."

Help.

"Help me first," he muttered.

The air changed, it grew oily, thick and distorted. The hairs on his arms stood on end and sparks flashed along the dashboard.

The radio switched on, a blast of senseless static, and Dave abruptly hurtled from the car, yanked from it as if grasped by an unseen giant. He took to the air, a flying monkey, screaming as he went. The scream stopped as he connected with the roof of the nearest house and Dave fell into the garden, twitching.

George let go of the vehicle and stumbled away and Len stopped his advance. "Wha...what happened?"

"I didn't do it," Jo said. How? What? "I...I..."

The car picked up speed, started to roll down the hill. George watched it go, hands in the air as if surrendering. Dave continued to twitch in the garden but there was less force to the spasms and blood pumped freely over the garden path.

Jo started to laugh. It went on too long and he wondered if he'd ever stop. The wheel barely moved, but he shoved his weight against it and navigated the BMW through the alleyway. The car bounced the curb on the other side, then they were through, speeding down the hill. Glimpses of the outside world, people lying in the street - what were they doing? - the helicopter overhead, far too low, the road wet and the wheels slid, skewing the car sharply to the right, then left. He straightened the wheel, past a man puking in his garden, a child draped over a garden gate. He was going to do it. Going to escape. Him and the voice in his head.

Len's hands encircled his neck. "Stop. The. Fucking. Car. Something 'aint right."

Terrible pressure as fingers closed around his windpipe. Unrelenting and so intense that for a second he forgot he was driving a car, forgot he was on a hill and forget he was Jo. He was just the pain. Until the car bounced off the curb, struck a police car and Len was thrown to one side. Blessed air rushed back into Jo's sore throat, although it burned as if on fire.

They were picking up speed, coming at the crossroads at least thirty, maybe forty.

Len went to grab him again, but the angle was off and he was stretched out inside the car. Jo pushed him to one side, then grasped his claw hammer, smashed it onto Len's outstretched fingers, snapping them like dry wood, skin split and bloodied.

Len twisted away, howling, and Jo shifted in his chair.

"That's what you get, motherfucker" he screamed, "that's what you get, you fuck."

Cursing, Len made another grab for him. Jo swung the hammer, but Len merely caught his wrist and yanked. Fire tore through the ligament and Jo dropped the weapon, his taunts dying on his lips.

A fist followed, great, wide, filling his vision, and he was punched into the seat, head smashing against the steering wheel.

Len appeared, his mouth churned and blood dribbled from between his lips. He cradled one arm as if it were a child soothed to sleep.

But before he had chance to act, Len's gaze shifted behind Jo, eyes widening in surprise, and in his dazed state Jo understood they had reached the crossroads.

An impact of metal against metal (possibly the fire engine), a glancing blow, something bright and red flashing past, then a hard knock to the front. The windscreen shattered. Jo slammed back into his seat, then into the roof. A crazy flow of nonsensical images followed. The roof, the sky, the roof, the door, Len, pain, fear, the roof, ending with a sensation akin to flying, then head butting the steering wheel and taking a face of airbag.

Merciful oblivion followed.

*

The world slid into focus from a thumbnail image in the corner of his eye. Jo was upside down, in the car that was upside down, looking through the wrecked metal and broken glass to a steep embankment and torn wooden barriers. The construction site. The BMW must have gone clean through and ended here. A drop of forty maybe fifty feet. He coughed and spat blood. Lucky to be alive.

Jo tried to move, but his leg refused to play along. White shards of bone jutted from his jeans. His groin and back were sticky and wet. He raised one hand and it dripped red with blood. He gave a soft moan as panic blossomed bright and deep in his chest.

Still alive. Focus. Where was Len?

On the slope, must have bounced free in the fall. Shit, he wasn't dead. He looked a sorry state, face all torn by glass, a shred of flesh hanging from where his top lip should be. No, wait, that *was* his top lip.

Len grunted, then sat bolt upright.

Panic from his injuries upgraded to blind desperation and dragging his leg behind him, Jo slid out onto the worksite, each movement agony, needles of fire racing through his thigh. He slithered onto dust-coated stone, gasping, sucking down air, tears of frustration obscuring his sight.

Len staggered to his feet. He wandered around in half-circles, leaning heavily to one side.

Jo dragged himself away from the wreckage. Going up was out of the question. Each motion and lump in the ground sent unrelenting agony spearing through his body. He closed his eyes, which was worse, then touched something soft.

A police officer lay before him. Head gone. Crushed as if in the grip of a powerful vice. Jo recoiled, unable to process the information.

None of them were worthy.

"Jesus." He put his hands to his ears. What was happening to him?

Further on, another copper lay discarded against a digger, at least what was left, little more than a pile of mince and bone inside a shredded uniform.

"What the fu--"

A sharp crack in the air and he was struck in the back. Jo flopped over. Blood swelled onto his shirt. Liquid gathered in his throat and dribbled out the corners of his mouth. Had he been shot?

Len headed towards him. Only now he waved a small snub-nosed gun in his hands. He fired again. The dirt next to Jo's head sprayed and his ear burned bright and hot.

Jo began to crawl, sliding his body further into the worksite, past the dead coppers, towards a pit. Len, if he even noticed the dead paid them no heed.

More dead: construction workers, bodies distorted into sacks of red grain. They lay scattered about in a semi-circle, as if they had simply exploded or imploded where they stood. None had had the time to turn and run or seek to escape.

And Jo was beginning to understand why. Enlightenment hovered on the edges of his consciousness: the voice, the woman in the mirror, even the giant from his dream, it was all connected, all leading to something. Had he been chosen?

Movement in the corpses. Those closer to the centre convulsed and shuddered. He thought of zombies, like in the movies, and wondered if the dead were about to sit up, clamouring for human brains. Instead, the corpses' chests exploded. Massive gouts of blood, bone and organs sprayed fifteen feet into the air. Emerging from this orgy of destruction and viscera were two figures, blinking in the daylight, soaked from head to foot, strange grins twisting across their newly-born features.

Another gunshot struck his leg and Jo's kneecap vanished in a puff of red and white.

All thought vanished in a sea of unrelenting agony. He slithered the rest of the way into the pit, past blasted chunks of rock and debris, more comatose than awake, past the strange creatures as they took their first uncertain steps into the world, until his head knocked against something hard.

A vast leathery object filled the bottom of the pit, oval like an egg, far taller than a man, easily the size of a house. It had cracked near the top, the leather thinning to transparency, chunks of it had broken free–pushed out from within – and whatever secrets it once hid had long clambered free.

His attention returned to his mangled leg and the pain coupled with nausea threatened to remove him from the world a second time. A sleep he'd not wake from -- that was certain.

Len stumbled into view, not looking much better, still holding the gun, waving it around like a drunk with an empty pint glass aiming for the bar.

Help me.

"I'm here," he gurgled, voice barely above a whisper, more in his head than any sound that escaped his lips. "What more do you want?"

Rebirth.

Sure. Why not? His world was ending anyway. And wasn't that the point, wasn't that what this voice was offering, a new chance, a new life. It had all gone to hell in a handbag. And what a shit life it had been, anyway, seeing out his final moments talking to voices in his head, face pressed against a giant egg. He'd hate to see the bird that laid...that laid...

Something unfurled its tail and stretched its wings.

Sense its power, its sexuality, driving through his mind with darts of white light.

Purifying. Beautiful. A woman reborn.

He cried. His heart stopped beating.

Jo died.

*

A furious jolt of images followed the darkness. Instead of merciful oblivion, the thing that had once been Jo glimpsed ancient tribes, all furs and face paint. They gathered in woodland clearings, working the flesh from naked men, hoisting glistening genitalia into the air like prized delicacies, drinking blood from goblets, dancing in the meadows, worshiping, fucking, killing.

Worshipping what?

Ishtar.

Roman centurions, armour glinting in a noonday sun, swords red with gore, creased sun-kissed faces. No emotion. None at all. A battle, a massacre, the burning of the forest, the spinning of the world. The steady advance of civilisation.

Ishtar.

And an endless sleep, returned to the stars, cradled in the arms of a terrible heat.

Ishtar.

Easter.

Ishtar fell upon him or perhaps more accurately into him, wings and tail folding tight. His mouth forced open and the goddess sank deep inside, penetrating Jo to his core, becoming him, ramming through his mind, exploding its seed so it consumed him utterly, filling Jo with its dark magnificence. When he screamed it wasn't really his voice but rather the voice of something else entirely. New life.

Len shot him again. This time square in the chest. It didn't hurt. How could it? Jo was dead. Rather, it awakened the creature he had become, *Ishtar*, the creature he had transformed into in one swift jolt.

While she waited for her host to find her, Ishtar had killed the construction workers, the police, even the ambulance crews because they didn't need to be reborn. That was obvious. Content in their lives, they slipped into the void of death, useless to her. But others, millions, in fact, were to be remade, and this was important, like Jo, they would cast aside the shackles of their previous existence and be reworked into what they really were, what they should have always been, deep inside when she peeled away flesh, muscle and bone and drew the *soul* into her light.

And what was this new form that rose from the mangled flesh of the dead? A prophet? A voice? Alive? Dead? Somewhere in-between?

All those things. None of them. She laughed, the sound tinkled and the air danced and swirled about her.

But first, Len.

With a hand that was more claw, the woman that once was Jo reached out and removed Len's gun along with most of his arm.

The screams that followed were high-pitched and went on for some time. But that was okay. There would be plenty of screams from now on.

Len sunk to his knees. His face had turned ashen white; he barely looked like Len, anymore. He stared at Ishtar with something approaching awe, repulsion and finally acceptance. Acceptance that his world was coming to an end, that he was ready to be reborn. A small part of her, the part that had been Joe, bucked at the thought. She allowed it to rush to the surface.

"Fuck 'im," it said.

She was inclined to agree.

The world was going to change. The old order torn down. Who needed it anyway? Jo hadn't. And nor did she.

She stretched. Not Ishtar.

She'd make sure of it.

THE END

Bio

Neil John Buchanan lives in the South West of England with three kids, three cats and a sympathetic wife. On weekends he describes dead folk and is all the happier for it. Neil has a zombie contingency plan for every home he has ever lived in and urges you do the same. When not scribbling out stories of madness, gore and plain unpleasantness he resides as dark overlord for Stormblade Productions, an audio and print small press specialising in the macabre and the short story form.

Educating Horace

By Matt Hickman

She awoke with a start, as a wave of panic and nausea crashed into her. Everything around her was enclosed in pitch black and she couldn't see a thing. Her face was constricted by some type of thick cotton-like material, she could feel the sensation of the fabric rising and falling in her mouth as she continued with her laboured breathing. The pain hit her rapidly and unbearably, all over her body - like dozens of sharp blades puncturing and penetrating her skin, all at the same time.

The sour, coppery taste of blood caught in her throat, coating her tongue and the roof of her mouth. As she ran the tip of her tongue against her ruined gums, and the remainder of her teeth she began to sob and moan uncontrollably. The majority of them had been yanked out, leaving nothing but gaping, throbbing holes. The wounds still leaked fresh blood, and the odd broken stumps of teeth and exposed nerves sent pain shooting through her skull. The contained heat of the makeshift hood over her head made her brow wet with perspiration as she continued to panic and hyperventilate. Rivulets of sweat began to run down her burning cheeks and neck.

She made an attempt to move, but her hands and feet were bound together tightly by some kind of sharp plastic or metal straps. The restraints dug into her wrists and ankles, restricting the flow of blood, and left her fingers and toes with a numb, tingling sensation. They were tight enough to rub and break the surface of her skin, threatening to lacerate and draw blood.

She lay in a warm room, the stuffy air intensified by her obstructed airways. The hood that constricted her head and view made it difficult to breathe. Despite her discomfort, she lay on a soft surface; perhaps a bed or mattress.

*

Horace sat alone at the large table located at the back of the school assembly hall, shovelling stale hot cross buns into his mouth, buns that had sat in the heat all day. He sat with his home-made Easter bonnet placed upon his head, the headpiece depicting a scene involving fluffy yellow chicks and pink eggs. He didn't pay any attention to the world around him. He continued to gorge as the other children on stage were singing Easter songs and saying prayers. Large crumbs fell from the stale pastry and rolled down his chin from the side of his mouth, landing in his lap, adding to the growing collection.

He sat listening to the next Easter song; something about the gift of life. He smiled contently, enjoying the Easter service. This was one of his favourite times of the year. He didn't really care for the Easter traditions or religious aspects, oh no. For Horace, it was all about the chocolate.

Horace Davidson was a large boy for his age. At fourteen-years-old, he was already weighing in at a portly thirteen stone. He wasn't particularly tall, and he was certainly no taller than some of the other boys in his year. He carried no muscle on his body to bolster his mass; Horace's weight was saggy body fat, plain and simple.

His shoulders were narrow, and almost didn't seem wide enough to carry the mass of his large cranium. His arms were flabby and dimpled, excess fat hung in place of firm triceps, and his forearms were similar in appearance to those of the cartoon character, Popeye. His hands were particularly small, with short, stubby fingers.

His vast paunch hung around his midriff like a large spare tyre. Despite his large abdomen, he had short, scrawny legs that looked as though they were about to buckle under the load above, at any given moment.

Horace wasn't a bright kid; he was the type of boy that gave the tyrants in his year a wet dream – he would often be referred to as a retard or a blockhead by his peers. The truth was, nobody knew whether there was anything medically wrong with him, or whether he was just a little simple-minded, or slow. Or all of the above.

He was being raised by his mother; a single parent since the disappearance of her husband, shortly after the boy was born. She was a skinny, hard faced woman in her mid-forties. Her grey, curly hair pulled back from her unwelcoming, dark green eyes and thin, pursed lips. The skin around her eyes was blemished with stress lines and wrinkles – the result of many years of worry and sleepless nights. With him being an only child and her sole responsibility, he had been reared as the epitome of a mummy's boy. She had done everything for the boy since birth, in all stages of his development, even if it did bridle his progress. She had taught him to tie his shoe laces, kick his first football, and dropped him off at his first day of school. She loved the boy with all of her heart, even though her love would often cloud her good judgement.

She would make up for his obvious lack of intelligence by making excuses that he was simply shy or withdrawn. When he was found staring strangely at people, making them feel uncomfortable, she would justify his behaviour by saying that he was inquisitive. Her flippant attitude towards her son's strange demeanour resulted in them both being classed as social misfits, by many people in the town.

He wore thick, black rimmed spectacles that had been broken and taped back together. His heap of curly, greasy brown hair hung down over his skull and face like an old, smelly mop. His cheeks were adorned with thick patches of ugly looking freckles, and a scattering of thin brown hairs collected upon his top lip. The lenses in his spectacles magnified his small, brown, rat like eyes, and their lack of any real depth or expression gave his whole gormless looking face a lack of any discerning quality or charisma. His mouth was small, and his lips thin and shapeless. The excess layers of skin and flesh hung around his cheeks and chin, his jowls wobbling when he spoke or ate.

Horace didn't mix well; he had no real friends at school – not that he minded, he enjoyed being alone. However, because he was an obvious target, he often found himself on the receiving end of many of the school bullies. Most days, whilst riding the bus home, he sat quietly amongst the other children while they were throwing items of rubbish off the back of his head, or stealing his property. He simply zoned himself out and became totally entrenched in a world of his own. A million miles away from the noise and carnage erupting around him. He never retaliated, he simply stared away, deep in his own thoughts.

As he continued to sit at the back of the assembly hall, shoving another hot cross bun into his mouth, the other pupils began to file out from the hall. As he stood unsteadily from his seat, he spotted three girls from his year walk past him, chatting. They were three of the most popular girls in his year, led by the beautiful Candice Smith; the only girl in the year to have a chest that was anywhere near the size of Horace's own. She was very popular with the boys in the year, mainly due to her slim attractive face, jet black hair, tanned skin, and athletic figure.

Horace stared as the girls walked by, admiring the view. His eyes locked with hers as she stopped walking and stared back. She gave the boy her most sultry look, and puckered up her lips towards him. Feeling his face suddenly redden with embarrassment, he glanced around him to check that she was looking at him.

Suddenly she spat at him. "I said, who do you think that you're looking at Horace, you fat waste of space?"

"Erm, what?" He asked.

Candice jeered. "Just then, stood there with a gormless, puppy dog look on your face. I've told you before to stop looking at me. God, you give me the fucking creeps."

"But you were looking at me, I just –"

"Why the *hell* would I want to look at you?" She spat, interrupting him. "Look at you, you're a complete fucking mess. Come on girls, let's leave this loser to ogle somebody else."

Turning on her heels, she stormed from the hall, her two friends following directly behind her. Horace looked around the room nervously and felt hundreds of sets of eyes burning into him as the entire canteen erupted into heinous laughter. One of the boys from his registration class walked past, knocking into his shoulder, sending him sprawling to his left.

"Way to go there, Horace. Always impressing the ladies," he shouted over his shoulder.

Horace didn't respond, he struggled his way through the crowd, ignoring the other children as they jeered. He threw his Zippy rucksack over his shoulder, quickly shuffling his way towards the exit, narrowly avoiding the dozens of feet that were thrown out in his path by other pupils in an attempt to trip him as he passed.

*

She continued to struggle, which made her sweat even more. Wriggling her head from side to side, she managed to get a corner of the material loose from around her chin; just enough to give her a view from her left eye. She appeared to be laid down upon a leather bed with no bedclothes or pillows. Inspecting herself, she was totally naked apart from her skimpy underwear and bra, her hands and feet appeared to be strapped together with plastic zip ties. With her one exposed eye, she could just make out where the sharp plastic had cut into her flesh, leaving red marks. Attempting to pull her hands apart to break the plastic tie, she yelped in pain as it cut into her skin and a trickle of blood ran down her wrist.

Wincing in pain, she called out quietly. "Hello?"

*

Back in the sanctity of his classroom, Horace sat in his seat, beads of perspiration gathering on his brow as the heat inside the classroom increased as the sun's rays poured in through the large glass windows. Sitting right at the front of the class, he got the best view of his favourite teacher – Miss Fingerhut. She had been teaching at the school for a few months, after transferring from a teaching assistant's job on the other side of town to a full time placement; an opportunity to forward her career.

From where he sat, he could smell the scent of her musky, sweet smelling perfume. She was a young woman in her mid-twenties. She had radiant blue eyes that sparkled and emanated a deep inquisitive nature, and vibrant spirit. Her straw-blonde coloured hair was perfectly straight and dropped down to the middle of her back, keeping it from falling into her eyes with a plain black headband. Her slim face had fresh, smooth skin with high, defined cheekbones, a small nose, and full red, pouting lips. She was absolutely stunning; a woman that oozed sexuality with the littlest of effort, while remaining natural and attainable.

As she stood, writing mathematical equations on the board, her short summer dress began to ride up as she stood on tiptoes in her flat leather shoes, exposing the top of her slim, toned legs. Horace's jaw dropped open in awe and he swallowed the lump in his throat, unfastening the top button of his shirt, allowing him to take in a mouthful of stuffy air.

She turned to address the group of pupils in the class.

"Right, settle down then, children," she began. "You boys at the back, stop talking. Stop it. Bruce, I *won't* tell you again."

Bruce settled, slumping in his chair.

She continued. "Thank you. So...who can give me the answer to number... Oh damn it, I've laddered my tights."

Taking a step forward, she cocked her leg up and placed the sole of her foot on the edge of Horace's desk. With her leg straightened, she proceeded to hitch up her dress and run the tip of her index finger down the ladder in the flimsy material. Horace found himself beginning to sweat as she exposed the top of her toned thighs, and he could make out the outline of the woman's light blue underwear beneath the dark fabric of her tights. Horace could barely control himself as he felt himself harden beneath the surface of the wooden desk. After glancing up, she noticed Horace staring between her legs, his eyes quickly snapped up to hers, and their gaze met.

She spoke to him quietly, in a soft, sultry tone. "Do you like what you see, Horace?"

She continued to inch up her hem of her skirt, giving him a better view between her legs. Then she slid the tip of her index finger into her mouth and slowly began to slide it backwards and forwards suggestively, never taking her eyes away from his. Horace thought that he would have an explosion in his loins at any moment.

"Oh God, yes, miss." He replied.

She suddenly asked him. "Horace?"

The boy was quickly snapped out of his trance, and found Miss Fingerhut staring at him with a stern, annoyed look spread across her face.

"Horace?" She asked again. "For the third time, can you give me the answer to number three? How many times do I have to tell you - stop daydreaming in class!"

"Sorry, Miss Fingerhut," he responded, "the answer is fourteen, I believe."

She rolled her eyes wearily. "The answer, if you had been paying attention, is twenty four."

Horace shrugged his shoulders and looked down at his desk. The rest of the class erupted into iniquitous laughter and cheering, at his expense. He sat quietly, staring vacantly at the board, ignoring their attempts to chastise him.

The sound of the school bell rang out, signalling the end of the day, and the end of the term.

Miss Fingerhut addressed her class. "Right then, boys and girls, everyone have a good Easter. Don't eat too much chocolate."

She looked at Horace and gave him a sly wink. He pulled himself up from his seat and made for the exit, his mind already wandering onto the subject of confectionery. As he rounded the corner of his school block to the main playground, he crossed the yard passing a few groups of other children. He was approached by three of the boys from his year. The largest of the boys put out his hand to stop Horace in his tracks.

"Oi, Davidson," he sneered. "What were you doing eyeing up Candice earlier?"

Horace didn't answer.

Taking a deep breath, he filled his lungs with air and took a step backwards. Planting his feet firmly on the ground, he dropped his rucksack from his shoulder to the floor. In one fluid motion, Horace threw a solid, overhand right hook, his fist connecting with the boy's chin. The boy collapsed backwards, his head thumping the playground with a sickening crack, opening up a large gash on the back of his skull. Blood quickly began to ooze out and gather in a sticky pool below his head. Horace didn't hesitate; he quickly stepped forward and began to stomp, bringing his heel down repeatedly on the fallen boy's face and neck.

Bone snapped, teeth separated from gums and plinked on the concrete beside the boys head as Horace stood above him, continuing to rain blows down on the boy from above. A menacing, evil look had spread across his face, and white spittle flew from the corner of his mouth. The boy on the floor had stopped trying to defend himself any further; he was out cold.

Horace snapped back from his daydream to find himself face to face with the boy.

"Did you hear what I asked you, Horace? Don't ignore me, you useless lump."

"What, sorry, I –"

Before he could complete his sentence, the boy nodded, and his two friends grabbed Horace by his shoulders, spinning him round. Bending him forwards, they held him doubled over, with his rear upwards, his shirt tails hung from the back of his trousers, exposing the top of his underwear and his arse crack. The boy standing behind him grabbed the top of his underwear and wrapped it around the top of his hand, and yanked the material upwards - hard. Horace yelped as the sharp edge of the material from his underwear disappeared up into the crack of his behind.

The boy behind him laughed. "How's that for a wedgie, Horace? Beg me to stop and I'll stop."

Still bent over, Horace bit his lip and refused to answer. Becoming agitated, the boy continued to tear at the boy's underwear, pulling it further into Horace's vast crack. He bit his lip and struggled to hold back the tears.

"You had better start begging Horace because this can go on all evening."

After a few moments of futile struggling, Horace conceded. He pleaded. "Please, let me go."

The other boy goaded. "Pretty please?"

Horace winced as the boy gave his underwear another sharp tug upwards. "Pretty please, with a cherry on top."

"Sad git," he spat, and let go of Horace's underwear as he released him. The boy stumbled forward a few feet. The bully added to his already toppling momentum and shoved his foot into the small of his back, sending him crashing to the floor in a heap. Every pupil in the vicinity snapped round and burst into immediate laughter. Once again, Horace collected his belongings from where they had fallen to the floor, frantically tucking his shirt back into his trousers as he walked away slowly and silently, attempting to remove the remainder of his underwear from his arse.

*

Nobody answered her first call. She lay patiently, silently listening. She called out again. "Hello, is anyone there? Can you hear me? Help."

No answer came immediately, then a few moments later she heard the sound of a door handle being turned, and the audible creak of a door opening. She lay still, terrified, her body beginning to shake in fear as she heard the sound of footsteps falling on a wooden floor, moving slowly towards her.

A voice spoke. "Was that you calling out?"

She didn't reply.

"Answer me or I will cut three of your fingers off," the voice replied sternly. "Was that you calling out?"

"Yes," she replied. Attempting to speak through her broken teeth and swollen gums.

"What do you want?"

"I'm scared. Where am I?"

"That is none of your concern."

"Please, I'm scared. What do you want with me?"

Suddenly, the hood that was covering her face was quickly removed, she squinted painfully as the light suddenly invaded her eyes. Her pupils quickly dilated and the blurred vision of her captor slowly came into focus. The black hood that had been snatched from over her head was held in her captor's gloved hand.

"Who are you? What do you want from me?"

"Just do what I tell you to do, as and when I tell you to do it, and you will be free to go."

"But what do you want from me? How can I be sure that you will stick to your word?"

Without any warning, a gloved fist struck her round the side of the head, bashing the temple. For a brief moment her world went black, before slowly regaining consciousness.

The figure slowly walked away. "I will return when it's time."

She heard the sound of a key in a lock being turned as she turned her head to the side and vomited. Then she passed out.

*

Easter Sunday arrived and Horace awoke early, excited. After all, the prospect of chocolate eggs for breakfast only happened once a year. He threw his bed clothes aside and wobbled downstairs as quickly as his chubby legs would carry him.

Reaching the living room, he looked around for his mother. She was nowhere to be seen. Turning, he spotted a pile of chocolate eggs stacked up on the living room coffee table and immediately began to salivate. Bounding over he quickly unwrapped a large Easter egg, hastily ripping away the cardboard and foil packaging as he proceeded to stuff the whole of the egg into his mouth. *Beats boring old crumpets*, he thought.

Taking another look around, spitting globs of spittle and fragments of chocolate from his mouth, he called out, "Mum, are you here?"

No answer.

Walking into the kitchen, the smell of cooking food invaded his nostrils and made his stomach growl. He headed over to the cooker surface where a large metal pot was slowly simmering away on the stove. Carefully, he lifted the lid and inhaled the beautiful aroma of the cooking meat. Licking his lips, he carefully placed the lid back down and called out again. "Mum, hello? Where are you?"

Again, no answer.

Horace smiled and remembered back to the previous years on Easter Sunday, where his mom had always put on an egg hunt around the house and garden. Looking around again, he beamed as he spotted a costume hanging from the front of the utility room door. Hanging from the coat hanger was a note written in his mum's familiar handwriting:

Horace, put this on, and head downstairs, and don't forget your basket. Love, Mum.

Slightly confused at the prospect, but obeying the instructions, Horace began stripping away his pyjamas, throwing them in a pile on the kitchen floor. He struggled as he squeezed his legs into the furry costume and continued pulling it up over his midsection. Eventually he managed to awkwardly slot his arms in and pulled the top section up over his messy hair. Pulling the zip right up to his chin, he caught a glimpse of himself in the reflection from the patio doors. He looked funny, an overweight, furry pink rabbit with two ears pointing from his head. One totally erect and pointing upwards, and the other flopping down to the side.

He laughed at his reflection as he waggled his head from side to side, making the ears flap around on his head playfully. Heading over to the kitchen surface, he collected the wicker basket that had been left for him, filled with a load of shredded, coloured paper. Inside, there was another note from his mum:

No peeking. Now come downstairs.

Intrigued, Horace walked across the kitchen to the door that led downstairs to the cellar. Opening the door, he called out. "Hello. Mum, are you down here?"

"Yes, honey, come on down." His mum's voice replied from downstairs.

Slowly, Horace began to descend the stairs that led down to the cellar. He continued along the dimly lit corridor that opened out to the room at the end of the hallway.

As he entered the room he stopped and looked in confusion. His mother stood before him wearing one of her old kitchen aprons. It was splattered with blood. In her gloved hands, she gripped a pair of pliers, and proceeded to rip the fingernails from the hand of his teacher, Miss Fingerhut, who was screaming through the gag wrapped around her mouth. She thrashed violently, naked on the leather bed.

"Mum, what are you *doing*?" He asked, confused.

"It's essential, dear. I had to remove her teeth and nails, we can't risk having her bite or scratch you."

Horace looked on, confused as his mother continued to viciously rip the nails from the woman's fingers, and toss them carelessly to the floor. Miss Fingerhut spotted Horace as he walked into the room. Her eyes widened, she mumbled something frantically from behind her gag.

The boy turned back to his mother. "Mum, I don't understand?"

"Today, my boy, you are going to become a man. Here give me a hand."

Horace placed the basket down on the floor and walked to the aid of his mother, who had proceeded to hold his teacher's left ankle and left wrist together.

"Grab that duct tape and wrap it around here," she nodded. "It's more than sufficient to hold her in place."

Horace grabbed the roll of tape and began to wind it around her ankles and wrists tightly. Once secured, he ripped the tape and continued to repeat the process with the other arm and leg as his mother held her in place. Once complete, Miss Fingerhut was left lying on her back with her vagina and arse pointing upwards, exposed.

His mother ripped the gag from the woman's mouth and threw it aside. The woman on the bed continued sobbing and pleading, an incoherent babble through broken teeth stumps and blood.

"Oh shut up, will you woman? Before I cut out your tongue."

The boy continued to stare on, incredulously.

"Right, Horace, grab your basket and take out your Easter eggs."

Complying with her instruction, the boy picked up the wicker basket from where he had placed it on the floor. He searched through the shredded bits of coloured paper until he found something. Confused, he removed the item from the basket before placing it back to the floor.

He held the plastic egg in one hand, attached to another device by a thin pink cable. As his thumb brushed past a switch on the device, the egg that he held in his left hand began to vibrate steadily. It felt a little strange, yet pleasant. On the device was a small dial, as Horace turned it with his thumb, the rate of the vibration increased rapidly.

He giggled. "What do I do with this Easter egg, Mum?"

His mother pointed to the woman's exposed genitals.

"Use your imagination, son."

Horace stood for a moment bemused, before suddenly beginning to understand.

He felt himself becoming aroused as he inched closer to the woman, an erection beginning to poke out from beneath the fur of his rabbit costume.

Miss Fingerhut looked at him, then his mum, then at the love egg in his hand.

She screamed.

Horace smiled.

THE END

Bio

Matt is an avid fan of horror fiction. He spends a majority of his free time reading books from both established and independent authors. With a diverse knowledge of the genre, he has now tried his hand at writing horror. With the support of his peers, some of which are established writers themselves, he now approaches a new career, one that will see him take horror by storm. His influences lead right back to traditional horror writers such as Edgar Allen Poe, Bram Stoker and William Hope Hodgson through to the more traditional horror writers such as Stephen King, Richard Laymon, Dean Koontz, James Herbert and Clive Barker to newer names such as Alex Kava, JA Konrath, Bryan Smith, Matt Shaw, Michael Bray, Iain Rob Wright, Graeme Reynolds, Tim Miller and Ian Woodhead right the way through to emerging writers who are currently starting out such as Stuart Keane, Jack Rollins, Kyle M Scott, Andrew Lennon and Shaun Hupp.

He currently resides in Tipton, a small town in the West Midlands with his partner and two children. He travels the width breadth of the UK on a regular basis as a Sales Manager for a construction company.

His writing debut, a collaboration with Andrew Lennon; Hexad, is available now as a digital download or paperback from Amazon.

He has since been featured in an anthology by Matt Shaw – Behind Closed Doors, which is available for digital download now from Amazon, and The Dichotomy of Christmas, featuring such established names as Graham Masterton and Kealan Patrick Burke. To be followed by inclusion into an anthology from Dark Chapter Press – Kids,

His first full length novella; Jeremy, is now available for digital download from Amazon UK & US.

Website – www.matthickmanauthor.blogspot.co.uk

Twitter - https://twitter.com/Matthewhickma13

Facebook - https://www.facebook.com/matthickmanauthor

Deb Loves Robbie

by Mark West

The egg arrived this morning, like I knew it would. Just like the past five years, it came wrapped in the same style of paper, with a little tag taped to it that read 'Happy Easter'. And inside was an old-style Cadbury's Caramel egg with the sexy lady bunny on the front who isn't on the adverts any more.

And just like before, the egg was almost five years out of date.

The Easter Bunny killed Deb Swales.

He didn't mean to, of course and I doubt he even saw her but that's what happened.

We'd been living in the flats for a few weeks by then and didn't know anybody other than our immediate neighbours. On the right, against the lounge, was an old couple who seemed to be very happy together and listened to their TV and radio at top volume. On the other side, against our kitchen and bathroom, was a couple in their thirties with a small child. He worked, she didn't, the kid screamed a lot. We were in our early twenties and in love and didn't need anyone else. Well, that's what we kept telling each other, Deb and me, but the reality was much more unpleasant. In truth, we didn't want anybody to know we were there.

We met at school, though we'd long been aware of each other because of our families. She had a sister and three brothers, I had three brothers and it was difficult to decide which family was the bigger bunch of arseholes. We were both the youngest and I never found out what caused the initial ruck but any chance to have a bit of aggro and one set or the other took it.

Deb said it was like that movie "Romeo & Juliet" (which I hadn't seen) when we had to do a Shakespeare play in fifth year and play the lovers. Loads of wolf whistling in the class and the teacher telling everyone to calm down and act our ages but something happened. I didn't really understand what I was reading, but the words began to make sense and when I looked at her, I started to see this really pretty girl who wasn't part of the Swales family, my mortal enemy, but someone kind and funny who smelled nice.

Two weeks later at the school disco I plucked up the courage to ask her to dance and she agreed. A week later we were caught snogging behind the design block and got detention. I then noticed my name was on her pencil case and it stayed there to the end of the school year when we both left.

We kept our romance a secret, meeting in the park or in town and keeping a low profile. She went to college, I went to apprentice in a local garage. Things seemed to calm down between the families when two of my brothers went to prison for trying to knock over a bookies and her sister got pregnant for the first time. We still didn't make a fuss but it did make life slightly easier.

When we turned eighteen, we talked about leaving home and setting up together somewhere. We couldn't afford anything grand - I was still at the garage, she was working in a local hairdressers between college courses - but we did see a flat going cheap on an estate on the other side of town.

We went out to celebrate. We were spotted. They were waiting for us when we left the pub.

"You dirty fucking pikey!"

Before I could turn to see who'd shouted, someone pushed me hard and I staggered forward. I managed to stay on my feet until I was kicked hard in the left thigh which knocked me sideways and gave me a dead leg. They'd timed it perfectly – we had already passed the front of the pub, I was pushed into the little service alley that ran up the side of it.

I heard Deb scream and someone shouted at her as I tried to stay on my feet, my leg barely holding me up.

"Fucking stay there," growled a voice and I didn't know if he meant me or her. Three big shapes blocked me from the brightly lit street. Another dark shape stood at the mouth of the alley, holding Deb tightly.

I staggered back. There was a door in the wall to my left, cracked and old and padlocked shut. A bare bulb hung over it, casting a sickly yellow glow.

"Thought you could play around, did you?" asked the middle shape, advancing on me and I knew who it was before he spoke again. "Thought you could dip your wick in our little sister?"

Gary Swales, the eldest of the kids, ran the group. He had a hard, handsome face though a deep cut above his right eye put a kink in his eyebrow and you could see his scalp through his thinning hair. He was snarling at me and I knew I was in real trouble.

"Gary," I said.

"You little fucking toe-rag, Robbie Hughes, how long did you think you could get away with it?"

"But I'm not doing anything wrong, we love each other."

It was the wrong thing to say. He made a guttural sound deep in his throat and launched at me, his fist rising and the light glinting off the big sovereign rings he wore on every finger. I tried to move but wasn't quick enough and he hit my left cheek. For a moment, the whole world went silent and the entire side of my face felt like someone had set fire to it. I staggered sideways as the sounds came back - yelling and shouting, my heart beat thudding, the sound of trainers on concrete. I was falling but tried to stay on my feet. The other brothers advanced and then Gary was in my line of sight again, his fist raised.

This time he hit my ear and the thud deafened me. I went down, my right temple hitting the slick concrete. I watched three pairs of trainers come towards me, felt someone grab the collar of my jacket and pull me up. A kick landed in my ribs and I felt something crack. Another kick caught my right shoulder, jarring my arm in the socket. Gary punched my forehead and I closed my eyes, tried to bring my hands up to protect my face. More blows rained on my arms and chest, more kicks hit my thighs and shins. Someone kicked me in the groin and blackened lightbulbs flashed across my field of vision, slowly turning red. Something ran into my eyes, blinding me. Another punch, another kick, another horrible cracking sound.

More black lightbulbs and then nothing.

*

I woke up in hospital. The first thing Deb said, after telling me she loved me, was that she'd lied to the doctors and said I'd been mugged. Her brothers beat me until I looked like a rag doll, then threatened her that if she told or was seen with me again, they'd fix her. She rang an ambulance from the pub and said everyone in there knew who she was but none of them offered to help.

The sovereign rings had done some damage but the pretty nurse who stitched me up did a good job and my broken ribs were taped. What nobody could fix was the damage done inside my head.

The doctors said I'd suffered a TBI, or Traumatic Brain Injury. I wanted to crack that old joke, the "what brain?" one, but I couldn't find all the right words and they said that was to be expected. TBI damage can be wide-ranging, they said and vary a lot. They told me I could have physical effects, like balance problems and headaches and dizziness, or my thinking and behaviour could be badly affected.

Was I sure, they asked, that I didn't know who'd done it? I took one look at Deb and the panic on her face - for me, for her, for us - and said no.

When I was released, Deb and I moved into the flat and neither of us spoke to our families. We laid low, to avoid the world for a while and lived our lives as I slowly built my strength back up - though I found it harder and harder to remember how to fix even the most simple of things at work.

The Thursday before Good Friday I was sitting in the lounge watching TV, as we'd found I needed to chill out after getting home from work otherwise I got ratty really quickly. Deb, in the kitchen, let out a shriek and came rushing through.

"You're taking me out for a Mickey D, my love," she said with a big smile.

"Why?"

"Because we need to call into the Co-op at the precinct, I've forgotten to buy Easter eggs."

I stood up, playing along. "Holy shit, why didn't you say it was an emergency?"

We grabbed our coats and left the flat in a flurry of laughter and snatched kisses. The balcony was deserted and we made our way to the stairwell, holding hands and deciding which eggs to buy. She fancied a Crunchie one, I was trying to decide between a Mars or a Caramel.

"Caramel?" she said, disbelieving.

"Yeah, I fancy the rabbit."

She laughed and stopped near the top of the stairwell. "You twat, how can you fancy a cartoon rabbit?"

I didn't have a chance to reply. The front door of the flat she was standing beside opened and someone wearing an oversized Easter Bunny outfit came out, tripping over his elongated feet. He bumped into Deb before lurching sideways and walking along the balcony with a couple of chubby girls wearing Easter chick outfits.

Deb fell forward, tried to regain her balance and twisted around. She was at the top of the stairs but I couldn't move fast enough as she began to topple back. She looked at me, her eyes wide, her mouth a perfect O and reached for me but we were too far apart. Her right heel slipped off the step, then the left and, her arms pinwheeling, she fell back, still looking at me and began to scream.

Her legs flicked up. The scream echoed around the stairwell and in my head, lasting until she landed with a sickening crunch that seemed to cancel all noise. I thought of the fists in the alley, the deafening silence after them.

She bounced off the step and fell further, landing on her shoulders, her body seeming to fold in on itself. She uncurled and slid down to land in a heap at the bottom, her legs tucked underneath, her arms splayed out.

"Deb!" I called and ran down the stairs. I knelt beside her head but didn't know what to do. Should I move her or leave her, should I ring for an ambulance or should I knock on some doors and get someone else here. The questions clustered in my head, confusing me until I couldn't think straight.

"Robbie," she said, slowly and calmly.

"Deb," I said and started to cry, "I don't know what to do."

"It's just an accident," she said, "we can sort it like we did with you in the alley."

"Yes," I said, willing to believe that it was exactly the same situation. "What can I do?"

"I don't know if I can walk so carry me back to the flat and we'll figure it out."

"If you're sure," I said. I was crying and my tears landed on her cheeks. I brushed them away. More fell, some into her opened eyes and she didn't even blink.

She was heavier than I expected and as I lifted her head there was a horrible sound like somebody peeling up something damp and sticky. There was a dark smear of blood and hair on the concrete and I pretended I didn't see it.

"Thank you," she said when we were through the door. I flicked the lights on with my elbow and she didn't blink against the light. "Put me in the bath, don't make a mess of the bed."

"But you'll get cold."

"No, because you'll keep me warm with your love, Robbie, you can make me whole again."

It all made perfect sense as she said it. "Yes I can, that's what I'll do."

I carried her into the bathroom and set her down, propping her against the wall. I took three towels from the airing cupboard, draped two in the bath and rolled up the last for a neck support. I picked her up and laid her gently in the bath and slipped the support behind her neck but her head rolled to the side, her cheeks loose. Her unblinking eyes were now half covered by the lids, as if she was getting sleepy and I really believed I could see love in there.

"Thank you," she said, "I just need to rest now."

"Well you've had a busy day," I said and laughed. I thought I saw the faintest of smiles at her lips and wanted to kiss her. "Are you sure you don't want me to call anybody?"

"No," she said, her voice sleepy, "it wouldn't help. And we have each other."

Tears pricked my eyes again.

"Don't forget it's Easter, a time for resurrection, remember? If you look after me, then I will come back to you. We can do it."

Tears rolled down my cheeks and spotted on her t-shirt. "I will do whatever I have to, baby."

"I know. Get some dinner, let me rest up, I promise I won't go anywhere."

I kissed her forehead and went into the kitchen to make a bowl of chicken soup and ate it watching the early evening news. Nothing I saw made any sense and the newsreaders didn't seem as if they were speaking English. The local news wasn't any better.

I must have dozed for a while because when I woke up my soup had congealed in the bowl. There was a terrible smell in the flat, like the drains had backed up. I thought I could hear weeping and went into the bathroom, the stench hitting me like a slap.

"I'm so sorry, Robbie, I had an accident."

I smiled and knelt beside the bath, kissing her gently on the forehead. Her skin felt warm and supple but she looked paler.

"Don't worry, I'll clean you up." I tried to laugh but the sound cracked halfway through and horribly resembled a sob. It was too much, I couldn't deal with this. "At least you're in the bath, eh?"

"Cheeky," she said.

I got some fresh clothes from the bedroom and Dettol from the kitchen. When I got back, the smell bad enough to make me gag, I could see a dark shape soaking through the towel she was sitting on.

"I'm so sorry," she said, her voice heavy with sadness.

I wanted to tell her it was okay but I couldn't figure out how to so I set to work. It took me an hour to strip her, clean her up and put fresh clothes on. I was sick twice in the toilet but said I thought I was coming down with a bug or something, to try not to upset her, but I could tell she didn't believe me. I noticed livid purple-red spots that looked like bruises on her buttocks and wondered whether to mention them. As she seemed so sad I decided not to make things worse.

When I was done, Deb and the bath were clean but I felt filthy. I got undressed, gave myself a strip wash in the sink, then put on fresh clothes.

I stood in the bedroom doorway, unsure of where to go since I didn't want to go into the bathroom again. Disgusted by my own behaviour, I put on my trainers and jacket. "Just going out for a minute," I called and went before she could say anything.

The balcony was deserted but I could hear music from somewhere and people were shouting in the carpark. I leaned on the wall looked at the lights of Gaffney twinkling in the night. My head was aching, as if someone was trying to twist it around like an unco-operative childproof lock. I felt tears in my eyes again and roughly wiped them away.

I couldn't think straight, to make the connections that would help me to see a way out of this, to sort everything and make Deb better again. I hit my temples with the heels of my hands hard enough to make my vision swim but it didn't make any difference.

I was outside for maybe ten minutes and didn't have a single coherent thought the whole time.

She called me as I went back into the flat.

"It's me," I said.

"Thank goodness, I felt lonely."

Tears fell again and I waited until they'd stopped before I went into the bathroom. I stood in the doorway, watching her as she stared at the ceiling.

"Hey," I said but she didn't turn her head. "Sorry I was gone so long. Are you hungry or thirsty?"

"No, just lonely. Come and sit with me."

I sat down, leaning against the bath and rested my hand on her forehead. Her skin felt cold. I got another towel from the airing cupboard and draped it over her.

"You're so thoughtful, Robbie."

There was something wrong with her eyes and I leaned down to see. A dark, reddish-brown strip had formed across the centre of both eyeballs that looked incredibly painful and made me want to be sick again. But she hadn't mentioned it, had she?

"Do your eyes hurt?"

"No, why?"

"Because, well, you don't seem to be blinking."

"Of course I'm blinking, how could I not. You're just not seeing it, that's all."

Was she right, had I made a mistake? We both knew my head wasn't where it should be and still ached but when I looked again, the strip was still there. I moved so the overhead light could catch her and her eyes didn't glisten. How could that possibly be?

"Go and get some rest," she said. "I'll be fine."

I didn't want to leave her again, it didn't seem right. "I'll sleep on the floor here."

"Don't be silly," she said, a smile in her voice, "go to bed. I'll make myself better for the morning."

Reluctantly, I got up. Trying not to look at her darkening eyeballs, I gave her cool forehead a kiss and went into the bedroom. When sleep finally overtook me, it was fitful and full of horrible dreams that I couldn't remember the second I woke up.

I spent the morning of Good Friday dozing. I got up at lunchtime and went into the bathroom. Deb still stared at the ceiling and the strips on her eyeballs had got darker. There was a patch of goose-pimples on her shoulder and when I touched her skin, it was cold and hard. Her cheekbones seemed more pronounced, as were her eye sockets, as if the skin had somehow sagged.

"Deb?" I said, quietly. When she didn't reply I nudged her shoulder. It was very stiff. "Deb?"

"Sorry," she said after a moment or two, "I was sleeping."

"I didn't mean to wake you."

"I know, I just need to rest. What day is it?"

"Good Friday."

"I still have time then, Jesus didn't rise until Easter Sunday."

I tried to remember the story but drew a blank. "If you say so."

She giggled, lightly. "How can you forget that? Go on, leave me be, let me rest."

"I love you," I said.

"Not as much as I love you," she replied, her voice already slowing as if she was dozing off.

I kissed her cold forehead, had a pee and a quick wash in the sink and went into the lounge. There was nothing on TV and the old folks next door were listening to something that caught me just right, nagging in my ears and driving me crazy. I put my jacket on and went out.

I don't know how far I walked that day but I kept going until it got dark. I had lunch at McDonalds, walked through the park, checked out the few shops that were open and nipped into a pub for a pint. There weren't many people about and the buses looked half empty. I wondered if everyone else was at home, enjoying time with their family, eating easter eggs and watching TV, talking and laughing and playing games. I couldn't bite back the bitter laugh that escaped - my family had turned its back on me and all that was left of it, my lovely girlfriend, was lying in the bath at home not looking very well at all.

I passed a church and could hear people singing. I stood by the front door for a while, wondering whether to go in or not and decided against it.

As the light faded, I got a burger from a hole-in-the-wall we used in town but only ate half of it before realising I wasn't hungry. I gave the remains to a homeless man outside the train station. He said something but didn't have his teeth in so it might have been "thank you" or "fuck off", I couldn't tell. As I walked away, he broke the burger in half and gave his dog some.

I knew something was wrong as soon as I opened the flat door. There was a smell

I couldn't place, like a butchers at the end of a long hot summers day but worse as well, like the time we'd discovered a badger dead behind the garages and spent a week watching it rot away.

I rushed into the bathroom and the smell made me stagger back, my hand over my nose. I gagged, swallowing back bile.

"I look bad, don't I?" she asked.

I clicked the light on and wished I hadn't. Deb's skin had turned green and her face was bloated. Her tongue was poking through her lips and her eyeballs, which had a thicker strip across them now, were bulging from under the lids.

"You look different," I said, trying not to scare her.

"Tell me, I know I must smell as well."

There was nothing to say. Breathing through my mouth, I knelt beside the bath but couldn't bring myself to touch her discoloured skin or look at her bulging eyes. I appalled myself, this was the girl I loved and I couldn't even bear to touch or look at her.

"Talk to me," she said and sounded scared, as if my silence meant I was going to run away. How long had I left her alone? Was she worrying where I was, if I was ever going to come home? How could I have been so cruel?

"I'm sorry, I went out to clear my head and time went too quickly, I didn't mean to leave you alone for so long."

"That's alright Robbie, you need some fresh air and I was resting. Two days and I'll be back!"

"I hope so."

"No," she said, in a scolding tone, "there's no hope about it, I will be back."

"Yes, Deb," I said and got to my feet. I felt terrible for not kissing her but the nausea was rising and I knew if I touched her I would throw up. As it was, I managed to close the bathroom door and get into the kitchen before I brought today's food back up in the sink.

Sleep was even harder to come by that night and I kept being startled awake by dreams.

At one point, I was aware of someone else in the bedroom. I turned and Deb was standing naked beside the bed, her entire body bloated and green. She held out her arms, the skin on her fingers drooping like badly fitted gloves.

"Do you still love me?"

"Of course," I said.

"Show me how much."

I woke up before she could climb onto the bed.

Someone was banging on the door.

I struggled to open my eyes. The clock read half past nine and I could hear things in the flat rattling. I could also smell something that seemed worse than yesterday.

I went into the hall. Before I could go into the bathroom the person at the door shouted in between his thumps. "Open this fucking door, you loopy twat, I know you're in there."

My breath caught in my throat, my heart rate quickening until it seemed to be pressing against my chest. Had her brothers figured out where we were? I pressed myself against the wall, to buy myself some thinking time.

"I can see you through the glass, you fucking idiot. Open this fucking door."

My head pounded, I couldn't focus or think straight. I needed to check Deb, I didn't want whoever was at the door to wake and scare her.

"Open it now or I'm breaking it down."

"Okay," I called, "I'm coming."

Slowly, keeping my eye on the shape I could see through the frosted glass, I made my way to the front door. I put the chain on and clicked the latch.

"Open it properly mate," said the man. It wasn't one of her brothers.

"I can't, I…"

"Jesus," said the man and gagged, "it is you. What the fuck have you got in there?"

He hit the door where the chain was connected, making it dance in its clip. The glass rattled and he hit it again. "Open it!" he yelled, "now!"

The screws holding the chain clip began to pull out. I put my shoulder against the door and tried to push it closed. He hit it again and again, each blow pulling the screws out further. I strained with everything I had to close the door but it was a losing battle.

The chain pinged off and he shoved the door open, knocking me down. I looked up at our neighbour and he glared at me, his face red. His expression changed and he looked panicked for a moment then turned and threw up against the wall.

I scuttled backwards, away from him and into the lounge, trying to keep him away from the bathroom. I bumped into the coffee table and rattled my soup bowl from yesterday.

"What's wrong with you man?" he demanded, stalking after me, his hand over his nose. "Can't you smell it? My little 'un has been sick half the night with it."

He passed the bathroom, stopped and stepped back. "Are you saving up a great shit or something?"

Pushing open the bathroom door he gagged again. He turned on the light and threw up down himself.

I got up, grabbed the bowl and ran at him, bringing it down on the back of his neck. He fell forward but regained his balance and turned, his eyes full of murder. Reaching out, his thick fingers closed around the neck of my t-shirt and he pulled me towards him. He punched me hard in the face and everything went black.

That was almost ten years ago.

I was arrested and tried for the murder of Deb Swales and GBH against Darren Driscoll, pleading not guilty to both. When they established Deb had died outside, though I maintained she hadn't, I was sent for medical reports. It was decided I wasn't insane but suffering from a mental disorder so I saw out my sentence in a secure psychiatric hospital. It could have been worse, I kept myself to myself and looked out of the windows and learned how to paint. They gave me tablets, made me do mental exercises and after a while, Deb stopped speaking to me. Five years ago though, the eggs started coming.

"How do you do this?" asked Nurse Fletcher as she put the egg on the dresser in my room. "You don't post it, you don't have contact with the outside world, I just don't understand it."

"I'm not sending it," I said and she smiled, clearly not believing a word. "Look at it, Caramel eggs don't even look like that now and it's years out of date."

"That's what I mean," she said, "I don't understand it."

A letter had been slid into the front of the packaging and she pulled it out. "What's this?"

"I don't know, you found it."

She handed me the thin, umarked envelope. I opened it and took out a single sheet of writing paper that had been carefully folded down the middle.

"Happy Easter, Robbie," I read, "see you soon. It's working!" I looked at Nurse Fletcher with tears in my eyes. "Did you hear that, she said it's working."

"I'm sure," she said and walked out.

I sniffed the paper, kissed it and read it again, tears running down my cheeks. It was working, it was finally working.

After all, I'd recognise Deb's handwriting anywhere.

THE END

Bio

Mark West lives in Northamptonshire with his wife Alison and their young son Matthew. Since discovering the small press in 1998 he has published over eighty short stories, two novels, a novelette, a chapbook, a collection and two novellas (one of which, Drive, was nominated for a British Fantasy Award). He has more short stories and novellas forthcoming and is currently working on a novel.

Away from writing, he enjoys reading, walking, cycling, watching films and playing Dudeball with his son.

He can be contacted through his website at www.markwest.org.uk and is also on Twitter as @MarkEWest

TRADITION

KYLE M. SCOTT

Easter was supposed to be fun, wasn't it?

Well, this sure didn't feel like fun to Billy.

Not one little bit.

Billy watched his older brother, Kevin; his perplexity growing with every moment. Kevin didn't look like he was having any kind of good time either.

In fact, Kevin looked scared.

His brother wore deep furrows of worry on his face that had no godly right to be there, and the strange blend of determination and anxiety seemed to age his sibling right before his eyes. Kevin was only fifteen, and as handsome and carefree as any boy could hope to be.

Usually.

Yet as he determinedly dabbed the water paint onto the smooth surface of the hard-boiled egg, he looked worn down, fretful. His eyes seemed to dart out periodically into the darkening woods beyond their back porch, as though scanning the tree-line for...

What?

Billy had no idea, but whatever it was, it wasn't something good.

Kevin was making him feel very uneasy.

The two boys had been sat out here for over an hour now, whiling away the early evening as the sun sank low. Twilight approached, casting its waning light across the mountainous terrain beyond the forest. The silhouettes of the jagged mountain peaks stood up like fangs biting into the purple-hued sky. It was both beautiful and somehow daunting to Billy, and only made more so by Kevin's mood.

Casting his eyes from the dark, towering peaks, Billy's eyes lowered to his own small patch of the world. Black shadows capered on the threshold between the boy's backyard and the old forest that was their neighbour in this new home.

Normally, the mysterious, deep woods transfixed Billy; filling his heart with boyish wonder. Abbington Wood was a place of infinite intrigue in his keen young mind. A place where anything was possible and where true mystery still resided, even in the age of IPads, the internet and Google.

Since moving to the small town during the early onset of winter, Billy had longed to explore the dark, unending woods. To make them his domain. A place of dreams where he could be anything and anyone he so chose to be. An elf battling Orcs for dominion of the realm, a wild mountain man of the old west, a soldier headed into desperate conflict with an enemy that only he alone could withstand. If the new family home was a place of comfort and warmth, the forest was something much more enticing. It was a canvas for his imagination. A place where, when springtime finally bled into an endless boyhood summer, he could run wild and free.

Well, here it was. It was springtime and the forest was in bloom. He longed to explore. To push forth from the edge of his home and experience the majesty of the old forest for himself. It rested right on his own doorstep like the gateway between worlds.

Billy huffed.

That had been the plan. To explore.

Only a week ago, Kevin had promised to take him out there beyond their yard. Together they would follow the small dirt path that led from their backyard, pass under the thick canopies, and follow the track to wherever it may go. Two fearless explorers, proudly treading into territories new.

That had all changed this evening, though, when Kevin had returned from school, loping into their home like all the world bore down on his broad shoulders. His brother had seemed depleted, shrunken somehow, and far less buoyant than usual. It was as though all the verve and fire had seeped from his pores in the short space of a day.

Billy sighed. This was the perfect time to go exploring, too. Their parents had warned them not to go into the woods alone, but tonight their parents were off with friends. They'd be gone until much, much later. At least one or two o'clock in the morning. Billy and Kevin had free reign of the house and of themselves.

And instead of venturing into the beckoning unknown, here they were sat on the rickety old porch while Kevin painted some lame Easter egg.

Even Billy, having just turned twelve the previous August, knew that this was an awful way to spend what could be an evening of unmitigated freedom. Why the hell was his older brother so damn hell-bent on painting that stupid egg?

And why was he taking the activity so seriously?

Worse than that, Billy was starting to feel a little afraid himself. Fear was like a virus. It spread and it wrapped its coils around anyone who let it in. He'd always looked to his older brother for support in such moments. Kevin was in many ways his idol. His hero. The older boy had been there for him during mom and dad's numerous fights in their previous home. He'd been there to reassure him when they secretly watched late night horror flicks in their shared bedroom. He'd protected him from any older kids that had tried to pick on him. Kevin was strong, brave, and resolute. He could be a jerk sometimes, and would torment his kid brother from time to time just like any older sibling, but the one thing Kevin was not, was timid.

Yet now, fear seemed to emanate from Kevin in waves, and it was creeping into Billy's world, too.

How could it not?

As Kevin worked, carefully teasing the red paint across the flawless surface of the egg's shell, Billy watched the woods beyond their home. Shadows crept across the small patch of grass that made up their yard like slowly grasping, elongated fingers, reaching closer and closer to the dimly lit porch where they sat, and for the first time, Billy sensed something else in the old forest besides adventure.

He sensed dread.

Unwilling to allow the fear to take hold, he pulled his eyes from the gloom of the treeline, and turned back to his older brother.

"Kevin?"

Kevin never looked up. His tongue protruded from his mouth in that way it always did when he was concentrating. "Yeah, what's up?"

Billy cleared his throat. "I was just wondering...could we maybe do something else tonight? This is sort of lame. Why don't we watch a movie or something? Wanna watch a scary film with me, or..."

Kevin cut him off. "No, Billy. I have to do this, okay. It's important."

"Important? It's just an egg, Kev. What's so important about it?"

"It just is!" Kevin barked.

Billy flinched. Kevin had never raised his voice to him before. Sure, he'd cajole him and taunt him from time to time, but he'd never seen real anger bubble to the surface in his brother.

Not like this.

The harsh clip in his tone seemed to echo out over the yard and into the forest. There was no other sound besides the soft chirruping of the birds nestled in the canopies, and it made the words hit all the harder.

Billy felt tears well up in his eyes, and with them, shame.

Asshole.

"Hey! I just thought we could have some fun! It's getting too late to go into the woods now, but we've got the place to ourselves, Kev. Let's at least do something cool!"

His brother seemed to compose himself a little, finally looking up from the small egg and turning to face Billy. The waning sun cast his handsome face in soft fire, and as he spoke, Billy detected a sure trembling in his voice.

"I'm sorry, kiddo, but I need to do this. Just trust me when I tell you it's really fucking important, okay?"

Billy gasped. "You said a bad word."

"I know. I know, and I'm sorry. I'm just a little freaked out right now, buddy. I didn't mean to shout at you, but time's wasting, and I've got to get this thing finished."

Kevin wasn't making any sense, and he sure didn't seem willing to talk about what he was doing. There seemed much more to this than simply following Easter tradition.

Billy tried a different approach.

"What are you painting on there, anyway?" he asked.

Kevin sighed, holding the egg up before Billy's face.

He took in his brother's work.

It looked like he was painting an image of a boy on there.

It was a rough likeness. Even though Kevin was quite an accomplished artist and had even gone so far as to win a few prizes in junior high for his work, the size of the egg and the evident trembling in Kevin's hands had taken a toll on his workmanship.

That said. Billy figured he knew who the clumsily painted figure on the egg's surface was supposed to represent. The little painting had soft brown hair down to its shoulders, and wore a red t-shirt and dark blue denims, just like...

"It's me," Kevin said, confirming his thoughts.

"Why are you painting yourself on an egg?"

"It's just...I have to. I'd rather not explain."

"Come on, Kevin," Billy groaned. "Tell me what you're doing? You're creeping me out."

Kevin's attention was back on the egg, now. He lowered his head and began dabbing the brush onto the egg again. This time, he was working on the small self-portrait's shoes. "You'd only be more creeped out if I told you, kiddo."

Billy huffed. "That's a copout and you know it! This is full on weird, Kev. We could've been out there exploring the woods. Now it's too late and instead we're sat here like jerks painting your stupid egg!"

Kevin continued his work. All his attention was on it. His eyes closed to no more than slits, as he worked the paint into his likeness.

"Kevin!?" Billy shouted.

The sudden rise in pitch almost caused Kevin to drop the egg. It slid momentarily from his grip, rolling across the tips of his fingers. With a small scream, Billy's brother clasped the egg in his hand. Sweat broke out on Kevin's forehead, running in tiny rivulets down his brow and into his eyes.

"Jesus. That was close..." Kevin whispered. It seemed he was talking to himself now. He held the egg tight, as though it was a brittle, precious artefact. His breath came in short hitches as he eyed it, scanning the surface for any cracks.

The soft swell of apprehension rising in Billy was giving way to anger now. He watched, frowning, as his brother composed himself and got back to work.

The hell with this!

"What is your problem, are you on drugs or something? It's just a boiled egg! If it drops and cracks, you can make another one. It's not like the painting is any good anyway!"

"You don't understand," Kevin muttered. "You can't."

"Then tell me!" Billy implored.

With a long, pained sigh of resignation that would befit their downtrodden father more so than his brother, Kevin's careful stroke of the brush came to a pause. He lowered the brush into the small pot of water sat by his side and then, ever so carefully, he sat the egg in the soft folds of a towel he'd placed by its side. To Billy, the effect seemed like one laying a delicate newly born baby down to sleep.

His brother must be on drugs.

He had to be.

Maybe he'd gotten hold of some of that marijuana the kids at school had been talking about. It was everywhere these days.

Made sense that maybe Kevin was on something. It would explain this crap, anyway!

When he'd laid the egg in its cotton nest, Kevin shuffled round on the porch, and faced Billy. His eyes were cast in shadow. The looming dark of the forest seemed to draw ever closer as the dying sunlight slipped over the horizon, as eager to be done with this day as Billy was himself.

Then Kevin's trembling lips parted, and he spoke.

Billy soon began to wish he hadn't.

"Look, what I'm about to tell you is going to sound fucking crazy, Billy, okay. It's going to sound like I've lost my mind, but you have to believe me, this is real. Can you do that, Billy? Can you trust me?"

Billy's pause was short. "I think so…yes. Yes, I trust you."

Kevin nodded, took a deep, laboured breath, and continued.

"Before I go on, just know that the other kids at school showed me proof. I'll get to that later, okay."

Billy was losing patience, and if he was being honest with himself, he was starting to wish he was inside the house and not sat out here on the porch while the shadows crept up the wooden awnings and the wind whispered insidious promises through the treetops only a stone's throw away.

Yes, he wished he was inside.

With the doors locked.

"Just tell me, Kevin...jeez! It's getting dark"

"Okay, but try not to worry, Billy. As long as I paint myself onto this egg, we'll be fine. That's what they said."

"Okay..." Billy prodded.

"Thing is, some of the kids at school, they...they told me a story about this place. About Abbington Wood. They said that the woods are old. Very old. And that they run deeper than meets the eye. They said that there are places in the woods, far back from town, where no one ever goes. They don't go there because they're scared."

"Scared?"

"Yeah. They said that ever since the first of the white settlers arrived, before there was even a homestead, never mind a town, people have been going missing. Children."

"You mean like...kidnapped?"

"Not quite. Apparently it started the very first spring the settlers arrived. At Easter to be exact. A little girl went missing from her home. All that was found was a trail of blood leading away from her bedroom and into the forest. Her father and a few men from the settlement took to searching for her in and around the old wood. They searched for days...weeks...but she was never found. No body. No nothing. It was like she had just disappeared from the face of the earth.

"It happened again the following year. And the year after that. In fact, Billy. It happened every single year since that first Easter, until one year, an old Maliseet Indian passed through town with his family, heading south down along what we call the Saint

John river, towards the border into Canada. He helped them, told them he knew what was taking their children – their first born children. He said that those old woods were home to many things not meant for this world. Not natural. Things that didn't belong. Things older than man himself. He said that the town sat on something the kids at school called a 'ley line', and that the threshold between worlds was thin here. So very thin that at some point, somewhere back in time, something had come through.

"And it set up its home in those woods, right out there..." Kevin nodded towards the old forest.

Billy felt chills kiss the nape of his neck as Kevin went on.

"No one knows what the thing is that lives out there, but they say it's an abomination. Something that predates even Christianity. Whatever it is, people around here say that it's the true spirit of Easter."

"Easter's a Christian holiday, Kevin." Billy retorted. "The egg represents..."

"I know what the egg represents, kid. Or rather, what it's supposed to represent. To us, it represents the resurrection, but all religions are an approximation of older myths that came before. Everything is hand-me-down, Billy. The same tales, or similar, are rooted in all cultures. They teach us all this at school. In the Pagan religion, Easter is the beginning of spring, the rebirth of nature after the cold grip of deathly winter. The egg represents fertility, new life. You see, each culture has its myths and its gods, Here, in Abbington, one of those myths is actually real.

"The Maliseet elder told the townsfolk what they had to do. It was simple really. The creature in the woods, it demanded that a rite be performed. His tribe had dealt with such a being before. They feared and revered it. Saw it as a lesser god of sorts. They understood the old ways before the white man came, and understood the being's desires. It feeds on the destruction of human tradition...human spirituality. Now, it wants to mock the holiness of the holiday."

Billy looked down at the roughly painted egg, chills creeping up his spine like liquid ice. He fought to compose himself. Kevin's story was getting under his skin.

Against his better judgement, he peered out into the now impenetrable gloom of the forest. Was it his imagination, or had the woods fallen still? The soft symphony of the forest seemed to have faded into silence. No birds sang in the trees. The rustling of leaves caught in the gentle springtime wind had ceased.

It was as though nature herself were holding her breath.

And he felt eyes on him, too.

Watchful. Baleful. Poison with insidious intent.

It was his imagination.

Had to be.

If Kevin had noticed the eerie stillness that had fallen over the woods, he never let on. He continued his story, speaking faster now, eager to be finished.

"Most of the people that live here are 'old blood'. That's what Lucy at school called them...'old blood'. It means that their families have lived here since the town was built. They go back generations. She said that they all follow a much older tradition here, and that they learned to do so through heartbreak and bloodshed. Many children had been lost before they began to take the old Indian's story to heart. These were stoic Christians, set in their ways. It wasn't easy for them to let go of their own rites and take up a new one. They saw it as an affront to their god, and that was the whole point. The thing in the woods, it wanted to replace their holiest of traditions with something... darker.

"Anyway, they learned to follow the old ways, but like any other town, new people would move in. People who didn't understand the way things work around here. The locals would welcome those families in, and when the time was right, they'd have a talk with them. Sometimes they'd tell the parents, but usually they'd tell the kids, knowing that kids would be more likely to believe them. They'd tell them all about the dark thing out there in the woods, and what they had to do to keep it from their door."

"And the families, the kids... they didn't listen." Billy stated. It wasn't a question.

"Some did. Most in fact. After all, why take the chance, right? Others, though... others thought the whole thing was nonsense, and kept the holiday in their own way. They came to regret it." Kevin paused, smiling ruefully. "Of course, I wasn't buying any of this shit when I first heard it."

"Stuff." Billy corrected.

"Sorry...stuff...I wasn't buying it, but Lucy and Ian took me to the school library. They've kept all the old records there of the town's history. All the newspaper clippings, going back till at least the turn of the century. They showed me the articles, Billy. They showed me the articles about the missing kids. And you know what?"

"What?" Billy asked, rapt.

"Every single one of them vanished on Easter Sunday. Every single one of them, gone, this very night..."

Kevin's final words seemed to hang in the air like black smoke. Billy felt his stomach fold over on itself. He couldn't help it. He was frightened.

Without another word, Kevin carefully picked up his egg and resumed painting. It was almost finished, by the looks of it.

While he watched, Billy played the story over in his mind.

His brother sounded like he meant it. He didn't sound like he was playing games, but then wasn't that exactly what an older brother would do to try and scare him?

Yes, of course it was!

Suddenly, the spell was broken. Billy breathed deep. In that moment, he realised just what his lame ass brother was playing at. Here they were, alone without their parents for the first time in a new home, right next to some very spooky woods, and

Kevin was trying to freak him out.

He was toying with him.

There was no old tradition.

No creature in the woods waiting to strike.

No Indian.

No nothing!

Now that he was thinking rationally again, Billy felt very stupid. He'd been suckered, and not for the first time, by his smarter, cooler sibling. It seemed like a prank more suited to Halloween, but he had to give Kevin credit for his performance. It was Oscar worthy.

Fighting to hold in his smile, Billy decided that he'd play along. He'd let his lame older brother think he was terrified. Let him think he was every bit as gullible as Kevin took him to be.

For now.

Kevin had finished painting the egg now. Holding it in his hands, he stood up from the wooden stairs where they sat, and walked out to the far end of the yard.

As he did so, Billy stifled a giggle. He watched as Kevin laid the egg down the thick grass, just before the threshold of the forest. The woods didn't seem so ominous now. They were just some regular old woods. Trees and animals and birds and flowers. They were still a little creepy, yes, but what woods weren't creepy at night?

And now, it truly was nightfall.

The sun had slid over the horizon, and only the faintest trace of its luminous fire kissed their world. All else was dark. A million stars shimmered above their heads, dancing their celestial dance, and the moon peered out from behind purple-tinged clouds.

Yeah, it was creepy, but it was just a forest.

He watched Kevin go about his silly charade, amused.

After laying the egg down, his brother clasped his hands together, closed his eyes and whispered a few words. Though he couldn't hear the words, Billy smiled, impressed. It was quite a show he was putting on. Billy felt almost complimented that Kevin would put in so much effort just to give him a good scare.

He hid his smile as his brother turned and made his way back to the porch, empty handed now. The egg lay before the wall of black like a tiny sentinel.

"Come on. Let's go inside, buddy." Kevin said.

Billy got to his feet, stretched and groaned. They'd been sat out here a long time. "Kev, can I ask you something else?"

"Sure."

"What's the tradition?"

Kevin frowned. "I'm not sure how it works, or what it means. All I know is that the first born child of any household, under the age of eighteen, had to paint themselves onto an egg and offer it up to…it."

"Like a sacrifice?" Billy asked, playing along. He was impressed by his own acting skills, as well.

"I don't know. I think so. People here think the egg represents the human soul, and you have to offer yours up to the thing in the woods. It's a mock effigy of sorts, they said. It's not really your soul, that's what the Indian taught them, but it's what the egg represents that the thing out there desires. All I know is that if you don't leave the egg out there by midnight, right by the foot of the woods, then it comes…

"It comes for you instead, Billy, and it takes the real thing."

"Scary." Billy said in a hushed tone.

Kevin frowned. "You believe me, right? I know it sounds crazy, but you said you'd believe me."

Billy mustered up his best, most sincere face. "I do. I promise.

"Good." Kevin smiled a little. It barely touched his eyes, but it was there nonetheless.

Great performance, Billy thought again.

"Let's go inside, kiddo. We're done here. We can watch a movie now."

Together, they left the porch and made for the warmth and comfort of their home.

As Billy entered the house, he cast a quick glance over his shoulder and immediately felt like a fool. He knew this was all make-believe, but still...

Still he imagined he could feel those watchful eyes, nestled in the gathering dark.

*

Kevin had been sat by the window for the last hour.

Billy found the whole charade very amusing. Since coming indoors, they'd spent the remainder of the evening watching a movie; an old classic starring Peter Cushing that both boys had agreed was much better than most of the modern horror fare. They'd eaten popcorn, drank soda and laughed together at the shoddy special effects. Billy figured the teeth on the vampire had been purchased in a fancy dress shop, and the cape too, but the tall actor who played the count had really sold the role.

By the time the movie was done, Billy was tired.

He'd have liked nothing more than to crawl into bed and drift off to sleep, but that wasn't an option. He was determined to let his brother's little game play all the way out.

After all, Kevin had wasted his time with the egg painting and the outlandish spook story, so why shouldn't he, in return, allow his brother to waste some time of his own?

Kevin had demanded they turn out the lights in their bedroom. He said he wanted to sit by the window in the dark, and watch the backyard. Billy, of course, had gone right along with him. Kevin peered out into the yard; the soft moonlight casting his face in a pale, translucent glow. He hadn't moved position in at least ten minutes. His foot tapped rhythmically on the carpet as he stared out into the darkness of the Easter night.

Billy was laid back on his own bed, propped up by two pillows. In his hands he held his IPad. The game he was playing was barely holding his attention, but he was steadily growing more and more bored with the ruse.

How long did Kevin plan to keep this up for?

Billy supposed it didn't matter. Looking at the clock by his bed, he noted that it was now two minutes till midnight. Kevin had said the 'thing' came for its prize at the stroke of the midnight hour, so soon, this would all be over.

Billy smiled.

It was time for him to play his hand.

He laid the IPad on his lap, clicking the 'off' button as he did so, and turned to his brother. Kevin was play-acting as though he was lost in his own world.

"Kevin?" Billy asked, breaking the prolonged silence.

His brother's voice was hushed. He never turned to respond, and instead just stared out into the moonlit yard and the wall of trees beyond.

"Yeah?" he said.

"Do you see what time it is?"

"Yes."

"I have something I have to tell you..."

"And what's that?" Kevin asked, with little interest.

"I know you made that story up."

"Huh?"

"I said, I know you made the story up. I'm twelve, Kev. I'm not a kid anymore. You almost had me fooled for a while. Almost, but not quite. I'm not as dumb as you think I am."

"You said you believed me."

Billy smiled in the darkness. "I lied."

Kevin peered out the window. "It doesn't matter. It's almost time now. It'll be here soon. It'll take the offering and it'll leave."

"You can drop the act now, Kev." Billy let the moment draw out, savouring it.

"It's not an act." Kevin's tone was dead flat.

Billy sat up in his bed. "I can't believe you thought I'd fall for it, but the jokes on you. I've been pretending this whole time that I was scared. You're not the only one who can play act, you know."

Kevin's reaction was muted. "Whatever."

Billy felt anger bubble up inside him. He'd hoped to get a better reaction that this. At the very least he'd hoped to make his brother laugh, or get mad, or...something. Anything but this.

Kevin just stared into the night, as though Billy's words had no effect at all.

"Kevin, you can come away from the window now. Let's go to bed. It's late, and there's nothing out there." Billy swung his legs over the side of the bed and planted his feet on the carpet. He reached to the bedside cabinet and opened the small drawer.

"I even brought your dumb egg back in for you when you were showering. Figured you might want to keep it," he said.

As Billy lifted the egg from the drawer, Kevin spun around on his seat, fast as lightning. Terror seemed to cast a burning light behind his horrified gaze, as his eyes fell on the egg.

Why was he still acting?

The joke was over.

He was acting, wasn't he?

Billy felt the first sickening stab of real fear soak into his psyche. His brother's face was a picture of horror. In the moonlight's glow, he looked like a ghost. A wraith, etched forever in terrible torment.

Kevin screamed. "Why would you do that?!"

Billy flinched from his older sibling's outrage. "D-do what?" he stammered.

Kevin's eyes darted down to his wristwatch, tears welled in his eyes. He was trembling uncontrollably; his whole body seized in the grip of a terror that Billy realised, with a rising wave of purest dread, could only be real.

What was going on?

Billy felt sick.

"It's too late!" The words came out of his brother's mouth like a long, agonised moan, soaked in a hopeless despair.

Billy was shaking himself, now.

"I'm…I'm sorry!" he stammered, as his stomach flipped over on itself.

What had he done?

"You've killed me, Billy!"

"I…I'm sorry." Billy begged. "I was only…"

The rest of Billy's words stuck in his throat.

His mind reeled as stark blind terror wracked his body.

He was looking beyond his terrified brother, now.

Outside the window.

There was something out there.

There was something out there in the dark.

It was a shadow with shadows, and as Billy watched, frozen in shock, the dark figure rose up behind his brother, separated from Kevin by nothing but the fragile pane of glass.

Billy couldn't make it out properly. The darkness clung to the impossible being like a second skin, but one thing was for sure.

It was not human.

Long, spindly appendages rose from the bulk of the black creature like the legs of a giant spider. There were more than Billy could count.

"B-Billy?" Kevin was crying openly, having seen the stark terror that gripped Billy. He never turned to face the looming thing outside their home, nor even made a move from the window as its vast shadow spread across the carpet like a hellish Rorschach, engulfing his own. It all happened so fast, and in his shock, Billy thought Kevin could no more move his body than the dead could shift their headstones from the depth of their sodden graves.

Suddenly, there was a thunderous crash. The window behind his brother shattered as the creature outside raised a huge limb, bristling with coarse insect hair, and thrust it through the glass.

Time slowed to an endless, awful crawl as Billy watched a long, razor sharp talon, like that of a mantis, slide around his brother's waistline. Below the huge grasping apparatus, a line of blackest crimson began to flow, dark as night, where the creature's tooth-like tubercles sliced the skin and opened Kevin's stomach as it held him.

Billy gagged as he watched the glistening intestines housed within begin to swell and push their way free of their prison.

The thing's head loomed in over his brother.

Billy screamed for his mom.

He screamed for his dad and for Jesus, for God and for himself.

And for his brother.

No help came.

Though the moon's light was low, Billy could now make out the abomination's features.

He wished he could not.

Its smooth dome resembled that of a spider's. The entire front area of the head was covered in a vast cluster of black, pitiless eyes that seemed to stare as one, right into the centre of Billy's soul. Beneath its countless, bulbous, black diamond orbs there was a gaping maw, almost perfectly cylindrical. A huge hole ringed with row after row of long, vicious looking teeth, thin as needles. Drool spilled from its meat-grinder mouth as it began to drag Kevin towards it. As he watched in repugnant, frightful awe, something moved within the dark abyss of its gullet, clicking together like pincers. A hideous mandible designed to tear and rend.

And feed.

It never made any other sound as it pulled his screaming, flailing brother close to its dark bosom, though the creature seemed to relish the terror it inspired.

It worked slowly, dragging Kevin through the shattered, jagged glass, piercing his skin and tearing his soft flesh to ribbons. As his screams of terror crossed over into mind-ripping exclamations of agony, the thing's cluster of abominable eyes seemed to shine with fresh fervour. His arms and shoulders spurted warm blood from a hundred wounds as the glass cut deep.

His eyes fixed on Billy, just for a fleeting moment.

It lasted longer for Billy than a million lifetimes. In his eyes, he saw the true depth of his betrayal.

His brother's eyes seemed to plead, and to question.

One blood soaked and shredded arm reached out toward him with shivering, desperate fingers. Billy reached out himself to touch his brother one last time, but before he could, the black thing's mandibles burst forth from its vile gullet and sliced into the skin and muscle of Kevin's shoulder. His brother's outstretched hand instinctively receded, clasping at the gushing wound. Ignoring Kevin's feeble attempts to protect himself, the hellish creature tore a chunk of meat free, working the food into its maw where it ground it to pulp. The geyser of blood that erupted from the vicious laceration covered his screaming brother's face in an arterial spray.

With lightning speed, it turned its abhorrent hide toward the woods. Holding Kevin close in its long front limbs as a spider would a fly, it scuttled off into the night in near silence, like a fevered nightmare suddenly dispelled.

Just as quickly as the world had descended into a madness of screams and chaos and horror, it was over.

A soft wind caressed the cracked and ruined window, causing the small ragged remnants of Billy's brother to sway gently, like tiny flags of skin waving farewell to their owner.

On legs that felt like lead, Billy got to his feet and staggered to the ruined window. Resting his hands on the blood-slick, wooden pane, he peered out into the night.

In the yard, he could make out dark splashes of blood from his brother's wounds, trailing towards the hateful black of the forest, and nothing more.

Kevin was gone.

Billy's eyes fell on the treeline, hoping beyond hope to catch a final glimpse of his poor, lost brother. The brother he'd condemned to death just as surely as if he'd loaded a gun, pointed at Kevin's skull, and pulled the trigger.

He thought about the thing he'd seen, the giant insect that wasn't an insect, but an abomination; a mockery of all that dwelled in the natural world.

A gun would have been better.

A gun would have been much, much better.

As though summoned from hell to affirm his thoughts, a scream pierced the stillness of the night.

He'd never heard such a pitiful, excruciating sound; not in a thousand horror movies nor a thousand nightmares.

It sounded like all the instruments of hell were being used on his brother, squeezing every drop of pain and torment from his quivering flesh.

In his mind, Billy began to form pictures, images to compliment the awful sounds leaking from the darkness of the old woods. He imagined terrible, unspeakable things, and the waking nightmare in his mind's eye played out every bit as long as his brother's suffering.

Finally, the sounds of his Kevin's agony died on the wind. The night grew still once more.

Billy thought back to what his brother had said.

'All I know is that if you don't leave the egg out there by midnight, right by the foot of the woods, then it comes. It comes for you instead, Billy, and it takes the real thing'.

The real thing...

He thought about those words and understood with terrible clarity that Kevin's true suffering would last a lot longer than his screams.

It would last till the stars fell from the sky and the oceans turned to dust.

*

Billy sat on the sofa, waiting for the familiar sound of keys turning, and for the front door to open. They'd be home soon, mum and dad. Home from their carefree night out on the town with their new friends.

The house was quiet now, and wreathed in darkness.

He'd turned all the lights off.

Billy knew enough about insects to know that many were attracted to the light.

He would sit there in perfect darkness, and wait.

In his hand, he held the small boiled egg.

He studied it in the gloom.

On the small, near featureless face, Kevin had painted a small smile. His way of seeing the bright side on all things, Billy mused. And it was accurate, after all. Kevin had loved to smile. And to laugh.

Billy wiped the fresh tears from his eyes, and cleaned the snot from his nose with a handkerchief. The egg felt lighter now than it should. It was strange, but he felt sure there was something else in there besides the boiled egg.

He shook it ever so lightly.

Yes, there was a sloshing sound.

Nothing like a boiled egg at all.

Perhaps Kevin hadn't boiled it properly, and some of the yolk was still soft.

Billy knew better.

Whatever was now housed in the fragile shell would remain in his protection. He swore he'd keep the egg safe. Whatever it was, it was all he had left of his brother.

Outside he heard a car pull up.

At this time of night, it could only be his parents.

He took a deep breath. As their soft laughter grew louder, there was a small squeal of delight from his mom, and a gruff snort from his dad, as one of them fumbled with the keys.

Billy reckoned they'd been drinking.

That was good.

It would make this whole thing a little easier to take.

He struggled to compose himself as the battle with the keyhole was won, and the door swung open and the lights came on.

A soft wind followed his stumbling, drunken parents over the threshold, and on it, he imagined he heard his brother, calling out in horror from a place far, far away.

On seeing Billy sat there, red-eyed and tearful, his parent's mirth died on their lips. Concern eclipsed the frivolity like ink spilled over white paper.

He tried to compose himself.

He really did.

Instead, Billy burst into tears and reached out instinctually, desperate to be held by his parents as the nightmare of it all finally overwhelmed him. As his arms stretched forward, hungry for embrace, the small egg toppled from his hand.

He watched in despair as it shattering on the hardwood floor.

Billy screamed then.

He screamed till his throat was torn and his vocal chords were all but snapped.

And when his mom and dad saw what poured from the cracked and splintered eggshell and seeped between the wooden floor panelling, they screamed right along with him.

THE END

Bio

Kyle M. Scott is a horror author hailing from the dark and desolate wastelands of Glasgow, Scotland. He spent his formative years immersed in the world of horror, devouring the genre in all its forms. A rabid fan of the underground authors whose work paved the way for a more visceral, hard-hitting style of horror, Kyle's love of extreme gore and boundary-pushing fiction fuelled his imagination and inspired him to forge his own dark path.

Kyle currently has four works available. Volume 1 and 2 of the 'Consumed' series - a collection of dark fiction that melds extreme horror with the blackest wit - and the full-length love letter to 80's splatter and monster movies, 'Devil's Day'. His second novel, 'Aftertaste', pushed the boundaries of depravity, combining social satire, suspense and a heavy dose of graphic horror.

In his relatively short career, his works have made him a favourite among readers with a taste for fearless, provocative fiction that evokes the classic works of those who shaped modern horror.

Among his many influences, he cites Richard Laymon, Edward Lee and Jack Ketchum as the writers who sealed his fate.

At present, he is working on the extreme horror novel, 'The Club'.

Kyle resides in Glasgow with his long suffering partner, an arrogant, half-demented cat, and an imagination that keeps him up all night contemplating therapy.

His parents are currently wondering what went wrong.

Kyle can be found causing trouble on Facebook at:

https://m.facebook.com/kylemscott123/

HEY-ZEUS

Duncan P. Bradshaw

MAUNDY THURSDAY

Guy passed the driving license to Ed, giving him the biggest of grins, "Here you go mate, get your eyes round that bad boy."

Ed snatched it, and turned it this way and that, checking for the quality, he nodded in approval, "That's some good work mate, real top notch, should be able to get our drink on later tonight huh?" Guy nodded enthusiastically.

"Wait a moment mate, why have you changed my name?"

"Duh, why do you think? If you get nicked, the last thing you'll want is for the po-po to know your real name huh?" Guy rapped his mate on the head with his knuckles, "Not the brightest bulb in the box are ya?"

"Why the fuck am I called Jesus though? Of all the names you could've gone for, you've called me Jesus," Ed whinged.

Harry nudged Guy in the ribs, "You didn't, did ya? Ha ha ha, that's well funny. It's cos of the beard isn't it?"

Guy picked up another slice of pizza and started to pick the chunks of pepper from it, "Yeah man, and besides Ed, it's pronounced 'Hey-Zeus', ya know, Portuguese or summat. You'll be fine, not as if anyone is going to challenge it eh? You said it yourself, it's top notch."

Ed launched a disc of pepperoni at Guy's face, catching him on the nose, "You're such a bell end. No one is going to fall for this."

"Only one way to find out mate," Harry butted in, "get down to the offie, pick us up some cans, we can neck 'em as we head into town. Maundy Thursday innit? Everyone goes out and gets pissed. Except this time gentlemen, we shall be amongst them. Heard some birds from college are heading to this pub called 'Hey Jude'. Reckon we head down and see if we can get some, you know what I mean?" As if to emphasise what he meant, he shoved an index finger into his other balled fist and slid it in and out.

"I think we understand what you mean, you dick," Guy whinged. With the pepper removed, he folded the slice of pizza in half and shoved it in his mouth.

Ed sighed and stood up, "Fine, I'll pop out now, give us some money though, not paying for it all myself am I?"

With a pocket full of shrapnel, Ed felt as though his jeans were going to fall down. The last thing he wanted as he entered the off license, was to begin proceedings by baring his Iron Man underwear to the proprietor. He was certain that any ID, regardless of its quality, would be rendered useless if the owner clapped eyes on his gaudily stained underpants.

As the door opened a bell rang out -and the shopkeeper, stood behind the counter reading The Sun, eyed him suspiciously. Ed could already feel beads of sweat blooming in his fringe as the door closed behind him and his palms were tacky. Striding past the counter, he managed a grunt of "Evening mate," before he walked down the aisle to the promised land.

With his entrance made, he looked around and saw, to his dismay, that he was stood amongst the wine. He could feel the eyes of the shopkeeper on him, so decided to act the part. Ed picked up the first bottle he saw, and turned it round, pretending to read the description. *Why the fuck would you buy something that had 'elements of jasmine and oak' in?* Tutting, he replaced the bottle on the shelf, though feeling it nearly slip out of his hands as he did so.

"Can I help you?" the shopkeeper called out.

Ed wiped his hands on his jeans and squeaked, "I'm looking for the lager," his voice coming out like he was thirteen again.

The man smirked and pointed with the folded up paper, "Over there mate." With the interaction complete, for now, Ed flounced round the back of the aisle.

A wall of cans greeted him, he felt as overwhelmed as he had when Emily had pulled her top off and volunteered her bra covered boobs to him. No matter how hard he pulled at the damn clasp, the promised land had remained stashed away. *Bollocks to it.* Ed knew he had twelve pounds and fifty eight pence in available funds, mostly in twenty pence pieces. Choosing from the wealth of garish coloured adverts available, he plucked three different four-packs from the shelf, did a last check to make sure they were in the same offer, then began the trek to the counter.

Time itself slowed down, each step a booming thud, the change slapped against his thigh, the shopkeeper, preparing for the inevitable, slung the paper onto a stool and crossed his arms, the words formed already.

Waiting for the right moment to be delivered.

With the cans dumped on the surface, Ed scratched his burgeoning beard, which grew sparsely on one side, and like a wild thicket on the other cheek. "Gonna need to see some ID mate," the shopkeeper asked. Ed gulped, pulled out his wallet and passed the driving license across, giving him as confident a grin as he could muster.

Like a hawk eyeing up a shrew, the shopkeeper turned the ID in the light, before sticking his bottom lip out in acceptance. Just as it was about to be passed back, his eyes screwed up, "Hang on. Jesus?"

Ed swallowed hard, "Yeah…erm, my parents are bible bashers, they erm…ya know…"

The shopkeeper smirked, "Don't suppose you could do me a favour could ya?"

Ed's mouth hung open, catching flies, the barman stooped down before slapping a bottle of water on the counter, "Could you turn this into wine? I'd make a killing." He looked at Ed expectantly, raising his eyebrows in time to 'Hallo Spaceboy', which was blaring out of the radio.

"Huh?" Ed asked dumbly.

The shopkeeper sighed, "Was only a joke mate," and passed the ID back, "if you want a carrier bag, they're five pence each."

"Yes please," he squawked back, before fishing around in his pocket and depositing enough change on the counter to keep a slot machine addict happy for a few hours. The shopkeeper tutted, rolled his eyes, and began to fish through the pile of coins.

"I fucking hate cider," Guy whinged. With every swig, he pulled a face afterwards as if he was going to throw up.

The trio walked through the park, the bag of booze swinging in Ed's hand, Harry laughed, "Shut it you nobber, everyone does, unless you're a farmer. Anyway, it'll get you pissed quicker though won't it? Hurry up, we're nearly there," he pointed to a lit up building beyond some wrought iron railings.

Ed belched, "There's no way we can drink this lot is there? Reckon we stash the others in a bush, pick them up on the way back, what do ya reckon?"

Guy and Harry nodded, and chinned the rest of their drinks. With the bag secreted in the hedgerow, out of sight, the three of them started preening. "So, we get in there, me and Harry will go find somewhere to loiter, and you go get the drinks in. Lager this time, OKAY? Otherwise, knowing my luck, I'll pull some bird only to yak up all over her as we're snogging."

Ed and Harry started to snigger. They pushed their way past the ostracised smokers and entered the building to the tune of 'Hey Jude'. It was bustling, Guy and

Harry pointed to a murky corner, Ed nodded and looked at the bar. It was two deep. He walked round the scrum and managed to squeeze into the throng, then bided his time.

"Can I see some ID mate?" the voice asked, stirring Ed from his thoughts about bra's and their infernal workings. Ed stuttered and dug the driving license out again, passing it to the smartly dressed barman. The instant he read the name, he raised an eyebrow, "Jesus?"

"It's pronounced, Hey-Zeus, it's Portuguese," Ed replied.

"No, no, it's fine. It is providence that has brought you here, to us today. Here, this lot is on the house. Take them to your friends and come back, we've got something special for you," the barman said.

Ed scowled, though it was short lived, free booze was free booze, they only had a tenner each, which wasn't going to last too long judging by the prices stuck to the pumps. The barman placed the second pint on the bar, and winked, making Ed feel a little uncomfortable, "Don't forget to come back," the barman reminded him.

"They're free?" Guy asked incredulously, Ed nodded. "Well where are you going?"

"The barman said he has something for me, be back in a bit," Ed answered, Guy shrugged his shoulders and went back to chatting to Harry about football.

Ed fought through the crowd again and got to the bar, though when he looked around, he couldn't see where the barman had got to. "Jesus?" a soft voice asked from behind him.

Ed turned around and looked straight into the buxom chest of a scantily clad lady, she looked down at him seductively, nibbling on her lip. Ed realised his mouth was open and promptly shut it, his teeth clacked together. Finally remembering the English language, he mumbled, "Yes?"

The lady smiled at him and grasping his hand, she winked and began to lead him off to a door marked, 'STAFF ONLY'. "Where are we going?" Ed asked, though not really caring.

She just smiled at him and pushed the door open, revealing a near pitch black room, "You just get in there Jesus, I've got something for you."

With a buffoons smile on his face, Ed walked into the room, the door shut behind him and clicked closed. "Hello?" he asked the darkness. There was a WOOSH rendering him unconscious.

GOOD FRIDAY

Ed came to and could feel air blowing over his back, opening his eyes, he could see stone tiles beneath him. He felt that he was laying down on his front, trying to stand up didn't work, and he realised that he was tied to whatever it was below.

"Jesus," came a stern man's voice from behind him, "so glad you woke up in time. It's Good Friday, and you have been delivered to us, by the ever knowing Judas Iscariot."

"Eh?" Ed asked dumbly, he tried to look around to see who was speaking to him.

"We have much to do Jesus, so let us begin," as the voice ended, Ed heard a cracking sound, splitting the air around him. He wracked his brain to remember where he had heard that sound before. CRACK.

CRACK.

CRACK.

That was it, Indiana Jones, it sounded like his whip.

Hang on.

"Erm, excuse me, but what are you going to do? I thought the lady wanted to... you know...have sex with me?" he said to the room.

A bassy laughing ran around him, covering him like a blanket, "Oh you're good, we know that you are pure and chaste. You have kept yourself this way. For the offering."

"What are you on about? What's the offering?" Ed asked.

"Hello?"

Another crack rang out, this time ending in a slash of pain running across his back, just below the shoulder blades, Ed cried out in pain, "What the fuck man?" Another crack, another fork of agony slashed his body, the lash wrapped around from one rib to the other. It continued. Each crack ended in another sting, the site would go numb temporarily, before warm liquid ran down his sides.

Ed lost count at thirty one, the sound was at a steady pace, and the end result was the same. His body rocked with each strike, the wood beneath him chafed his skin, rubbing it raw. Thick strands of spit and blood dribbled from his mouth, spooling from the beard hair before spiralling to the stone slabs beneath him. Eventually he lost consciousness and the world went black.

He was lost in a dream where he was trying to find his way home. Ed was in the park with Guy and Harry, they staggered about the place, cans in hand, swearing at him, telling him to stay out and not be such a baby about going home. As he crossed the divide between park and street, a blinding white light seared his eyeballs.

His own screaming brought him to. The cracking had stopped, but he could feel coarse hands rubbing his back. Thick fingers pressed into the gashes and lacerations, fingernails dug under his skin, seeking out the meat beneath. They smeared a gritty powder into his wounds, "Salt the flesh, make it clean," he could hear the gruff man chanting to himself.

With his strength expended, he saw a robed figured kneel down in front of him, and unfasten the rope which bound him. Once he was released, cold hands were thrust under him, turning him onto his back. As he was spun around, he could see that he was in a basement; tall oak casks were stacked against a far wall. He saw that he had been lying on a thick table, still wet blood glinted in the thick wooden grain.

The pain which coursed through his body as his mutilated back was placed beneath him, nearly made Ed pass out again, he cried out, hoping that someone would hear his cries. His eyes were forced open by cold salty fingers, he looked into the face of the barman, "Jesus. You have gone through stage one of the preparation. Behold, stage two. The bleeding."

Ed felt clammy hands hold his near lifeless arms against the table top, with his eyes released, he tried to see what else was around him, nothing except stone, beams and stacks of barrels. The barman appeared in his eyesight again, "Behold, a crown fit for the King of the Jews."

A coronet of metal was held above his head, something sparkly was wrapped around the circumference. As it was brought closer, he could see that the metal ring was laced with barbed wire. Ed tried to squirm, but hands held him firmly in place. The barman disappeared from view, though he could feel his damp breath against the tips of his ears.

Then he felt it. Barbs dug into his head, gently at first, more like an irritation, but it grew in ferocity, before he could feel it scratching against the bone of the skull. "Stay still now," the barman's voice warned.

TAP TAP TAP

Ed couldn't work out what was making the sound, perhaps it was someone trying to save him. The barman appeared in his eyesight once more and he saw that he was holding a hammer.

TAP TAP TAP

The jagged metal bit further through the skin, embedding itself in his skull, he could feel blood trickling down his head, dripping off his hair and onto the table beneath him. The barman worked his way around, and then stood over Ed, "There, that's better, you look like a true King now. Not much more to endure, then your journey will be complete. I promise."

There was a clap of hands, and Ed was released, the relief was temporary as the same clammy hands hauled him to his unsteady feet. "Please mate, I'm not really Jesus..." Ed begged.

The barman raised a hand, "You're not? But your driving license says it is? You're not trying to deceive us are you?"

Ed sobbed, "No...yes...look, please, it's been a terrible misunderstanding. Please... let me go."

Hands dragged him across the floor, towards a treadmill, "You cannot fool us with your lies Jesus, we know who you are. Do not be afraid, we have been waiting for you for some time. We can finally complete the ritual, and *He* will be awakened."

Two robed figures dumped Ed onto the treadmill, before disappearing off to one side. "Who will be awakened? What are you on about?"

"Judas of course. He will be reborn, the true apostle will walk amongst us once more, and guide us anew," the barman lectured, he gestured to the two shadowy figures who bowed and knelt down.

"I don't understand..." Ed whimpered.

"That is of no consequence. Now. Jesus, the deceiver, it is time for you to walk the way of suffering, I hope you have kept some of your strength. For now you will need it."

There was the sound of wood scraping against stone, Ed tilted his head and saw the two robed men materialise out of the gloom, dragging a large wooden cross. The barman walked to the head of the treadmill and punched in a target distance of one mile into the display, "Arise, false prophet," he commanded.

When he did not, the barman punched Ed in the face and hauled him to his feet.

The figures stood to one side, with the crucifix running in parallel to the treadmill, they lowered the corner of the cross onto Ed's shoulder, the weight nearly forced him to his knees.

"Now Jesus. Walk," the barman commanded, he hit 'Start' on the machine, and it whirred into life. Step after agonising step, Ed plodded on, the pace was slow, but persistent. As he staggered onwards, the three figures would take in turns to spit on him, clout him around the head, or push down on his burden.

Ed sunk to his knees a number of times, after each collapse, the machine would be stopped, he would be pulled to his feet, and it would begin again. After what felt like eternity, the machine beeped that the journey had been completed.

"Good, you have arrived Jesus," the barman cried out.

Ed looked around, "But I haven't gone anywhere…"

"I think you have, both in body and mind. Now, the final act," his eyes darted to each of the robed figures, who dragged the cross off Ed's blistered shoulder and rested it on the floor.

"You have done well, now you have but to embrace the end. Your end," the barman picked Ed up under his armpits and dragged him backwards. His legs were leaden and every time he tried to stand, they faltered.

Ed felt his back rub against rough wood again, splinters wormed their way into the red raw wounds. His arms were splayed outwards, and his feet straightened. "No, please…no…" he murmured through fat lips.

He felt something cold press against the palm of his right hand, like a fifty pence piece, he heard a clang and felt something be driven clean through, he screamed. The hammer came down again, until the nail was flush to the skin. The other hand was next, before his trainers were ripped off and thrown into the corner of the room. As his feet were nailed to the cross, he floated between reality and dream.

Another scraping sound woke him up, he saw the ceiling flip and turn the right way up. As gravity took hold, his body sagged, pulling on the nails, opening the meat of his hand up. "And lo, it has been completed. Die well, Jesus."

Ed fought to keep his eyes open, but each felt like they had weights attached to them. His head sunk to his chest, and he gave in.

EASTER SUNDAY

"Well he can't have just disappeared, can he?" Guy grumbled, rummaging through another bin bag. He recoiled as his thumb sank into the decomposing body of a rat, "This is gross."

"Look, last I saw, he was going off with that fit bird in the pub, just saying that if he got murdered and hacked into pieces, it stands to reason he'll be out back, won't he?" Harry said matter of factly. He was in his element, supervising his mate, "They bloody love their oak casks huh? I bet they store human blood in 'em."

"Shut up you nobber, have you gone through the dumpsters yet?" Guy asked, wiping rotting entrails over his trousers.

Harry shook his head and walked to the nearest one, he clambered on top of a barrel, and opened the lid, "Fucking hell, smells like your mum in here."

"Are you going to take it seriously? Our mate has vanished, probably been forced to have sex with that bird until he died or his knob fell off. It's our duty to find him, he's still got my iPod the little bastard," Guy argued.

Harry dragged a black bin bag aside, "Shit, Guy, think I've just found Ed, or what's left of him." Nestled in amongst rotting vegetables and mouldy fruit, Ed's pallid, blood soaked face looked back.

"What are we gonna do? Call the filth? Gotta do something haven't we Guy?" The pair had dragged Ed's body to a nearby garage. The three of them had been there before, smoking joints and swapping scraps of porn mags they had found by railway sidings.

Guy stood over Ed, his fists were balled in rage, "No man, we're going to fuck them up. It is not okay for them to offer our mate sex and then murder him like a bunch of sickos."

Harry laughed nervously, "Are you joking, there's only the two of us, if they did that to Ed, I'm pretty sure, that all we'd accomplish is being turned into dumpster buddies. Fuck it, let's call the filth, they'll sort them out."

"NO," Guy screamed. "Not a chance, I've got an idea."

"What?"

"We're gonna use voodoo and bring Ed back, then we'll get him into the pub and he can have his revenge."

"Voodoo? Are you retarded? You got the Ladybird book of Voodoo rituals or summat?"

Guy shot Harry a look, "Look, it's Easter, ole zombie Jesus came back didn't he? Ed was sort of like Jesus."

"Only cos you told Scabby Pete to put his name down as that."

"That was for a laugh weren't it? Look, are you gonna help me or what?"

Harry shrugged, "Guess so, nothing else to do eh? I lent Ed FIFA, won't be getting that back in a hurry will I?"

Guy smiled and slapped Harry on the arm, "Good man. First, we need to beef Ed up a bit, they've done a right number on him. I've got an idea, come on..."

"Cheers mate," the delivery man pulled off the top copy and passed the invoice to the barman. With a toot of his horn, the driver pulled away and headed home, the last delivery of the day complete. The barman folded up the invoice and shoved it in his pocket. Pulling on his thick leather gloves, he tipped the first barrel onto its side and rolled it into the open warehouse.

"Now you knobber," Guy hissed. Creeping out from behind the bins, the pair rolled their barrel towards the fresh delivery. They managed to stand it up just as the barman made his way outside again.

"Can I help you lads?" the barman asked, squeezing his gloved fist with his free hand.

"Nah, you're alright mate," Guy muttered, before they slunk off down the alley.

"Chancers, looking to take advantage of some free booze," the barman watched the pair turn a corner, before turning back to the collection of barrels. He sighed, this was part of the job he hated, no matter how many he took through to the warehouse, the number never seemed to go down. He huffed and tipped the next one on its side.

*

With the barrels indoors, the barman pulled the doors to, locked them, and then wrestled a thick wooden bar to hold them into place, "You want a hand?" the manager asked, pulling his robe off and hanging it on a hook behind a door which led to the bar upstairs, he was joined by a lady, who also disrobed.

"Yeah, please," the barman answered, "get this done then. Any sign of...you know who?"

The lady shook her head disappointedly, "No, not yet, though it can't be too long now. I reckon he's been out, seeing what has changed with the world. A lot to take in has old Judas."

BANG BANG

The trio breathed in sharply, looking at one of the barrels.

BANG BANG BANG

"Praise be! Our prayers have been answered, he has been delivered to us," the lady cried aloud.

"I wasn't quite expecting him to be in a barrel," the barman added, with a slight air of disbelief.

"Our sacrifice has been heard, he is amongst us once more, I have yearned for this d-"

The top of the barrel creaked open, the wooden disc clattered to the stone floor, the trio prostrated themselves on the cold stone floor, "PRAISE BE," they called as one.

"MMAAAAAAAA," the barrel moaned.

The barman looked up, puzzled, "Mmaaaaaa? What does that mean?"

"Perhaps it's the language of the ancients?" the woman offered.

Metal clacked against the edge of the wooden barrel, fingers ending in six inch blades, fashioned from shoplifted kitchen knives, gripped hold of the wood.

The three acolytes stood up uneasily, trying to peer into the void of the barrel. The metal ending fingers gripped and hauled Ed free from his temporary home, smelling of stale beer. His blue face, with purple eyes and drooping gums looked at his killers.

"Judas?" the woman asked blankly, unable to compute what she saw.

Ed stumbled out of the barrel and stood on awkward legs, his chest was puffed out, something stashed beneath his tracksuit top. The manager snapped off the staff from a broom and charged the intruder, clocking him around the head. Ed's head cracked to one side, before slowly looking back to the front, crusty flakes of blood fell off his forehead.

"Shit," the manager mumbled.

Ed slashed his right hand across the manager's throat, who collapsed to the ground, hands pressed to the wound. Blood poured through his fingers, turned white through the pressure of trying to hold the inner workings of his throat inside. He looked up at the dead kid and tried to ask 'why', managing nothing but a series of gurgles and blood bubbles.

A hand stabbed the manager through the face, lancing the eyeballs, Ed picked the man up with no effort at all. Hands slapped against his side, blood from his ruined throat squirted over Ed's face, who didn't so much as blink. He lashed out with his free hand, and severed the head clean off. The lifeless body hit Ed's legs before falling to one side, blood was pumped out of the ragged stump. Ed discarded the head and turned his attention to the survivors.

The woman went to run, but Ed was on her quickly. He dived to tackle her, and took her left leg off at the knee. She screamed as she rolled around the cold stone floor in agony, fingers tried to pinch the sliced arteries and veins closed, trying desperately not to bleed out. As she howled with pain as her long fingernails scraping against the inside of her leg, Ed crawled beside her. He raised his hand in the air and brought it down on the base of her spine.

This made the woman try to feebly fend him off, but it was no use. Ed slammed his other hand into the base of her neck, and then pulled apart, separating the woman into three pieces.

"You're supposed to be dead," the barman yelled. He ran at Ed as he tore the woman apart and kicked him on the back of the head. Ed slid across the floor, coming to a rest on his back. Try as he might, he couldn't right himself, the blades were screwed into his fingers and he couldn't push himself up.

The barman cackled, picking up a fire extinguisher, he walked slowly over to the stricken revenant, "I'm gonna have to kill you again Jesus, ruin your second coming," he promised.

He stood over Ed and raised the extinguisher, Ed spun to one side and executed a near perfect leg sweep. The barman landed on Ed's chest, the extinguisher hit the floor and rolled away. "Huh?" he could feel something biting into his chest, he looked down into Ed's dead eyes.

"MMAAA MAAA MAAAA," Ed cackled, and pressed a button sewn onto his tracksuit top. The circular saw whirred into life and chewed through the barman, sending chunks of raw meat into the air. It easily sliced through his ribcage, and soon was spinning in thin air, the barman rent in two.

The door from the bar opened, Guy and Harry crept out, "Fucking hell mate, it actually worked!" Harry shouted.

The pair pulled the chewed up remains of the barman from Ed, and helped him to his feet, "What do we do with him now Guy?" Harry asked, picking stringy bits of chewed up lung from Ed's tracksuit top.

Guy smiled, "Well, I say we get Ed here back to the garage and clean him up a bit, we are going to make a killing at Halloween."

THE END

Bio

Fie! That rapscallion Duncan P. Bradshaw has slain me once more. From yonder Wiltshire, where he lay his codpiece down, to the sundering moors of Somerset, where he did track me to my doom. His beastly cats did corner me unto this place of solace, only for his mighty strength to render the door to matchsticks. As I lay here dying, he speaks to me still. Strange stories of things which scratch away inside his skull. Be they monsters? Nay, they are the thoughts of a loon, I wouldst have done well to appraise them whilst I was alive. How can thou make good on my mistake? Visit his website at http://www.duncanpbradshaw.co.uk or regard his ghastly form at http://www.facebook.com/duncanpbradshaw. He is one of the Sinister Horror Company, and you can uncover their tomes of mystery at http://www.sinisterhorrorcompany.com .

FELDMAN'S RABBIT

RICH HAWKINS

The car broke down as the rain turned to sleet, and Feldman smoked his last cigarette in a fit of expletives spat over the steering wheel. And after all that there was laughter rising from his throat and bursting from his mouth, but it didn't last long and he ended up punching the top of the dashboard in frustration. Then he fell silent and watched the cigarette burn down between his fingers. He wound down the window and threw the butt onto the snow.

He looked outside. The snow covered the fields and the road, the trees and the hedgerows. Gathered atop fences like spiked ramparts. As it fell, the wind spat it in all directions, and soon the car would be blanketed and he would eventually freeze to death. Someone would find him once the snow had thawed: a frozen effigy in a glass and metal tomb. And his elderly parents would say it was his own fault, because he was weak and careless, and forgetful and foolish. They would gather for tea with the rest of the family and nod their heads and say what a nice man he had been, while lamenting his mental issues. Poor chap, they would say. Never stood a chance in life. Bad genes from his mother's side. She had three insane uncles, don't you know?

His fate would be remembered for years, as a cautionary tale for the children.

Feldman shook his head. No, it wouldn't happen, because he was not going to die in the squalid interior of a rusting Vauxhall Vectra while listening to Neil Diamond's greatest hits. So he gathered what belongings he could carry and abandoned the car. Before he left, he locked the car. And he set out into the white fields, keys jangling in one deep pocket. He glanced back once to look at the car, but it was already lost in the falling snow. He mouthed a silent goodbye then moved on.

*

The snow was up to his ankles, and each step pulled at his leg muscles and drained the strength from his bones. His feet were numb with cold. His shins ached. Shivering in the orange coat, Feldman grimaced at the sky and the fields around him. No houses in sight. No buildings to punctuate the land. Not even a barn or a stable. A nagging voice inside his head told him he would die; it scratched at the inside of his skull until he was shouting for it to go away. He thought he was already half-mad.

You are half-mad, Feldman. The doctor told you, remember?

He shook his head and spat. Wiped his mouth. Carried on, grunting and wincing as he struggled.

He found some meagre shelter under the boughs of oak trees, but he was always too cold to stop moving for long, so he blundered back into the falling snow and kicked his way through rising drifts and up shallow hills. He lost track of time. The light waning in the sky and all about him. The air turning colder, biting at his pudgy cheeks and around the soft flesh of his mouth. His teeth chattered. When he opened his mouth, the cold air stung the back of his throat and made his gums ache.

He was hopelessly lost, stumbling and tripping, his exhaled breaths like fog. Mouth trembling with the cold. His body winding down like a broken clockwork toy. He longed for heat and comfort, a hot drink and apple crumble. A fire to warm his hands upon. But there was nothing; just him and the snow, ever falling, and the great coldness killing him by plunging degrees.

Feldman only realised he was crying when his vision blurred and the snow formed watery shapes to harry him from all sides.

And that was when he caught sight of the house far ahead.

He had to wipe his eyes to be sure.

*

He stood hunched like a vagrant in the overgrown garden before the house, his breath shuddering in his chest. Snow gathered upon his thick shoulders. The house gave no shadow and loomed above him. Dead ivy vines strangled the broken guttering and scarred brickwork. Upon the roof of black slate, the chimney sat squat and stubborn against the weather.

The four windows – two on the ground floor, two upstairs – were clouded with grime and too dark to see beyond.

He limped to the front door, passing the shapes of garden gnomes concealed under the snow. The pond was green ice and frozen weeds. Utter silence around him. All he could hear was his frantic heart. The paint on the door was flaking away, revealing the dark wood underneath. A brass handle and a rusted knocker. Feldman breathed out, glanced around, then rapped three times on the door and waited. When no one answered he knocked again, a little harder, and cleared his throat.

He knocked several more times before he lost patience, opened the door and pushed it inwards. He stood in the doorway, waiting for someone to emerge from inside the house, but no one came, even when he called out with a frail voice that didn't sound like his own. And he stepped inside, glad to be out of the snow and wind, then shut the door behind him.

Standing in the dark of the hallway, Feldman called out again, but his voice disappeared into lightless rooms and passages to leave him alone, shivering and half-frozen.

*

A throat of stairs led up to deep shadow. Little daylight entered the house. Everything was ill-defined and blotchy with darkness. He thought it might be his eyes.

"Hello?" he said. "Is anyone here? I'm sorry to intrude, but I had to get out of the snowstorm. I abandoned my car somewhere back there. It's the worst snow I've seen for quite a while…" He waited, breathing too loud. "Hello?"

No one answered. The house was silent.

Feldman brushed the snow from his shoulders and hood, and it fell around his feet. Shuddering, he slumped on a stool by the stairway and rested his legs. Gusts of wind slipped through cracks in the walls to whistle and moan. A cold draught swept across the hallway.

"Fuck you, Mother," he muttered. "Feldman's tougher than you think. Feldman's going to be just fine."

*

He flicked the light switches, but remained in darkness. With the small flame of his cigarette lighter held out before him, he searched the downstairs rooms for signs of life. The kitchen was full of shadows when he stepped inside, glancing around furtively. He pulled back the curtains on the window over the sink. The grey daylight revealed dust-covered surfaces, a rusted iron sink, and a dining table that looked like it'd been carved by hand. Smell of damp and neglect all about him. A feathery corruption somewhere under the floor.

He turned the taps in the sink and waited. Water pipes rattling in the walls. A scraping, like something was trying to claw its way out of house's innards. He looked down at the taps, but didn't expect to see any water rushing out, and he was proved right.

He opened wall units to find plates, bowls and cloudy wine glasses. No food in the cupboards. A desiccated beetle lying on its back. He pulled open a drawer full of rusting cutlery. Grimy teacups on a mug-tree painted a dull shade of green.

Everything was covered in dust. Dead insects on the windowsill. His feet scuffed on the dirty linoleum floor. Dust balls gathered along the skirting boards.

Cracks in the walls. Flaking paint and peeling wallpaper. Crumbling plaster scattered on bare floorboards.

There was a rabbit's skull on the dining table. It looked to have been bleached. Skinless. As frail as old paper and furred with dust. Two enlarged teeth in the middle of the upper jaw. Around it were grey hairs and fur and more dust balls. His mind suggested it'd been left as an offering for him.

Feldman left it alone.

He stepped into the living room. The brown carpet matted with grime, clinging to the soles of his shoes. A sofa and two armchairs. The air was thick with dust, and he felt it stick to the inside of his throat when he took a breath. There was no television. The stone fireplace was cluttered with old pieces of coal and blackened wood. Porcelain figurines of rabbits lined the mantelpiece.

Feldman looked around at the paintings on the walls. Pastoral scenes of green hills and curving rivers, lush meadows and fields of wheat. One was of a flower in the first warmth of spring.

There was a laundry room at the back of the house. Piles of old towels and blankets. He looked out at the back garden, which was bristling with tall weeds and knotted bramble thickets.

When he returned to the front of the house, he tried the door under the stairs, but it didn't give, so he left it alone and then climbed the wooden steps to the landing. He searched the rooms and found nothing but the possessions of someone who'd left the house a long time ago. Dead flies upon a layer of thick dust on a small bed. Reeking blankets. He entered the bathroom and reeled from the stench of backed up pipes and stale urine soaked into rugs and rags.

Feldman went downstairs. He gathered some musty towels and blankets from the laundry room and brought them into the living room. He sat on the sofa and pulled off his coat, shoes and socks. Grimacing at his pale shivering feet, he covered them in towels then slumped on the sofa with the blankets wrapped tight around his shoulders. It took a while for his extremities to warm and the shuddering in his torso to stop. Then he closed his eyes and listened to the wind-blown snow pattering against the windows.

*

There were dreams of walking through the house to follow the smell of chocolate into a room that hadn't been there before. But when he entered the room there was nothing but a ragged, furred figure crouching in the corner, enshrouded by shadow, pawing carrots into its mouth. Then the figure finished eating, stood and turned around, but Feldman had already fled from the room.

*

Feldman woke sucking on air and swaddled in the blankets. His stomach gurgled with hunger.

The house was dark. Night had fallen outside. He rose on unsteady feet to look for some candles.

*

He found candles in a kitchen drawer. He lit them in the living room and drew the curtains. Then he sat down on the sofa and ate the two packets of crisps he'd taken with him from the car. He had half a bottle of Pepsi too, and took sips from it as he pondered what to do while the snowstorm seethed outside.

As the night wore on, the wind and snow flailing against the house, he slowly drifted into an exhausted sleep.

*

Feldman woke in the morning, desperate for a drink. He swigged from the Pepsi bottle until there were only dregs left, then decided to save what remained for later. A ravenous hunger burned in his gut. He craved chocolate and sweets. Longed for a decent sugar-rush.

He rubbed his face and scratched around his fleshy chin. He remembered fragments of a dream about a motionless figure with cone-shaped ears atop its head standing outside the front door, its bloated shape seen through the frosted glass, as though it was waiting for an invitation to enter the house. But he had the sense that the figure didn't need an invitation, because it already lived and belonged here.

Shaking off the memories of the dream, he pulled back the curtains from the living room window and looked out at the falling snow. Deep on the ground, covering the fields beyond the overgrown garden. And a sudden feeling of isolation and loneliness overcame him until he was hugging the blankets tighter around his shoulders and arms for what little comfort it offered him.

He turned away from the window, shuffling on sockless feet clad in damp shoes, and walked about the downstairs rooms to encourage the blood into his extremities and warm his heart. A suspicion that the bloated figure from his dream would be standing outside the front door was dispelled when he ventured into the hallway. He sighed with relief, thought himself foolish, and then realised that the little door under the stairs was ajar even though he hadn't opened it.

*

"It might just have come loose by itself," he muttered, more as a vague comfort to himself than anything else. But it hadn't worked, and he stood before the open door, hunched in his musty clothes and borrowed blankets, eyeing the darkness past the threshold under the stairs.

He returned to the living room and lit one of the candles, dripped wax onto a saucer and stood the candle in the wax until it held fast. Then he went back to the door under the stairs. He hesitated before he stepped through the doorway, the candle held out before him. He kept sniffling, and wiping his nose.

Past the threshold was a room no wider than the inside of a phone box. The smell of dust and rodent droppings. And, strangely, chocolate. That wasn't possible. Couldn't be possible. Saliva gathered at the back of his mouth.

There was an old wooden door to his left. It was stained black and would have been unseen in the dark if not for the candlelight. He pulled the door towards him then leaned forward, and the flickering flame near his face revealed a stone stairway descending into darkness.

Feldman swallowed. Took in a breath. Started down the steps.

*

He descended to a cramped basement and stood at the foot of the stairway, casting the candle about to light the scene before him. Stone walls cold to the touch. The dirt floor was cluttered with cardboard boxes filled with children's toys from decades ago. Plastic figures and stuffed animals tatty from age and wear, board games from the Seventies and Eighties, yo-yos and wooden spinning tops. Old water stains dirtied the boxes. Fluff balls drifted on the floor.

Feldman almost jumped out of his shoes when the candlelight revealed a pink tattered figure slouched upon a chair by the far wall. His heart climbed into his throat. He gasped then let out a relieved breath as the light gave the seated figure definition and showed that it was merely some forgotten rabbit costume meant for a fancy dress party. It had been propped upon the seat, and its legs dangled to the floor. Tall floppy ears. A blue bowtie around the neck. A round hole where the face would have been. Scraggly and ruffled, stained with dirt and other dried fluids.

Feldman wrinkled his nose. On the floor next to the chair was a long handled wicker basket of brightly coloured Easter eggs.

The candlelight threw shadows that danced and writhed on the walls.

He approached the rabbit costume with little steps that slowed as he reached its slumped form. The costume smelled musty and ripe, yeasty and vaguely meaty. He reached out and touched its matted fur then quickly pulled back, frowning and muttering, irrationally fearful that the costume would suddenly come to life and lunge for him with flapping arms.

He crouched to the basket and picked up one of the eggs. It was wrapped in red foil. Raised it to his face and sniffed. His mouth watered. He found a seam in the wrapping and pulled it back and peeled the foil from the egg. It was chocolate. He cracked a section of the egg and put a piece into his mouth and let it dampen upon his tongue. He closed his eyes as his taste buds fizzled with the sweet taste of the chocolate. It was exquisite. He chewed.

Before he realised what he had done, he had devoured the egg and there was only scrunched up foil in his hands. He was breathing hard, his heart beating fast with abnormal beats. A vague feeling of shame overcame him, like he'd just finished masturbating to a photo of a friend's wife.

He climbed the steps back to the room under the stairs, two Easter eggs cradled in the nook of one arm against his stomach.

*

Swaddled in the blankets on the sofa he gorged upon the two Easter eggs, and when he was finished his fingers were sticky with chocolate and his stomach ached with dull cramps.

He lay back on the sofa and closed his eyes, groaning softly. He smiled to himself and patted his rotund belly, listening to his guts gurgle and squirm.

*

He spent the rest of the day on the sofa, holding his stomach and licking smears of chocolate from around his mouth. The snowstorm continued and seemed like it would never end.

He fell asleep sometime before midday. A dream of hurrying through the snow towards a distant figure with its back turned to him. As he got closer he realised that the figure was wearing the tattered rabbit costume. The ears flapped in the wind. Feldman called out to the figure.

And the figure began to turn around.

*

Feldman opened his eyes and couldn't remember where he was until he saw the discarded tinfoil wrappers on the floor. The stomach ache had faded and he was hungry again.

He returned to the basement, licking his lips in anticipation. He fell upon the basket of eggs, tearing at the wrappers with his hands, stuffing chocolate into his busy mouth. When he had finished eating, there were no eggs left, and he wavered on his knees as the realisation hit him. There were tears in his eyes.

"No more chocolate," he whispered. "No more eggs. No more Easter." And he put his hands to his face and sobbed quietly. He lay down on the cold floor, his chest hitching with shuddered breaths, lamenting the empty wicker basket and the scraps of tinfoil.

*

When he came to he found himself on his knees, grasping the rabbit costume in his trembling hands and holding it to his face as he inhaled deep breaths like he once did with women's underwear when he was younger.

He dropped the costume and realised he had to leave the house.

*

Without a clue where to go, Feldman dressed hurriedly and went out into the storm to escape the house. And he wandered, hunched over against the snow that fell upon and against him, stumbling through the drifts that reached past his ankles. The wind bore teeth, pinching and swiping at him, roaring around him like the gathered voices of immense monsters.

He roamed and staggered for what seemed like hours, shivering in the terrible cold, hallucinating the faces of his parents and old friends. His vision down to no more than a yard past the furthest reach of his arms. He cried to the sky, sobbed to the ground, and implored the invisible gods of the fields to guide him to new shelter.

Close to collapse and on his knees, pulling his exhausted body through the snow, he emerged before a house. There was a moment of ecstatic relief and joy until he realised it was the house he'd fled hours ago.

The worst part for him was the renewed hunger for chocolate eggs.

He shouted and screamed, cursed every name he could pull from his mind. He experienced such a feeling of dread and futility that he broke down in tears. It took him quite a while to crawl to the house, rise to his coldness-numbed feet, and open the door to slip inside.

He dragged himself to the sofa in the living room and closed his eyes to the wailing of the wind outside.

*

In Feldman's dream, the figure turned around to regard him, and it was his own face he looked upon.

*

There was a chocolate egg on the coffee table when he woke. He stared at the thing for a short while and after very little consideration tore away the wrapping and consumed the egg with both hands stuffing it into his mouth. Afterwards he felt happier than he could ever remember.

He went down to the basement, giggling and rubbing his hands together like an excited child. The wicker basket had been replenished with Easter eggs. This made him cackle into his hands and dance a little dance of rapture.

He laughed and grinned as he pulled on the rabbit costume, and it fitted perfectly over his doughy limbs and bulging stomach. It warmed him, swelled his heart, and made him dizzy with glee. And when he was finished he stood on the stone floor, joyous at the wonderful thing he had become.

*

The storm had passed and the sky cleared to perfect blue in its wake. There was bright winter sunlight upon the land, and the snow melted and the ground began to thaw, like spring had arrived early.

Resplendent in the tattered rabbit suit, Feldman flung the front door open and dashed outside, giggling as he swung the wicker basket of Easter eggs in his hands. He cavorted in the sunshine, kicking through the receding snow, his eyes glazed over with idiot joy and his mouth covered in chocolate. Scrambling and pawing, dancing on the road, having the time of his life. And he never wanted it to end.

He was too busy spinning in a circle and whooping to hear the approaching rumble of a large engine.

*

The twenty-six tonne lorry was travelling too fast around the bend to stop in time when the man in the raggedy rabbit suit appeared in the road, throwing brightly coloured eggs around. The driver had been drinking. There wasn't time to brake.

The lorry hit the man with such force and speed that he was obliterated where he stood. He burst like a wet flesh-sack and showered the road with viscera, blood and tufty scraps of pink fur.

The lorry skidded to a halt. The driver climbed down from the cab. He looked around at what remained of the poor individual. He gasped at the round, wet object on the road.

The severed head of the man in the rabbit suit stared back at him, eyes open, ears floppy, with chocolate smeared around the manic grin of his mouth.

THE END

Bio

Rich Hawkins hails from deep in the West Country, where a childhood of science fiction and horror films set him on the path to writing his own stories. He credits his love of horror and all things weird to his first viewing of John Carpenter's THE THING when, aged twelve, he crept downstairs late one night to watch it on ITV. He has a few short stories in various anthologies, and has written one novella, BLACK STAR, BLACK SUN. His debut novel THE LAST PLAGUE was nominated for a British Fantasy Award for Best Horror Novel. Its sequel, THE LAST OUTPOST, was released in September 2015.

He currently lives in Salisbury, Wiltshire, with his wife, their daughter and their pet dog Molly. They keep him sane. Mostly.

On the Third day

By

Graeme Reynolds

"Get a move on!" Barrabas hissed to Simon. "We gotta be there and back before sunrise."

"I can't see a bloody thing!" the small man complained. "I've already stubbed my toe on a rock and I stepped in something that's gotten right into my sandal. I can feel it squishing around in there! Why can't we use the lantern?"

The larger man slapped his companion across the head. "Because then the guards would see us and arrest us for grave robbing! Look – I only need you to help move the stone, so can you please try to keep quiet and keep up until we get there?"

"Alright – but I hope you realize that this is really unpleasant. I think I stood in goat..." Simon stopped abruptly as the moon appeared from behind a cloud and revealed Barrabas's murderous expression. "I'll be quiet now," he muttered.

The moon bathed the landscape in a cool monochrome as the men slowly picked their way across the rocky slope. Occasionally one of them would lose their footing, and a small landslide of sandstone pebbles and fist sized rocks would cascade down the hillside.

Eventually they arrived at their destination. A large boulder leaned against the sheer wall of a small outcropping of rock, away from the path and shrouded in shadows.

"Right – we're here then. Let's get that boulder out of the way and get on with it" Barrabus said.

Simon's mouth fell open "It's bloody HUGE! How the hell are we going to move that?"

Barrabus leaned around to the side of the boulder and produced two large wooden poles, a grin spreading across his face.

"With these. Any more questions? No? Good."

Simon and Barrabus wedged the ends of the poles into a gap began to push.

"So why exactly are we robbing this grave?" Simon asked. "Is he an Egyptian immigrant who was buried with all of his money?"

"Na!" replied Barrabus. "He was a prophet."

Simon dropped his pole. "A prophet? A bloody prophet! I could go into town and find you a dead prophet in any backstreet between the fish market and the Thirsty Camel tavern."

"You don't get it do you – he had hundreds of followers. Rich followers. Do you have any idea how much money his sandals will be worth? Now shut up and push!"

The boulder began to move; slowly at first but then gaining momentum until it rolled free and bounced away down the hillside, gaining speed as it headed towards the town below.

"Shit!" said Barrabus, as the avalanche descended upon Jerusalem.

"Do you think that bastard Barnabus is guarding the east wall tonight?"

"I really hope so!"

The moon passed behind a cloud, and a wave of darkness swept across the hillside.

"Great – now I can't see anything AGAIN!"

"Shut up – I can hear something. Let me just light this lantern."

Simon's eyes strained against the curtain of darkness, willing them to see what lay beyond its veil. He could hear the sound of Barrabus searching in his pack and something else. A slow scraping sound like a sack of wheat being dragged across a dusty stone floor, followed by a short, sharp sound that seemed like a footstep.

The sounds were definitely getting closer. The long dragging sound followed by the lurching step.

"Can you hurry up with that lantern?"

"Almost got it...there!" Barrabas struck the flint and the lantern ignited.

Barrabas turned towards the cave and let out a small involuntary shriek. Standing right next to him was a tall, bearded man.

The man was around six feet in height, with long dark hair and was draped in a white funeral shroud. His eyes were milky, opaque orbs. A large centipede crawled out of his right nostril and fell to the floor. Blood stained the man's shroud, and a loop of intestine was visible through a large wound on his side.

Barrabas looked in horror at the creature before him and started to back away. The thing's arms shot out in front of him – searching and grasping the empty air until they connected with Barrabus's tunic. Its hands gripped tightly and it pulled itself towards the terrified grave robber, then sank its teeth into the man's neck.

Barrabas began to scream as he flailed wildly at his attacker. The creature responded by clenching its jaw and violently whipping its head from side to side. The skin on the grave robbers neck stretched and split – finally giving way as the creature tore its head back. A fine spray of arterial blood misted Simons face, staining his tunic a deep wet crimson and Barrabus fell to the ground – no longer screaming, but simply making a surprised gurgling sound as his essence drained away into the sand.

"What the..." Simon stammered, his stomach lurching and his legs suddenly becoming numb. He stumbled backwards, unable to take his eyes from his friend as the bearded man pounced upon him and tore a ragged hole in Barrabas's cheek with his teeth.

The heel of Simon's sandal caught on a small boulder and he fell backwards, arms flailing until he landed on the rock strewn hillside. A particularly large pointed rock fortunately prevented his head from striking the ground. Simon's eyes rolled back in his head and he passed into oblivion.

Simon slowly awoke. It was as if he was being pulled from somewhere warm and comfortable into a world of burning pain. He didn't want to wake up, but the terrible searing agony in his legs and abdomen would not let him sleep.

He opened his eyes and immediately wished that he hadn't. His legs were no more than bones, stripped of their flesh apart from a few fibers of muscle that had not yet been devoured. The strange bearded man and Barrabas had their hands deep into his stomach and were feasting on the strange bulging tubes that they were pulling out of the hole in his middle.

Realization combined with the terrible pain and Simon returned to reality. He started to scream. The scream was cut short however as his former friend reached into his chest cavity and tore Simon's lungs from his torso.

*

The sun was still low in the sky, but already the temperatures were soaring as the four figures left the east gate and started their journey.

"I still don't understand why we had to wait three days to go and move the body"

"He was very specific about it, John. I asked him the same question and he said that it was really important that we didn't go anywhere near the body until sunrise on the third day, otherwise, and I quote, 'Bad Things would happen.'"

"What kind of Bad Things?"

"I don't know – he started going on and I stopped paying attention. Something about demons inhabiting the empty shell I think, and it taking him three days to sort all the paperwork out. I was just nodding and smiling at that point. He wasn't making a great deal of sense."

"Do you have any idea what three days in a cave will do to a dead body? Can you begin to imagine what the smell is going to be like?"

"That's why we brought Mary with us." Peter nodded his head in the direction of the woman trailing behind the two men. She was talking to Mark, who was, in turn attempting to coax a belligerent looking donkey into motion with a carrot on a stick.

"She brought a load of spices with her, to try and cover the stink."

"Great" said John without much conviction, "instead of liquefying rotten corpse stench we get curried liquefying rotten corpse stench. That will be an improvement."

The group trudged on in silence, the heat from the sun robbing them of the energy to hold a conversation. The quiet only occasionally broken by sporadic cursing from Mark when the donkey decided to bite him or turn round and go back the way it had come from.

After an hour, the group arrived at the cave.

"Where's that boulder gone?" said John. "There was definitely a big boulder here".

"Like that one they were trying to move down by the east wall this morning?" said Mary. The one that came down the hill in the middle of the night and crushed that guard?"

Peter and John exchanged worried glances and hurried inside the open cave.

"Where are the other two?" panted Mark as he appeared over the crest of the ridge, physically dragging the donkey behind him.

Mary looked up from her nails, a bored expression on her face.

"Inside. I suppose they are going to go get the body or something. When exactly am I going to get paid for this?"

"I already told you. You will get paid when... hang on a second, where did all this blood come from?"

There was blood all over the dusty ground by the entrance to the cave. Several large puddles were thickening in the morning sun, along with areas that seemed to have been covered in a fine spray adjacent to the large pools. The air was thick with flies and a pungent coppery tang that was unmistakable. One of the pools had a wide trail leading away from it as if something had been dragged through it. Along the course of the trail were a number of small red and brown chunks that Mark really did not want to look too closely at.

Mary's eyes widened as she registered the scene before her, and, clamping a hand firmly over her mouth, ran for the nearest boulder.

"We'd better check this out, in case anyone's hurt" said Mark, but was only answered by the sounds of Mary being noisily unwell behind a large rock.

"Why don't I take a look" he mumbled to himself and set off to follow the trail, the donkey trotting along behind him quite happily now that he had let go of the reins.

The blood trail carried on for almost 100 yards, across the loose rock of the hillside and around a large outcrop of sandstone. Mark nervously peered around the rock and almost screamed as the donkey came up behind him and nudged him to one side so that it could get a better look.

The trail ended at a man, or what was left of him. His legs were no more than bones covered in strips of red sinew and his pelvis and waist were stripped of flesh up to his rib cage. This would have been disconcerting enough without the fact that the man was dragging himself along with his hands, down the hillside towards Jerusalem. As he clawed his way along something that looked suspiciously like his liver plopped out of his chest cavity onto the dusty ground.

"Erm... are you alright?" Mark asked.

The injured man looked over his shoulder and, on seeing Mark, turned and began to scramble up the hillside towards him.

The man didn't look much better from the front. His eyes were an opaque white colour, and dried blood was caked all around his mouth and chin. His teeth were stained bright red, and as he moved up the hillside (surprisingly quickly for someone with no legs, Mark thought), fresh blood welled up inside his mouth and streamed in rivulets down his face and neck.

"Maybe you should lie still..." Mark said, backing away from him

The man ignored him and, now only a few feet away, launched himself into the air at Mark. Something slithered from his open chest and landed with a squelching sound behind him in a wet, red heap.

Mark instinctively ducked to his left, and the creature landed next to the startled donkey, sinking his teeth into its foreleg and tearing off a long strip of fur and flesh.

The donkey let out long bray of pain and outrage, and, as John and Peter came hurrying around the sandstone outcrop, turned around and kicked its attacker firmly in the centre of his forehead, caving his skull in. Gray particles of brain matter oozed through the splintered bone and the ruined body finally lay still. The donkey kicked him again anyway, for good measure, and then fled down the hillside, leaving a cloud of dust and the receding sounds of angry braying in its wake.

John and Peter looked at one another.

"I think we might have a problem" Peter said.

*

Thomas sighed as he headed towards the market. The events of the last two days had been catching up with his friends and some of them were beginning to sound quite unbalanced.

"They should go away for a few days, have a nice long lie down away from the hot sun," he muttered. "I mean, I know we're all taking this hard, but to suggest he's come back from the dead and is wandering around Jerusalem – it's just bloody stupid!"

The market was now only a few streets away. Already the deafening noise of the place was growing in intensity – from a faint murmur a few streets back, to sounding like a hive of angry wasps that someone had kicked into a herd of camels. Thomas would catch the occasional scent of spices and animal excrement on the breeze.

He hated the market.

Thomas pushed his way out of the crowded street into an empty alley, immediately savouring the cool shade of the high walls. The alley was deserted apart from two men at the far end that were shambling in his direction. Thomas began to walk towards them, when he stopped and looked at one of the men.

"Is this a fucking wind up?" he said.

The men did not reply and instead carried on down the alley. Their heads were tilted at an odd angle, with their arms held out in front of them, clawing at empty air.

"Yeah – NICE ONE PETER!" he yelled, looking around. The bastards were all having a good laugh at his expense. They would pop over the top of the walls and point and laugh any second now.

Thomas hated it when they pointed at him and laughed.

"OK smart arse" he said to the man with the beard and the bloodstained white robe who was now only a few feet away from Thomas. "If you are REALLY him, show me the wound in your side from that big fucking spear they stuck you with."

The man lurched forwards, and put his hands on Thomas's shoulders. Thomas pushed his right hand into the side of the man, and his eyes widened with horror as it slid inside something cold, wet and slippery that felt like a squirming bucket of eels. He yanked his hand out, pulling the tubes out as he did. They began to unravel into a wet pile on the floor besides the man.

Thomas opened his mouth to scream, but before any sound could come, the bearded man drove his head forward and bit down into Thomas's tongue.

He squealed in pain, trying to push away from the strong arms that held him fast and those terrible, tearing teeth, but to no avail. The man that appeared to be his dead friend tore Thomas's tongue from his mouth, swallowing it in one go, before thrusting his head forwards towards his victim's throat.

*

The first thing that he was aware of was an agonising pain in his head and the crush of bodies around him. His stomach lurched, and he snapped open his eyes – immediately wishing he had not as the burning light of the sun shone into the room through the partly open shutter. There was a persistent banging on his front door that was making his head pound in time to it. He clambered over the two sleeping prostitutes on his bed and stumbled towards the door, kicking over a half full gourd of wine as he went.

"This better be good" he growled as he slid back the bolt.

Of all the things he had expected to see when he opened the door, the two worried looking men standing before him were pretty far down the list.

"Peter? John? What the fuck are you doing here?"

"Hello Judas. Can we have a word?"

*

The morning was taking on a rather surreal slant thought Judas as he took another sip of the strong coffee and looked up through bleary eyes at the two men before him.

"So what you are telling me is that he has come back to life and is now attacking the living – and when they die they also come back to life. Is that about right?"

"Basically yes" said Peter, his eyes cast down at the floor.

"When he spent all that time going on about life after death we didn't expect things to be quite so... literal" John chimed in.

"And you want ME to stop him?"

"Well, yes, if you wouldn't mind" said Peter, looking up with a hopeful expression on his face.

"Why the hell would I do something like that? Go and beat his head in yourself. He used to call you his rock – so go and find a big pointy one and get on with it."

"Well, the thing is... that wouldn't look very good from a public relations point of view. You already more or less killed him once, so all we are really asking is that you do it again. Just more permanently this time. Before things get out of hand."

"Thirty pieces of silver was your fee I believe" said John, holding up a small brown leather purse and jingling it in front of Judas's face.

Judas looked at the purse and sighed. "Bugger!" he said, taking it from Johns outstretched hands.

*

The sun beat down upon the heads of the three men crouched behind the wall.

Judas turned to his companions. "Did I mention that this is a bloody stupid idea?"

"It might be stupid, but it's the only idea we have. Anyway, it was YOUR idea!" said Peter. "Do you think we got them all?"

"Let me take a quick look" said John, and pulled himself up so that he could peer over the wall into the alley below. The sight made his stomach lurch.

There were more than fifty people in the alleyway, and all of them were missing parts of their bodies that would normally be considered important. Most had large sections of their throats missing, the wounds slowly dripping with thick black ichor. Others had limbs that had been stripped of their flesh or that were missing all together. Some of the worse ones however were the people whose internal organs had been torn from gaping holes in their stomachs and chests.

The people were wandering around in the tight alley, seemingly confused as to how to leave again. Wagons had been positioned at each end blocking off their escape routes. On catching sight of John's head peering over the wall, they moved almost as one towards him, their arms waving and grasping the air as they reached for the man. John squealed in terror and popped his head back down behind the wall once more.

"That looks like all of them" he said, "let's get on with this".

The three men lifted a large barrel of oil and heaved it over the wall. There was a small wet squelching sound as it landed on one of the undead without legs, followed by the splintering of wood as the barrel cracked open, spilling the oil across the ground.

Four more barrels followed in rapid succession, but as the men began to lift the final barrel, they heard the sounds of angry voices at the far end of the alley.

"You had better go and see what's happening" John said to Peter

Peter ran to where Mark was attempting to calm a growing crowd of people who were gathering around him.

"He is risen! Halleluiah!"

"Give us eternal life lord!"

"Look," Mark yelled above the cries of the crowd "There is nothing to see here, so why don't you just go home. I hear there is a good stoning on by the West Wall this afternoon? Why not go and see that instead?"

An overweight man with a grime encrusted beard shoved Mark in the chest. "Bollocks, he's trying to keep the eternal life to himself!"

"Get Him!" cried another man, and the crowd surged forward, hurling abuse and the occasional rock at Mark.

"No! You don't understand!" cried Mark as he fell to the ground. The mob ignored him and began to push the wagon clear of the alley way entrance, and, once the gap was large enough, pushed and shoved their way inside.

Beyond the makeshift barricades, the heads of the zombies slowly turned towards the commotion, and they lurched towards the fresh meat that was in turn, running directly towards them.

Mark, dazed and bruised from being trampled, was lifted to his feet by Peter. "Are you OK, Mark?"

"I'm fine. Only a couple of broken ribs, I think. What happened?"

Peter gestured past the wagon into the alley. "Take a look for yourself."

Both men gazed in horror at the carnage taking place. The people were running towards the undead hordes, throwing themselves into the mass of tearing teeth. The screams of those being slowly torn apart filled the air, and, as their ruined corpses then staggered to their feet, those still untouched by the dead pushed their way forward with greater determination. At the front of the pack, stood an all too familiar figure, covered in blood and holding two fists full of dripping red meat that he was cramming greedily into his mouth.

Mark and Peter exchanged glances. It was too late for anyone left alive in the alley now, and the numbers of the walking dead had more than doubled in the last few minutes. Soon there would be no stopping them.

"Light it up!" yelled Peter.

A small puff of smoke appeared from over the top of the wall, and Judas's head popped up briefly, before taking cover again. A flaming torch tumbled through the air, its arc almost seeming to be in slow motion, before it bounced off the far wall and landed in the throng of feasting corpses.

For a moment, nothing seemed to be happening. Peter and Mark looked at each other nervously. Then the oil ignited, and the barrels exploded.

The fireball expanded upwards and outwards – tearing along the narrow confines of the alleyway and rising over twenty meters into the air. The wagons at each end burst into flames and were blown over by the blast wave. Seconds later, fist sized chunks of meat began to rain down on Jerusalem.

A woman who had been trying to force her way to the mass of living dead picked herself up and looked at the now empty alleyway – empty that is, apart from the burning meat that plastered the walls and dripped from the roofs. She turned to Peter.

"But where is the lord?" she said.

"Erm…Heaven…that's right! He has ascended into Heaven!" he said to the woman.

He turned to Mark. "I think we may have to edit this bit for the book".

"Amen to that" Mark replied.

*

The donkey had run until it decided that it was far enough away from the annoying human that had dragged it up the mountainside, and the human that had bitten it. The donkey still could not believe it. It was supposed to bite humans, not the other way around!

The throbbing in its leg had gotten worse and it was feeling quite unwell. Its mouth was dry and the water it had drunk from a nearby stream had not made it feel any better. Eventually, it decided to lie down in the shade of an olive palm and have a long sleep.

The donkey lay on the hard ground and tried to sleep. Its breathing became shallow, and eventually it stopped all together. Flies gathered around the donkey's corpse.

The moon was rising over the desert as the Donkey unsteadily got to its feet. It wanted to bite something, it decided. It wanted to bite something HARD!

It turned its milky, opaque eyes to the sky and let out a long menacing bray, before heading off towards the small human settlement in the valley below.

THE END

Bio

Graeme Reynolds has been called many things over the years, most of which are unprintable. By day, he breaks computer programs for a living, but when the sun goes down he hunches over a laptop and thinks of new and interesting ways to offend people with delicate sensibilities. He lives somewhere in England with a random cat that seems to have decided to move in with him.

Graeme is the author of the massively successful High Moor series, that is widely acknowledged as the best werewolf horror series in existence (according to his mum) and owns Horrific Tales Publishing, a well respected UK based small horror press.

http://www.facebook.com/horrifictales/
http://www.graemereynolds.com
http://www.horrifictales.co.uk
http://www.amazon.com/gp/product/B016IF0DH0/

Easter Eggs

By Chantal Noordeloos

The rain drummed down on the dented silver Ford Taurus SHO as it turned off the German highway onto a small country road. The car, like the road, had seen better days, and Polly Green wished –not for the first time that day—that she had stayed in Los Angeles. She glanced at Lukas, her fiancé, who was staring at the road with a deep wrinkle across his brow.

Everything had gone so fast. She and Lukas had met less than six months ago, at a party of a mutual friend. There had been a spark between them from the moment their eyes met. *Like magic.*

He was perfect in her eyes. Sweet, handsome, a little clumsy at expressing himself –English wasn't his first language—and he adored her. They mostly spoke English with each other, though Polly could understand a fair bit of German, thanks to her grandmother. She knew her *Oma* would have loved Lukas. Even if she might not have approved of how fast their relationship was developing.

After dating for four months, Polly found out she was pregnant, despite the precautions they had taken. Teetering on the edge of a panic attack, she hadn't been sure how to tell him. When she finally worked up the courage, Lukas had surprised her by sinking to one knee, and asking if she would marry him. It couldn't have been more perfect.

There had been some doubts in those first days. How well did she know this man she was about to spend the rest of her life with? But now, two months later, she realized it was the right decision. Lukas was a dream come true, and she really wanted this child more than anything in the world.

Her hand touched her flat stomach. It wouldn't be long now before she started to show. She already suffered from extreme morning sickness. The horrible overwhelming nausea would hit her at random times; it was crippling. At home, Lukas would make her his own herbal remedy that he claimed was good for the baby and would aid against her nausea. It never helped, but she drank it anyway; he tried so hard to help. As if summoned by her thoughts, a wave sickness flowed through her, but she'd already made Lukas stop at Gorlitz half an hour ago and didn't want to bother him again. Besides, they were almost at their destination.

Lukas wanted to introduce his fiancé to his family and tell them all the good news about their baby in person. It would be perfect to spend Easter in Germany, he assured her. They had some wonderful Easter traditions. She had always wanted to go to Germany, and Lukas promised they'd visit her grandmother's birth town too. She would have shared his enthusiasm if she didn't feel so damn ill and tired all the time.

Aside from the nausea, the hormones gave her terrible nightmares, which made sleeping problematic. When she closed her eyes the images of an old woman forcing her gnarled hand –cracked and brown as if it were made out of wood—into her womb and ripping the delicate baby out haunted her. The old woman held the undeveloped child in front of her, all limp and alien looking, and she laughed before she slipped the fetus between her cracked lips, letting it lie on her tongue before chewing.

The nightmares toyed with her mind, leaving her frazzled and clinging to sanity. The last thing she wanted to do right now was travel to a strange place with strange people. She'd hinted at maybe going at some later date, but Lukas, in his excitement, hadn't picked up on the signals.

Polly hadn't pushed the matter, though in the end, due to her health, they had gone a few days later than planned. She would manage, she told herself; things could be worse.

Lukas took a right and drove through a filthy looking village. Garbage littered the streets, and uninspired graffiti decorated the walls of the grey houses. There was something bleak about the whole place. A hint of relief washed over her when they didn't stop in the village, but drove further North-East.

*

The rain stopped, as if by magic, when they drove onto the Opfergabe family estate.

They drove onto a muddy lane, and Polly held her breath at the sight of the land. It was mid spring, frost had only left the air a few weeks ago, but the meadow around the farm already bloomed with the most beautiful flowers. An almost luminous green covered the trees and grass, as the rays of sunlight touched them, turning the remaining raindrops into sparkles.

It's like driving straight into a fairy story, Polly thought.

They drove past an apple orchard, where pink and white blossoms kissed the deep brown wood of the branches.

"This place is beautiful," Polly gasped, her face only an inch away from the glass. She felt like a little girl pressing her face against the show window. "You told me it would be, but I never even imagined."

"This is why I wanted to come here. Our land is very special. I promise you, it will look even better after Easter." Lukas winked at her.

She laughed, "I don't see what difference two days would make?"

A smile curled around his lips, but he didn't explain himself.

"Did you grow up here?" she asked.

"Yes, I lived here until my late teens and helped out," he said in his strong accent, "I'm very much a part of this land." He pushed his round glasses further up his narrow nose, and shot her a crooked smile. "Many of my seed has been spilled here."

This time she laughed despite herself. A mild sense of shame made her cover her mouth with her hand.

"Did I say something funny?"

"A little," she admitted. "You might want to rephrase that last sentence. It just sounds..." she struggled to find the words to explain it, "... it sounds a bit dirty."

"Soil is very dirty," he said, nodding in agreement.

"Not that kind of dirty," she giggled. He frowned, and shot her a questioning look. Polly didn't know how to explain, so she just bit her lip.

A grand house loomed up in front of them. Instead of a small cottage, or a typical farmhouse, a mansion greeted them.

"This is your family's farmhouse?" Polly asked, her eyebrows arched. "Is your family royalty?"

Lukas smiled and shook his head. "No, but the farm has provided for my family with great wealth over the years. Our land is fertile and business is good. The house was built by my great grandfather. He liked to show off his riches." He leaned a little towards her, barely taking his eyes of the road as he spoke in a conspiratorial low voice: "I don't think my mother is comfortable with any of the splendor. She is a little more... humble."

He stopped the car near what looked like the back door of the large building.

"Mutti!" Lukas shouted as he opened the car door. Then he continued to speak in German. "We are here, and I have brought you a great surprise."

The back door, a big wooden monstrosity, opened and revealed a shrunken old woman. The sight of her made the blood drain from Polly's cheeks; she couldn't help thinking of her dream. Behind the old woman was a younger one, who obviously was Lukas' mother. Both women had hard faces. Stern grey eyes stared at her. Polly stepped out of the car, her nausea lessening as she breathed in the fresh air. She met the younger woman's eyes.

"Hi..." Polly said, trying to keep the tremble from her voice, "I'm Polly." She held out her hand, but the younger woman stood rigid with crossed arms. When Polly moved her hand to the older woman, she just spat on the ground and said, in harsh German: "Does she speak German?"

"Well enough to understand you," Lukas said, "But holding a conversation is... problematic."

Two pairs of grey eyes looked at her with undisguised contempt. She couldn't help but feel an instant dislike for both women.

"I can learn," Polly said in heavily accented German, but inwardly she thought: *Not that I would have to, since I'll be living in the States, far away from you people.*

The old woman eyed her suspiciously, and Lukas' mother rolled her eyes.

"You better show her the room we have prepared," the mother said to Lukas. "We're very busy making the last preparations for tomorrow's Easter ritual." She turned around without so much as hugging her son, and walked back into the house, the older woman on her heels.

"Is your mother mad at me?" Polly whispered. She thought Lukas' may have told his mother that she was pregnant before they were married. Perhaps the woman thought that Polly was 'that kind of girl'.

"No, you are not to worry. My mother is just a bit, how do you say it?"

"Curtly?" she offered.

"Yes, exactly... curtly." He tried to hide a smile. "She means well. You'll have to forgive her. We Opfergabers are just a little... different. She'll warm up to you." He winked at her.

"Not all of you. You're not like that."

"I've always been a bit different." He kissed her forehead.

Lukas led her into the big house, his hand gently on the small of her back, and whispered in her ear: "You will love the Easter Ritual. It's my favorite thing about being home. It's really the most magical time of year in this place."

Inside the house, Polly caught herself holding her breath. They had entered through the dark kitchen. There were Easter eggs everywhere. Hanging from the rafters, placed in large bowls on the counters, and dangling from thin twigs placed in large vases. There were hundreds of them, each decorated with a different ornate pattern of symbols. She reached out, gently touching the tip of her finger to one of the colorful shells, marveling at the intricate artwork on them.

"We will bury the twelve eggs before sundown," Lukas' mother said in German, holding up a large wooden bowl, "So hurry. I want you there for this. You can bring her too." She nodded towards Polly, who was mesmerized by the eggs the woman was holding. The eggs were even more ornate than the ones around them, decorated with vibrant colors and rich gold. For a moment, Polly imagined she could hear the eggs palpitate, like hearts, but she knew she was just imagining things. The sight of the things made her uneasy.

Lukas must have noticed something, because he looked at her with worry in his eyes. "Do you need to lay down?"

"I wouldn't mind."

He took her hand and led her upstairs, to a small austere room. There was a single bed, which was made up with a grayish white sheet tucked tightly at the corners and an embroidered off-white throw spread on top. A round table and one chair stood to one side of the room, and on the other side was a sink. The window was narrow, and the faded blue curtain hung half closed, letting in only a sliver of light.

"There were a lot of Easter eggs down there, are you going to hide them all?" Polly asked, as she took her coat off and put it on the chair.

He laughed. "Yes, we will hide some of them for the children of the village to come find. They always come Easter Monday, and then bring their loot to the breakfast table. But that's not the main part of the ritual." Gently he maneuvered her to sit on the bed. The bedspread was coarse and cold to the touch. "Most of the eggs you saw are just decoration. We use them to cheer up the house, and it is believed there is good fortune in decorating your house with eggs. The twelve eggs my mother was holding—one for each month of the year—will be buried all over the field today. According to superstition, the eggs will provide both the land and my family with health and fertility. Now, those twelve eggs are no ordinary eggs." His warm grey eyes, so different from those of his mother and grandmother, sparkled. "We use the Ukrainian tradition of Pysanka, which is a wax-resist method, to decorate the eggs. My family is a mixture of Ukrainian and German heritage," Lukas explained, "and the Pysanka is a strong part of our identity, as it is with many Ukraines. *My* people believe there is a little magic in the ritual, and we will each make a small sacrifice during the egg painting."

"Sacrifice?" Polly couldn't keep the worry from her voice.

"It's not a big one," Lukas laughed. "Everyone's sacrifice is their own choice and they all do something different. Some will mix a drop of blood into the wax, while others will give up some money, or donate a lock of hair. Just little things. I promise you there is no reason to worry."

"You didn't make one of the eggs…" she said, frowning. "Was it important to you?"

He touched her cheek with gentle fingers and smiled. "Yes, this tradition is very important to me." He winked at her. "Don't worry, I get to make an egg too. There is a thirteenth one, and it's quite an honor that I get to make it, for it's the most important of all. We bury it at midnight tonight, which will give me plenty of time to decorate it."

"Can I help?" she asked and he beamed at her.

"Yes, you can, but I will show you how tonight. First I need you to rest a little, so you can be there for the first ritual. We want to bury the eggs before the evening."

"I hope I feel up for it." Her stomach churned, and the thought of running through a field, burying eggs, wasn't appealing.

"I'll make you my famous drink." He snapped his fingers, and stood.

About ten minutes later he returned, holding a large stone mug. She took it from him, holding it under her nose.

"This is not your famous drink," she said, as the vapor hit the top of her lip. There was something sickly sweet in the scent of it.

"This is my *mutti's*. It's even better. Her *krauter*..." he looked at her questioningly.

"Herbal," she translated.

"Her herbal skills far outdo mine." He smiled, but the look in his eyes was intense, as if he were afraid she would reject the drink his mother made. Carefully she took a sip, moistening her lips more than anything else. The brew tasted less sweet than it smelled, but it really made her stomach turn.

"It's delicious," she lied, "It's very hot, though. I'll have to let it cool off."

"Just make sure you drink it" He kissed her forehead, "I'll be downstairs for the preparations, so you rest, okay. I'll pick you up in an hour, when we're ready to go into the fields."

"Okay." She lay down on the narrow bed, and shot him a smile. He blew her a kiss and left the room. She glanced around, her eyes resting on the sink. Without hesitation she got up and quickly tipped the hot brew over, and washed it down with water. Her hand rubbed the last few drops of evidence away, before she turned to the narrow window. It gave a beautiful view over the lands, and she could see the farm lands to the back of the house. People were already getting ready for the celebrations, it seemed. At least a dozen men, women and children walked around, carrying boxes and baskets.

The nausea hit her hard, and she decided to lie down.

*

She had drifted off, slipping into one of her dark dreams. As the nightmarish old woman, whose face was never quite clear, cut open the skin of her stomach with one long dirty fingernail, a strong hand grabbed her shoulders and woke Polly. She sat up in her bed, startled. It was difficult to shake the nightmare off, as she stared at the cold face of Lukas' grandmother. She almost screamed at the sight of her, convinced for the briefest of seconds the old woman had come to take her baby. She needed a moment to snap out of it, and with all the strength she could muster, Polly forced a smile, trying to think of something to say.

"Hello..." She realized Lukas had never properly introduced them, and Polly didn't know what to call the woman.

"Here," the woman said in brusque German, "Drink this." She pushed another mug of the same concoction in Polly's hand. "Then you must get up. We're going to perform the Easter ritual in a few minutes."

"Th... thank you," Polly stammered. The old woman glowered at her. Polly put the cup to her lips and pretended to drink, but as before, she only wet her lips. The woman nodded satisfied, and walked out of the room. Polly waited until she heard the footsteps retreat, and dumped the rest of the liquid down the sink, leaving a bit more than a sip in the cup. She waited a few minutes, giving herself enough time to have drunk the beverage, before going downstairs.

A strong smell of roast pork hit her nostrils, and Polly cursed how sensitive her pregnancy made her to scents. Normally she enjoyed the aroma of roasting meat, although this did smell as if it was on the cusp of burning. Her stomach turned but she held her own as she made her way down.

Lukas greeted her at the bottom of the stairs, and she handed him the cup.

"I couldn't finish all of it," she said. He looked in the cup and smiled.

"We're about to go into the field," Lukas nodded towards his mother, who was holding a basket with the eggs. Next to her stood a fair-haired young woman, a few years younger than Polly, with watery blue eyes. Polly guessed she was a cousin or something, since she didn't resemble the others. Perhaps just a family friend, Polly thought. She didn't like the way the girl looked at her, the pale blue eyes were filled with loathing. *Great, another German woman who hates my guts.*

Polly realized she'd had enough of this place, and couldn't wait to go home again. She didn't like anyone she had met so far, and she didn't want to stay here anymore. She would talk to Lukas after the ritual.

"Follow me," Lukas' mother said, and she led them all outside. There were dozens of people all around, and it looked as if most—if not all—of the neighboring village had come for the ritual. Most people were still in their work uniforms, as if they had just dropped what they were doing before they came. The butcher's apron was covered in dark red stains, which made Polly's skin crawl. There were a couple of police officers walking about, which was oddly comforting.

"How are you feeling?" Lukas whispered.

"Uncomfortable," she admitted. "It's very different from anything I'm used to."

"Yes, it must be." Lukas wrapped his hand around hers and squeezed her fingers. "This must be quite the culture clash."

"In America, this would be a great scene for a horror movie," she said, nodding at the sinister-looking butcher.

Lukas laughed. "I can imagine. Though, in the defense of my culture, there have been plenty of moments in America that have felt equally weird to me."

She smiled. Of course it had. That was all it was, they were having a cultural difference, and she was having problems with dealing with it. No biggie. She was just being pregnant and melodramatic. Even an innocent Easter tradition. It wasn't as if they were burying anything scary. They were just eggs.

"Don't worry," Lukas kissed her on the cheek, "This will only be for a few days. Then we go back to America, and you can frighten me with your mother."

She giggled. Her mother wasn't as stern as Lukas' mom, but Danielle Green was a whole different kind of scary.

In a long procession, of perhaps a hundred people, or more, they walked towards the fields. The people all looked rather glum. There was no happy chatting or laughter, Polly noticed, and it made the event feel more like a funeral than festivities.

Lukas guided Polly along and told her where to stand. People glanced at Polly, their solemn faces eyes filled with hints of curiosity. No one came up to make acquaintance, and after the faux pas of offering Lukas' mother her hand, Polly didn't dare to introduce herself. None of them seemed particularly friendly, anyway.

The ritual was an odd one, and Polly wasn't sure why Lukas was so enamored with it. She, along with most of the attending people, stood in a large circle. They were each given a sprig of what looked like an evergreen bush. The waxy leaves pricked her skin.

Seven men and six women, Lukas, his mother and grandmother among them, stood in the center of the circle creating their own circle. Lukas stood dead center, and was handed the basket. He, in turn, handed an egg to each of the twelve who surrounded him. It was Lukas' mother who spoke. Her words were so fast, and she was far away enough, that Polly found it difficult to follow what she said. She heard snippets, and only when the woman was facing her direction.

The mother held up her egg. She yelled something, then turned. Polly gathered that the eggs were an offering to some Goddess called Eostre.

It surprised her that Lukas' family were pagans. He had never told her about this. His mother kept talking about the offering. There was something about giving life to gain life, or the circle of life, or something like that, Polly only half listened. A wave of nausea hit her again, and she swallowed hard to keep the acidic taste down. Her tongue stuck to her dry palate.

The ritual took forever. The twelve people poked sticks into the soil, trying to find the right spot to plant the eggs. Finally, they each dug a deep hold and placed their egg inside. When this was done, all the people in the circle helped to cover the eggs with dirt. With glum expressions they stomped the dirt in place, though they looked rather half hearted about the whole thing. Polly just stood to the side, watching everything.

Lukas slid a hand around her waist from behind. "Tonight will be our turn," he said. "Tonight is special."

"Do you mind if I lay down again?" Polly said. "Your family must think me horribly rude, but I just feel so sick."

"I think it's a great idea," Lukas said. "I'll have mother fix you one of her drinks."

"No, that's okay…"

He squeezed her tighter. "I insist."

*

She didn't drink the new beverage –which was different from the previous two—either. Instead she just fell back on the hard bed, and closed her eyes for a moment. She dozed, not quite sleeping, but when her door opened she kept her eyes closed, pretending to be sleeping. It could be his grandmother again.

"Is she asleep?"

Polly didn't recognize the woman's voice, so she did her best not to move a muscle.

"She should be. I gave her enough to sedate an elephant." It was Lukas' mother's voice. Polly struggled in her pretence to sleep.

"Is that not harmful for the baby?"

"No. The baby will be fine. I know what I'm doing. We will put the foetus in the final egg, so we can bury it at midnight." Footsteps indicated that they had entered the room. "Honestly, why did you bring us one who speaks German? I had to censor myself in my own house."

"I slept with six girls, mother. She was the only one who was pregnant on time. This is not an easy task." To her horror, Polly recognized Lukas' voice. Her blood ran cold.

"I hate that you have to sleep with these women," the unknown woman said.

"I'm sorry, my love, but there is no other way." Lukas let out a snort. "Do you think I enjoy sleeping with these American pigs?"

The words cut straight into Polly's soul.

"Why can't you just impregnate one of the captured girls?"

"They are too sickly and poor. My sacrifice needs to be a more significant one and I can't risk leading the wrong people to this farm. This stupid sow's family thinks she's somewhere in Berlin with a man called Lukas Opfergabe. They'll never find her."

"This is not the time or the place for this discussion," Lukas' mother intervened. "We won't have much time to extract the fetus. I need you to go see if the oven is clear yet, so we can put her body in there when we're done. Clean out any of the remaining bones. Officer Kruger will know what to do with them. I will help grandmother prepare."

Polly didn't open her eyes until she was sure they had left the room. Her mind was spinning, her heart was pounding and part of her wanted to curl up and just cry, but she refused to give in to that part. She wasn't the kind of girl that gave up, and her survival instinct kicked in. She had to run. A panicked voice in the back of her mind wondered where she could go. She didn't have the keys to the rental car, and she didn't dare look for them.

She couldn't go to the authorities, since they were most likely involved as well. The only thing she could think of was getting out of the house. She would make up the rest as she went along. As she slipped on her coat, she put her hands in her pockets for her phone and wallet, only to find them empty. Lukas must have taken her belongings, just in case. She took a deep breath to fight the panic. Nausea made her stomach turn, but there was no time to give into it, not if she wanted to live.

The window was narrow, but wide enough to let her squeeze through.

Not bad, for an American pig, she thought bitterly. She banished the thought of Lukas' betrayal from her mind. There would be time to worry about him later, now all she could focus on was her escape.

Her room was only on the first floor, so the drop wasn't too high. She had once been the top of the cheerleading pyramid, in her high school days, so this was barely a challenge. She scanned for a good place to get down, away from any potential downstairs windows. The last thing she wanted was to have any of those psychos see her leave. With trembling knees, she made her way further down the ledge, then carefully lowered herself.

She pulled her dark coat over her blond hair and ran in the direction of the road. The sound of an approaching car made her veer off her path. She couldn't risk getting seen by anyone. Not until she was at a safe distance from both the farm and the village. She considered running across the meadow, but the idea of being out in the open frightened her. Instead, she ran towards the large barn that stood off to the west of the farm. It looked pretty abandoned, and would provide her with at least some protection until she had figured out a better way of escape.

Please, God. Don't let anyone be inside.

There were no lights, which was a good sign. She hurried around to the door and peered inside. It was very dark, but Polly couldn't detect any movement, so she took her chances and slipped inside. She wished she could just stay there, at least until it was light, but she knew she'd have to run under cover of darkness. The only question was... when would she risk it? Outside she heard shouts that made her heart race. *They already know I'm gone. That was faster than I had hoped.* She suddenly regretted hiding in the barn; if only it was further away. *What was I thinking?* For a moment she considered sneaking out, but she heard voices outside and couldn't determine how far away they were.

Quickly, and as quietly as possible, she made her way to the back of the barn. The darkness hid the details from her, but she could see the outline of what looked like a pile of hay. Then she moved around the pile, overwhelmed by the strong sour scent of the dried grass, looking for a way to get in. She noticed a dim light shining through the crack of a hidden door. Someone on the other side made a hushing sound, and the light went out.

Whoever is in there must be hiding too...

In a moment of desperate insanity, Polly pulled open the door. She didn't know what she thought she would find, or if she put herself in more danger, but had to find out.

Inside was darkness now, and she heard a whimper.

"It's not them," a female voice whispered in German. "She's not one of them."

"She must be the sacrifice," another girl whispered back.

"Please," Polly said, in her best German. "I need help. They're trying to kill me."

There was a sound of a match striking stone, and a small flame caused Polly to shield her eyes. The flame lit a candle, and then another.

"They will find you in here eventually. There is nowhere you can run." A dirty face, hovering over the candle, looked at her through matted hair. "They own everything and everyone around here."

"Others have tried to run over the years," the second girl said. Polly counted four girls.

"Who are you?"

"We are part of next year's victims," the first girl said. "We lost our babies too soon, so we couldn't be sacrificed."

"They wanted to take your babies too?" Polly said. Her fingers caressed her stomach with a light touch.

"They put the babies in the eggs. They rip them from your womb, and then they kill you—chop you up and burn your body parts. I don't know how they get the babies in the eggs... it must be some kind of magic," a third, equally dirty, girl muttered. "Then they bury the eggs as a sacrifice.

"That's... horrible..." Polly raised her hand to her mouth. "And no one has ever tried to stop them? No one has ever come looking?"

"W don't know... but I don't think so," said the first woman. "We only know what happened to the previous girls. Maybe she knows...?" She pointed at the darkest corner.

"Only one way to stop them... break the ritual." An older voice said, and a woman of undeterminable age, sat forward. The light hit her face. Polly wondered if this woman had been pregnant too.

"How do I do break the ritual?"

"Smash all the eggs, kill the babies inside."

"Are you telling me the babies in the eggs are still alive?" Polly asked, mortified.

"Yes, very much so. Not only are they alive now, but they stay alive after they're buried. They feed the land, and it will feed them in return. The children become part of it; they grow into trees, foliage, richer soil, you name it. But they stay alive until that which they are connected to dies." The old woman gave her a bitter smile, showing a row of rotten teeth. "I tried to stop them once. Couldn't deal with it anymore, all that murder. I've ripped the unborn from the bellies of their mothers. The blood that sticks to my hands will never be washed off." She looked at her filthy hands. "They couldn't kill me when I tried to stop them, so instead they locked me in here, with the victims. My own sister..."

"You want *me* to kill those babies?" Polly's knees threatened to buckle; she thought of her own baby. "I could never..."

"Then you'll die, and they'll take your baby." The woman shrugged. "Killing them is your only hope. And you best make up your mind fast. The infants will be part of the land at midnight. That's when she wakes... the lady of the soil."

"The Goddess they were sacrificing to?" Polly said, "Eoster, or something? Isn't she meant to bring life to all?"

"Ha," the woman let out a bitter laugh. "She doesn't give life, stupid girl... she takes it, and converts it." The woman let out a sharp laugh. "Gods can do many things, but they can't grant life. That's all a lie. That's why we humans are so important to them, the life we create is so powerful." She shook her head. "You better hurry. Your time is running out. It's almost midnight, and it'll be a challenge to find all the eggs.

"Go," encouraged the first girl. "If you stop this... you could save us all."

"Why don't you come?" Polly asked, "We'd have more chance finding the eggs if there's six of us." It would be less scary if she didn't have to go alone.

The girl shook her head and held the candle in such a way that it illuminated her legs. Polly held her breath. Bones protruded from the skin of the broken, doll-like, legs, which were cleaner than the rest of the girl, so someone must have cared for her. The wounds had healed, badly, and it was obvious girl would never walk again. Polly looked at the other girls; their legs were all broken too. All except the woman.

"No need for legs," the girl said bitterly. "Go."

Polly didn't want to look at the girls anymore. She didn't want to be one of them, nor did she want anyone to take her babe.

"I'll come with you," the older woman said. "I can help."

"They didn't break your legs... why didn't you stop the ritual yourself?"

"Because I was afraid."

Polly nodded. She understood. She would rather run too, but she wasn't sure if she could get away.

The older woman led the way out of the barn, and they both ran towards the large field. "Isn't everyone at the field now?" she whispered.

"They're still looking for you, girl. Besides... the thirteenth egg isn't buried in the field, but somewhere... else..."

There was something eerie about this land that looked so beautiful during the day. The wind whispered menacingly, and the moon covered everything with a cold silver light that banished the darkness from the land.

It took her a while to find the spot where she believed one of the eggs was buried. The soil was still loose, and came away easily as she dug frantically. She almost threw the egg aside, but she caught herself just in time. It lay in the palm of her hand—white in the light of the moon—and radiated heat. A mixture of fear, inquisitiveness and disgust rose in her all at once, as she put pressure on the egg with her thumbs. The shell cracked under the weight, and Polly peeled it away, driven by her own morbid curiosity.

In her hand, warm and covered in some sort clear sack filled with mucus, lay a half-developed baby. It wasn't quite an embryo anymore, it looked too human for that, but it wasn't fully formed either. The translucent skin showed black spots where its lungs were. All its bones were visible as dark lines. Her baby would look something like this, too. The hormones raged through her body, and crippling Polly at the sight of it. The baby moved in her hand, not yet dead. The thought of having to kill it was too much for her. She knew she had to do it, but she just needed a moment. The old woman grabbed the baby from her hand, held it up, and squeezed. Blood oozed over her hand, and Polly yelped in terror and sadness.

"It had to be done," the old woman said. "Find the next one."

They never had the chance. Something happened to the land. Polly couldn't quite describe it, but it felt almost as if some invisible force rippled through everything. It was as if the world around her was waking up, as if it was becoming aware.

"You're too late," a familiar voice said in perfect English. Polly turned around to look at the dark figure of Lukas' mother. "It's midnight, and the children are now part of the land. There is nothing you can do to stop it."

"We killed one of them, your ritual is broken," Polly said.

"Its death is unfortunate, but not all is lost" The woman shook her head. "Do you think I would let you stop us? Risk the wrath of Eostre? You have no idea what is at stake here. Not just for us, but for all those who depend on us."

"You're killing people…"

"Our children all grow up healthy. Those we provide for don't suffer poverty, illness or anything bad in their life. They are blessed and filled with luck. We save hundreds of people at the cost of thirteen. I say those odds are good. Where you come from people kill more people for less."

"I stopped you," the other woman said in German.

"You've stopped nothing, sister," Lukas' mother said. "I still have my sacrifice."

"You won't have enough," Polly said, scrambling to her feet.

"Yes, I have," the woman said calmly. "I don't have to sacrifice babies. The only reason I pick the unborn fetuses is because I'm not as cruel as you think I am. The children I take don't have a consciousness yet. Their existence really doesn't change when I plant them from one womb to another. The death I give the mothers is merciful and fast."

"I... I don't understand." Polly wondered if her legs could hold her, or if they would buckle.

"To put something with a consciousness in the ground, would be condemning them to the worst of hells. They would be captured between life and death, in pain, and aware of it, until that which they are linked to dies. Imagine becoming part of a tree? They can live for hundreds of years... some even thousands. You'd be trapped under the soil, in pain, for all that time. There would be no crying for help."

"That's... sick..." Tears ran across her cheeks.

"The fetuses don't know any better." Lukas' mother said softly, "They simply become a part of it all. But you...."

"I won't let you kill me..." Polly said, and she clenched her fists.

"I don't intend to kill you, silly girl. Haven't you been listening." The woman took a deliberate step back, her eyes no longer fixed on Polly, but at something behind her. "The Goddess needed two more lives. Your baby is the twelfth sacrifice, and you are the thirteenth."

The snapping sound of twigs made Polly turn and, to her horror, she stood eye to eye with the land... or at least something that had come from it; something that had shaped itself into a woman. Her face was hideous. Instead of skin, it was covered with soil, in which insects crawled restlessly. Wooden roots had made a skeletal frame, and her skull-like face had a feral mouth filled with rows of sharp teeth. The smell of wet soil and clay hung pungent in the air. The thing reached out to Polly with wooden claws.

The roots, sharp as needles, which were shaped as ribs, legs, arms, even veins, shot out at her, penetrating Polly's soft skin, pushing inside of her like wiggling maggots. Polly didn't even have time to scream, as the creature pulled her inside of her. Polly struggled, but the woman melted into the ground, dragging her along. Every nerve sang with pain as the earth applied pressure to Polly's body, breaking all her bones, tearing her lungs to shreds, mixing flesh with earth. Every orifice filled with dirt, preventing her from screaming. How she was still alive was beyond her. Something dark and hard pushed against her eyeballs, bursting them, so that the liquid mixed with the earth. Each drop that spilled out was still part of her. Her brain, mangled as it was by roots and the pressure of dirt, still functioned, still thought. The mother had been right, this was a true form of Hell. Everything happened slowly, deliberately. Her body branched out, as if she was made of nothing but roots herself. She would grow, she realized, and be part of this land –while at the same time, she would never truly belong. The baby in her stomach stirred. She was more one with it now than she ever had been, of every move it made. It would grow too, and be part of her and part of the strange creature that had swallowed them both. What remained of Polly could sense the other babies too. There were thousands of them, some hundreds of years old. She even sensed some of the dead ones, that hadn't quite rotted away yet.

An overwhelming sadness came over Polly's remains, and she wished she could have just died in her bed. If only she could be a corpse in an oven, so that her torment would end. But there was no end to her torture, she wasn't even sure what she would become, what her role would be. If she could have, she would have cried. Instead, she tried to pray.

Please, God... don't let me turn into a tree.

THE END

Bio

Chantal Noordeloos lives in the Netherlands, where she spends her time with her wacky, supportive husband, and outrageously cunning daughter, who is growing up to be a supervillain. When she is not busy exploring interesting new realities, or arguing with characters (aka writing), she likes to dabble in drawing.

In 1999 she graduated from the Norwich School of Art and Design, where she focused mostly on creative writing.

There are many genres that Chantal likes to explore in her writing, but her 'go to' genre will always be horror. "It helps being scared of everything; that gives me plenty of inspiration," she says.

Chantal likes to write for all ages, and storytelling is the element of writing that she enjoys most. "Reading should be an escape from everyday life, and I like to provide people with new places to escape to, and new people to meet."

Links:

Facebook: **http://tinyurl.com/pon4e66**

Blog: http://chantalnoordeloos.blogspot.nl/

Twitter: C_Noordeloos

Amazon page: **http://tinyurl.com/puy2t87**

Easter Hunt

JR Park

It was set to be a glorious Easter Sunday as the villagers slowly woke from their sleep. The fire-red sky from the previous evening had lived up to its folk tale promise and brought about a morning so magnificent even the mist that had settled across the surrounding fields shone yellow; lit up in a golden glow by the majestic rays of the morning sun.

Old Pat was already up and making his way through the low level cloud with a sack full of chocolate eggs. He smiled as he picked out one of the treats and regarded it for a moment before hiding it within a thicket of long grass.

He couldn't remember how many years he'd been making the early morning trek to set up the children's Easter egg hunt, but it could be counted in decades. He'd started whilst Edna was still with him, and when she died, succumbing to a sudden and aggressive cancer, he carried on the tradition. Bringing happiness to the children of the village seemed like a fitting memorial to his wife, and one that he knew she would approve of.

Times had certainly changed.

When he first came up to these fields all those years ago he had carried a basket of real eggs; their shells carefully hand-painted with rainbow swirls and dusted with glitter. Today their sparkle came from the brightly coloured foil, wrapped at a factory and bought from the local shop. Some of the magic seemed to have died with the moving of modern times, but the beaming smiles from the kids hadn't changed, and neither had that feeling of joy he felt watching their innocent games.

Even this morning as he picked out the hiding places for his chocolate treasures he felt the air tingle with the same excitement of old.

Finding new hiding places had become increasingly difficult with each passing year, and he was thankful this time he had a new canvas to work with. Heavy rain storms last autumn had caused severe flooding. The ground had swelled and slipped in the wash, bringing forth new dips and gradients; nothing on a disastrous scale, but enough to pull down fences and remodel the terrain.

The subsequent work on a new drainage system, hastily organised by the council, was still ongoing and would no doubt lead to an even more altered landscape, but for now that was out of bounds. The red-tape fences clearly marked the building site, encircling the huge craters that had been dug for the laying of pipes by a good few metres.

As long as he kept the eggs away from the red tape the children would be safe.

Old Pat clambered over a wooden stile and peered through the mist.

Strangest I ever did see, he thought as he regarded its custard-like colour.

His skin tingled as he swallowed his own saliva in a vain attempt to rid himself of the strange sour taste that prickled his tongue.

Bending down to re-tie a loosened shoelace, a movement caught his eye. Looking up he watched as a silhouette emerged from the foggy surroundings.

Kid couldn't wait until after church, he smiled to himself. *Come out here early to get first pickings.*

'Who's that?' Old Pat called out. 'Annie, is that you? Edmond? Your father won't be happy about you sneaking out this early.'

Silence met his questions as the figure staggered towards him. Feeling his knees creak as he straightened up, Old Pat walked towards the figure. His eyes locked onto its face as he squinted through the yellow vapour. The mist swirled across the plain, continuing to conceal the identity of the oncoming stranger.

It had to be one of the children, even with such obscured visibility he could make out their height, just reaching his chest.

'Edmond?' he called again as he drew closer.

A gust of wind blew hard across the field and momentarily the mist cleared. As the stranger's face was revealed Pat's cheeks grew a chalky white.

The old man didn't have any time to react before he heard the slop of his intestine falling from a huge gash, torn across his stomach. In shock he reached forward, trying desperately to grab hold of the fatty tube that spilled from his own body. But his grip slipped, his fingers failing to find any purchase on the slimy, gristly texture.

The chocolate eggs scattered on the ground as he dropped to his knees.

A sliver of sanity returned and with it the thought to scream; to call for help. He opened his mouth and bellowed, but a slice across his windpipe reduced his cries to a rasp. It became a gurgle as blood poured down his neck and into his lungs. Red crimson bubbles frothed from the gaping wound as the old man struggled to breathe.

He felt a large, wet sack fall through his hands and splatter onto the ground.

He knew it was his stomach.

Daring once more to look at his attacker, his face contorted with terror. Old Pat fell forward as his thumping heart beat its last; his lifeless corpse landing face first into a pool of his own blood.

Even on such a beautiful spring day the church was cold inside. The sun had been blazing since dawn, managing to burn off the mist that had glowed with such a radiance it'd become a talking point as the families met for the Easter Sunday service.

Annie didn't care about some stupid fog. It was Easter and it was time to go hunting for chocolate.

She shivered as she sat restlessly on a hard, wooden pew, swinging her legs back and forth. The sun shone through a stain-glass window creating brightly coloured patterns on her legs. She held them out, admiring the kaleidoscopic image. It warmed her skin, teasing her with the pleasures to be had outside.

She looked at her mother with a face of abject boredom. The warning look that glanced back said it all. *Sit quiet and shut up.* The priest's sermon had long become a mindless drone, buzzing in her ears. Annie quietly sighed and gazed back at the pattern. The reds and greens sparkled, just like the foil of a chocolate egg.

Annie was eight years old when she'd entered the church. The service had crawled at such a pace that she swore she'd turned nine before she was allowed out with her friends to play in the fields.

'How boring was that?!' Megan scoffed as she took Annie's hand and ran through the long grass.

'We're here now,' replied Annie, excited to be free from her parent's watchful eye for the next few hours. 'We've got to get a move on otherwise Bruce and Edmond will get all the treats.'

Reaching the tall Ash tree, they saw the two boys with their hands already in the bushes, pushing back brambles in search of the sugary treasures. Ian must have got there first, or just been lucky, and already had an armful of silvery wrapped orbs, whilst Derrick looked on with jealous eyes.

'Gertie and Brad aren't coming,' Megan informed, taking pride in her knowledge. 'Brad was sick coming out of the service and Gertie's in trouble for pushing him into his own puke.'

Annie couldn't hold back a laugh. 'They're always fighting. I wonder if I'll fight with Adam when he's no longer a baby.'

'Probably, but you'll win,' Megan replied, her mind on the eggs. 'I reckon I know where Old Pat's hidden them this year.'

With that she sprinted across the field.

'Wait for me,' Annie called out, running after her.

A cry stopped them all in their tracks.

Annie and Megan turned to see Ian floundering on the ground, surrounded by a dozen chocolate eggs that had been scattered by his fall. Above him stood the oafish Derrick, puffing his chest out and smiling a cruel smile.

'You leave him alone,' Bruce was the first to voice his support as he stopped his search and ran towards the pair.

Edmond, Annie and Megan weren't far behind.

'Don't be an idiot,' Edmond berated the wannabe bully as he caught up. 'Play the game fair. If not you'll have me to deal with.'

'Oh yeah?' came Derrick's reply through clenched teeth. 'You've been asking for it for a long time.'

He launched himself at Edmond, grabbing the boy's shirt. The pair tumbled through the grass, kicking and punching as they wrestled each other.

'Stupid boys,' mocked Annie. 'Come on Ian, I'll help you up.'

She took his hand and slowly brought him to his feet.

'Ugh! What's that on your shirt?' Megan pointed at a red smear running down his top. 'There's more on the ground.'

Intrigued by the strange substance, Megan set off, following a trail across the grass and towards the stile at the top of the field.

Ignoring Ian and the girls, Bruce turned and ran towards the duelling pair of boys. Edmond needed help to escape the fists of his much larger foe.

'Bruce, come back,' Annie called trying to catch his hand as he ran past.

Bruce stopped at her touch.

'I don't want you to get hurt,' she implored.

'But he's my friend,' Bruce answered.

Paying no heed to the going-ons around him, Ian dusted himself off and picked up one of the Easter eggs that lay on the ground. Carefully unwrapping it, he let the chocolate melt in his mouth. It tasted good as the treat dissolved on his tongue. Closing his eyes, he silently savoured the moment, lost in his own private pleasure.

Opening them again, he squinted at the light, finding it hard to believe what he saw.

'But it's not your fight,' Annie tried to reason with Bruce.

'His fight is mine,' came the retort.

'You always say that. Don't be so stupid!' she huffed.

'Um... guys,' Ian's quivering voice was muffled by a mouth half-filled with chocolate.

Something had caught his attention, shocked him from his moment of bliss. Ian watched as it came closer, but a sense of disbelief kept him rooted to the spot.

Edmond cried out as Derrick's fist caught him, square on the cheek.

'Guys,' Ian called out again, his nerves growing fraught.

'Not now,' Annie shouted him down before returning back to her argument with Bruce. 'Why can't you just grow up? You're better than all this fighting.'

'You wouldn't understand,' Bruce said shaking free from her grip and running towards his friend.

Mesmerised by the nightmarish figure that bounded across the grass, Ian pinched his own hand. The feeling of pain as his fingernails dug in told him he wasn't dreaming. But how could that be?

'Guys!' the tone in his voice had changed. A resonance of fear vibrated through his words with such primal power even Edmond and Derrick stopped fighting and looked up.

Only metres away from where Ian shook, standing on its hind legs and just a few inches taller than the terrified boy was a rabbit-shaped beast with wild, piercing eyes. Its mouth foamed with a bubbling liquid that oozed down its chin, matting its white fur into a yellowish mess. Pointed incisors protruded like knives and it swung its arms, slicing the air with its lethal claws.

In an instant the creature was on top of Ian, knocking him to the floor. Its bulk kept him pinned as he stared, helplessly into its glowing eyes.

Thrusting its arms forwards, the gnarled claws buried deep into the boy's shoulders. He screamed as the pain coursed through his body. Waves of agony were ignited afresh each time he tried to wriggle free.

The monster leant closer, its nose twitching as it sniffed at the soft flesh of Ian's exposed neck. Thick drool dripped onto the boy, stinking of something wretched. Bruce ran to his aid, but was too late. Its long front teeth sank into Ian's milky white skin. Blood sprayed high in the air as the creature tore into his throat.

A scream echoed across the field. Annie recognised it as Megan and ran towards the sound.

She heard another cry, distorted by the wind that rushed by her ears. She knew it was Bruce. Tears ran down her cheeks as she dared herself to look back. Confirming her worst fears, he lay face down on the ground, his jet black hair swimming in a puddle of blood that collected round his head.

The monster had worked quickly and was already upon Edmond, his chest a mess of broken bone and savaged flesh. Its teeth gnawed at the stringy innards pulled from his stomach. Edmond's head rolled to one side and looked at Annie. She gasped as she saw his lips move. He was still alive!

Her vision was blurred with grief as she glimpsed Derrick running down the hill towards the village. *Coward!*

She felt no better than him as she turned and ran towards Megan, but she had to help her friend. The others were already lost.

Climbing the stile she saw Megan transfixed by the remains of a mutilated corpse. Trails of flesh had been pulled from the body and its face had been shredded. Brain matter dotted the area like a horde of pink maggots. The starlings had already taken its eyeballs and were making short work of the rest.

A sack of Easter eggs laid by the body's side, giving the only clue to its identity.

'Old Pat?' Annie asked between gasps as she caught her breath.

'I-I-I guess so,' came Megan's response, her voice quivering with fear.

The girl burst into tears, but a hand from her friend held her mouth.

'Shhh,' Annie warned. 'We've got to be quiet. What did that is still out here. It got the others. Killed them, like Old Pat.'

Megan's sob intensified, but remained muted by Annie.

'We've got to be really quiet,' Annie continued. 'Promise?'

Megan wiped the tears from her eyes and nodded.

Slowly Annie removed her hand from her friend's mouth. As she had promised, Megan kept quiet, wiping her long brown hair away from her tear sodden cheeks.

'What do we do?' she asked, her voice trembling.

'We've got to get back to the village,' Annie tried her best to sound confident. 'Tell our parents what's happened. They'll know what to do.'

Carefully the pair climbed the stile, keeping themselves as low as they could.

'Try not to look,' Annie whispered back to her friend as she cleared the stile first. 'Keep your eyes on the ground.'

Curiosity gripped Megan as she ignored the warning and scanned the landscape. Silent tears fell down her cheeks as she saw the boy's lifeless bodies strewn across the field.

The wind carried birdsong, their melodies unmoved by the tragedy around them. It bowed branches and directed the grass in waves, like a landlocked sea; the dark patches of blood resembling oil spills, polluting the natural beauty of this once comforting place.

The monstrous apparition was nowhere to be seen.

Megan jumped down from the stile, landing on shaky legs. The adrenalin made her senses keen, ready for flight, but it made her muscles quiver. The ground beneath her feet felt soft, unreal.

Annie took her hand.

'Keep close to the hedgerow,' Annie whispered. 'We'll follow it all the way down.'

Slowly they crept across the field. Their ears, now attuned for danger, made their footsteps sound like thunder. A snapping twig echoed round the hills. They squeezed each other's hands as they crept, hardly daring to breathe.

'Annie,' Megan whispered.

'What?' her friend asked.

'What does it look like?'

'Like the Easter bunny,' Annie replied. 'A big, evil, slobbering Easter bunny.'

'Where did it come from?'

'I don't know,' Annie's tone grew irritated.

'Where is it now?'

'Megan,' Annie stopped and turned to her, 'just because I saw it doesn't make me an expert. All I know is it has teeth and claws, and eyes that look like hell.'

'You didn't mention the blood soaked fur,' Megan retorted.

'What?' Annie asked, puzzled.

'And the foaming mouth,' Megan's eyes grew wide as she looked past her friend.

Annie turned to follow Megan's gaze.

'Run!' she shouted pulling the other girl along by the hand.

The pair turned and ran back up the hill, away from the murderous beast that was galloping towards them on all fours.

Their young legs carried them swiftly but the monster's speed was unmatched. It quickly gained distance and with a mighty leap, pounced towards them.

Its claws caught Megan's back, pushing her forward. Annie turned to catch her friend but was knocked over by the force. She landed on her back, with Megan crashing on top of her.

They faced each other, powerless to move as Megan cried for help. Unable to see past her best friend's face, Annie could feel the weight of the monster as it sat on top of them. She could hear the sound of flesh being ripped open by its awful claws.

'Help me,' Megan mouthed, her voice finally lost to the terror that beseeched her.

Her eyes were like saucers, her pupils dilated with fear. Try to ignore it as she might, Megan was acutely aware of what was happening to her.

Her gaze remained fixed on her best friend.

Blood splashed around them and Annie screamed as Megan's head went limp. A serrated claw smashed through the top of her skull, showering the pinned girl underneath in a confetti of bone, brain and blood.

Gnashing teeth made jittery, but brutal bites to the corpse's neck, slicing through the spinal column like it was nothing more than a tough piece of gristle.

Annie held out her hands, pushing at the creature's snout in a desperate attempt to fend it from feasting on her as it had her friend. But its skittish attack seemed impossible to deflect as it edged closer, nipping at her fingers as it did so.

With a final act of determination she clenched her fist and mustering all the strength she could, she launched a punch, landing it square on the beast's nose.

The creature reared up on its hind legs and briefly studied its prey, holding its claws out ready for the lethal blow. It opened its ever-chewing mouth and a guttural roar bellowed from its lungs. As it launched towards her a rock struck the side of its head, halting the attack. Another rock quickly followed its predecessor, this time smashing directly into one of its glowing red eyes.

Recoiling in pain, the monster fell to the floor, momentarily stunned.

Annie rolled from under the decapitated body of her friend and looked up to see Bruce launching another rock at the creature.

Blood dripped from his head and a jagged wound tore down his left arm, which hung uselessly by his side.

'Come on Annie,' he called out. 'I've only hurt it.'

Climbing to her feet, Annie ran towards her saviour.

'You're alive!' she yelled with excitement.

'Yeah. The bastard wounded me. Knocked me right out,' he explained. 'But luckily for me it didn't finish the job. That'll teach the bugger.'

'Bruce!' Annie was shocked by his language, but felt herself blush for a different reason.

Taking Annie's hand, Bruce ran through a gap in the hedge and pulled them both into a ditch by the border of the field. It was damp and muddy at the bottom, but it was also dark.

'We've got to get home,' Annie whispered once they had caught their breath.

'We'll never get to the village,' Bruce whispered back, wheezing from exhaustion. 'That thing's fast. God knows if Derrick made it.'

Annie started to protest, but stopped herself. Climbing up the slope, she peered over the top of the ditch for a moment eyeing the village, bathed in beautiful sunlight. It had never looked so welcoming. It had never looked so far away.

'Careful up there, Annie,' Bruce quietly called with concern. 'This ditch used to be the end of the field until the floods. There's an old barbed wire fence lying in the dirt. Don't cut yourself on it.'

Her eyes caught the rusty lines of needle sharp barbs trailing the slope. Beside her was one of the old fence posts. The wood had rotted in the damp, becoming home to a teeming population of woodlice. It had been pure luck that Annie hadn't cut herself on the spikes.

'What do we do?' she asked.

'Wait here,' Bruce replied. 'We can stay here until our parents realise we're missing.'

Pulling his penknife from his pocket, Bruce began slicing the end of a stick, sharpening it to a point.

'But it's distracted,' she called back, still looking over the edge. The monster was making short work of Megan's head. The child's skull cracking as it bit into her face. 'We can make it.'

'Town is up wind,' Bruce said, pulling her back into the safety of the ditch. 'Even if we're really quiet it will smell you.'

Satisfied with the makeshift spear, Bruce picked up another stick and repeated the process.

'Can rabbits smell good?' Annie asked, genuinely unsure.

'I guess so. It's always twitching its nose,' he shrugged. 'And *rabbits* don't look like *that*. Whatever that thing is, I don't want to take any chances. Besides,' he braved a smile, 'even I can smell you from here.'

Annie's face cracked into a shadow of fun as she playful pushed him. The relief was fleeting as the horror of the situation proved overwhelming.

'We can't just stay here. What if Derrick didn't get home? It will eventually find us,' her voice quivering with a growing panic. 'We've got to do something.'

'Maybe you're right,' Bruce picked up another stick and sliced the wood to a sharp point. 'The construction field's over there, right?'

'Uh huh,' Annie recalled seeing the red tape flapping in the wind. 'But that's out of bounds. It's dangerous.'

'Exactly,' Bruce replied. 'We've had it drummed into our heads that the new drainage works is a dangerous place to play. As dangerous for us as it is a mutant bunny?'

Annie's eyes lit up with a sense of hope.

'Listen,' Bruce placed another sharpened stick on the pile, 'I've got a plan.'

If Annie had turned nine whilst waiting for the church sermon to end she reckoned she was eleven by the time she counted to five hundred, as instructed by Bruce, and slowly crawled to the top of the ditch. She'd had her eyes shut all the while she counted, listening intently to anything that would indicate the success of Bruce's progress. But she'd heard nothing expect the birds overhead and the blowing wind.

Carefully crawling past the fallen barbed wire fence, Annie gripped the spear Bruce had left her. It was crude, but sharp. The rest he'd taken with him.

She peered over the top. Just like he'd promised the red tape had been cut, but the fence post was left standing; a marker for her. It seemed so far. Did Bruce really sneak all the way across there without being seen?

Annie thought about how brave he had been and she felt her heart glow with a pleasing rush that momentarily caught her breath. Now it was her turn to be just as brave. It was her turn to prove herself.

Slowly rising to her feet she looked around for the creature that had killed her friends. Through the hedge she could make out the remains of Megan spread across the undulating field. Jackdaws and crows fought over the scraps as they pulled at the soft tissues. Annie's stomach convulsed, but she held back from retching, swallowing back the salvia that pooled in her mouth.

Come on, where are you? she thought as she walked out into the open, knowingly making herself a target.

She squeezed the spear and held it in front of her as she circled around, trying to keep sight of every direction at once. The creature could come from anywhere.

A rustle in the hedgerow made her turn. The branches and foliage concealed the form, but a pair of eyes glowed in the dark between the leaves. Annie staggered backwards as fear fleetingly enveloped her mind. She turned to look over her shoulder, eyeing the fence post that marked her destination.

The snapping of branches made her look back. The monster had burst from its hiding place and sprinted towards her on all fours in a blur of teeth and menace.

Without hesitation she turned and ran. The pounding of the creature's claws shook the ground and echoed in the sky, but Annie remained focused on the fence post.

Just run towards the post, Annie. Run, run, run. And when you get there don't stop running. Don't look back, don't rest. Run.

That's what Bruce had told her and that's what she did.

Her legs stretched as far as they could, her lungs burnt and still she could feel the monster gaining on her, its strange snarl growing closer and closer behind her.

Got to reach the post, she screamed to herself as she climbed the hill.

Taking the brow as her legs wobbled, she reached her destination, but didn't slow down. The ground beneath her disappeared, opening up to a sheer drop. The whole field in front of her had been dug out, three storeys deep, with a criss-cross of trenches and half-made pipe networks.

She tried to stop, but the momentum carried her over the edge, momentarily flying through the air before she felt herself fall.

A hand caught her dress and pulled her backwards.

She landed against hard rock and felt a pair of arms hold onto her tight. Instinctively Annie held still as she lay on a small ledge in Bruce's protective embrace and watched the beast follow her descent. Without a guiding hand to pull it back, the creature careered down the long drop, finally crashing onto a set of wooden spikes at the bottom.

The pair climbed back to the field and watched as the animal writhed amongst the spears that had impaled it.

'It worked,' Annie cried, hugging Bruce.

'You did amazing,' Bruce hugged her back.

Releasing from their celebrations, he looked into her eyes and smiled.

'Still got my spear,' he laughed.

'This thing,' she held up the handmade weapon. 'First present you ever gave me. I'm keeping hold of this.'

Bruce's smile grew wider.

'Well, maybe it won't be the last. You're really something, you know?'

Annie was flattered by the praise and found herself unable to resist leaning closer to kiss him. She watched as he reciprocated the action, gently puckering his lips to meet hers.

Savouring the moment, she closed her eyes, waiting to experience the moment she had dreamt of for months.

An ear splitting scream forced her eyes open.

She fell to the floor; pushed to safety by Bruce.

Behind him stood the creature, its face gnarled and broken by the spikes. Blood dripped from its wounds, rasping as it struggled to breathe.

Bruce stood little chance of escape as the creature drove a claw through his stomach.

'Nooooo,' Annie screamed as she stabbed her spear into its throat.

Throwing Bruce aside the monster swiped at its attacker. Annie fell to the floor as her thigh gushed a crimson spray. She gripped the wound under her dress and ran.

The pain was agonising as she sprinted across the field. Every step opened the wound further, but she had no choice. The monster bounded after her, slowed by its broken, hind leg, but still giving chase. Gradually gaining ground, it gnashed at her heels, causing her to trip.

Annie rolled over to face the beast, crawling backwards with her hands as she frantically tried to keep distance between herself and the creature.

A claw caught her foot. It sliced her shoe, but she tumbled backwards as she found herself sliding down the ditch that had previously offered her a thin veil of sanctuary. As the rabbit-like beast curled back its mouth, displaying the full length of its lethal fangs, that sanctuary was obliterated.

Blood poured from her leg as Annie tried to escape but there was nothing left. She was drained, exhausted by the attacks, the chase and her injuries.

The monster crawled over the lip of the ditch and down towards its beaten prey, seemingly enjoying the moment; relishing the kill.

Closer it crawled, inch by inch, until it stopped still and eyed up its quarry. It leant back on hind legs ready to pounce on the defenceless girl; ready to deliver the death blow.

An evil sparkled in its eyes, whilst drool continued to foam from its mouth, a bubbling liquid with a strange yellow colour. It stunk but Annie could no longer smell; as desperation set in she was close to catatonia.

Her hand dropped to her side, landing on the soft wet wood of the old fence post.

Of course!

As the monster leapt towards her she sprang into action. With a strength summoned from the pit of her being she pulled at the post, pulling it from the ground and releasing the barbed wire links from the dirt. Like a net of twisted, metal knots, the old fence ensnared the creature. It tried to free itself, but the more it struggled the further entangled it grew.

Already wounded, the monster was weakened further as the barbs pulled tight, tearing across its hide and pulling open savage gashes.

Annie got to her feet and dug a large rock from the earth. She held it above the monster and with a vengeful glee, brought it crashing down onto its skull.

Again and again she drove the rock into the creature's head, obliterating the cranium into a ragged, shapeless mess of fur and blood.

Pulling rabbit brain from her hair, she climbed the slope and staggered back to Bruce, satisfied the monster was finally dead.

'It's okay,' she said as she sat down next to him, smiling and holding her hand comfortingly against the wound on his stomach. 'The grown-ups will come and sort everything out. We'll be fine.'

'We did it?' Bruce weakly smiled back.

'Yeah we did it, alright,' Annie replied.

She leant forward and the pair kissed, beginning a relationship that would last for the rest of their lives.

A hail of bullets flew through the air with such ferocity they lifted Annie off the ground. Ripping through their flesh and bone like it was soft butter, the artillery tore them both to pieces, splattering their child corpses across a three metre radius.

A group of figures in yellow HazMat suits surveyed the carnage holding automatic machine guns in their gloved hands. The barrels of their M60s still smoked from their fresh discharge.

'The gas spread further than we thought,' one of them spoke into a radio. 'Even infected some kids.'

The ground rumbled beneath their feet as around them the earth churned up. Rabbit-shaped creatures with glowing red eyes emerged from the dirt and sprinted from the hedgerows, disturbed by the gunfire.

Moving at such speed, the numbers weren't easy to count.

'That's about twenty,' the man spoke into the radio once more. 'Containment measures are not working. It looks like the infected are headed towards the village.'

He squeezed his radio in anger at his failure.

'God help them.'

THE END

Bio

J.R. Park is an author of horror fiction and co-founder of the publishing imprint the Sinister Horror Company. His novels Terror Byte, Punch and Upon Waking have all been well received by readers and reviewers, even if the sick bucket hasn't been too far away from their bedsides.

Art house, pulp and exploitation alike inform his inspirations, as well as misheard conversations, partially remembered childhood terrors and cheese before sleep.

He currently resides in Bristol, UK.

Find out more at JRPark.co.uk and SinisterHorrorCompany.com

The Jesus Loophole

By Luke Smitherd

It was the smell that told Harry he was somehow back in his office. Amazingly, that knowledge penetrated his brain seconds *before* the realization that he couldn't see. His eyes were covered and something was tied around his head, over his mouth. This was swiftly followed by the knowledge that his hands and legs were tied to a chair (*his office chair*).

Naturally, panic came next in the chain of realization-to-response, and as he began to open his mouth (the tape covering it pulling painfully taut across his cheeks) to let out a smothered but hysterical scream (the cloth in his mouth muffling the sound), he remembered, in a detached way, where he had been last. He had been leaving his house, heading to the car. *No.* He'd gotten into the car, hadn't he? That was right. He had driven to ...the office! That was right, he'd—

You're tied to a fucking chair! You're in your own office, bound and gagged and tied to a fucking chair! What's going on! Fuck! Fuck!!

His heart - not in the best condition after too many oh-why-not steak dinners and only exercised with leisurely rounds of golf - pumped like he was running a marathon of terror, the madness of his situation settling into his brain. He jumped and strained in the seat., his strangled, cloth-filtered screams sounding like those of a bellowing cow. His hands grasped at the armrests they were tied to, pointlessly trying to break them. His head ached, and there was a woozy feeling behind his eyes, and a lingering chemical smell under his nostrils. Had he been drugged?

The cleaners! The cleaners! When are they coming in?

It was the weekend. The place was empty. No one was coming. He'd gone in to put a few tweaks to the Liefeld pitch – he was handling that one personally, for it was the biggest potential contract in his small company's history. Yes, he could have done it at home, but he worked best in his own office space, and the kids had their idiot friends round for a Saturday night sleepover. The noise had been horrendous, his usual sleep-deprived headache making it—

What the fuck are you going to do?! What the fuck are you going to do!? Who did this? What do they want?

There was no safe onsite. It couldn't be about cash then. Blackmail, perhaps, a transfer, but why here? *Fuck it. Get loose and don't have a heart attack in the meantime!*

The sweat was already soaking his collar, tight as it was, his neck fatter than he realized or would admit to himself. He strained and grunted and struggled and yelled for all he was worth.

"You're going to choke. Stop screaming."

Harry froze. He wasn't surprised by the voice, as such – it made dull sense that if he'd been tied to a chair, the person responsible was likely to be nearby – but he was frightened into an animal's response by the confirmation of it, instinct pointlessly telling him stillness meant invisibility. He fell immediately silent, his breath rushing in and out of his nose due to the tape covering his mouth.

"Thank you," the voice said. "I'm going to take the tape and the blindfold off you now. Alright? And you're going to stay silent. If you don't. you'll regret it. There's no one that will hear you if you scream anyway, so it's not worth it on either count." The speaker sounded middle aged, the same as Harry, perhaps a little younger More worryingly -, Harry noted this as adrenalin flooded his mind, – there was a slight shake to the person's voice, as if the speaker was using a great deal of effort to communicate clearly. Or calmly.

Oh shit. Oh shit. Ohshitohshitohshit—

Harry knew the speaker was correct. No one would hear. The office was in a small industrial estate – and it *had* to be his office, the smell was the same, the feel of his ergonomic chair was the same, contoured specially to fit a lower back that ached little bit more with every passing, inevitable year, paying the price for his two decades as a driver, helping build this place – and he knew there would be no one onsite now. Security was well out of earshot, located by the main gate. Even if one of them had passed by on one of his laps of the premises, he wouldn't come close enough to Harry's office to hear anything through closed van windows. The privacy of the office was one of the main reasons Harry had picked the unit.

"Tape first. Brace yourself, this stuff is very strong."

The tips of gloved fingers pushed into the flesh around Harry's mouth. The leather material was making it difficult for Harry's captor to gain purchase of the tape's edge. Harry's flesh was pinched painfully many times in the process, but he only yelped once. He didn't want to take any risks, already going into survival mode.

Don't scream! You heard him! Don't scream! Just play along, cooperate and maybe—

The tape was suddenly torn from Harry's face, and the speaker hadn't been lying. It *was* strong stuff. It didn't take any skin with it, but it felt as if Harry's mouth had been slapped with a hand coated in sandpaper. His bitten-back scream came out as *Affff.*

"Told you," the voice said, and there was a pleased sound to it that turned Harry's blood to ice water. "Blindfold now. I don't know why I bothered with it really. In hindsight, I think I only used it because it's the sort of thing that you *imagine* doing when you kidnap someone. I've never done this before. That said, you should really pay more attention to your surroundings when you're unlocking somewhere important." The gloved hands returned, grabbing Harry's head roughly, and Harry could get a better feel now for the fingers and the size of the hands. They weren't large; not the hands of a fighter or bruiser. Were circumstances slightly different, Harry would have felt encouraged by this for Harry *was* a heavyset man, not too tall, but broad and doughy. He would outweigh his unseen assailant for sure, but it meant nothing when he was tied securely to a chair. The blindfold came away, and the sudden brightness of the light, contrasting with the darkness of the figure before him, made Harry momentarily think that he was seeing things.

In front of him, seated on a chair that had presumably been taken from the main office, was a slender man wearing a black sweater, black trousers, and black gloves. What added an air of the surreal to the image was the manner in which Harry's kidnapper had concealed his face.; It wasn't a mask, or a balaclava; instead a number of black rags had been wrapped around his head, giving him the appearance of an Egyptian Mummy. *No, not a Mummy,* thought Harry, noting the sunglasses that the man was wearing to hide his eyes. *He looks like the guy in that movie. The Invisible Man.* The whole thing would have looked almost comical if not for the man's posture. He was leaning forward intently in the chair, arms resting on his thighs, back rising and falling with each controlled breath. Everything about the mystery man's body language screamed intensity, eagerness ...and this was the man who had drugged Harry and tied him to a chair.

"As I said," the man added, holding Harry's now-removed blindfold up slightly, "not much point in this, as you can see." The man's voice, Harry now noted, was only slightly muffled by the thin black rag covering his mouth. The material must have been very thin to have such a minor effect on the man's speech.

Don't worry about the fucking bandages! Worry about keeping this guy calm.

Look at him!

Harry's heart – hardly the most carefully tended organ in Harry's body – reminded him of its presence once more, seeming to spasm and squeeze in new ways.

Hold on. Hold on. Calm your heart down or it's going to kill you. You can breathe. Breathe.

But the next thought didn't help:

Why is this happening? Why? What is going on?

"W-" Harry began, speaking instinctively, and then almost bit his own lip in his haste to cut himself off. He'd been told to keep quiet, and threatened with retribution if he didn't comply, yet here he was—

"That's good behavior Harry, and I understand the question," said the man. Other than the slow, deliberate breathing, the rest of his body was completely still. The jaw moved beneath the rags and the gaze from the sunglasses never left Harry's face. He looked alien. "You *are* allowed to talk by the way. By that, I mean you just have to be quiet when you do it. Obviously, you want to know why you're here. I'm going to tell you."

Harry nodded quickly, nervous little jerks of his chin that were barely nods at all. Sweat began to bead along the bottom of his chin, running into the small folds at the front of his neck.

You're going to die.

You don't know that. You could just be a hostage, a ransom.

Then—

No. You're in the office. He wouldn't hold you hostage here when he knows people are going to come into work in the morning. He's going to kill you.

Harry pissed himself, the jet of it hitting his thigh and seeping through his trousers, pooling warmth and wetness in the seat of the leather chair. The damp spot would have been difficult to notice against his black trousers, but there was the smell. If the Bandaged Man noticed, he didn't show it.

Harry thought of Linda, lying in bed and dozing fitfully with the remnants of a fever. She'd had the flu all week, and Harry had been looking after her, even taking time off during the Leifield preparations, even with his usual sleep problems (he never slept these days). The worst of it had been over for a few days now – over enough that she insisted it was ok for him to get caught up, enough that she'd agreed to allow three of Ben's friends from football to stay over for the night – but she still hadn't been sleeping well. There she was, with no idea of the nightmare her husband was going through a few miles away. He ached for her in that moment more than he had ever ached for anything in his life.

"Please," Harry whispered, tears springing to his eyes. "Please don't kill me."

The Bandaged Man moved suddenly, causing Harry to flinch in response. He jolted like a startled rabbit. The Bandaged Man waved a hand, irritated.

"You asked a question. At least have the decency to wait until I've answered it," he said, his voice now sounding as if he was gritting his teeth slightly.

"Yes, yes of course." Harry said, frantically.

"There are a few reasons *why,* Harry," the Bandaged Man said, his arms resting on his thighs once more. "But one of them is that this is an *experiment.* A long-term experiment, yes, but an experiment nevertheless. There are two principles I'm putting to the test here. Two. You're a religious man, Harry. I know you are. So am I. Very much so. And that's part of it."

"H-how do you—"

"Harry, *seriously,*" the Bandaged Man hissed, his entire body tensing as his hands curled into fists, "Shut. The. Fuck. *Up.* You asked me a goddamn *question.* Are you going to listen to the goddamn *answer?*"

"I-I'm sorry, I'm sorry, I won't speak again until you're done, I promise!" Harry hated the pleading sound in his voice as he barked desperately. He thought of Linda again, of Ben and Sally, and suddenly the pleading sound didn't seem so bad. If he had to kiss this guy's ass to stay alive and get back to his family, he'd do both cheeks and say thank you for the opportunity, sir.

Then shut the fuck up and play by his rules! Let him speak! You might be able to get out of this!

"You go to church, Harry," the Bandaged Man said. "Every week. You help with the events."

This guy ... he's seen you at church? He's part of the parish?

A very cold feeling began at the base of Harry's spine and began to creep upwards. He remained silent, however. His verbal reflexes had finally got the message, it seemed.

"Yes. You're a regular church goer. A good man. A *family* man. Loyal to your wife for...twenty-five years, yes?" The was silence in the room, the Bandaged Man's frozen body language and the blank rag-covered face like that of a large black ant behind the sunglasses. Harry froze too. Was he supposed to respond? He didn't dare.

"You can answer that," the Bandaged Man said, seemingly realizing Harry's confusion. "I want to know the answer."

"Y-yes," Harry said, and it was true. He had never cheated on Linda. "Twenty-five years."

This motherfucker has done his homework. He knows about you. This isn't a random thing at all.

Hope dimly blossomed. This could be about money then? This guy had done his research as part of some kind of shakedown? Not a robbery, but some kind of ransom situation?

Better that than a knife in the guts, Harry thought, his mind mentally breathless, adrenalin in his veins, his frantic flight instinct held in check due to his bonds. *I'll pay it. I don't care.*

"I believe you Harry. I believe you," the Bandaged Man said. "Father of two. I've seen you all together lots of times. I can tell a family man when I see one. You're loyal. You understand the importance of that. And them ...I've seen the way they look at you. You're everything to *them,* too."

The chill and anger at the mention of Harry's family – that they'd been *watched,* his *kids* too – was offset by the last sentence. Here it came. *You're everything to them?* It *was* a ransom situation. Uncertain whether his permission to speak still stood, Harry nodded in response. The Bandaged Man leaned further forward in the chair, an ominous creaking sound emanating as he did so - from the chair or the floor or *somewhere* - that simply enhanced the Mummy effect in Harrys mind.

"But the *last* time I saw you, the last time I *watched* you," the Bandaged Man said, "was yesterday. I watched you last night. You played a board game, the four of you. Didn't you?" They had. They'd played Scrabble.

The fucker had been outside all along.

Harry's anger bubbled, his own fingers clenching impotently now, but he tightened his jaw and said nothing.

"You can answer," the Bandaged Man said.

Harry still said nothing, thinking of his children without a father and worried about what his anger might make him say to help that thought become a reality. The Bandaged Man nodded as if Harry had spoken.

"I know you did and *you* know you did. What you *don't* know is this.: How do you know you're the same person?"

Silence.

"...what?" Harry blurted, surprise getting the better of his restraint.

What the hell kind of a question is that?

"The same person as yesterday. How do you know you're him?"

Silence again.

"...*what?*"

"Bear with me, Harry. I'm making a point. You know you're the same person from the day before because you *remember* the day before the feelings, your clothes in a pile on the floor from the night before or in the laundry basket. Barring some kind of cosmic trick, you know you live your life in transition from night into day into night into day and you are still you. Right?"

Not knowing what else to say, and wondering where the hell this was going, Harry said:

"...right."

"But here's the thing," the Bandaged Man said, holding up a finger. He seemed to have relaxed slightly, the previously visible tension no longer there ...but that steady breathing continued. "Would you say you were the same person as you were five years ago? Ten? Twenty? I don't mean the same body: the same bones and eyes and brain. I mean the same mind, the same personality? Think about it. Really think about it."

Despite the situation – and perhaps, in some way, because of it, needing to please his captor – Harry did just as he was asked. Was he the same person he had been twenty years ago?

"Well ...I-in some ways ...n-no. A lot of ways. W-who is, right?" The question came out over-earnestly, desperate to find common ground, to say the right things. The Bandaged Man was clearly crazy. "Y-you grow older, wiser, things happen ..."

Oh, God.

Harry went fish belly white in an instant. Because something *had* happened three years ago.

Could this be ...oh my God, could this be something to do with—

But that *had* been three years ago, and he'd—

"Of course," the Bandaged Man continued, either not noticing or pretending not to notice the utter transformation of Harry's complexion. "Something happens, doesn't it? Some subtle change, some metamorphosis without any real tipping point, some steady *change* as invisible as the movement of the big hand on a watch. It's not today, tomorrow, or the day after that, or the day after *that,* or the day after *that,* because then you're still close enough to you to be *you*. No. It happens over a *long* time. And you only *see* it – only *know* the difference – once you're far away enough to look back and notice. *Once enough time has passed for the person you* are *to be come the person you* were."

Harry's eyes goggled in his head as he tried and failed to hide his stunned expression.

It can't be him.

This couldn't be about revenge because the only man who would *want* revenge was dead.

This can't be anything to do with that! Breathe! Breathe!

"Do you understand, Harry?"

Keep it together!

"I ... uh ...I think so ..."

"It's like an existential conveyor belt," the Bandaged Man said, with a sigh that sounded ...rapt. "They're titles. *The Past You. The Present You. The Future You.* Moving, always moving, always from right to left, the present becoming the past and the future becoming the present. Once the change happens, the man you *were* doesn't exist anymore."

The finger came up again. "I said there were two principles at work here. That's the first. They're intertwined, but this is key. Past, Present, and Future You. That Past You can become a stranger, an island. Imagine criminals that turn to God and become pastors; drug dealers that become drug counselors; rapists become feminists. What is the *key* in all of those transformations, Harry? What is needed for those changes to work? As I said, normally, the change is slow, unnoticeable, and those transformations – those examples I just mentioned - *do* happen at speed, but these cases are different, to be fair. Either way; for all of these changes to happen, what is needed?"

Oh, shit. Oh, fuck. Oh, God ...

"Remorse," Harry whispered. The Bandaged Man's gloved finger jabbed forward, approving and condemning.

"*Remorse*," the Bandaged Man breathed. "This is both a huge part of the second principle, and a huge part of my problem. That's W why we're here. How have you been sleeping, Harry?"

It ...it can't be him. He's fucking dead, oh God ... Harry thought, simultaneously as the answer to the question came: *I haven't had a restful night of sleep for the last three years., Lliving a lie will do that to a guy and then you have to lie even more to cover the change in yourself and it goes on and on and on ...*

Tears sprang to Harry's eyes, and he began to sob.

"Please ..." Harry begged, "*please*. I have a family. I'm *sorry*. Please. *Please don't kill me.*"

"Ah. You know what this is about now, don't you Harry?"

"... *yes*..."

"So you understand that you will never leave this room, don't you?"

"*Take it off!*" Harry suddenly screamed, spit flying from his lips. "*Take that fucking mask off! You look like a fucking dick, take the mask off! At least have the balls to look me in the eye!*"

"You have got to be kidding," the Bandaged Man murmured, and this time his teeth clearly *were* gritted, but his words weren't referring to the request to remove his disguise;. his hands were already up and around his head, removing the sunglasses and undoing and untying. "You're going to talk to *me* about having the balls? *Really?*"

"*Fuck off!*" Harry screamed, manic now, rationality thrown to the wind. "*You're dead! You're dead!*"

"Obviously not," the-slowly-becoming-less Bandaged Man said, his blue eyes burning into Harry's as he spoke, "I did very much want to do a reveal. To see you shit yourself in front of me, but you already guessed. Another waste of time." The last of the bandages came away and revealed a face that Harry knew well. It was the one he'd seen in his dreams for the first year of the last three and, slowly, less and less frequently after that. It was always the look on this face that Harry had seen inside the courtroom. He hadn't been there to see the return of that face to church. Harry had been in jail at the time, and, despite his faith, he could never face the people of his old church once he was out. Not after what had happened, forgiveness or no forgiveness, and they'd moved to another *city* for crying out loud ...but his old congregation had seen the return of this face. Oh yes.

They had never forgotten it. When it came back to church, two months after ...*it*, a face that everyone in there had turned to stare at as the body it was attached to had shuffled in and taken a pew at the back, moving like a man with the life scooped out of him. *So brave,* they all thought *And keeping his faith! First his wife, and then so soon after, his daughter. So brave.* Then, two years after that, after the suicide note and the disappearance: *so brave, but it wasn't enough. The poor man. May God forgive him and put him with his family.*

"You don't have to do this, Michael," said Harry, his face slick with tears, his voice hoarse. "Please. I'm sorry, I'm *so* sorry. Think of my wife and children, they haven't done *anything*."

Michael Ormandy had returned to sitting in the same position he'd assumed when he was still wearing the mask. His hair, almost uniformly black when Harry had last seen him, was now nearly completely grey, transformed inside the space of three years. He looked sixty instead of fifty. His face was gaunt, and those previously hidden blue eyes looked haunted.

"It's not your family that I'm worried about, Harry," Michael said, nostrils flaring as he resumed that steady breathing once more. "Not yet, anyway. No, not like *that*," he added, shaking his head as he heard Harry gasp at the remark. "Never mind..,, forget I said that. I'm not going to touch your family. I promise. In some ways, I feel that I really should, but I'm not a monster. It *would* make us even though, wouldn't it? Tit for tat? What you took from me, I take from you? Well, you didn't take my wife, that happened before you, but you took care of the rest."

"Michael ... M-michael ..."

"There's nothing you can say, Harry," said Michael, solemnly. "Only God can forgive you. I know it was an accident, but when the person that committed that *accident* is eight times over the legal limit, it's not *really* an accident, is it?"

Harry could only stare at Michael, his mouth working silently as his own rapidly hitching breath contrasted with his captor's smooth and steady breaths.

"I mean ...even then ... I think ... I *think* ... with God's help ...I could have forgiven you," Michael said, his eyes watering a little now, "if you had just been ...*honest and confessed* ... that would have been something. But you weren't man enough. And you have money. And a membership at the golf club where some guy knows another guy who knows a guy who knows a judge. And the fucking *joke* of a sentence you got ... when mine ... is for *life* ..."

Think. For the love of God, Harry, think. Please.

"You can't do this," Harry sobbed. "Murder ...think of your *faith*, Michael. You went back to church, I heard about it ..."

"I did, didn't I?" said Michael, sniffling back his own tears now, but keeping his composure. "Can you believe it? Even when it was just me. Even after the cancer took Eloise. Then you happened. Can you *imagine?* I have to admit it. I came *very* close to abandoning ...all that. Not just because of what happened to my family, but because of just ... *how* ... *badly* ..." Michael closed his eyes and his fists here, the words shaking and almost at a whisper, "I wanted ... you ...dead. And knowing how *unfair* it was that you would live, and that I would have to live with the *torment* of you living and *wanting* to kill you *so* much ...but knowing that I couldn't. Because then I would go to hell." He opened his eyes. "And then I would never see my family again. Removed from them, separated for eternity. The ultimate divorce, if you will." He smirked, a small flash of bitterness that flickered across his face and disappearing ... and then, amazingly, replaced by a slowly growing smile.

"And then I figured it out," he said, and despite the trembling and the now-heavier breathing, the smile made him look peaceful. "The loophole. And how the *existence* of that loophole – the fact that God could *miss* that – meant that, despite His greatness and His glory ...God didn't get *everything* right. There were a few errors. And sometimes we have to put the pieces together for ourselves. We have to make it work. God helps those who help themselves, after all."

"Loophole? Loophole, Michael, what are you talking about?" Harry babbled, seeing a potential loophole of his own. "Murder is *murder,* Michael, and you're right. If you kill me you'll go to Hell and you'll *never see either of them again.* Don't do this—"

"Why did God allow Jesus to be crucified, Harry?"

"You know why!" shouted Harry, wanting to get back on track, to convince this madman of what Harry knew to be true: that Michael's course of action would damn him. "You've known it since Sunday school, and so have I!"

"Actually, no," Michael said, shrugging slightly. "Not me. I came to Christ late in life, in my twenties. Former drug addict. Not that I ever wanted that going around the village parish, particularly, so you wouldn't know. *God* forgives; *Man* ...less so. It was God's goodness that saved me from that life and His love that opened my eyes, but it was Jesus' sacrifice that meant God *could* forgive me for my sin, wasn't it? People talk about the *true meaning of Christmas* every fucking year, but they forget that the single most important part of the Christian faith is the *Easter* story." Michael sighed bitterly.

"Forget bunnies and eggs and hot cross buns. *Easter* is about Christ's torturous, *agonizing* death as the ultimate sacrifice.. That horrible death of the Son of God as atonement for all the sins of man, before and after, allowing us to ask for forgiveness and to receive it. Plus the promise of eternal life in His miraculous return, yadda yadda, but that isn't the point here. The point is that the Easter story means we can ask God's forgiveness for our sins and receive it. *Remorse* again, Harry, *remorse* that allows the transition from sin to righteousness."

"Yes, yes, that's right, Michael!" Harry blurted, sensing victory, a catch, a rule that could save his life. "But if you kill me, it isn't some murder in anger that you can regret afterwards! This is premeditated. You *want* to do it! How do you regret that?! You can't! You have to regret the *sin,* Michael, and *mean* it, not just feel bad that you can't get into heaven!"

The gloved finger came up again.

"That's the catch," Michael said, the smile now frozen on his face in a manner that made him look exactly as insane as he really was. "That's precisely the catch. Remorse, and the Past, Present, and Future Me. Present Me is here, right now. He's in charge, driving the bus. Present Me understands the truth here, and that truth is: you *have* to die. Justice demands it, *and I can't let you live as the idea makes me want to* scream. Injustice like *that* is one of God's mistakes--the universe *isn't* just. It isn't fair. He loves us; He made us; but His universe obviously isn't fair. My wife and daughter died horribly and they were far better people than me."

"B-but, but, Michael," Harry gasped, "they're with God now. The life after means so much more than the life before. You know that—"

Michael moved suddenly, striking like a cobra. Leaping up out of his seat, he reached under his right leg as he did so and produced a medium- sized hammer. Michael brought the weapon down with a sickening crunch onto Harry's fingers, hitting them three times in quick succession. Harry rocked and screeched like a stabbed dog. His fingers immediately splayed into jagged angles, broken and useless, the skin split in several places. Michael stood and watched for a moment, and then sat down, laying the hammer across his lap.

"Don't mention them," he said quietly. "Don't mention them again." Harry continued to scream in response. Michael waited for several minutes until the volume died down, turning into whimpering breaths.

"If you have faith, Harry, why are you even scared to die?" Michael asked. "Is it because you're going to Hell for what you did? Is your remorse not strong enough? I can believe that." He sighed. "Anyway, as I was saying," Michael said, resuming his previous flow, "Present Me knows you *have* to die. But the *Future* Me ...the Me that will have the responsibility of remorse after the fact ...that's the problem. You see, I already *know* I will feel no remorse. I'm looking at you screaming like that, looking at the pain you're in right now, and it makes me feel calmer than I have in years."

"Fff ....fff ...." gasped Harry, trying to speak but in too much pain to do so.

"No remorse means no access into Heaven," Michael continued, his voice now flat and dead. "And I *would* risk that, you know. I can't imagine an eternity knowing that you... *you* ... lived a long life with your family ... Insane in Heaven, can you imagine?"

"*You're insane now!*" Harry screamed in pain and fury, red-faced, veins bulging in his neck. "*Fuck you!*"

Michael struck again, this time bringing the hammer down with great force onto Harry's kneecap, cracking it like a coconut. Harry's screams hit a previously unheard pitch, and as Micheal resumed speaking, Harry heard none of it over his own bellows. Michael spoke anyway, knowing Harry was beyond listening, but going through his thoughts as if he were performing some kind of final check.

"But what if ...what *if,*" Michael said, looking through the twisting, shrieking man in front of him, "it was possible to 'game the system', so to speak? To play by the Easter rules – God's rules – and win?" He stood, and walked around to the back of the chair he'd been sitting on, putting his hands on the backrest and letting his arms take his bodyweight. He hung his head low, sighing heavily, as if a great weight was leaving him. The hammer lay in the vacated seat.

"If by some chance Future Me actually does feel remorse., that's great," he said quietly, his eyes closed, his breathing shaky once more, confirming his plan to himself as he spoke pointlessly to the screaming man sitting a few feet away. If Harry could hear – and if his senses weren't overridden with pain, – he would have heard the robotic nature of Michael's speech, would perhaps even have known that this was a mantra that had been repeated many times, over and over, Michael talking to himself in whatever lonely room he had lived in for the year following his faked suicide.

"That's what I need. But I doubt Future Me will feel it, at least not by himself. That's the problem. Just as *justice* is the role of Present Me, *remorse* is now the job of Future Me. I need to make sure both roles are fulfilled. *My* role,as I become Future Me,is to do my very best to *foster* that remorse.; to feel it enough to truly ask for and earn God's forgiveness, and receive the reward promised by the Easter story. If I can make that happen ...then I will have gamed God's system and won. Do you understand?"

He looked up, watching Harry writhe for a moment, and then scooped up the hammer. Coming around from behind the seat, he marched straight to Harry and grabbed a fistful of his hair, pulling the other man's bellowing head back.

"Tell me why I shouldn't kill you," Michael said, his eyes wild, his voice breathless.

"*My kids! They're not even in high school yet!*" Harry screamed, realizing this was it - his last chance - his fear overriding even the terrible pain in his shattered knee. "*You've seen them, Michael, you've seen them! Oh God, think of their faces! Think, think, think of those faces when they find out what happened to me! Please!*" Michael nodded slowly in response, staring intently into Harry's bloodshot eyes.

"Yes," Michael said eventually, "that ...*that's* exactly the kind of thing I'll need. Thank you, Harry." Still holding onto Harry's hair, the hammer came down on Harry's unbroken knee, and then Michael went to work.

*

Linda watched the children play on the front lawn, keeping an eye on the space between them and the road. She scrubbed at the baking tray she'd had soaking in the sink. She knew she was a worrier, although who could blame her these days. The road was pretty quiet, the kids well-drilled on matters regarding running out into it as well. Even so, she watched, and the reason wasn't only concern.

It had been two years since Harry had disappeared. Her only light, her only way *back* had been the kids. As she watched the darkness begin to lift from them the last few months, lifting with every game they played, she felt it lessen just that little bit inside her too. She knew it would never go away. Some days it took all she had to get out of bed and get them dressed, but at least now she began to believe that they could be themselves again someday. She felt like a shadow of her former self, but at least she felt something, and maybe the kids were young enough to come back completely.

He might still come back one d—

No. There had been no body, but the police had been clear. It was a murder scene.

But if there was no body—

SHUT UP.

She closed her eyes, then breathed deeply and resumed watching the kids, smiling sadly as Sally chased her brother. Linda watched as Sally's running turned into walking, then a full stop. She saw Sally's head drop and start to nod, making small and rapid movements that meant only one thing.

Linda dropped the tray into the sink, and tried to compose herself as she opened the front door and made her way over to Sally. She had to stay calm and be the anchor, had to keep it together, had to let Sally know it was okay to cry. Linda dropped to one knee on the grass, pushed Sally's brown, tangled locks out of the way of her sweaty, flushed face. Ben stood a few feet away, looking awkward and confused, shuffling his feet and wondering if he was somehow in trouble.

"Hey," Linda said. "Hey, Sallyface. Are you ok?" Sally's lips pressed together tightly as her blue eyes filled up.

"Mm," she whimpered, "mm, mm, just, just ..."

"Daddy?" Linda asked, knowing the answer. She'd seen these shutdowns many times. "Did you think about Daddy?" Sally nodded silently in response and began sobbing. As Linda drew her daughter close, she began to do the same. Ben started to sniffle too, confused, but starting to understand what this was about, even if he didn't understand how it applied here. Linda stroked her daughter's head as the tears began to soak her blouse, and wished yet again that whoever was responsible - the one who had never been caught - would burn in hell, even as she questioned that such a place existed at all.

And Michael, watching all this from his car - he watched the house most days of the week - saw the diorama of suffering before him, and his heart went out to the family of three on the lawn. He tried, as he always did, to *nurture* that feeling, to internalize the pity and let it go to work on the memory of his actions. He was sure he felt *something* shift, but, as always, it wasn't enough. He didn't regret a thing.

Two years, he tolf himself, *isn't anywhere near enough time. Don't worry.*

Of course, he was still too close. He was not far enough removed from Past Me to be anyone else. He had years to transform before he died. He had enough time to work on it, enough time to change. To *feel.*

But will you ever change enough? How much do you need? *How much is enough to get in?*

That was always the question. And as he turned the key in the ignition, checked his mirrors, and switched on his indicator, the same answer came again. It was as predictable as the fact of change itself.

I'll guess you'll find out eventually, won't you?

THE END

Bio

Luke Smitherd is the author of the international bestseller THE STONE MAN, shortlisted for Audible UK's Book of the Year Award 2015. His other novels include IN THE DARKNESS, THAT'S WHERE I'LL KNOW YOU as well as A HEAD FULL OF KNIVES, THE PHYSICS OF THE DEAD and the short story collection WEIRD. DARK. (Those titles are clickable, by the way. Straight to the Amazon purchase page. Hint, hint.)

A former singer and guitarist, Luke now writes full time for a living. He a: can't quite believe it, and b: has to remember that he shouldn't drink before lunchtime. Not on a weekday anyway. He currently travels and writes, and ignores cheap jibes about not having a 'proper job'. Follow his pasty white ass and keep up with his nonsense on Twitter (@lukesmitherd) on Facebook (Luke Smitherd Book Stuff) YouTube (Luke Smitherd) and at his website lukesmitherd.com, where you can sign up to his Spam-Free Book Release Newsletter to get occasional free stuff. He will stop saying Luke Smitherd now.

He's watching you as you finish reading this, and the second you complete this sentence he's going to kill you.

Made in the USA
Charleston, SC
10 August 2016